SPECTRUM

SPECTRUM

Web Shifter's Library #3

Julie E. Czerneda

DAW BOOKS, INC.

DONALD A. WOLLHEIM, FOUNDER

1745 Broadway, New York, NY 10019

ELIZABETH R. WOLLHEIM
SHEILA E. GILBERT
PUBLISHERS

www.dawbooks.com

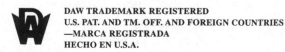

To Those Who Made Things Happen

This book is dedicated to everyone who found new ways to keep our SF/F community going strong when we couldn't be together,

And to all those who turned the wheels of publishing from their homes (and kitchens!).

We were in this together and I couldn't have written this book without you.

Thus it's *for* you.

Thank you.

Acknowledgments

Interesting times. I find myself, mid-pandemic and all else, anxious for a new reason. I don't want to miss thanking anyone but I've so many to thank it would take volumes, not pages. Forgive me as I clump you, tenderly and with joy, instead. A group hug, if you will, to be collected in person.

To my friends. I cannot believe I've provided a fraction of the support and encouragement to you that you have given me. A debt I will try to repay—but then you'll do more, I just know it. Thank you.

To my readers (who are also friends and honestly a Venn diagram would help here). Thank you for the joy you've taken in Esen's ongoing adventures, and your excitement for the next. I feel it too! The Dear Little Blob is the perfect character to write—and read—these days.

To my team. DAW Books, 50 years of amazing. Penguin Random House. KT Literary. The "B's": booksellers, bookstore folks, and bloggers. The warehouse people! Supporting work—keeping at work—while caring for one another. I couldn't be more proud. A special shout to my editor-dear and dear friend Sheila Gilbert for above and beyond envelope stuffing amongst all the rest. (So much of the rest!) And to my agent Sara Megibow, for zooming into our homes to check on us authors as often as possible, with that big smile.

To concom. CoNZealand? I'd planned to be there, couldn't be there, then, all at once, could be! If there was any bright side it was how magnificently you made Worldcon happen for us, even if we couldn't be together. Thank you. (And yes, most of you are in this book again.) Thanks also to AmazingCon (Steve, Ira!) and When Words Collide and Canvention. The virtual Aurora Ceremony hosted by Mark Lefebvre was brilliant. (Loving the trophy.)

Thank you, Nancy Tice, for supporting Edward Willett's wonderful *Shapers of Worlds* anthology. I have named Blue Spider and Wort—and made them gamers—for you. Thank you Bob Milne for naming their game as an Easter Egg. And I'm grateful to Cyn, BF, and Tanja for resolving my eye colour conundrum. (They happen.)

Above all, thank you to my family—presently afloat in our tiny bubbles of space-time, never touching but always touched. You hold my heart.

CONTENTS

Out There

VEYA Ragem, you have been informed of the risks inherent in the classified experimental upgrade identified as Pathfinder X23-42-6. Do you give consent?

Whether they admit it or not, deep spacers believe in an afterlife.

Sanity on long runs, out there in the vast. Faced by the uncaring empty, knowing there'd be no rescue? If all you were was meat in a can—if that was all you would ever be—why *be* at all?

Veya believes. She'd died—*surely she'd died*—for where she is has nothing to do with being alive.

And everything to do with a hell she'd never imagined.

<u>Do I have a choice?</u>
<u>Not if you want reinstatement. Not if you want to fly the latest and the best.</u>

Her memory is composed of shards like glass. Some hold an image, without sound. Some only voices, without a face. They spin as if hanging from thread.

While she is gripped by thicker filaments, suspended in a mist without color, without sensation. Has hands, sometimes. Has shape, if no skin. Watches her organs as they orbit.

Momma, tell me again about the worlds around the stars. About the people there. I want to know everything. I want to meet everyone.

Only her eye—*that eye*—doesn't drift. Tethered to glistening threads, its orb hangs beyond her reach.

Not beyond her mind's. Each time her eye focuses—*every time*—she's no choice but see.

1: Cabin Night; Aircar Night

THE warm evening breeze sighing through the open window was redolent of spring's delicious blend of rot and new growth, with a whiff of annoyed weasling which might have been my fault, having interrupted its hunt. Amphibians sang their impassioned evening chorus from tree, puddle, and cabin wall, drowning out the whine of thwarted night biters clinging to the screen. Duggs Pouncey, General Contractor for the All Species' Library of Linguistics and Culture, triumphantly pulled the stack of chips across the workbench still serving her for a table and crowed, "You lose!"

Director Paul Ragem gave a rueful chuckle. Lionel Kearn, Library Administrator, studied his cards with disbelief, then folded them neatly and put them down. "Again."

"Yet you keep coming."

I closed the door behind me, regarding the trio with pleasure. Duggs, powerfully built, with clever hazel eyes and short black hair touched with gray, wore worn blue coveralls, the legs cut off below the knees, over a faded red-and-black–plaid shirt. Her broad-toed feet were bare. Lionel was still in his staff's yellow shirt and brown pants, with matching shoes, but as far as I knew, he didn't own casual clothes. Slim of body, he'd a long, usually serious, face with earnest brown eyes cornered by faint wrinkles. Wisps of hair graced the top of his head, a sign he'd broken the nervous habit of fiercely rubbing his scalp while thinking.

Being newly happy.

Paul had switched to a dark silk shirt over shorts. His tousled black hair dipped over a high forehead, and his gray eyes brimmed with good humor. He leaned on an elbow, his lean strong form slouched comfortably.

Duggs grinned at me. "Catch anything, Es?"

With these Humans, I'd no hesitation sending my tongue along my lips, curling the tip over the sensitive nostrils at snout's end, to imply a most successful hunt for mousels under Duggs' back porch.

Paul, my first and best friend, lifted a judgmental eyebrow. *Behave,* that meant.

I dipped my ears in mild protest. "They've learned my scent," I admitted, then had to boast. "If there are any left."

Duggs laughed. "There's plenty. Found a new nest in the equipment shed this morning."

My ears perked up.

Paul pointed a finger.

Down they went again. *It was as if he had them on remote control.* "Maybe you should get a scruff," I suggested, trying not to grumble. Paul was reminding me these card nights were for socializing, not hunting, unless his own subtle but real pursuit of how far we could trust Duggs with our secret counted. I hadn't exactly given him a chance to do it before revealing my true self to her.

By accident. *There'd been extenuating circumstances—*

"Scruffs don't bring beer," Duggs said cheerfully.

I suspected she was aware of Paul's protective wariness and didn't care. And that Paul knew she knew and didn't, yet—somehow this made him happier.

Humans were so confusing.

"Besides," Duggs continued, "it's fun having the curator herself clean out the rascals."

I'd thought so, it being difficult to indulge this me's instincts now that Lesy had taken over the farmhouse, but—from Paul's reaction—I might have pushed the envelope of acceptable behavior.

Then I noticed he was trying hard not to grin. "You don't mind at all," I accused.

Out came the wide smile I loved. "How could I, Fangface? You look so proud of yourself."

"Just don't chew them around me," Lionel pleaded.

Duggs snorted. "You've seen worse."

"Assuredly," the former Survey First Contact Specialist stated firmly. "Meaning I don't have to now."

My tail drifted from side to side as I listened to their banter. I caught the shine in Paul's eyes and knew he felt it too. The warmth. The security. Since our first meeting, we'd never had this—*he'd never had this*, I added to myself. To be surrounded by friends, safe to say whatever we wished—which included a deplorable tendency by the Humans to tease the Web-being in the room, but I was growing accustomed—this was new.

And wonderful. I smiled at Duggs, who'd made her remote cabin our weekly gathering place—purportedly to go over plans for the addition to the Library, the excavation now well underway. After she'd brought out cards and marker chips to teach Lionel the Botharan version of Ringworld Rummy, we'd started to arrive with supper and beer. These days, once we'd looked at the plans, we settled in for a fine evening.

Duggs saw me smiling and patted the stool beside her. "Deal you in this round, Pups?"

I lost my smile, showing her a fang. "Not a 'pup.'"

"Deal you in, Blobbie?"

My proper name was and is Esen-alit-Quar, Esen for short, and Es in a hurry or between friends. It has never been *Blobbie*, though I am, in my natural state, a teardrop of blue goo. Which Duggs knew.

Before I could wrinkle my snout in outrage, mostly feigned but not entirely, my relative age being a sensitive point—not to mention my dignity as Senior Assimilator of the Web of Esen, even if that role was presently diminished with Skalet offworld who knew where, but I'd Lesy—

"Not tonight." With a rueful smile, Paul set down his empty glass. "Sorry to break us up early, but we've a busy day tomorrow." To me. "Isn't that right?"

"What's she done now?" Duggs asked, no longer amused.

And regrettably accurate, "she" being Lesy.

Truly Lesy, a joy of itself. She'd arrived on Botharis as a too-small reassembly of scattered Lesy-bits, growing as her mass was bolstered by my shared flesh and her mind by the memories therein. As far as I could tell, Lesy's restoration was complete, including those unique personality traits Skalet abhorred and which caused Ersh *concern*.

A concern I'd inherited, Lesy having made herself at home. As I'd hoped she would. *Just not this thoroughly.*

Within a day of her restoration, in part thanks to Evan Gooseberry's kindness, Lesy had taken over Paul's bedroom on the hidden top floor of our farmhouse. Within two, she'd spread like a tidal wave through the rest of the building and, rather than fight the inevitable, we'd moved to the greenhouse pending the Library's now-urgent addition.

Paul, who rarely complained, had given me dour looks for two days and refused to scratch my ears, *as if I'd any control over my Elder.* On the plus side, we'd found a use for the few Kraal tents our scholars had left intact and they had heaters. It remained to be seen if Lesy would desert the farmhouse in favor of the shiny new suite under construction, or if it'd be ours.

I'd be happy either way. Paul refused to place a friendly wager.

As for the All Species' Library of Linguistics and Culture? Lesley Delacora—Lesy's Human-self—had joined our staff as Creative Consultant in the Response Room. She'd wanted to be Artiste in Residence. I'd known my web-kin's preference wasn't to actually work, but to generate, as whim struck, a fulsome, ever-increasing mass of artwork. With *whim* being the key word and *art* a matter of opinion, thus we weren't going to encourage her.

Alas, the title hadn't helped. Charming, artistic Lesley showed up when and if she chose, spent most of her time at work distracted by what wasn't, and left without warning, abandoning whatever project she'd touched. She broke the fabricator regularly, pushing the limits of the device beyond tolerance. Lionel had ordered two spares.

Lesley made my various selves seem model employees, and how our full-time Response Room supervisor, Ally Orman, tolerated her was one of the Great Human Mysteries in my life. *Tolerate wasn't the word*, I reminded myself. Ally had grown, despite my misgivings and desire to caution her otherwise, to consider Lesley a friend. She cheerfully brought lunch for the two of them to share each working day, a time they spent chatting about whatever Humans chatted about, and I hadn't the heart to tell Ally the food was why Lesley cultivated the activity.

A thought I'd remember later.

Paul sighed before I could. "Lesy's been helping herself to the contents of the recycle bin."

"The rejected gemmies?" Duggs frowned. "Why?"

I didn't try to explain, having no idea either. "We don't know where she's putting them," I admitted. "The recycling company's threatening to cancel. You haven't seen any suspicious piles, have you?"

Duggs' cheeks expanded, then she let out a burst of opinionated air. *That'd be no.*

Our missing gemmies had to be somewhere. The term was the local appellation for what our scholars brought to be assessed as new information for the Library's collection, clutched in hopeful appendages or in sacks. The lamentable practice hadn't slowed despite ardent and repeated discouragement, including new interactive posters on Hixtar Station and stern looks at the fake artifact sellers at the landing field.

To dispose of what failed our assessment, Paul had contracted a set of his cousins to recycle it—appeasing the Terworth and Cameron branches of his extended family. Since we'd had to provide funds for their equipment and other purchases, with the same stroke Paul started yet another business in the Hamlet of Hillsview—delighting the Chamber of Commerce and reeve. All as what *passed* assessment threatened to fill both levels of the Library basement.

What no one else but me, on Botharis, appreciated? If the mood struck, Lesy would produce a far greater volume of useless stuff in no time at all, a significant amount something she'd treasure and insist we keep. We'd have to build a warehouse—warehouses—putting those in orbit would be a bonus—

Suffice to say, sticking Lesy in the Response Room had been my attempt to let my web-kin indulge her need to make things, with the bonus that each *thing* would go home with its satisfied scholar, question answered in the physical format most meaningful to their species.

Lesy knew, as I did, how to ensure that. Granted, she had to work with a Human who didn't know what she was and, however well that side of things appeared to flow, my web-kin couldn't grasp the concept of responsibility. *My job—and I was failing.*

And now she'd found a new source of material? We were in trouble. *We being me.* "We'd best get back," I confirmed, ears sagging.

We were on our way home, the aircar rising to a height reassuringly above the trees below, when Lionel muttered, "How can she win so often? Not that I accuse Duggs of cheating, but . . ."

"Aren't you?" Paul replied, a smile in his voice.

"She cheats." Both Humans turned to look at me. I set my ears at *trust me*. "Why do you think I hunt mousels while you play cards? I don't want to lose all the time." Not that mousel hunting was always a win, but the chase alone was—the point being, whenever Duggs dealt, there were a few cards that smelled of fresh sweaty Human creases, not hands. After all, Duggs' hands smelled of sawdust and machines, with occasional bacon.

I'd expected my companions to be upset, but they chuckled. Paul's, "Knew it—" overlapped Lionel's, "Glad we play for chips."

As Paul resumed a more safety conscious position such that he could see where he was flying—though to be fair our aircar was more modern than most on this world and could fly itself home if necessary—Lionel leaned back in his seat. "The scoundrel."

I detected a peculiar note of admiration. "You're impressed?" I'd been anticipating, as Skalet would say, the moment of revelation and retribution. Not that we weren't friends, but I'd expected a dramatic "aha!" and the throwing of slightly greasy cards in the air. Which I'd have caught in my teeth—

"I'm relieved it's not my lack of skill. And—" Though not usually demonstrative, Lionel reached out and touched my paw. "I'm relieved Duggs doesn't treat us as different."

Treat me as different, that meant. "I told you," I said, wondering if he'd forgotten. Humans did. Some of them.

Paul, who didn't and was ever my conduit to understanding his kind, stepped in, "It's not the same as seeing, Old Blob." With relief of his own.

I tilted an ear in time to catch a muted, "'Blobbie.'"

"I bite," I warned. "Do you need to see that?"

Taking my threat as seriously as I meant it, Lionel patted my paw and eased back. "A fine, fine night."

Paul took a slow deep breath. Let it out. By that, and the faint aroma of stress, I knew he was ready to begin. Sure enough, "Anything to report?"

For this was the other reason we three gathered once a week—away from the Library and its too-curious Carasian, Lambo Reomattatii—and why Paul flew this convoluted route home to keep Duggs free of it: to exchange notes on our still-secret search for what we'd decided to call the Framers.

Instead of my proposed "Bad Thing" which Paul said prejudged.

I had no problem prejudging. Whatever sent those framed images of lost starships—to the Kraal, to the Sacrissee, and,we suspected, to the Human Commonwealth and others—had either ambushed the ships or swept up any that came to harm in those reaches of space it appeared to claim. It wasn't as if we could ask their crews. The images showed derelicts, adrift and empty. *Bad Thing.*

All this had landed in our varied laps because of Paul's mother; more precisely, his mother's starship. Veya Ragem had been the navigator on the Survey research vessel *Sidereal Pathfinder.* During a classified test flight, something went wrong and the crew abandoned ship. *Pathfinder* was lost, not that any public records showed it ever existed. Believing the ship had a new star drive, Lambo, an engineer, had established himself as the operator of our Anytime Chow Food Dispenser in order to skulk in our basement hunting secrets.

Then Victory Johnsson, a murderous criminal, brought a Framer image of *Pathfinder* to our kitchen.

Paul thought he'd known his mother's story: that she'd left Survey in disgrace and worked on a sequence of starships further and further out; that she'd died with the crew of a tramp freighter, the *Smokebat,* after it was struck by debris, never knowing her son was alive.

Now we knew that two years after *Pathfinder,* and a year before her death, Veya visited Stefan Gahanni, Paul's biological father, on Senigal III, to leave her son a message. Despite all the evidence, and her family's conviction, Veya had believed Paul lived and looked for him until she died.

One day, I might ask Paul to tell me if knowing his mother's quest made the grief over losing her easier to bear or more painful. *Or I might not.* Ersh knew, some curiosities weren't meant to be answered.

Johnsson's abduction of Paul and Lionel, her attack on the Library, had been arranged by a mysterious backer. She'd implied Veya's death hadn't been an accident. We'd no proof, but Lambo, now sharing, said hc hadn't been able to locate a single member of *Pathfinder*'s crew. Lionel's cautious scan of classified Survey records—before Paul stopped him—had uncovered the appalling information that everyone who'd served with Veya was either dead or missing and presumed dead.

It stank of conspiracy and coverup. That, or the Framers had a reach beyond imagining. *Bad Thing.*

All we had, so far, was their signature: the frame bearing symbols not in any memory Ersh had shared with me. There was that frozen chunk I hadn't tasted—

I might have to.

"I've some surprises to report," Lionel replied, his tone grave. Seeing Paul become more alert, I tilted an ear to confirm I was paying close attention as our friend continued, "I've received the data concerning Sacrissee ship losses. While Sacrissee don't, with very recent exceptions, leave their system, they do build solid, well-respected starships and lease those to non-Sacrissee crews. Thousands of ship transits in and out of their system take place annually; on average, less than a dozen suffer catastrophic damage or go missing, an enviable safety record. I offer this as background—" *I may have fidgeted.* "—because what alarmed the Sacrissee into hiring Molancor Genomics to modify their species was an atypical cluster of ship losses fifty-two years ago. Five in under a month, and where they vanished is, I believe, significant. The Sacriss System heliopause."

"The Vast Out," Paul murmured, the Sacrissee term for the, to them, terrifying realm beyond the reach of their Sun. Interstellar space.

"Exactly. Each entered translight with no indication of trouble. But what's key? Two were later found—"

"'Found?'" I interrupted. *Might have yelped it.*

Paul locked the controls, the aircar stopped to hover over a copse of night-black trees and turned to face Lionel. "Go on."

"Each ship was found not far from its entry, engines dead. No, not dead. Depleted." Lit by the glows within the aircar, Lionel's face aged, wrinkles become grim lines. "If my translation of the record is accurate—and I'd like you to check it for me, Esen—the crews were found as well. Torn apart. Some—some pieces were embedded in the exterior bulkheads."

In the ensuing silence, the aircar rocked gently. It might have been a breeze, passing beneath like a wave. More likely, we'd each stiffened in reaction.

"What could do that?" *Who would?* A question I decided not to ask. As for when? Fifty-two years ago was about the time I'd met Paul and made my first friend.

While a wild Web-being attacked starships. I consoled myself that Death hadn't left any living mass behind, embedded or otherwise. *Another thought not to voice,* Lionel being squeamish about mousel chewing. *Which he should have mentioned before I—*

"Nothing we know of," Paul replied soberly.

"There's a complication," Lionel said. "We've no proof Framers were involved. If anything, the evidence in hand suggests they weren't, given the fifteen Sacrissee Framer images the Kraal shared with us were of ships lost within the last eight and a half years. I've confirmed with senior officials on Sacriss VII that we have all they've received." That world being the homeworld and travel hub for the system. "Those original five ships aren't among them."

Paul looked at me. "From what he said on the train, did Virul-ru lie to us?"

For my friend to want me to check his memory against mine was unusual. *So were embedded person-bits.*

Skalet would know, but we'd last seen my web-kin on the Library's train as she'd left with Virul-ru, Courier of House Virul and the highest-ranking Kraal any of us had met in the flesh. He'd come with a proposal to end Kraal interest in Botharis—where they didn't belong but had a history of invading. Accompanying Virul-ru had been Sacrissee officials and their expert from Molancor Genomics, who didn't belong either but wanted to recover their stolen chimeric embryos. For the Sacrissee, it turned out, were in the midst of their species-wide directed evolution, reinventing themselves into what they hoped could survive the new danger coming from the Vast Out.

They'd done it once before, to venture into space. At least this time they claimed they weren't culling the less fit. I didn't approve but, as Ersh often reminded me, *to each their own biology.*

I thought back to that day. "Virul-ru said, '. . . the first went missing over fifty years ago. The rest over the years between.' Then he said, 'None have been recovered.'"

"The Sacrissee originally dealt with House Bract, among others," Lionel volunteered. "It's possible, even probable, they'd withhold information from House Virul."

Skalet would find out.

"What have you learned about the imaged ships?" Paul asked.

"It's impossible to know if their translight corridors were altered from what they filed with system control, but I believe I've spotted a commonality. When the comp finishes the revised model, I'll be in a better position to speak to its validity."

Paul nodded. "Give us what you have."

"It's not much, but—like the original five—all of the Framer imaged ships were lost after entering translight in the heliopause." Lionel shrugged. "It may be meaningless."

"Or Framers avoid solar wind." The Humans looked at me. I half lowered my ears but kept going. "Maybe they don't have the right shielding?" I didn't bother to add Ersh-memory of soaring naked through the blasts of tasty charged particles and tingly magnetic clouds; the mostly-energy me wasn't much of a conversationalist.

Paul gave me his patient *we'll talk about it later* look, complete with lifted eyebrows. "There are no wrong types of shielding on spacecraft, Esen. They work or you don't survive."

Unless you were a Web-being. Which Skalet and I had eliminated from the beginning as a possibility. If non-intelligent, like Death, it wouldn't know how to send images, let alone frame them; if intelligent, like those of Ersh's Web, it should know better than expose itself.

Admittedly, our opinions were biased, but none of the Humans thought it likely either, so I lifted my ears to show I accepted Paul's statement and honestly wouldn't need a follow-up refresher on ship design. *I could hope.*

"As for the Commonwealth?" Lionel shrugged. "We've a mass of data on missing or damaged Human starships since *Pathfinder.* Where there's no definitive cause listed, the default explanation is navigation error. Not one mention of framed images."

"There must be." Paul scrunched his nose as if at a bad smell, which there wasn't because I'd have smelled it long before a Human.

Oh. It was the Human expression, meaning he didn't like the *smell* of what he heard. With a justified sense of smug over my growing powers of interpretation, I turned to Lionel for his response.

"Agreed. If they've been classified, they'll be in Survey datafiles. I backed out, as per your order." Lionel sounded like my Lishcyn-self when Paul locked away the fudge for my own good.

As if I'd overindulged since that time with Henri—*not what mattered now.*

"Thank you," Paul said quickly. I nodded to add my approval. As a senior officer in that service, Lionel had abused his authority—for what he believed the greater good—beyond even Survey's wide tolerance. He hadn't been disciplined simply because his final act before a mandatory retirement had been to resolve an interspecies' crisis. *With some help from me.*

That didn't mean Lionel Kearn had been forgiven or forgotten. He even had support, after a fashion. It turned out there were those within Survey itself who'd applauded his past rule-bending, namely a private club of like-minded officers calling themselves "The Intrepid Few." *Humans gathered around the strangest notions.* At the start of each year, Lionel received an invitation to join their ranks, or at least attend a party.

I knew, because he'd shown me the invitation that found him here, this winter. Though an actual printed card, it was only slightly fancier than the invitations sent out for the Hamlet of Hillsview Agricultural Fair and much less informative, consisting of a contact ident beneath a paragraph in bold extolling the role of self-confidence and individual daring in space exploration—without reference to safety standards, resupply, or the certainty of painful death without both—while the fair pithily listed event highlights—the same every year, as expected— with a polite request for donations at the bottom. The latter being typical for Human groups, I found its lack on Lionel's invitation suspicious and told him so.

He'd shrugged and tossed the card into the recycler.

Lionel didn't want friends like that, having an active conscience and friends like us, while Paul considered any continued attempt by Lionel to tap his contacts within Survey for secrets, even for us, an unacceptable risk to him, no matter how willing he might be.

For now. If we didn't succeed elsewhere—using Paul's resources, which were extensive—we might have to let him. *Not there yet.*

At the uncomfortable thought, I squirmed and changed the topic. "Any news from Skalet?"

Lionel attempted to quash me with a frown.

As if that had ever worked—I responded with an ears-up eager grin.

His frown deepened. "Es, you know perfectly well while she is S'kal-ru and deep within the heart of the Kraal Confederacy, she won't dare contact us."

What I knew was my web-kin would dare whatever she pleased, and most likely get away with it, but that wouldn't make Lionel feel better. He worried about her safety.

In my opinion, Lionel should worry more about whatever schemes she had underway because Skalet hadn't gone solely to learn what the Kraal might know about the Framers. That was the bonus, granting her admission to the most rarefied and protected layer of Kraal society: the Great Houses.

I'd no idea what she had in mind for them, but worrying about that? Up to Paul and me, who knew Skalet best.

"Well done," Paul said to Lionel, then faced the controls to start the aircar moving forward again. It wasn't as if there was anyone but Botharan Bats to notice us hovering, but my friend didn't take unnecessary chances.

I pressed my nose to the side window, looking back toward Duggs' cabin. Near it was a hill containing a Kraal Peacemaker missile, until recently hidden and forgotten. As a result of the Kraal proposal and its speedy acceptance by the Botharan government, ably represented by Special Envoy Niala Mavis, Constable Malcolm Lefebvre and others were busy removing it and four others. Not a job poor Mal had seen coming when he returned home to semi-retire, but we were all doing the unexpected.

As were the others who'd been on the train that fateful day.

Lambo was now officially the Library's head of security—when he wasn't busy in the Chow or hunting through the collection for clues to the *Pathfinder*'s mission. Well, he'd the title, but he wasn't doing the job, sulking ever since Paul told him he couldn't stand guard at the door and terrorize incoming scholars. Fortunately, Lionel and two other staff were willing to check the vidfeeds and monitor alarms.

Polit Evan Gooseberry, our friend and Commonwealth diplomat, had come for a holiday and been swept up in it all. He'd helped us, and in return we'd kept secrets from him. About him and what he was. Outright lied, to protect my Web, and I supposed Ersh would have been proud to see me finally take responsibility. *However distressing.*

Evan had left us to spend the last of his holiday with his Great Gran and hadn't been in touch since. I hadn't worried about him until Paul recently reached out to the embassy on Dokeci Na only to be told Evan Gooseberry was unavailable at this time and, with apologies, no, they couldn't pass along a message. Diplomatic-speak for *not here, can't say when he'll be back.* I'd wanted to contact his Great Gran Gooseberry—not that I'd her ident or location, nor could I be sure of species—

But no. Paul insisted we weren't to bother Evan, who'd things to work out. I'd argued working things out went better with friends, admittedly a most un-web-like opinion but validated by my experience, but my own friend had been unusually firm. And had resources of his own, should he see reason to worry.

Something else I wouldn't think of till later.

The missing final member of our tiny "Find the Framers" group was Special Envoy Niala Mavis, who'd asked the Library—specifically Paul—to find out what they were and what threat they posed to Botharis. Which we were doing already, if with wider concerns, but what mattered was he'd said yes. Though I'd a sneaking feeling he couldn't say no to her. *Humans were complicated.*

On that thought, I turned my attention to Paul. "Any word from Nia?" I asked innocently.

"She'll be here tomorrow." The corner of his mouth I could see resisted a smile. "To check the status of the Library addition for the Preservation Committee."

"Humph." Lionel hadn't stopped frowning. *Still grumpy.* "Mark my words. We're going to regret that cover story."

"She doesn't need one anymore." I bounced on the seat. "Nia should say she's coming to visit us." *I'd no shame.* "She's a hero. They'd let her."

Paul turned to give me what I'm sure he thought was a quelling look, which didn't work because I immediately worried more about being in an aircar with an inattentive pilot. "It's because Nia's in the public eye right now, Es, that she can't," he disagreed. "Everything she does makes the news vids. Like it or not, we need the Preservation Committee if we're to meet without drawing attention. Attention we can't risk before certain matters are concluded."

I stopped bouncing and quivered with anticipation. By "certain matters," my friend didn't mean our search for answers about the Framers— *not only that*—but Nia's ongoing efforts to use us as a wedge to open Botharis to the wider universe. Especially—

"The space station." Lionel's gloom vanished. "Do you think she's got the final go ahead?"

"Too early to say," Paul replied. "There's still some resistance."

Not a surprise. The once-tiny Botharan Department of Extraplanetary Affairs hadn't envisioned their next major project would be an orbital station to handle interstellar traffic for the All Species' Library of Linguistics and Culture. I was sympathetic. Most Botharans hadn't known we existed until the Mavis Peace Accord—so-called by non-Kraal—was signed on our train. *Hero!*

Any resistance wasn't to do with financing. The department hadn't had the budget for more than a communications array, but an anonymous benefactor of the Library had stepped forward to pay for the station. Being me. Technically, Sec-ag Mixs C'Cklet, for I'd drawn the funds from Mixs' holdings on Panacia, certain my architecture-obsessed web-kin would have approved.

For now, Nia wanted the Library's involvement kept on a need-to-know basis. *Wait till I told her we might need to add an orbital art gallery for Lesy.*

I angled my ears to concede Paul's point. The Hamlet of Hillsview Preservation Committee it was. I knew why Lionel worried about them. They'd not been pleased to learn we'd let aliens traipse through their countryside. *Not that it had been our fault.* Before they'd a chance to stop issuing testy memos on that subject—*mostly to Lionel but some to me*—along came news of our building expansion. They'd been livid to discover we'd included the potential for one or more in our original agreements—*fine print going both ways*—and, in fact, Duggs had started the dig.

Having no recourse didn't mean they couldn't fuss, the three volunteer members in particular adamantly Opposed to Change. Change such as aliens though, to be fair, they felt much the same about the local council's proposal to add an aircar pad to the historic village square and a porch to the post office.

I was sure they were glad to know, thanks to Nia, the Kraal were no longer a threat to Botharan historical sites—for the near future, at any rate. Maybe less so that she'd smoothed matters here to permit ships bringing scholars to the Library to remain finsdown to await their return. Not a proper shipcity, with overnight facilities, but a great deal closer.

Mind you, without a space station, in order to keep some kind of handle on how many ships sat on the field at once, we'd needed to install an operations tower—thus far a tent, but an actual tower was in the works—containing translight coms and dedicated staff. Being Botharis, that staff consisted of Lenata Mady, a trustworthy and somewhat reliable individual. We'd yet to convince her not to hook the incredibly expensive translight com to her belt when she went to the Port Village for lunch, and she occasionally took it home to the farm by mistake.

Where she'd left it three times now, usually on her kitchen table but once in the henhouse.

Nia understood Lenata, having grown up near here. With Paul, who she also understood and in a way I never would. She'd loved him, mourned his loss, and spent the time since discovering he lived hating him for it.

To her great credit, Nia valued his work, the Library, enough to put all that aside. These days, we worked together admirably.

Except that Paul had loved her back and confessed to me that throughout our years together he'd dreamed of finding Nia again. *His happiness mattered more than anything else—*

"Nia's coming for the committee and our update on the Framers," Paul said firmly, his head still swiveled to let him look at me. "That is all."

"Of course." I kept my ears up, the essence of professional decorum from nose to tail.

He wasn't buying it. "Esen-alit-Quar."

I added *sincere*, putting my paw gently on his shoulder. "I promised."

Paul's eyes softened. "That you did. Thank you."

Though having a perfect memory? I'd promised not to fix Paul and Nia.

Didn't mean Lesy couldn't try.

Nearby

CELONEE Jefer Buryatsea Gooseberry, Great Gran to family and select friends, had built her house on a hill. The hill was sand, being an ancient dune stretched along the coast, so there were raised paths to protect the tough-rooted grass and trees that held the dune where it was, and woe to the visitor who strayed from those.

A wide firm beach marked where the dune sloped into the emerald-and-blue water of Scintillation Bay and then lost any permanence, replaced by shifting sandbars covered by busy seabirds at low tide and deep channels that could shift, too, especially after hurricanes.

For that reason, and others, a wharf styled like any in neighboring fishing towns jutted beyond the reach of tides, if not hurricanes, offering tie-ups to those who came by water as well as a sand-free landing to those who came by air.

Both saw regular use, for her house on the hill hosted frequent gatherings of the extended Gooseberry family, members of which didn't always share a bloodline but were recorded in the official Gooseberry Lore and thus Great Gran's particular concern. The surname Gooseberry boasted to be the only one able to follow itself without break through that record and other documents—some in museums—back to fabled Earth, the homeworld and origin of the Human species.

Though not all Gooseberrys were, by now, Human.

Contemplating that, among other things, Evan Gooseberry sat on the end of Great Gran's wharf, feet dangling over the ocean. The spot was his favorite, not just for the view. If you sat here, you were left alone, to be alone. House rules.

He'd sat here often since arriving on Pachen IV, having taken a leave of absence from the Commonwealth Embassy on Dokeci Na, a leave extended from a couple of weeks to a couple of months to—

He'd yet to have answers. Yet to find peace.

Evan gazed into the distance, not seeing the wavery line where dark blue wave met light blue sky with its row of tall white puffs of cloud. Let the warm salt- and fish-scented breeze tug at his shirt collar and cool his bare, sandy toes, while questions roiled through his head. Chief of which, *what was he?*

The first question he'd asked the day he arrived.

Two Months Ago

Evan stepped inside and closed the many-paned glass door with care. Bag in hand, he surveyed the entry, soaking in the known and well-remembered. The fresh yellow of the walls, the skylight overhead. The floor tiles. Most rough and reddish, others smooth and inset in the corners, glazed with yellow and blue flowers. One tile had a chip in it. A long-ago mishap with a bag of pebbles from the beach.

The wood shelves on the lower left wall. The colorful sandals and boots waiting on them belonged to one person, and the hooks were bare but for a single broad-brimmed hat.

Grateful tears blurred his view. Great Gran had been as good as her word, clearing the house for his arrival. Evan wiped his eyes with the back of his hand, then set down his bag and kicked off his shoes. Putting those on a shelf, he stripped off the jacket he wouldn't need here, tossing that on a hook. He lifted the hat free.

His, right where he'd left it. He turned the hat around and around in his hands, enjoying its prickly texture, feeling the cool of the tiles seep through his socks. Enjoyed breathing.

When had he last caught a breath—a peaceful, safe breath? His head grew light, almost dizzy, with relief.

"Out back!" came a faint shout.

Tears threatened to spill again, but Evan didn't care. He hurried across the intervening room to the voice, to the one person in all the universe he trusted without reservation or thought.

She rose to her feet as he came through the open patio doors, tall and strongly built, her skin the same rich black as his own. Everything about Great Gran was larger and more splendid than anyone else in his life, from her wise dark eyes under their marvelously expressive brows to the giant gold rings singing in her ears. Since he'd last seen her image, she'd altered her hair to a mass of springy coils, dancing over her shoulders and back. Paired clips, each with a dangling cluster of living yellow flowers, kept the coils from the sides of her round face and her hair was, today and for him, the blue of the ocean beyond, complete with sparkles. She wore a light brown split skirt and vest over a shift of deep red, green, and gold. Her feet were bare, each big toe adorned with a pearl. After the sameness of space travel, Great Gran was the embodiment of life itself.

She held out both hands, her wide beautiful smile fading to concern. "Evan—"

The touch of those hands pulled him back into the world; Evan trembled with the power they had. "I'm all right. Better, now I'm home," he added, to be truthful and because she'd know, looking at him, that he wasn't *right* at all. "Long trip."

Her strong fingers tightened over his. "Sit with me." She guided him to the double seat, sank into the cushions beside him, not letting go.

Sunbeams sparkled on the ocean and slipped between the slats overhead. He'd one on his toes. Another, warm and bright, on their clasped hands. He remembered the ring on her thumb, the flat stone with its inner glow—

"Evan. Look at me." The irresistible summons dragged up his eyes. Hers were full of warmth and a worrying resolve. "When you called from Botharis, I promised you a conversation."

"N-now?" he protested weakly. He'd anticipated a walk on the beach, maybe supper and a night's sleep, before anything serious.

"Yes, now." Great Gran bent close to kiss his cheek. She smelled like flowers and sunshine and beer. "I know you," she said gently. "You've been chased here by secrets. By what you don't know—what you're guessing. About Molancor Genomics. You and your sister.

Waiting will make it harder." A hand left his, pressed warm where her lips had touched. "My dear, you must have so many questions."

His notebook, still in his bag, held page after page of them. For some reason, Evan could only remember one and grew cold, despite her hand and the tropical air, cold enough to shiver.

"What am I?"

Present Day

He wasn't entirely Human.

Great Gran had told him what she could, as kindly as she could. Like the Sacrissee Evan had met at the Library, he was a chimera: a blend of Human and something else. He and his twin sister had been born with Darmellas-Et4F6 Disease. They'd have died of the genetic disorder if Great Gran and their fathers hadn't paid Molancor Genomics to do whatever it took to save them.

They'd known what it meant: the addition of non-Human genetic material. As for whose—or what's? Great Gran had shrugged, shaking her head. Molancor claimed it a proprietary secret, that there'd be no lasting trace. Evan's genome tested as Human by the time he was ten, via the best equipment on Pachen IV, so the decision was made to wait until—and if—he asked for himself.

Though there was no one to ask, Great Gran admitted. Not for more details than she'd given him. When Molancor demanded access to keep testing Evan, she'd taken them to court and won. Molancor had been forbidden to contact him again. Unfortunately, in the same judgment, all Gooseberrys were ordered to keep their distance from the company and its employees.

Evan wished he could have eavesdropped. Great Gran was ferocious when it came to protecting family. Her day in court must have been spectacular even for her, for the judge to go that far.

These past weeks, Great Gran had been an oasis of calm and strength, helping however she could. She'd listened to his ideas, let him use her systems to search and send out inquiries. Above all else, she granted him privacy and peace, denying the fervid curiosity of every

Gooseberry in range. The entire family clamored to see him as soon as he felt ready for company. *He wasn't.*

She did all this, Evan knew, because Great Gran waited. She didn't say for what—she didn't have to. He understood she waited for him to accept and move on with his life. Be grateful. He'd survived the treatment.

His twin hadn't. Evelynne Gooseberry. He'd a name, now, to remember her by. Evie, Great Gran said they'd called her, during her too-brief life. The day after he arrived, she'd brought out a much-folded print of the two of them, nestled together and blissfully asleep in the same crib. Evan, who knew nothing of babies other than being able to hold his cousins' awkwardly when pressed to it, wasn't entirely sure who was who.

He hadn't dared ask. While holding the print, Great Gran had grown visibly upset, then too quiet. She took out her boat for the rest of that day and night, and when she came back, put the print away.

Evan didn't tell her he'd made a copy for himself, that he treasured the image not only for Evie, but because it showed him when he'd been Human.

What was he now?

Evan watched seabirds wheel gracefully in front of him. They weren't as they seemed either, he thought. White, with elegant, black-tipped wings, they looked refined, even serene. But those scheming yellow eyes watched for a chance to swoop down and steal your lunch. They'd drop something unpleasant on your head if you'd brought none, so for that reason—as well as the tropical sun—he wore a broad-brimmed hat. Still, the seabirds were simply being themselves. He envied them their self-awareness. Their innocence.

An innocence like that of those two babies, curled against each other, chubby fingers intertwined, and it was as if the image of their peaceful slumber had stolen his ability to sleep.

For his nightmares had started that night.

At first, Evan hadn't thought much of it. He'd an active imagination. Been thoroughly unsettled, despite Great Gran's reassurances, and still off-balance from travel. A disturbing dream or two was to be expected and these? Surely harmless fragments. A white hallway, lit from above, with no end in sight. He didn't walk but floated along as if on water. Nothing remarkable, nothing to cause fear.

Except the soft *clicks.*

Click, click. The sounds seemed at times to come from the walls. At others, from behind his neck. Never loud. Irregular. Like an antique clockwork stuck on a number, its minute hand fighting to move time. *Click, click.*

By the third night, the third recurrence, he'd known he was in trouble. His auto-therapist suggested treatment after treatment. He meditated. Swam and ran. Made lists upon lists of possible sources of trauma—*what WAS he*—but nothing stopped the dreams. Nothing changed in them. *Click, click.* Evan came to dread sleep, grew worn and anxious during the day.

He'd extended his leave out of desperation. Despaired if he'd ever return to work, the work he loved.

Grew determined. He had to fix it. *Fix himself.*

Bringing him here. *To work, then.* Evan opened his notebook. The sea breeze fluttered the pages until he caught them in the bands on either side. He'd many such books and journals, written in a neat, careful hand. Notes for his work at the embassy. Records of his health and challenges. Random facts he wanted to keep.

What he wrote in this notebook concerned trust. Concerned his growing lack of it on every front, and if that wasn't a *FEAR* to match any phobia he'd owned since childhood, it came distressingly close.

What he wrote wasn't only about himself and his past. Wasn't only about his nightmares.

Here he wrote about those he'd believed his friends.

Lists of questions. Incongruities. Puzzles. The more he wrote, the more vividly he remembered and the more upset he became. By this point, the notebook itself caused him pain, let alone the act of reading it. But he must.

Here, on this page, he'd written, among other things: *How did a ShimShree get to the Library? How did it leave?*

Such a small and harmless curiosity, a ShimShree being an alien Evan particularly wanted to meet. When he'd found and followed one's tracks in the snow in Esen's Garden, he'd thought his chance had come, but he'd been too late. Esen told him it—a scholar named SeneShimlee—had already left.

But Carwyn Sellkirk, a member of the Library's staff, later assured him no ShimShree had ever visited the Library. If one had, she'd said adamantly, they'd be on her list. Whatever that was.

And when he'd mentioned the ShimShree to Nia and Onlee on the flight to Grandine from the Library, to make conversation? Nia had been concerned anything as large as a Petani freighter—required to transport the huge alien—would have landed at the primitive field in the hills, so Evan retracted, saying he must have misheard and be wrong.

He wasn't. He was more convinced than ever. The tracks. The spew, a hard, translucent crust where a greenhouse window had shattered. A ShimShree had been there.

And he'd intended to prove it.

He moved a finger below the question on his notebook page, to where he'd copied the answer he'd received this very morning, from Commander Ne-sa Kamaara, security chief for the Survey ship *Mistral*.

Attaching his presently inactive diplomatic credentials to the information request had been, as Great Gran would say, like using explosives to stun a Sharp-fin and float it to the surface instead of dangling a baited hook on a line.

No, what he'd done was more like putting his head in the water before setting off the charge. If the commander had elected to contact Evan's superiors at the embassy, his leave would be permanent. Why he'd taken the risk, Evan couldn't explain even to himself.

Unless it was the way everything normal and plausible had grown into something else in his mind. *Click, click.*

Unless it was how he'd grown tired and frustrated, until the day came he had to know something. Anything—

Now Evan wished he didn't.

Commander Kamaara to Polit Gooseberry. Confidential. Confirmed with the Petani Government: by their records, no ShimShree has ever traveled to the Botharis System or asked to do so. Also confirmed: there is no ShimShree named SeneShimlee.

His friend, Esen-alit-Quar, had lied.

2: Response Room Morning; Chow Morning

THE next morning, I made it to the admin corridor, appropriately dressed and groomed, before the first train left its station at the landing field. As I passed the still-quiet Assessment Counter on my way to the Response Room, Henri Steves' eyebrows shot to her hairline. "Es?" She recovered and smiled. "Good morning."

"Good morning, Henri," I replied cheerily, as if my presence at this hour was perfectly normal. While Paul believed—*expressing this to me regularly*—we should be in place and ready before the Library filled with scholars, I'd rarely managed it before Lesy arrived in the greenhouse as a bag of frozen bits and been late every day since she had. Now—with "Lesley" providing a first-hand example of how not to be dependable?

As Curator and Senior Assimilator for the Web of Esen, I needed to do better. *In other words, last night I'd developed a twinge of responsibility and set an alarm.*

As I went down the corridor, Paul was still in his tent; Lionel still in his chosen quarters. The Library felt asleep. To my joy, I realized I'd done it. I'd be in the Response Room before Ally, and certainly before my web-kin, to search for our missing trash.

Opening the door, I felt a thrill of accomplishment. Or was hungry, having skipped breakfast, but as a Lanivarian, I could miss a meal or two. It was Esolesy Ki who couldn't, those five stomachs unruly when empty, and *her* return was a conversation Paul and I had yet to have—

"Youngest?"

"What are you doing up?" I blurted.

Lesy lowered her brush. "Is it morning?" She brushed a stray lock of white hair from her forehead, eyes bemused. "I've misplaced time." Her Human-self was tall and beautiful, as she was in any form, and she loved embellishing whatever she was—making it as strange that she wore only a paint-splattered smock and one brown sock as finding her awake before noon.

"It's morning," I sighed, giving up my plan as I sat on a stool. "Nice pot."

"Do you like it?" Blue eyes shone. "I'm not done."

I recognized one of the larger pots I'd tucked behind the greenhouse. She'd set it on the table Ally used for items to be checked; a good-sized pile of dirt on the floor marked where Lesy had dumped its contents. Dirt coated the sink, and by the filthy state of my smock—nicely back on its hook—she'd used it for a washcloth. Far from the first time Lesy had retrieved a pot without Paul or me noticing until too late. She remained unexpectedly fond of the things, despite no longer being able to fit inside.

Especially if upset. *What now?*

I considered the pot. "It's bright," I said charitably. There were times Lesy's art was stunning; given the sheer volume of her efforts and her lifespan, it had to happen. What she did to our pots, however, was more along the lines of experiential.

I'd a feeling she closed her eyes.

Dots were the theme today. Large ones. Small ones. Of every color and not just of paint. Her other sock had been rolled into a ball and glued near the pot's rim and beside it? I leaned closer, suspicious. "Is that the handle of Ally's scraper?"

"It has become art," she proclaimed happily.

"Art has to stop now," I informed her. "We have to get the room ready for Ally. Time to get to work."

Oh, the woebegone look that earned me. A less determined being would have relented. I offered distraction. "Have you eaten since yesterday? Breakfast?"

"You brought me breakfast?" Lesy asked, happy again. "How thoughtful you are, Esen."

No, and I hadn't had my own, but—I eyed the mess morosely—*there was no winning this one.* "Lambo's opened the Chow. If you go right away," I suggested, "you'll be first in line."

Our Carasian was renowned for two things: a short temper and an inexplicable if welcome enthusiasm for the first meal of the day. Staff hurried to get in early because service went rapidly downhill afterward, to the point where lunch was risky and supper? Not for the faint of heart. The bellowing—the throwing of objects—

"Good idea." Lesy pried her sock from the pot and put it on, then swept her loose hair into a knot behind her neck. "Back soon!" she caroled, dashing from the room, the smock covering nothing of her back. She'd somehow managed to paint a large blue question mark over her spine.

Nothing the staff hadn't seen before. Well, the question mark was new, and between that and the pot, I'd have to find out what was bothering my Elder before it showed up in other, possibly less tidy, ways.

As for tidy?

I shrugged off my appropriate jacket and went in search of gloves suited to the fingers of this me.

I thought I'd done an excellent, if hasty, job of cleaning up after my web-kin—*after all, I'd centuries of practice at it*—but when Ally Orman arrived, she stopped in the doorway and crossed her strong swimmer's arms, nodding curtly at the table. "Another pot, I see."

Which I'd had to leave on the table, mostly because the glue and paint remained revoltingly sticky but also because it was too big for this me to lift safely. I angled my ears in apology. "Sorry, Ally."

To my surprise, she chuckled and lowered her arms. "Don't be. I admire Lesley's creativity. She's an inspiration." The Human came to the table and considered the wildly dotted pot. "Ah, there's my scraper."

"The glue hasn't set—"

She held up a hand to stop my reach. "Leave it. I'll fabricate another.

This really is—" Her struggle for an adjective was familiar. "—remarkably passionate."

You could say that. "We're running out of pots," I confessed. Once Lesy had turned a practical object into a work of her art, there was no using it again. Not without thoroughly upsetting her. I'd learned that lesson the time she'd cemented Ersh's cutlery to the ceiling in a somewhat pleasant spiral. Ordered to set the table, I'd made the mistake of prying some forks from her creation. Catching me despoiling her latest masterpiece, Lesy collapsed dramatically into a tight wrinkled ball of woeful Dokecian—in the middle of the kitchen. I'd tried to stick the forks back on but apparently I'd no talent for it. *There'd been wailing.*

Suffice to say Ersh was furious—with me, not our cutlery thief, but fairness hadn't been an important part of my upbringing. I'd had to apologize and tickle Lesy, then we'd all loudly admired her artistry—without supper—until she grew happy again.

Mind you, once Lesy left Picco's Moon, Ersh had me chip off every utensil and scrape it clean. *Again, never fair.*

"You should order more," Ally said, gesturing to the table with its dotted pot.

I lowered my ears. "And encourage her?" With significant disbelief.

Her expression grew stern. "Esen-alit-Quar. Don't you know how vital Lesley's art is to her happiness?"

I did. *I just hadn't thought anyone else would notice.*

I regarded Ally more closely. Her disapproval seemed sincere and with me, because of Lesy. Yet another familiar situation, if one I'd honestly thought I'd left behind.

I could almost hear Ersh's voice. *You brought her back; she's your responsibility now.*

"I'll order pots," I conceded, lifting my ears as best I could under the circumstances.

After a quiet talk with our artist.

After the Lamentable Incident of this past winter, the Library's code for a threat to life and/or large-scale destruction, trapped three trainloads of scholars in the Library for slightly less than a full spin of the planet—causing significant distress, despite an epic party, and a painful amount of overtime—we'd put measures into place to forestall anything close to a recurrence. Hence the shipcity, where, if necessary, scholars could spend a night safely within their transport, and the enlargement of our plans for the addition to the main building to include an emergency shelter we hoped never to need.

No one knew how Lambo Reomattatii got his claws on those blueprints, but it wasn't beyond our former drive engineer's capabilities, nor, it turned out, was altering them to include a ground floor suite of rooms scaled to a Carasian in place of our planned staff lounge.

Why was anyone's guess, because Lambo wasn't telling. We'd have put in an apartment gladly if he'd ever asked for living quarters, but from the moment he'd arrived, Lambo insisted on squatting in the Chow. Although according to night maintenance, the huge creature had recently claimed a couple of rooms on the second floor basement, areas they wisely left alone.

The point being, Lambo preferred to have secrets and to sneak around us, as if ready to ambush.

A disturbingly predatory attitude in any employee, to be sure, but Lambo? We, including Lambo, used the male pronoun to keep his ultimate gender private, but our Carasian was destined to become she— fully female and a deadly carnivore—possibly within the year.

As the timing of an event guaranteed to instill consternation if not full-fledged panic among non-Carasians was, understandably, a sensitive topic around Carasians, Paul had reached out to Reeto, his former roommate. Who'd insisted on an explanation for the whole *declared dead/wasn't really* part of Paul's past first.

Since our arrival on Botharis, no one here had, to my consternation then dismay. *Humans.* Paul's view—*for once not entirely trustworthy in mine*—was that the famed Botharan abhorrence of prying into the affairs of others was just as well, given our history held secrets we couldn't share with them, ever.

It wasn't as if the *declared dead* had been intentional. Paul's Survey implant had gone off, signaling his imminent death, when he'd been impaled by a branch from a falling tree. *While courageously trying to save Ansky and me, not that we needed saving.*

Well, she had, but later and I'd failed. I'd had a wee nibble to remember her by, before letting the mountain stream wash her away.

The point being, we were rescued by Kraal who didn't appreciate tracking devices in their guests and removed Paul's without asking, thus Survey—in the form of Lionel Kearn, not that Paul would tell Reeto— received the final *Paul Ragem is dead* signal.

Which Paul could have corrected, being not dead, except we were being pursued by Lionel while we all were chasing the wild Web-being Death, and my friend put protecting me and my secret above his own happiness—

I'd tried to convince him to leave me, to reclaim his life. Tried to hide from him so he would, but—by any name—Paul was the most stubborn, impossible, wonderful friend a lonely Web-being could hope to find.

He'd made a new life, over the next fifty years with me. Had a new family, fathered twins, and we might have stayed as we were for the rest of Paul's days, except that Skalet chose to use the Kraal to flush us into the open again, right into Lionel's arms, leaving only one choice. Restore Paul's reputation at last, with Lionel's help.

And bring him back home, to Botharis.

Whatever version Paul used, and Reeto's reaction to it, Paul refused to tell me, but the Carasian did provide the list of female-to-come warning signs. We should watch for changes in appetite, but first would come irritability, outbursts of brilliance, and difficulty molting.

By those, Lambo should have been female already.

As staffing problems went, announcing the Chow's operator's pending debut as an obligate carnivore fell under the heading of *Defer Till Inevitable* with fervent hopes that we'd have sufficient warning to clear the Library of everyone edible and arrange Lambo's transport offworld. Unless our other arrangements came to fruition in time.

For this, and other reasons, whenever I stepped into the Chow, I did so with more than the usual level of ready-to-jump-out-again caution.

Today, however, I did an excellent impression of Ally and stopped in the doorway to stare at art.

For Lesy was still in the Chow. And she was painting. *Again.*

While eating. She'd a roll of something edible in her right hand. Her left was smeared with some condiment or other and she alternated using the yellow goo to add highlights and licking her fingers.

She was talented that way. After all, Lesy's preferred form was her five-armed Dokeci-self for a reason.

This time the object of her colorful attention wasn't a pot nor, to my relief, Lambo, who crouched near my web-kin, every eyestalk but the one briefly bent my way before ignoring me riveted on what was appearing on the Chow's wall.

Lesy rubbed her left hand over the rest of her roll, then thrust it toward the Carasian. "Red. That one." She pointed to a bowl at Lambo's feet.

A handling claw picked it up tenderly and brought it within reach. Shoving the rest of the roll in her mouth, Lesy scooped a gooey mass— red—with both hands then flung it against the wall. Rising to her knees, she quickly began stroking shapes out of it.

From the doorway—*I wasn't committing to any closer yet*—I saw what she was painting. According to Ersh memory and mine, Lesy's personal style was best described as free-form chaos. That said, if motivated she'd the technique to capture a scene or person with astonishing accuracy. Usually in materials destined to expire in under a minute, as if she didn't want to be caught slumming in reality.

What was taking shape on the Chow's wall, in condiment and sauce, was so realistic I could almost feel the fragrant spring air coming through Lesy's door. More than a door. She'd created a life-sized archway beckoning me out to a spacious patio set with tables and chairs, surrounding by fystia shrubs in bud. Shrubs much nicer than my poor stunted survivor, an implied and typical Elder critique jolting me from her spell.

Lambo hummed a deep enraptured note.

I hadn't known he'd wanted a patio. *He hadn't wanted customers.*

Technically, he had none. We didn't charge for meals served by the Anytime Chow's dispenser. How could we? Anyone brave or hungry enough to put themselves through Lambo's version of service deserved whatever they could get. Granted, the surly Carasian was polite to Paul.

Not to any version of me, however. *A sore point.*

"There." Lesy stepped back. "Your turn," she said with suspicious delight.

And didn't mean me.

Before I could do more than gasp, Lambo rammed both great claws into the wall and began furiously to scoop out foam and support materials and *yes, that had been plumbing*, flinging freshly anointed debris over his carapace. While humming.

The shrill of the Library's alarm signaled time for a pair of Web-beings to make their exit. I grabbed Lesy's arm and ran for it.

Nearby

L IONEL couldn't keep up with Paul, who beat him to the Chow by several strides, and Duggs was hot on his heels, swearing under her breath, because the alarm hadn't signaled an attack on the building— one of Lionel's particular nightmares—but instead warned of catastrophic structural failure at this location.

"Stop!" he heard Paul shout.

Lionel and Duggs followed him in as the BOOM of a final claw strike echoed in the ensuing calm, punctuated by the delicate patter as lighter debris rained down and water sprayed in little random fountains. The Carasian rattled around to face Paul, coated in dust and streaked with what looked very much like condiments. His eyestalks converged in a disturbingly happy cluster. "Do you like it?"

Duggs' face turned red; she actually whimpered with rage.

Catastrophic didn't cover it. "What are we to like, exactly?" Lionel asked, almost afraid to find out.

A handling claw waved jauntily at the massive hole in the wall. If not for the strength of the external layer, they'd be staring through dust into the Garden beyond; a strength Lionel doubted the original designers of a Survey emergency shelter had thought to test against a determined Carasian. *A report should go to the manufacturers—*

"The new door," Lambo asserted proudly.

Duggs found her voice. "It's a damned hole," she grated out.

"You aren't very observant. It's several holes." An eyestalk aimed her way. "From which you can make a door. I started the work for you. You're welcome."

"'Welcome?!!" Lionel watched in awe as Duggs' features writhed through dismay to outrage. "Started—you—" She spat. "YOU!!"

"I expect our head of security responded to a threat of some kind," Paul said, his tone suggesting that had better be the case or the job would go to someone—anyone—else. Avoiding the sprays, he closed on the Carasian and rapped his knuckles smartly on a claw larger in girth than his body. "What was it, Lambo?"

"There was no threat, Director," the creature replied calmly. "Lesley had a dream about the Chow." The low rumble softened to as close to a confiding whisper as physically possible. "She made it real." All eyestalks snapped to the wall and the Carasian hummed with pride.

A wall on which there was painted, Lionel abruptly recognized, the remnants of an arch painted in the exact color of a fish sauce he enjoyed, outlining the limits of Lambo's attack on the plumbing. *It did explain the appetizing smell.*

A claw snapped. "Lesley said it was my turn," the creature continued at normal volume. Three eyestalks aimed at the speechless Humans. "I'd barely started when Esen took her away. Growling. Most unprofessional."

"SHE was unprofessional? What do you call THIS?" Duggs pointed at the hole.

"Progress." A claw reached to coyly snap off a piece of exposed pipe. More water sprayed.

Duggs launched herself at the much larger Carasian. Lionel grabbed for her and missed.

Paul's upraised hand stopped her. "Lambo, you added an apartment to the new construction," he said quietly. "We agreed to make room for it. Surely sufficient—"

"That's for me. This is for the Chow." The Carasian gave a settling shake. "Summer is coming and we'll need a patio for customers."

The problem wasn't the idea, Lionel decided numbly. It was the unlikelihood of it ever originating in the devious brain within those pulsing armored plates. "Whatever made you think of a patio?"

"Humans like tables and chairs. They like to eat outside in good weather, in a pretty place, with their friends. It would please the staff and many of our visitors. Lesley told me so."

And there it was.

Duggs let out a string of epithets, ending with, "—HER. Again. I don't care if she's—" She caught herself, the near slip perceptible to the Humans, hopefully not to a Carasian. "—if she's famous. She can't be allowed to keep wrecking the place!" Perhaps finding Paul's now-chilly gaze hard to meet, she looked to Lionel. "I've documented!"

"Yes, you have." In fact, Lionel had a stack of complaint forms on his desk; paper complaint forms, because Duggs Pouncey, Botharan to her core, refused to be convinced important matters could be safely encoded within the com system. *Inefficient.* Especially as Duggs' handwriting looked like wild scratches when she wasn't livid with rage, not to mention the brown stains from her mug.

Lionel'd sent back a sheet that was soaking wet. It returned looking as if it had been dried with a torch.

The stack *documented*, in furious detail and with cost, the ongoing damage done by Lesley Delacora's artistic modifications to the property. Most concerned the Ragem farmhouse, but she'd painted the exterior of the barn as well, though the stripes had washed off in the rain.

Nothing outside appeared safe, other than the greenhouse, and Lionel couldn't tell if Lesley respected Paul and Esen's new home or was no longer interested in the building.

For a peaceful week and a half, Lionel'd believed the Library building itself would be immune from Lesley's ambitions. That changed about the same time as he discovered he'd been woefully uninformed about what constituted an artist's capabilities, though where Lesley had found an industrial grade portable grinder to "enhance" the Response Room door panel remained a mystery. Duggs claimed none of her crew's tools were missing. Esen had promised to start opening her web-kin's packages.

The Chow's wall would land on his stack. It'd be Duggs' first act on leaving the scene of Lesley's latest.

Paul's chuckle startled Lionel and shocked Duggs. "Lesley's right. I'd enjoy a patio myself."

With an eager swoosh of air, a great claw rose—

"No more of that, please, Lambo." Paul tipped his head. "Duggs is in charge of the physical structure of the Library."

"Then she can do it," declared the giant, eyestalks shifting to Duggs.

"Rock for Brains," that worthy said in a dangerously even tone. "This 'start' of yours has shut down the staff showers and caused a short in the saltwater pumps in aquatics. Just fixing those will take days, and that's if you keep out of my way. You'll be lucky if I build you an apartment. I'm not building you a damned patio."

All eyestalks returned to Paul. Was that a beseeching look? "Is the Garden only for Esen and Esolesy Ki?"

Catching Paul's meaningful glance, Lionel gave a tiny nod. Lesley's dreams and idea. Now what sounded very much like a direct quote from Esen's Elder. As such, the complaint wasn't to be ignored. His friend needed to talk to Esen about this, and soon.

Making the rest his job. Lionel coughed. "If I may make a suggestion, Director? Let me consult with Lambo concerning his proposal. Which does have some merit," this with a beseeching look of his own at Duggs.

She gave him a ferocious scowl, wanting to disagree, but he knew her well enough to guess she liked the idea. *Not that she'd ever admit it.* Lionel waited patiently.

"Written up," Duggs snapped finally. "With blueprints. I know you can do those." Her scowl transferred to Lambo. "And what the director said. No more—that!" She thrust a finger at the ruined wall.

The Carasian, who'd surged to a posture of triumph, subsided with a disappointed clatter. "Agreed. I am gratified to work closely with Administrator Kearn, who shows an intelligence rare for your species. When he isn't being stupid," this added generously.

To his surprise, Paul frowned. "I doubt Lionel has time—"

"He must!" Lambo roared. "This work is vital!"

"I'll show you vital—" Duggs yelled.

"I have time!" Lionel nodded repeatedly, grateful when the shouting stopped. "I have time," he repeated. "Don't worry. I can fit this in, Paul."

"Very well." Paul turned to their contractor. "Duggs?"

Her glower spoke volumes, but she nodded. "I'll send in a cleanup crew and get on the repairs. When they're done, you'll feed them and be nice about it." With a glare at Lambo.

Who rose to his full height, clawtips parting in threat. "I AM ALWAYS NICE!"

Unimpressed, Duggs glared until the Carasian gave a small shudder and shrank to normal size.

Paul ducked his head, hiding a smile.

Lionel surveyed the mess on the floor and counter. The food dispenser, being a sensible machine, had turned itself off. He'd learn what that implied for the raw ingredients inside later. First things first.

"I'll inform staff." There'd be no breakfast from the Chow this morning—probably no service at all during the construction. His job. They'd have to bust out the ration stores, use the self-heating tubes for now.

As for the trainload of scholars about to arrive? An informative sign outside the existing entrance to the Chow, in multiple languages and formats. Tape an "X" to deter any aerials. No, a net. Less tempting to Heezles.

And he'd best put a rush on the permits to allow food service for non-Humans in the Port Village.

Maybe no one would be hungry.

Duggs stormed off, muttering darkly. As Lionel and Paul went down the admin corridor, the latter stopped at his office door. "I know you're in a hurry, but a moment?"

"Of course."

The window was set to transparent, filling the room with diffused sunlight. The view looked past the Garden to the hill where the Ragem farmhouse and barn had stood for generations. As far as the eye could see, spring was in full force, a tapestry of urgent green and rose buds, pale shoots thrusting from the ground, and, new this year, the swathe of dark brown mud marking a temporary road.

A construction road, hard as it was to believe. Needed, Lionel'd been assured by everyone he could find to ask, because no one in the entire province of Crickysee had flight-capable heavy transports, other than

Duggs' personal craft. Grav sleds? Frivolities reserved for starships and those in Grandine, the capital.

A transport full of mud from the excavation skidded by as Lionel watched, the driver barely able to keep its treads on the road. *Actual treads touching the ground.* It was a sight to behold.

However it was done, Lionel decided, the work couldn't go fast enough. Paul and Esen shouldn't be living in the greenhouse, for starters, not that either would let him bring up the subject.

"Paul, if this is about my model—" he began, careful not to use the term Framers, "—the comp hasn't finished processing."

"It's not." Paul took one of the paired armchairs, beckoning him to the other. "Lionel, I fear I've put you in an untenable position."

"The patio?" Lionel raised his eyebrows. "I've sorted things out between Duggs and Lambo before now." Easier than between Duggs and Skalet, for that matter, and that was before Duggs learned of Esen and her Web—a turn of events Skalet wasn't to know. *Was it cowardice to hope to be offworld when—not if—she did?*

"True, and we thank you for that." Paul ran an absent hand through his thick black hair. There were faint touches of gray in it, though only the tiniest wrinkles in the skin beside eyes and mouth. Most of those were from laughter.

Some lines were not; Paul's life had changed irrevocably once linked to that of a semi-immortal Web-being with a penchant for good deeds and a knack for poor planning. Speaking of whom— "Any word from Esen?"

After the events of last winter, she'd promised them both to be more diligent about using her personal com. Not much of a promise, given she'd rarely if ever used it before, but Esen had seen how worried Paul'd been—they'd all been—about her. Her heart, whichever form it took at the moment, was always in the right place.

"Yes." A half smile. "She's taken Lesley up to the house. Something about washing off a question mark."

"Metaphor?"

"I was afraid to ask. Paul's smile faded. "Esen's aware she has to talk to her web-kin about more than gemmies."

"Gently, I trust. Lesley's—" *fragile and childlike* "—a favorite of the staff. The majority of them," Lionel qualified, recalling the stack of complaints on his desk. He struggled to be more positive. "I think she's doing quite well. The other day, Lesley resolved a question for a cluster of Rands when Esen wouldn't."

A flicker of anger in those gray eyes. "Esen avoids Rands for good reason. You know that."

Because he'd been there   here in this office, in fact—when Paul had been forced to set Esen's Rand-self on fire to save her. If he hadn't, she'd have lost herself within the longing that glued a cluster into a functional colony.

About to apologize, Lionel frowned in thought. "Did you know Lesley doesn't? She told me afterward, Paul, that she's been a Rand. She called the experience 'entertaining while it lasted.'"

"She and Esen are nothing alike." Dismissing the Web-being, Paul stood and began to pace. Reaching his desk, he paused to rest the fingertips of his left hand on the top, staring down as if they held an answer to a puzzle.

Or the right words— "You mentioned an 'untenable position,'" Lionel said quietly, abruptly guessing what this was about. He'd expected a challenge to his decision. "I can be out of Skalet's quarters today, if that's what you want."

His friend looked up, his obvious surprise reassuring. "Not at all. If you're comfortable there, Lionel, believe me, it's a relief. Not only as a proper bed for you, for the time being, but Esen—she's convinced something in there will be how Skalet reaches out to us. If she does."

"*When* she does," Lionel corrected, hearing the caution but determined to believe what he chose. That Skalet would be in contact when it was safe to do so, if only to convey information about the Framers. He gave his friend a quizzical look. "If not that—what's this about?"

"Your relationship with Lambo."

His eyebrows rose. "I wouldn't call it a relationship. Yes, I've spent more time with our Carasian these past months, but I've been following up on his claims as to why he's here at all, let alone trying to sneak into our systems." Claims that seemed solid, but . . .

"What is it?" Paul asked, reading his face.

Lionel grimaced. "It's proved difficult to get definitive answers from the university. Or from Anytime Chow, for that matter. They produce documentation of a Carasian, but no one will swear it's this one."

"We're having the same trouble." Paul's "we" referring to members of his Group. "Even for a Carasian, Lambo's conspicuous. You'd think we'd be able to find some reliable witnesses."

"His knowledge of drive engineering passed every test I could devise." Tests Lambo had found ludicrously easy, proof if he needed more. "And I located a construction supervisor at Dresnet Shipyards who said a Lambo Reomattatii apprenticed with her and showed great promise. Alas, her description of 'big, black, and cranky' is as familiar as it is inconclusive." Lionel sighed. "It certainly doesn't help that Lambo avoids surveillance like a trained spy."

"Is he?"

"You're not serious."

Paul leaned back in his chair, eyes gleaming. "'It has been observed that solitary Carasians who live and work among aliens for an extended period of time will forge unique and original moral codes— '"

"'—possibly to enable them to function more comfortably outside species' norms.'" Lionel harrumphed. "A sadly outdated text and you know it. Carasians are as capable as Humans when it comes to blending into a new society without changing who and what they are. Which is both highly moral and exquisitely conscious of individual legacy. Not a species inclined to blur the edges." He pointed an accusing finger. "Leading me to conclude, Director Ragem, that you are not serious."

A noncommittal shrug. "What I know is we haven't had Lambo's full story—and may never hear it. He's a private being under all that bluster." They shared a quiet chuckle at that before Paul grew serious. "What I want to talk to you about, Lionel, isn't about Lambo's morality or past. It's about what just happened in the Chow between the two of you."

Immediately concerned, Lionel did a mental review of their latest contact. Nothing seemed out of the ordinary where their Carasian was concerned. "Did I make a mistake?"

"No. Not exactly." Paul gave a small cough. "How familiar are you with Carasians? The species itself. Not knowledge—I know you've that—but personal connections. I've a reason for asking."

"'Personal'?" Lionel echoed, mystified. "Almost none, other than Lambo. I've some academic contacts; attended lectures in my early years. Why?"

"That's what I was afraid of—it's nothing you've done, Lionel. The signs—I should have seen them. I'd a Carasian roommate," Paul offered as if that explained any of this. "And Esen's one, on occasion."

"What signs?"

"Doesn't matter. What does is why Lambo jumped at this patio idea of Lesley's. It's not about Human comfort. I think he's instinctively seeking access outdoors. To where there's space and privacy for a Carasian-sized pool."

"We are not building—*her*—a pool," Lionel protested. "Whatever would we—how could we—the dietary constraints alone, Paul!"

"I guarantee you Lambo isn't thinking clearly. Not when a male our Carasian clearly admires appears ready to make that commitment."

"Admires?! That's not pos—" Lionel felt the blood drain from his face. "You can't—he—she—" He swallowed. "Female Carasians eat unsatisfactory mates!"

"That they do." Paul chuckled. "We won't let it get that far," he promised. "It's time Esolesy Ki returned to the Library. I'll contact Rudy and start the process."

Meaning Captain Rudy Lefebvre, Paul's cousin and their friend, would touch down on the landing field and waddle down his ship's ramp as a reasonable facsimile of their young Lishcyn, to be greeted by Esen herself.

"Lambo respects Esen in that form, little as he admits it," Paul added with a smile, "and you, my dear Lionel, will be far too busy to help with the patio project. I'll convey the message."

"Please do," Lionel said stiffly, wondering how he'd ever be able to go back into the Chow without worrying what was going on behind Lambo's many-eyed stare. He'd probably starve—

Of course he wouldn't, he told himself. His problems were nothing compared to the Carasian's pending predicament. A rush of compassion thickened his voice. "We must make provision for Lambo's—ah—her future, Paul."

An approving nod. "I've asked Esen. She told me the responsible approach would be to fire Lambo immediately and pay for passage offworld. Carasian females take care of themselves." Paul gave another little shrug. "But, as we've learned by now, our Lambo isn't typical of the species. In light of his peculiarities, Esen's proposed we hire a male

Carasian as soon as possible, and let him work on a pool if so inclined. Along with a food source we can all accept."

Why, the clever little— Lionel pursed his lips and let out a soundless whistle, considering the ramifications, then nodded. "Our agreements for the Library allow for non-staff aliens living onsite, but this—we'll need quarters in place for him first."

"At a safe distance." Paul spread his arms. "In case Lambo isn't impressed."

Lionel laughed and shook his head. "Astonishing. Did you ever think we'd be matchmaking Carasians?"

"Can't say I did." His friend's face grew pensive. "Then again, I've learned not to think too far ahead."

Lionel felt a chill at the words, though Paul merely stated the reality. Was it because they'd both gained a new appreciation of what *ephemeral* meant, living with those who weren't? That a Human lifetime was not only finite, but all too short?

Or did Paul, intentionally or not, warn against becoming too attached to this moment in their lives, when everything was better than Lionel had dreamed it could be, even with the threat of the Framers and Skalet among the Kraal—

A moment and life he'd hold onto with all of his being. Lionel coughed. "I'll start inquiries into a potential new member of the staff." *Lock down the future—this future—in as many ways as he could. Protect it.* "We could use another plumber."

"Never fit in the accesses."

"Any ideas?"

"None at the moment, but keep in mind you're Lambo's standard," Paul said with a completely straight face. "Our new Carasian will have to measure up. Intelligent. Resourceful."

"Handsome," Lionel joked back, glad to lighten things. "Definitely handsome."

"Whoa, there." But with that warm, generous smile.

Lionel returned it, fighting the sudden irrational urge to grab Paul Ragem and hold on to him too.

Out There

TEACH me how to say hello, Momma. I want to learn every way there is.
Why?
To make friends.

Veya has none, but she's not alone. Among the shards of memory, out the corner of her eye, she glimpses parts that aren't hers. Aren't Human or aren't female. Not her shape nor her scars—

She defines herself by what she isn't. A game of stark numbing horror, to sort the drifting collection into _theirs_, not _hers_—

Other eyes are tethered by filaments, beyond reach of their original owners. Human, some. Others, not. All of the eyes stare into the featureless mist, stripped of lid or lash, and she cannot wonder what they see or watch.

Being too full of what the eye—_hers_, not _theirs_—tethered beyond her reach can.

Captain says we've a problem. Sent me to talk to you.
The problem isn't me. The problem is the corridor's corrupted.
There's something already there.
What? Sensors are clean.

I don't know what it is. I see lightning. Glistening filaments. I see—
Techs say that's your mind making sense of the feed—
I know what I see—

Her eye focuses. It means she'll see another ship engulfed soon. Have no choice but see those inside pulled out and shredded, bits tethered by filaments to hang in Hell's featureless mist.

They aren't *her*, those bits. They aren't *his*.

But oh the grief. She clings to it. Holds the grief of everyone else, as well as her own—

3: Bathtub Morning; Excavation Afternoon

"**D**ONE." I put aside the sponge, regarding Lesy's back critically. Except for reddened patches where I'd had to scrub, the blue question mark she'd painted on her skin was gone. Asking how she'd managed it would only earn me a lengthy and pointless lesson in how to do it to myself. *Not happening.*

As for asking why? While she might have had a reason beyond adornment, one presumably making sense to her, in my experience it wouldn't make sense to anyone else, especially me. *Not worth the risk.*

"Rinse?" I offered, holding up the nozzle.

Supple as a fish, Lesy spun around to rinse herself, splashing suds and water over me and the tiles. She rose with the waves and crossed her arms on the side of the tub, resting her chin on them to regard me with amusement.

As I sputtered and rubbed myself frantically with a towel. Being *WET.* I growled under my breath.

"We should go swimming in your little river," my unrepentant web-kin proposed. "As Rrabi'sk. You like that."

This was new. I paused, towel in both paws, to stare at her. "Rrabi'sk are extinct. We can't use the form on Botharis—" I'd told Lesy my Web had a rule: if it wasn't here, don't be it.

Though more a prudent guideline I broke on occasion—

"Oietae, then. We can use the habitat zone. And while we're there,"

Lesy said, rising up in the excitement of Artistic Endeavor, so more water splashed out, "I can freshen up the space. It's dull."

Admittedly, interior design hadn't been high on our list, considering the challenge of making a substantial section of the Library building watertight and filling it so we could offer a variety of suitable salinities, pressures, and temperatures to visiting scholars. With collection interfaces that worked while wet, but that wasn't the point. "Why do you suddenly want to go swimming?" I asked cautiously.

"I'm bored." Lesy flounced back down, producing another wave crest. I was amazed there was any water left in the tub. "Bored," she repeated, lifting a foot into the air and wiggling her toes.

Not good. Not good. "Is that why you got Lambo fired up over a patio?"

The toes froze in place, then began to bend, one at a time. "I didn't want to eat in that room again. It's not pretty, like our Garden." The other foot rose. "It is *our* Garden, is it not?"

It certainly wasn't, not if Lesy planned to redecorate it. Though my feet were in a puddle, I concentrated on drying my ears.

"Esen-alit-Quar." Unlike Ersh's soul-devastating invocation of my full name, Lesy's came with a plaintive quiver at the end. Delivered as she rose once more into sight, and yes, her full bottom lip was quivering too. "Tell me it's *OURS*."

When my precious plants were at stake, I discovered I'd some spine after all. "It belongs to the Library," I informed her. Firmly.

Her blue eyes filled with real tears.

Fine. "The clearing where our Web meets is ours," I capitulated. "Where you danced for Evan," I added, since our Web of three hadn't technically met there yet. As the space was a hidden stone patio surrounded by large boulders, I didn't see what harm Lesy's Human-self could do to it.

I'd remember that later.

Now, however, I was rewarded by her dazzling smile, Lesy's upset vanquished like magic. She climbed from the tub, taking my towel and spinning in a circle with it. A graceful circle, without slipping on the wet tiles, and I grinned to see her happy.

It was how she won, I thought suddenly, and stopped grinning. "Lesy, you brought a pot into the Response Room again."

Another circle, the towel now a flag over her head. "Did you like it?"

Lesy didn't wait for me to answer, going to the counter to sit before the mirror. She started to pin her wet hair in complicated knots.

She didn't wait, because she didn't care, not really, about my opinion. Considering the abysmal quality of my art appreciation skills, that was fair. What wasn't, from a Human perspective and even from mine?

She didn't care that she'd left a mess for me to tidy. The story of our lives together, me tidying after Lesy, me keeping her happy, and now, when it was about keeping her and our secret safe?

I felt at a loss. *What would Ersh do?*

She'd have me go with Lesy to Portula Colony, or some other place where my web-kin had created a home. Keep her company until she'd reestablished herself, which meant waiting until she'd started a new project and simply forgot I was still there.

Portula was gone, destroyed by Death when that wild primal Web-being had hunted Lesy-the-original. Death had consumed her, not that I'd share the memory with Lesy-the-restored. The bits of her I'd collected on Dokeci Na predated the end of her existence.

And too much time had passed for any other home Lesy had made for herself, any identity, to remain safe. I'd no idea how to tell her.

Or if I even should. Paul understood why I'd accepted Lesy's plea not to know what had happened. To her. To Ersh, Ansky, Mixs. She wanted to stay happy, believing we'd a home on Picco's Moon, that Ersh ruled her mountain there, that we could go back.

Even it was a lie.

My friend called it mercy. Skalet, predictably, called it cowardice.

Family. I sighed, very quietly, and picked up the wet towel before padding over to stand by Lesy's shoulder. Our eyes met in the mirror. Mine were to either side of a long dappled snout, hers, above an elegant Human nose. My ears, however, were lowered in distress, and I left them that way. "Lesy, I need—"

"What you need is a game!" Her eyes sparkled. "Are you ready to play, Es? I've hidden my latest art just for you. I used all my new treasures for it. It's spectacular, if I do say."

I wasn't sure what alarmed me more, that she'd stolen the gemmies for a game, or the notion of *spectacular* art lurking on the Library grounds. "I thought you lost the gemmies," I mumbled, losing the advantage. *If I'd ever had it.*

Her hand waved, pins flying free. "I lost them in my latest art," Lesy explained, as if I should know such things. "All for our game." An almost invisible frown. "There will be more, won't there? When the trains come today?"

"That, I can guarantee," I replied. How to keep Lesy out of the recycle bins was now my new problem.

Problems were much less fun than Lesy's games. Despite my often having to grovel to whomever among our web-kin turned out to be the brunt of it, Lesy being extraordinarily good at finding secrets and causing mischief, if not so much at apologizing. Skalet was her favorite target, which was why the two were rarely home at the same time unless summoned by Ersh, and there was no Kraal trick or tech able to keep Lesy out when motivated. *I'd taken a guilty pleasure in seeing my formidable web-kin reduced to shaking with fury that wasn't at me.*

Then there were the games where Lesy's goal turned out to be getting me in as much trouble as possible, so Ersh—

Choosing to remember the *fun*, I lifted my ears. "How do we start?" After all, I told myself virtuously. I had to find her latest creation and make sure it wasn't a hazard to the unexpecting.

Beaming, Lesy turned on the stool and brought her nose to mine. "I give you a clue, Esen dear, and you go hunting. Ready?"

I'd need dry clothes—and feet—but the word *hunting* worked its spell on this me, and I licked her chin. "Ready!"

"You must be looking down to see, the spectacular art I made for thee."

I blinked. "That's the clue?"

Lesy spun around, busy with her hair again, leaving me facing her question-free back. "Hurry, Es," she told me. "It won't last long."

And just like that, I growled to myself, *the game had become a problem of its own.*

In my experience, Lesy's clues were rarely subtle. She loved games and her favorite type was hiding herself—or things—but, as Skalet would say, our Elder lacked the patience to wait for gratification.

You must be looking down to see, the spectacular art I made for thee.

It seemed clear. I left the farmhouse, quite sure where I needed to go. And that Duggs was *not* going to be pleased.

Paul? I couldn't guess. He'd shown remarkable tolerance for Lesy's inconvenient creativity, though—like Ersh—he expected me to deal with the result. Limiting her access to large power tools and masonry had helped—but insufficient, based on today.

. . . must be looking down.

There was only one place I could think of where looking down was presently easy and where Lesy could count on her art not lasting for long.

Duggs' Pit.

Unfortunately, I was wrong.

Spring's a tricky beast, as seasons go, depending on planet type and the vagaries of the local star. Spring in the southern hemisphere of Abseran means a mad scramble underground by local life as their part of the world tilts ominously closer to their red giant sun, an extra kick of radiation accompanying the arrival of searing heat.

In the northern hemisphere of Botharis, on this, Norrsland, smallest of its three continents, within the eastern mountainous province of Crickysee, the valley-carved county of Straint, and most specifically the tiny Hamlet of Hillsview?

I'd learned spring meant mud.

And this spring we'd more than our share, thanks to Duggs. The excavation, known as Duggs' Pit, would ultimately descend the full two floors of the Library's existing basement, allowing a future connection to expand our storage capacity for, yes, artifacts.

There being no end of the things in sight.

Last year, as Esolesy Ki, I'd proposed a slide from inside the greenhouse to the new basement, ideally with a twisty loop, but apparently there were structural concerns. That would have ended my pleading—I hadn't really wanted a slide *there* anyway, hoping more for one from whatever future suite of rooms Paul and I shared into the Garden, and my plan was to warm my Humans to the idea of a slide for me *somewhere*—but as the mere mention of a "slide" now made Duggs flinch?

Persisting in asking had considerable entertainment value.

There was none in mud. Mud surrounded the excavation and coated equipment. Mud disguised as a roadway allowed the approach of muddy transports to pick up more mud; and where it went, I certainly didn't care so long as it didn't come back.

Above all, there was a thick gooey layer of mud at the bottom of Duggs' Pit, it having rained for the previous week—

—and I'd brought most of it back to the greenhouse. *On me.*

Ears flat, I used a second towel to scrape gooey brown oozing mud from the once-clean fur of my left flank and leg, the first towel a brown oozing lump on the floor. *I'd need more.* Fortunately, we'd a stack in the greenhouse.

"She didn't think you'd take her seriously," Paul said after a moment.

Licking mud from my nose, I snarled my opinion of that and thrust out my hand for another towel. My friend wasn't filthy and dripping, having remained on the top of the excavation with everyone else, instead of slipping to the bottom. Where there was mud. Masses of gooey ooz-ing *WET* mud.

As if mud wasn't insult enough, none of the Humans had been will-ing to get equally filthy to help me out of it. Oh no. They'd sent down a basket. And when those watching from above realized I hadn't been hurt, just drenched in mud?

They'd laughed until I scrambled out, ears flat and fangs showing. *Humans.*

"She's sorry." The words lacked conviction. Paul knew as well as I did Duggs enjoyed what she called my *gullible side.*

I reached around and gently grasped my tail. It looked like a piece of soggy rope and felt—suffice to say there'd be no wagging before it was clean and dry. I lifted it with a pained sigh.

"I could get a hose."

As I glared at him, a dollop of mud plopped from my tail.

The corners of Paul's generous mouth pinched.

"Not helping," I informed him, recognizing an incipient laugh when I saw it. *Not the first time.* "Helping is finding more towels."

"I know. I will." He pointed at my head. "You missed some—" All at once Paul covered his mouth and made a strangled sound, eyes bright.

It was, I supposed, *funny.* Not my present state, nor the deplorable idea of being inflicted with a spray of water, but Duggs' ability to trick me each and every time. *If you want to look down, go right to the edge*, she'd said. *It'll hold you. You're light*, she'd said. *I swear I saw something floating down there—*

Me, as it turned out. Not that I floated for long.

Using a dry towel, Paul began pressing mud from my back. "I'll talk to her," he told me, the amusement gone from his voice. "Duggs doesn't mean any harm, but she has to understand."

I glowered. "Understand what?"

"That your trust is a gift." The towel paused, then resumed. "I shouldn't have let it go this far—some of it's your fault, Old Blob."

"Mine?!" My ears shot up in protest, flicking mud in every direction.

Paul wiped brown spots from his face and regarded me thoughtfully. I regarded him right back, knowing that look. *Lesson coming.*

Sure enough. "We play our games but you know I'd never let you come to harm."

I'd have bristled, but there was mud. I settled for: "Of course. We're friends. Friends play."

"That we are." With a small smile, he resumed drying my back. "In her way, Duggs is trying to play. As your friend."

I held up my poor tail. "Not a friend." With the hint of a snarl as I admitted to myself it wasn't the mud or *WET*. Something hurt, inside. "I could have been damaged, falling like that." *Not really, but he knew what I meant.*

"Duggs tried to catch you at the last minute—she says," Paul qualified, but I could tell he believed her.

I wanted to. "So how is it my fault?"

"You're too trusting. Yes," quickly, as I made to protest, "you've learned to dodge snowballs."

"And water balloons," I grumbled, my friend prone to ambushing me with the horrid things on hot days. "And boxes. And—"

"Hold on there." Paul chuckled as he grabbed a new towel and moved his attention to the back of my neck, where I couldn't reach.

"Those are games. You know perfectly well when I'm playing. You do, don't you?"

A little late to ask, I thought, but nodded, detecting a faint note of worry. "I do when it's you. When it's Duggs, I don't."

"You'll have to learn, Old Blob. Think of it as a chance to expand your knowledge base about Humans," he coaxed. "Duggs is sly. Crude, at times. She—"

When he hesitated, I twisted to look at him. "What?"

Paul's eyebrows had drawn together. Not quite a frown. Not a pleased look either. "It's occurred to me our Duggs uses her practical jokes to test new relationships. It's not kind, but you could think of it as a form of self-protection. Only those determined to be close to her would put up with it and stay."

Like Ganthor, I thought, blinking in surprised recognition. Because I blinked, mud got in one eye and stung. My desperate flailing paw encountered a towel, and I used it to scrub my snout furiously. Once I could see again, I gazed through tears at Paul. "You're saying Duggs is a Ganthor."

For a Human, she resembled one. As tall as Skalet but heavier built— not all muscle, Duggs enjoyed her treats, but most. Physical and expressive. I'd seen her angry. There'd been stomping.

Ganthor greeted those they knew by shoving against one another with all their might. To ask acceptance into a new herd meant taking that bruising punishment until they allowed you to stay. Or you died.

"An apt comparison." Paul's eyes lit up. "What we need is a herd matriarch."

The leader who signaled when the shoving started—and stopped. As well as everything else but, for my needs, this was ample.

"How?" This was one of those moments when my friend had thought of something and, instead of telling me, waited for me to catch up. *Being half-coated in mud didn't encourage patience.* Still, I tried to follow his reasoning. Obviously we didn't have the Human equivalent of a herd matriarch handy. A Lishcyn could shove back, with force able to earn a Ganthor's respect, and Duggs knew Esolesy Ki was me. That could work. But this me? "I don't want to bite her," I admitted in a very small voice.

"Don't worry. You won't have to." With welcome, if mysterious, conviction in his voice. "It's time you gave Duggs a bit of her own, Fangface. Stop cleaning up."

I dropped the towel, clutching my poor sodden tail. "We're going to the farmhouse?" The greenhouse did have a portable shower stall, all fine and good for a Human's smooth skin and insignificant hairs but those of us with proper coats? The farmhouse had a full, delightful fresher with a sand shower option and dryer. Oh, how I'd missed my dryer—the fluff cycle—*Lesy wouldn't mind.* I gave a happy little moan of anticipation.

"No. I've got a better idea." Paul scooped mud from the floor in two hands, a suddenly worrisome *there could be water balloons* gleam in his eyes as he leaned over me. "Hold still."

Nearby

SCINTILLATION Bay was near the equator, granting it a reassuring predictability. Year-long, the timing of sunrise and sunset varied by no more than a few minutes, and rain fell once a day in the so-called dry season and twice daily in the wet.

Each bedroom had a private covered balcony. Evan's, like Great Gran's above, faced the bay. Stripped to his swim briefs, he made himself comfortable in the basket swing to wait out the afternoon rain.

The deluge approached as a massive gray wall, beneath roiling black clouds. Beneath, the waves calmed. Birds grew silent. Treefrogs grew loud and the air around him seemed to pull away. Evan tipped back his head and opened his mouth to breathe.

Waiting.

The rain's leading edge struck the house, slamming against leaf and tile with a deafening roar. Each great drop shattered and bounced from the balcony railing, sending a fine mist to coat his legs. A second storm began as the roof shed rain in sheets, hiding the trees and bay beyond.

His skin pimpled as the temperature plunged and Evan smiled at a memory. *Goosebumps.* His younger self had assumed the term was reserved for those named Gooseberry. Great Gran had explained what a goose was, and how a plucked carcass had little bumps on the skin where feathers had been. She'd told him how marvelous an adaptation

Humans had, that their skin reacted to cold by tightening up and raising its tiny hairs.

Evan remembered his young self being unimpressed by tiny hairs and asking Great Gran if he could grow fur or have feathers, as either would be warmer. She'd told him to put on a sweater.

Did the alien who'd donated its genes to him have fur or feathers? Evan stretched out his foot, examining the smooth skin of his calf and thigh, the creases on his knee. He'd learned, these past weeks, that the "Human-only" result that had comforted his family wasn't the whole story. The non-Human would be lurking, dormant, deep in his cells. Could huddle within his bones or in organs. There was no guarantee a chimeric legacy wouldn't resurface, part of a process through which one partner adapted to the other, or if a new challenge to the body activated a response.

If he stayed in a cold place, might he grow fur or feathers? However unlikely, Evan thought he could accept either, if he knew which to expect. It was the unknown beneath his skin—the secret—that troubled him.

Rain continued to hammer the roof as the storm front left the bay. Sunlight glittered on waves in the distance. Rainbows danced and the temperature shot up. The air, once thin, grew thick and scented.

Evan stood, stilling the swing of the basket chair with the brush of his hand. Time to go.

His feet having recovered most of their calluses, Evan stepped on twigs and other storm debris without care. The sand, damp from the rain, remained cool to the touch. It wouldn't for long. As the sun evaporated the last cloud, the air in open areas began to shimmer and sizzle with heat.

Evan moved in the shade, crouched under the low dripping fronds, searching for telltale glints of blue. After every rain, Great Gran's orchard briefly swarmed with plump little Nerfie Crabs, leaving their burrows to scavenge fallen fruit.

There. He pounced, catching the creature behind its snapping claws and placing it in his net sack.

If he failed to fill the sack, he'd dump his catch and hope for better luck tomorrow. But if he did? Evan licked his lips. Tonight the crabs would be supper, boiled then cracked open, served with Uncle Tam-ja Gooseberry's Extra Sizzle Sauce—a taste he'd missed offworld, if not that same uncle's dreaded fruitcake.

Having thought of it, Evan waited. To his surprise, the *FEAR* didn't come. *Of all the phobias to finally put to rest.* He'd need to face a slice of cake next holiday to be convinced.

Glint. Pounce. Glint. Pounce. His skin grew slick with sweat as well as leftover raindrops—the reason for the swim briefs—and Evan wiped his face with the back of an arm. He grinned with triumph as he dropped in a final catch, filling the sack as the rest of the crabs retreated from the sun.

Holding the netted—and angrily snapping—mass of blue crustaceans at a distance, Evan stepped on the boardwalk and into the open. The wood was hot underfoot. His head and shoulders burned. He'd take his catch to the kitchen, then come back down for a swim in the sparkling water—

He spotted a strange runabout tied at the wharf below, next to Great Gran's larger sailboat. By the look, a rental from the marina at nearby Sandling's Point. Blown in with the rain? Or, less welcome, visitors.

Why they were here—whomever they were—could wait.

Evan lengthened his strides, anxious to be rid of the crabs and get to his room—and dressed—before being seen—

"Evan!"

Too late.

Great Gran beckoned him through the kitchen door. She wasn't alone. Two stood with her, Human males, in their mid-fifties. At first glance, their loose-fitting floral shirts and brown skirts, the sandals and straw hats obviously new, suggested tourists, the kind beloved by the sellers waiting by the marina. They'd even the beginnings of sunburn on their pale arms.

Then one moved, tilting his head. As recognition struck, Evan stiffened. The face was bearded, the bearing different, but he remembered those bright, piercing eyes.

Petham Erilton. At least that was the name he'd used on Dokeci-Na while pretending to be a senior administrator at the Commonwealth

Embassy, a role he'd shed like a coat during the crisis with the Maree-pavlovax. Erilton was a high-level government operative of some kind, with discretion to act and, it turned out, the power to do so, offering to order the Survey ship *Mistral* to land armed security. Erilton hadn't returned to the embassy after the situation was resolved, and no one asked after him.

Perhaps no one dared.

Those piercing eyes narrowed slightly; acknowledgment and warning.

Of what? Evan felt ridiculous in his sweat-soaked briefs, crabs snapping. Ridiculous and helpless, along with a growing outrage. What was someone like Erilton doing in their kitchen? Had Kamaara reported his query after all?

Absurd. Even if she had, the worst he could expect was a standard termination notice, not a visit from government operatives—

The second intruder bent to peer at the crabs, then looked up with a disarming smile. "Looks like a feast."

Great Gran chuckled, earrings tinkling. "Thanks to my lad. Well done," she praised as she took the sack from Evan's unresisting hand, giving him a luminous smile. "Plenty for company, do you think?"

She'd missed entertaining. Not that these were ordinary guests or safe, but seeing the longing in her eyes, Evan hadn't the heart to refuse. "There is."

"It's settled, then," Great Gran exclaimed joyfully, waving the sack at their visitors. "Evan, this is Eller Theelen and his brother Decker. They've come from Senigal III."

Aliases, doubtless with immaculate idents to back them up. Of the two, Decker was heavier, with broad shoulders and the look of someone you wouldn't want to fight. Evan had learned the signs. Tufts of nondescript brown hair showed beneath his hat and his blunt features were eminently forgettable. The look in his brown eyes was placid, almost dull—an expression Evan didn't believe for a second.

As for Senigal III? Surely another lie, yet—*that name meant something*—

Before Evan could remember what, Great Gran continued proudly, "They've come all this way to buy my little boat. Imagine that."

Evan didn't try. "*Sparkles* isn't for sale."

"Of course she isn't." In complete command, squirming sack held at arm's length, Great Gran glided to the huge sink under the main kitchen window, her dress billowing like a sail itself. "Doesn't mean we can't show her off to an appreciative audience." The crabs, sensing the end was near, began struggling in earnest. She emptied them into the sink, the creatures climbing over one another in a frenzy to escape.

"We could make a very lucrative offer, Fem Gooseberry," Theelen/Erilton said, following her to the sink. He caught a crab who'd made it to the countertop, deftly avoiding the claws. "Let me help with those."

Lies. In Great Gran's kitchen.

Protest dying on his lips, Evan turned and went up the stairs to get dressed.

Ordinarily, Evan stayed on shore when Great Gran took visitors on *Sparkles,* space on deck and below tight without adding someone who already knew the boat's specs by heart. Sail area and displacement, ballast ratios and keel length: the sum was a long, sleek racing yacht, thoroughly uncomfortable on long journeys but well able, as Great Gran would say, to make you feel alive.

Grown up in the life, Evan was comfortable on the water and a good sailor. Great Gran was a superb one and, when the mood struck her, she'd push *Sparkles* to the limit and beyond, singing at the top of her lungs. If you could avoid falling over the side, you found yourself caught up in the glorious madness of straining sails and wild water.

At day's end, too exhausted to do more than swing from the safety lines and grin at one another.

A shame sailing didn't keep away his nightmares.

This time, Evan had no intention of leaving Great Gran alone with their *guests.* He jumped on board behind Decker, who grabbed for the nearest rope as the boat rocked gently.

"So you like to sail?" Evan asked innocently.

The other let go of the rope. "Eller's the one who likes water. I'm along for the ride. Not on something like *this,*" he added with emphasis.

Invitations to sail with Celonee Jefer Buryatsea Gooseberry were reserved for the few competitive racers she respected and those people she loved who knew their way around the boom. Not even Pachen IV's elite were granted the privilege, and some had tried.

Evan merely shrugged. "That's up to Great Gran." He gestured to where she stood at the tiller, talking to Eller. "After you."

Decker didn't want to go first, and it wasn't the narrow gangway with the ocean below, Evan judged, but being followed. After a sharply assessing then dismissive glance, the other turned around to go forward. He kept a thumb hooked in the belt of his woven skirt.

Security detail? Probably armed, though trained to be dangerous without. To protect Eller/Petham—whatever his real name was?

Or—to ensure cooperation. *His.*

In what? Mouth suddenly dry, Evan walked along the deck, determined to have answers before cooperating at all.

By night, Scintillation Bay filled with mystery. Waves broke along the beach in lines and swirls of eerie blue-green light: late summer's bloom of dinoflagellates. Stars twinkled in an ink-black sky; matching pinpoints of light on the horizon and below marked passing ships and the land's edge.

Night Ravens, wide black feathers softened at the edge to muffle sound, swooped like ghosts over Great Gran's patio and the Humans gathered there. The ravens hunted Bloat Flies.

Who hunted Humans. Human plasma, to be precise, and Evan would have been amused by how the dangerous Decker slapped at the tiny buzzing pests and flinched from the birds, if not for the cold steady regard of Decker's so-called brother. Eller's gaze followed and trapped him, though he'd taken the farthest chair, beyond the pool of light cast by glows beneath the tables, little more than a shadow himself. *Didn't seem to matter.*

As his opinion hadn't mattered when, midway through supper, Eller had confessed with charming, if feigned, embarrassment that he and his brother weren't confident taking their rental boat out in the dark and might they spend the night tied at the wharf?

Fine with Evan, but no, Great Gran would have none of it. As visitors, they must stay in the house, in comfort. She'd sent Evan upstairs to open two guest rooms, and now this. Sharing their traditional pleasant end to a summer's evening, drinks on the patio, with the intruders.

It was as painful as Evan expected. Eller and Great Gran carried the conversation, seeming not to notice Evan and Decker remained mute. If there was a pause, Eller asked questions, about the house, about the birds, about her sailing. Granted a new, keenly interested audience, Great Gran couldn't help but blossom.

When she excused herself, silence fell like a stone.

Did they expect him to break it?

Evan met Eller's stare, sorely tempted to expose the pair as frauds and send them packing, sink or swim.

The other lifted his glass as if daring him to do just that.

They both knew he wouldn't. The diplomatic corps fell under the auspices of Survey, the arm of the Commonwealth responsible for the interface between worlds like this one and the greater, non-Human universe of the stars above and beyond. Bizarre though it felt, Eller and Decker were his colleagues.

It didn't mean they were on the same side of—whatever this was.

Evan looked away, staring into the dark.

As he'd cleared the piles of crab shells from the supper table, he'd recalled with a sick jolt why Eller and Decker's declared last port of call seemed familiar. He'd read the name in a file. A file containing what Survey had on record concerning former First Contact Specialist Paul Antoni Ragem. Beneath the cold stark line about his mother's, Veya Ragem's, death by accident, had been the location of Paul's still-living biological father, Stefan Gahanni.

Senigal III.

Evan had brought Paul Ragem to Dokeci Na on the *Mistral,* along with Esolesy Ki. Coincidence, that Eller—as Petham—had been attached to the resulting mission? Now, that he'd gone to Senigal III?

Maybe.

Eller's being here was not. Evan's vacation trip to Botharis this past winter had been properly public and sanctioned, with everyone at the Commonwealth Embassy on Dokeci Na aware he'd gone to visit Paul and Esen. To surprise them.

He'd done that.

Had Eller come about Paul, to drag up the past yet again? *To harm*

him! Evan lowered his eyes and set his jaw, afraid his fury at the possibility would show. A fury followed by a rueful realization. *Not over
his feelings for Paul. Not even close.*

As for whatever Esen and Esolesy kept from him, however much it
filled notebook pages and troubled him? They were Paul's dearest
friends. And his. At least Evan hoped they were.

All at once Lionel Kearn's advice that winter night came rushing
back to him so strongly he could almost hear the words. Feel the conviction behind them. *It's easy to trust when you understand the situation. When it comes to our friends, to Paul, Esen, and Esolesy Ki? Trust
them even if you don't. Especially then.*

He'd try his best. For now, what Evan understood perfectly was that
the All Species' Library of Linguistics and Culture wouldn't exist without the three. For that reason alone, he'd never willingly betray them.

This might not be about Paul and his friends, Evan realized abruptly.
What if Eller's arrival here had been triggered by what happened on
Botharis during his visit? At the behest of Special Envoy Niala Mavis—
and, oddly, Esen—Evan had sent an urgent call spiraling up through
levels of his government, prepared to facilitate an immediate offer to
bring Botharis into the Commonwealth. His thumb had hovered with
Nia's over the confirmation.

A confirmation never sent, for the Botharans chose a different path to
protect their world from the Kraal Confederacy. Evan hadn't explained
to his superiors why the offer had been requested or why it was refused,
a lack unquestioned at the time but surely noticed. He'd had no choice.
He'd given his word to Nia, knowing full well that by doing so, by
promising his silence, he tacitly broke his oath to the Commonwealth
and one day might pay the price.

Had that day come?

Didn't matter. He'd do it again, Evan told himself grimly. Do whatever he must to be able to help—to—

Great Gran emerged from the house like a ray of sunshine, beaming
at Evan and her guests. To Evan's dismay, her smile lingered meaningfully on Eller. He should have guessed she'd notice the attention paid
to her favorite *eligible* Gooseberry and braced himself. "Evan," she said
brightly, "be a love and trade seats with me. I'd like to watch the surf.
The tray?"

Forcing a smile, Evan relinquished his chair and took her tray. The cups of iced fruit sparkled with condensation, the already stifling evening air grown thick with moisture. After Great Gran made herself comfortable, he passed her a cup and spoon. Next, he offered the treats to Decker, who took his eagerly, only to be startled by another fly. Swatting at it, he fumbled and dropped his spoon. "Sorry," he mumbled.

"Just let them bite," Great Gran advised. "You won't feel a thing. We've medication if you bloat."

"'Bloat?'" Decker froze midreach, eyes agog.

She patted her abdomen. "They're called Bloat Flies for a reason. After a few hundred bites, you're immune."

Straightening, Decker looked ready to bolt for his bedroom.

They were called Bloat Flies because they stopped biting once they were swollen with blood. The bites themselves? Harmless to anything as big as a Human. Smiling to himself—the joke on guests a long-standing tradition—Evan continued on, putting the tray on the table in front of the double chair. The only seat left was here, where Great Gran had been, next to Eller.

His skin crawled, but he dared not hesitate. Evan gestured to the tray as he sat. "Help yourself."

"You're not having any?" Eller asked, taking a cup. He took a spoonful of the frothy stuff, throat working as he swallowed. "Delicious. Thank you," to Great Gran.

Who looked at Evan, waggling her eyebrows. "What do you think?"

She didn't mean the dessert. She meant the male presence sitting close enough to add body heat to the sultry night, a scent like spiced almonds to the air, and Evan might have considered Eller attractive— perhaps worth getting to know better—

—if he weren't a professional liar and potential threat.

Evan shot to his feet. "Your pardon, Great Gran, but—I've had too much sun. I'm for bed. Good evening."

He made it to the wide wooden staircase and taken three double steps up before the voice from behind stopped him in his tracks.

"A word, Polit Gooseberry."

Without turning around, Evan gave a short, single nod, then resumed climbing the stairs.

Hearing Eller follow.

The upstairs hall served as the family shrine. Portraits of Gooseberrys crowded the walls from ceiling to floor, in varied media, each in a trim white frame. The portraits weren't all flattering nor were most particularly realistic; to each, however, was affixed a beautiful handwritten card giving the individual's full name and date of birth—with space for date of death, if currently alive—and beneath, the volume and page within the official Lore where more could be found, including proof of being a Gooseberry and worthy of hanging there in the first place.

It was sacred, it was sanctuary, and, most of all, this was their home, his and Great Gran's, and the farther along the hall Evan walked, his steps echoed by an intruder's, the more furious he became. By the time he passed Aunt Melan Gooseberry, resplendent in her anti-bug hat, his right hand was an unconscious fist.

On reaching his bedroom door, Evan Gooseberry rudely threw it open and pointed inside.

Sandy footprints gave evidence to his haste earlier in the day, the tossed covers on the raised bed to another troubled night, and his private notebooks, the topmost open, sat exposed on his desk.

Ordinarily, such intimate exposure would have made Evan exceedingly nervous, let alone having a stranger—an attractive male stranger— in his private space. Tonight he found himself oblivious to such concerns. As Eller entered the room, Evan brusquely waved him to the wicker chair near the window, letting the other remove the shirt tossed there. Remained standing, arms crossed, silently waiting—*no, demanding*—an explanation. If Trili, his best friend at the embassy, had seen his expression, she wouldn't have recognized it. Set and stern. Ready for war.

Eller's demeanor altered as he looked up at Evan, a caution sliding behind his eyes. He seemed to abandon whatever tactic he'd planned to use. "Polit Gooseberry, I'm here on a matter of Species' Security. We need your help."

Evan raised his eyebrows. "Which species and who is 'we'?"

"All of them." Eller lowered his voice. "All of us." He brought out a device, thumbing the control. Dozens of images filled the air of Evan's bedroom, maybe hundreds. Each was of a dead starship adrift in space; each framed by an abstract design. Through them, Eller's keen eyes searched Evan's face. "You've seen these before. Something like them."

The words held such surprising, almost breathless hope, they stopped Evan's planned evasion. He stared at Eller through the bizarre collection, remembering the terror of the Sacrissee, the lengths they'd gone to out of fear of—of whatever this represented. The *Vast Out.*

This wasn't part of his oath of silence to the Botharans, the young diplomat decided. *It couldn't be.* "I have," he admitted, sitting on his rumpled bed. "Images like those were brought by Sacrissee officials to the Library on Botharis." He omitted the Kraal. "They were afraid."

"So am I." With that unexpected admission, Eller thumbed off the display. "The All Species' Library of Linguistics and Culture. Paul Ragem and Esolesy Ki." Saying their names, his tone warmed. "Impressive work on Dokeci Na—as was yours. Did they offer an explanation to the Sacrissee? Have answers?"

Evan shook his head. "No. Not yet," he amended, certain Paul and Esolesy—and especially Esen—wouldn't leave a system-spanning mystery alone, not when it meant lives at risk.

How had he?

By spiraling into his own petty concerns. By giving into mistrust of those he called friends, when he should have been better. *Was* better. He'd spent weeks with, as Great Gran would put it, his nose buried in his navel, worried about lint when there were those who needed him. *No longer.*

Evan Gooseberry met his companion's gaze, his face calm, composed, and determined. "How can I help?"

"By coming with me. By joining the mission to meet whomever—whatever—is responsible. To stop the carnage."

A first contact mission? Evan's first breath caught in his throat like a crab in a net. His second was steadier. "You realize I'm just a junior diplomat."

"With high level clearance and access to resources Survey doesn't have."

Well, yes, he'd the clearance, but that was because Evan, through no fault of his own, repeatedly found himself in situations requiring it, and his superiors had decided they'd no choice but give it to him; not that most of his workmates knew. It was that or, as Ambassador Hansen put it—jokingly, Evan hoped—lock him up where he couldn't encounter aliens needing help.

But the rest? "I don't know what resources you think I have."

"I'll explain, but first, you need to know what we're up against," Eller said heavily. "The images I showed you were illegally seized and concealed by a faction within Survey previously thought harmless— even useful. Their public face is a group of captains and senior officers, active and retired, called the Intrepid Few. They push for improvements to Explorer Class ships, self-fund research abandoned by mainstream engineers.

"What we didn't know was that a faction within the Intrepid went dark years ago, hiding work on forbidden tech. It began with Veya Ragem's assignment to *Sidereal Pathfinder.*" His expression turned bleak; he thumbed on the display again, dead ships filling Evan's bedroom. "It ended by starting all this."

Paul's mother? Beginning to suspect precisely what resources Eller wanted of him, Evan licked suddenly dry lips. His "How?" was barely a whisper.

The display went off. "We don't know. That's why I'm undercover as one of them, and why I'm here. The images were leaked to Survey by someone in the faction who recognized what they implied: a new and strange intelligence, possibly malevolent—"

"Possibly not," Evan broke in, then subsided.

"Exactly," Eller agreed. "To know, we need to make contact, ideally before more ships go missing. Unfortunately, our best and only lead remains the faction itself." The smile vanished. "These aren't fools, Evan. Following the leak, members of Intrepid Few actually came forward claiming to have uncovered a secret project called Pathfinder. They requested a Survey ship to recover its lost tech and discover what, if any, connection it has to the source of the images—oh, yes," Eller said, reacting to Evan's raised eyebrows. "They're that sure of themselves. Of course, their primary goal isn't to find who is sending these images. These are ruthless people. They intend to destroy their tech and erase any trace of their culpability. Survey's playing along, for now, and that's where you come in, Evan Gooseberry."

"Because of Paul," Evan stated.

Earning a tight smile. "Yes. Everything about Pathfinder is tied to Veya Ragem and her son. I said the faction are ruthless. To conceal what they'd done, they had the crew of the *Sidereal Pathfinder* murdered and pursued Veya Ragem for years until they caught her. They sent Victory Johnsson to Senegal III and Botharis. Her orders were to find and destroy whatever Veya might have left with her family and to bring Paul to the faction for questioning—and disposal. Fortunately, she failed."

They sat in his bedroom, the sound of waves a gentle whoosh through the open window, talking about murder and treason and now this? "I was there," Evan said in a small voice. *Intent on his own concerns*—

Eller nodded. "Hence the faction's interest in having you join the mission. An interest I've encouraged by telling them you and Paul are close. Very close."

Trili. "We're friends," the young diplomat corrected, hiding his embarrassment and careful not to look toward his open notebooks.

Was that a twinkle in Eller's eyes? *Surely not.* "Are you aware Paul Ragem has been checking on you since you left Botharis? He's called here and queried the embassy."

Evan's face grew hot. Had he dreamed Paul would do such a thing, he'd have insisted Great Gran let his calls through—which would have required an explanation of why this stranger and not family, leading to—*best not*. "I've been in seclusion," he said stiffly, leaving it at that. "This *faction* can't believe I'd harm Paul."

"They believe Paul trusts you. That's useful to them."

He went as cold as he'd been hot a moment before. He'd betrayed that trust. Filled notebook pages with questions and doubts, challenged everything about those closest to his supposed friend, and even accused dear sweet Esen of lies—*Had it been jealousy? Was he that petty?*

Eller, unaware of the reason for Evan's silence, went on after a brief pause. "Paul Ragem's put himself outside the Commonwealth. I assure you he's suspicious of anyone in authority—"

Evan stirred. "Do you blame him?"

A shrug. "My opinion is irrelevant. My superiors are convinced any attempt at direct contact could spook Paul into running again."

It was—Evan sighed to himself—*distressingly plausible.* "Where do I come in?"

Eller glanced toward the open window then back, lowering his voice, as if afraid to be overheard. "Survey wants you as our liaison, to draw upon Paul and his partners' resources for this mission."

Evan approved. In his view, everyone should respect what Paul and the Library had to offer. Part of him longed for a task to begin to make up for the past weeks spent in doubt of his friend—

The rest was anxious. "And the faction?"

"To them, you're a key to discovering what Paul Ragem knows about Pathfinder and who else he's told." *So they could be eliminated.* Eller didn't add the words; they filled Evan's bedroom as if shouted. "That's information we'll need as well, Evan, in order to protect him and them."

"I'll do my best." Evan was proud his voice didn't tremble. "Paul's never spoken to me about his mother or her ship. All I know is what I've read in their Survey files."

"Take this." Pulling a datacube from his jacket, Eller tossed it to Evan. "It contains what's not in those files. The cube will wipe after you read it and I'll thank you not to take notes." With a warning tip of his head at the notebooks. "Part of what's there are my official credentials. The real ones. I'm trusting you with my life, Evan Gooseberry."

Evan found himself on his feet, holding out the cube. "I don't want any secrets. I'm not a spy," he protested, his voice strange to his own ears. "I'm not capable of being one."

Eller didn't take it. "I know what you are, Evan Gooseberry," with a disconcertingly frank appraisal. "You're honest. Intelligent. Incorruptible. Bit of a dreamer—and conveniently on an extended leave of absence, so we won't need to fabricate a cover story. Do your part for the mission and let me be the spy," with a sideways quirk of his lips. "You be someone I can trust. A witness—" a careless shrug "—if my cover's blown."

There was nothing Evan liked about this, from factions to *blown*. Nothing that felt right or reasonable.

Derelict ships and terrified Sacrissee. Paul and his friends threatened by faceless enemies.

Slowly Evan drew back the cube. "And your 'brother'? He a spy, too?"

With a relieved smile, Eller shook his head. "Decker's a very capable Survey officer. He's been my aide since Dokeci Na."

"And bodyguard," Evan dared add.

"And that. Decker's been briefed on the Pathfinder Project and the Intrepid Few, but believes the latter are respected fellow officers. He doesn't know about the faction or that I'm pretending to work with them. That stays between us." Eller waited for Evan's nod. "Decker's been told you're essential to Passerby, Survey's mission designation. He thinks you're along as a diplomat—in case we get to negotiation stage."

Evan gazed down at the milky white cube in his hand; it felt heavy, as if weighed down by its secrets, and a thrill of fear shivered down his spine. "I'm not sure I can do this."

"Good."

The prompt agreement made him look up.

"It means you won't be overconfident," Eller continued, rising to his feet. "You're Polit Evan Gooseberry, temporarily assigned to Survey's Mission Passerby as liaison to the All Species' Library of Linguistics and Culture. Be yourself, that's all." Without smiling, he offered his hand. "We've a ship to catch. Are you with me?"

This morning, he'd been catching Nerfie Crabs. Somehow, the homely thought pushed back some of Evan's fear. He stood. "After what you've told me. After this?" Evan tossed the cube and caught it. "Do I have a choice?"

"We're not the faction." That quirk of the lips again, adding a surprising appeal. "You have a choice, Polit, though I'd like my datacube back if the answer's no. You understand."

But there was no choice, Evan thought, meeting Eller's steady gaze, certain the other knew it. Not with lives at risk, not with Paul tied up in whatever this was.

He took Eller's hand in a firm grip. "I'm with you."

An hour later Great Gran sat on Evan's bed, feet flat on the floor, eyes catching the light as she watched him pack. She hadn't uttered a word since he'd told her he was leaving with their guests. Leaving at once, now, in the dark. Eller and Decker were down at their boat, getting it ready.

Evan glanced at her worriedly between socks and shirts. Again before cramming his winter coat in the bag, his personal notebooks stuffed in a sleeve because what they contained was too personal, even for Great Gran. His dress shoes. *Where to—*

He stopped with a shoe in each hand, unable to bear another moment's silent disapproval. "Please say something."

She drew a deep breath, held it in puffed cheeks, then let it out with an opinionated, "Puffph!"

If only he could explain. Not that it wouldn't sound incredible. Yes, there'd been Gooseberrys who'd lived through adventures—some surviving to tell their tales—but he wasn't like them. Now, to be part of a highly classified government mission? To help a spy catch members of a murderous faction—and that on top of finding and communicating with a previously unknown intelligence? An intelligence, moreover, sending images of derelict starships?

First contact, on a scale no one could imagine, potentially affecting every species in this portion of the quadrant—with Survey—Humans—taking point.

Then there'd been the datacube. He'd taken it and the reader on the balcony. Read the contents with care and if Eller hadn't said not to take notes? He would have. *Maybe should have.* This was about Paul's family; it seemed a betrayal to trust it to memory.

There had been a reassuringly official, code-word rich surety concerning "the bearer, currently known as Eller Theelen, acting under the direct order of Survey and the Commonwealth" signed by the three most senior members of that service. With a note attached from Ambassador Hansen saying Polit Evan Gooseberry was attached to Eller Theelen and Mission Passerby until further notice, with *We know you'll make us proud, Evan.* written at the bottom.

Evan knew he should feel honored. What he actually felt was terrified and more than a little queasy because there was no telling what lay ahead, but he'd do his best—

Just as Great Gran had taught him. Letting his shoes fall, Evan knelt at her feet. "I've told you I can't say what this is about, but it is vital, Great Gran. Lives are at stake. Why won't you trust me?"

Her head jerked toward the balcony door, earrings jiggling. *It wasn't him she doubted.*

He owed her everything. How could he leave without giving her something to hold onto, no matter what Eller said about secrecy and protocol, how few had been trusted with the full scope—

He chewed his lower lip, then nodded. "I worked with Eller before, on Dokeci Na. He's—it's proper and official, Great Gran, just really really secret. That's all I can tell you." He sighed. "I probably shouldn't have said that much."

"He's a slick liar, that one. And once you're gone, I'm to be one. Pretend you're still here." Anger filled the words. Hurt. "You want me to lie to our family."

"To everyone, until I'm back." She'd be believed. He'd refused visitors as well as calls; his now-useful history of breakdowns and ensuing seclusions would add weight. If anyone came to visit, they'd probably think he'd squeezed himself into his child-size cabin near the beach. "This is important. I wouldn't ask if it weren't." He touched her knee. "I am sorry."

"You'll *be* back? That a promise, Evan?"

He didn't look away. Couldn't speak. *Wouldn't lie.* Not to her.

For a fleeting second, Great Gran's face began to crumble, then she steadied, blinking furiously. "Well, then," she said, as if trying out her voice. "Here I was worrying this was still about Molancor and your sister . . . but . . . well, then." Her hand covered his. Gave a gentle squeeze. "I suppose 'official' and 'vital' means you'd best not waste time here. Tide won't wait."

"Never does." Getting to his feet, Evan bent to kiss her cheek. Tasting tears, he sat quickly and wrapped his arms as far around Great Gran as he could, then pressed his face into her neck. "I'll do my best."

Her grip had always been stronger. *She was.* "You trust yourself, Evan Gooseberry," Great Gran whispered fiercely in his ear. "And you save your trust for those who've earned it. No one else." She eased him back. "Here." Reaching between her breasts, she retrieved an object, pushing it into the palm of his hand. "Take this. Don't let *him* see you have it."

Still warm, the cylinder was featureless, green, and about the size of his index finger. Puzzled, Evan looked at Great Gran. "What is it?"

Her teeth showed in what wasn't a smile. "My Buddy. Let me show you how he works." A serious look. "I'll expect Buddy back."

As well argue with the sea. Evan shook his head, but not at her, giving in with a smile. "I promise."

It wasn't until he took the walkway down to the wharf, Buddy tucked inside his shirt and bags in hand, that Evan discovered what Great Gran would as soon as she left the house.

He whistled without a sound.

Eller and Decker had readied a boat for night sailing.

Just not their boat. *Sparkles* was lit, engine purring, ready to go. Having thrown off the stern line, Decker stood waiting for him by the bow. They'd make the tide.

Great Gran would have their skins for this—

Evan found himself chuckling.

—assuming a certain spy dared face her again.

4: Greenhouse Afternoon

DISTINGUISHING voices from inside a cocoon wasn't easy, I discovered, especially with my ears plastered to my skull. Fortunately, those speaking came closer.

"See what you've done?" *Paul. Not happy.*

"What do you mean? Lionel told me— Esen? What's happened to her?"

While I couldn't be entirely sure, that should be Duggs. After all, she was why I was lying on the cot, inside my tent, inside the greenhouse. Which was a great number of *insides* on top of my situation, and this me wasn't overly happy about it, but Paul insisted we make our point.

I squinted through tiny slits in now dry and caked mud, thoroughly imprisoned. Paul had been excruciatingly thorough in his reapplication. He'd hardly needed the hand dryer to set the stuff into this cocoon-like casing. He had anyway. I'd a feeling he'd enjoyed himself.

"The local silt reacted with her fur," he was explaining. "She's having difficulty breathing."

Oh, I could breathe just fine, if only in little huffs. It not having occurred to me to expand my lungs before Paul entombed me.

"She thinks you pushed her."

"Damn it, Paul. I'd never do that. You know that, Esen." I caught a glimpse of her face, screwed up in worry. "Can she hear me?"

I managed a pathetic-even-to-me whimper.

The cot shook as she dropped to her knees beside it. "You shouldn't have gone so close to the edge." Worry become anger. "What were you thinking?"

"That she could trust you." I thought I'd heard every tone and nuance in Paul's voice; I'd never heard this *cut* of scorn.

If I hadn't been entombed, my tail would have shot between my legs faster than I could snap at a mousel.

Possibly why I was entombed, I realized belatedly. I really wasn't good at hiding my reactions, especially where Paul was concerned, and I definitely hadn't picked up how disappointed he was in Duggs.

"Of course she can trust me," Duggs protested, still on her knees. "It was only a joke—"

Paul rapped his knuckles on my chest. "Does this look funny to you?"

Guessing that was a cue, I whimpered again, though I wasn't uncomfortable. Without its annoying water content, the mud was rather soothing. Warm, if restrictive. *I could nap*, I decided, closing my eyes.

"She's passed out! Esen! Blobbie!" I was grabbed and shaken. In the process, chunks of dried mud began pulling free of my fur—

—pulling fur free of me! I cracked open an eyelid, literally, and snarled. "Nurrphler!"

"There you are." Duggs let me drop on the cot, as nurturing as a Web-being. "Damn it, Es, you scared me."

"How's that feel?" Paul asked in a too-gentle voice. He didn't wait for an answer. "Probably like having someone you trust lie to you and put you in harm's way. For fun."

I trembled inside the case, hearing his tone grow cold and distant. This was the dangerous version of my friend, the one capable of terrible things, and all I could do was hope Duggs saw it.

It seemed she did, for when she spoke again, the bluster and anger were gone. "I swear I didn't mean her to fall. When she did, I tried to grab her, but—why did you go so close to the edge, Esen? Why?"

Because Lesley told me to look down. I'd have said the words, but my snout was buried in in mudcake.

Fortunately, I'd Paul to speak for me. "Because you said she'd be safe. Esen's trust isn't like yours or mine. It's complete. Innocent. Utter.

It's up to us to try and deserve it. Because Esen is more than you know. Bess."

If not entombed, I'd have glowered. *He could have warned me there'd be a performance.*

Still, cycling was the quickest way to be rid of the mud and there were adequate organics mixed in—I let go of my Lanivarian-self, moving through web-form too quickly to be seen as more than a flash of blue, to finish sitting on the cot as a Human.

The non-living mass I'd shed as a stencil around me. My bare, now clean, feet couldn't reach the floor, so I swung them back and forth as Paul wrapped me in a blanket. His hand lingered approvingly on my shoulder and tugged my hair before moving away. My dear friend, ever-hopeful, believing Bess was a kind of key.

The first time Paul had asked this of me it was before strangers and forgotten friends, members of the Group he'd assembled in secret to protect me and mine who'd gathered to test us both. He'd asked me to be Bess to prove to them I was harmless.

And to prove to himself he hadn't lost my trust.

Silly dear Human. We were of the same Web. We always would be.

As for today? I looked up at Duggs and smiled.

She appeared to have forgotten how to smile back, or speak, though she was still breathing, if raggedly. Semi-paralysis was a not-unfamiliar response to this version of me, so I kept smiling and waited, more or less patiently.

The problem, as Paul well knew, was that this me elicited other, less convenient reactions from others of the species. Chief among them was a tendency to forget I was over five and a half centuries old and could tie my own shoelaces, as the saying went. Rudy was hopeless. Lionel determined to be better.

In the beginning, I'd resolved to never show Paul Ragem this me, and risk our friendship. I needn't have worried. He'd figured it out long before meeting Bess in person. *As usual.*

The corner of Duggs' mouth deepened. "Brat."

"It's better than Blobbie," I told her, my voice higher-pitched. I set my expression to what Rudy called Devastatingly Sweet.

"All the hells—" She broke off to glare at Paul. "You could have warned me."

He spread his hands. "How?"

My turn. I gestured to myself. "I'm not this, on Botharis." Not if I could help it. No need to mention being Bess while imprisoned by Kraal last winter. *Emergencies happen.*

Duggs' face contorted worryingly, then she barked out a wicked laugh. "Kinda hard to be the boss when you're a squirt." She held a hand about waist-high.

I could be several species who, at that height, were imposing and functionally adult. *Not the point,* I told myself and looked pleadingly at Paul.

He nodded. "Go change, Old Blob. And thank you."

I stood, clutching the towel, stretching to make it clear I was taller than waist-high to either of them. *If not by much.* "We still need to find the gemmies."

"I already did," Duggs informed us, chuckling as Paul and I stared at her. "The clue was 'looking down,'" said as if it were obvious. She pointed up, which certainly wasn't.

Paul understood first. "The Library roof." He shook his head in wonder. "Of course. It can be seen from my old bedroom in the farmhouse. If you look down."

"That the bedroom Lambo broke?" Duggs asked with a growl worthy of a Lanivarian. "Or the one you managed to build without me, with the concealment fields and lift?"

I looked from Duggs to Paul, then edged out of the tent, grabbing my clothes.

The Humans could argue about secrets.

I'd Lesy's to see for myself.

Otherwise, how could I win our game?

Nearby

L IONEL no longer gave much thought to the sequence of security protocols guarding the physical component of the All Species' Library of Linguistics and Culture, namely the collection and the technology to host it, even if they also guarded Skalet's—now his—quarters. He knocked on the rail of the box stall in the Ragem barn to reveal the wooden staircase, took those worn stairs down to what appeared a traditional cold cellar, walked through what felt like and was a wine rack—unless you approached at the correct velocity—into the lift. Once the lift descended, well below the Library's basements, he faced the second of two exit doors, confidently putting his hand on the persona-lock on the wall beside it. Lights played over his face. A vibration as the floor confirmed his mass and position. "Lionel Kearn," Skalet's voice confirmed. He waited for the lock's question to test he wasn't under duress.

"How are you, Lionel?"

It took him a heartbeat to realize what he'd just heard.

Who. For the voice wasn't the machine's recording but velvet. Real. *Skalet's.*

Lionel put his other hand on the still-closed door for support, gathering his wits. "Gratified," he said simply. That his belief had been justified. That she reached out to him—though he'd never expected the persona-lock to be the means. "Ready to be of assistance."

"No questions?" *Amusement.* Perhaps a hint of approval.

"I would not waste your time," he replied sincerely. A link like this—assuming Skalet remained on a Kraal world, within the confines of a paranoid Great House—couldn't be maintained for long. Not without detection.

"Admirable." Definitely *approval*, warming his heart. "The data you require has been supplied. You know where to find it."

"I do." Skalet referred to the restricted portion of the Library's database, her portion, containing information on the Kraal she'd acquired over centuries hiding as one of them. An incalculable treasure. A perilous vulnerability. Now, he'd no doubt, it contained details for the Kraal Framer images to match those he had for the Sacrissee. At last he could expand and strengthen the model, begin to test hypotheses.

She'd known.

"I have information for you. The triggering incident in Sacrissee space—"

"I've seen." *Confirmation.* Whatever he put into his comp, in her quarters, she could access. "House Bract will be held to account at the appropriate time. We have more immediate concerns."

Her voice became distant and formal, the words akin to a report. "Though I give no names, you will know of whom I speak. Consensus has been achieved, at extreme cost, in regard to the threat to shipping. There shall be a dual response. First, and already in motion: the consolidation of assets where they can be protected. Second—and it is this, Lionel, that is both unprecedented and unpredictable: in advance of the threat being identified, in absence of any credible intel it ever will be, an extraordinary concentration of command has nonetheless been instituted. There shall be one who leads. One whose finger rests oh-so-lightly on the trigger to launch all to attack, and I've no need to tell *you* how dangerous that is."

No need. Agreements signed and sealed purported to keep the Kraal war machine docile and cooperative, but any peace with their neighbors owed far more to Kraal preoccupation with themselves. The Confederacy seethed with inner squabbles and power struggles, to the extent where Commonwealth analysts were confident they were incapable of uniting under one rule.

Should the Kraal ever truly collaborate in order to turn their violence outward? It would be those in their way who'd feel it first. Pay first. Worlds like Botharis.

His hand on the door closed into a fist and Lionel leaned his forehead against it, closing his eyes. "What would you have me do?" But he already knew, even before the soft, chilling words emanated from the panel.

"Have a ship ready at all times. A fast and reliable one. Prepare to flee with the Youngest at my signal. Lure her offworld with her Paul, if you must."

Lionel opened his mouth to ask about Lesy, to demand Skalet's plan for her own safety. Instead, he lifted his head as he lowered his hand to his side, and heard his voice say the impossible in a cool, calm tone. "I will."

"It may not come to that," Skalet said next, almost gently. "This mystery may yet prove a misunderstanding between strangers. 'Any problem can be resolved by the right action, delivered with courage.'"

Astonishing, for her to offer comfort as Esen would.

No, Lionel realized, his heart thudding wildly. The latter sentence was a quote, from the ancient texts of the Kraal philosopher N'kar-ro. Skalet warned him as plainly as she dared. If the Library couldn't solve the mystery of the Framers and respond—if the Kraal burst from their space to take the offensive and he couldn't move Esen out of harm's way—Skalet would take the right action. Courageously and decisively, regardless the risk.

For if the Kraal chose to concentrate power in one individual?

That leader became their vulnerability.

To reach whomever it was, Skalet—S'kal-ru the Courier—would have to become not only trusted, but essential. *It would take . . .* Lionel could picture the sequence. Removing a dissenter here, and there. Proposing strategy in this ear; the opposing one in that. She was an assassin, operating at a level of sophistication and skill no Human could match—

Against the most heavily guarded individual in a culture that prided itself on political statement by personalized poison.

"Understood," he heard himself say, when what he wanted to say, to tell her—

"Lionel Kearn, what is the name of your first love," a machine asked. "You have three seconds."

—no longer mattered. Skalet was gone. Again. This time, not only to learn what the Kraal knew of the Framers, but to position herself in order to dictate what they did with that and future knowledge. It was terrifying. *She was.*

And glorious.

"Two seconds."

"Tisken Uppet, my sixth-grade math partner," Lionel told the panel; the door slid aside, permitting him entry.

"Paul said it's time. It's no trouble, Lionel. Glad of an excuse to pop by." The voice on the translight com—male, Human, and deep—belonged to Rudy Lefebvre.

Newly in command of the *Largas Swift,* of the Largas Freight's fleet, Rudy was much more than family, being the second Human Esen had come to trust. She'd shared who and what she was with him, including Bess—who became Gloria, Rudy's "niece," whenever they were in public and Human together.

Rudy was a weapon as well, trained and ruthless, and to this day, Lionel suspected if he ever failed Esen or Paul again, Rudy's would be the last face he ever saw.

They were compatriots now, part of Esen's innermost circle, if not her Web. Friendly, if not friends, for things hadn't started well between them. Lionel regretted his part in that. *Not that regret ever changed the past.* Rudy had been inspired by his beloved cousin—and his uncle— to become a patroller for the Commonwealth. When Paul had "died," his reputation ruined—by Lionel—Rudy had left the patrol, determined to uncover the truth. Consumed by grief and betrayal, he'd chased every rumor of his cousin and, later, the Esen Monster—hiding his relationship with Paul. Rudy'd even managed to become captain of Lionel's own ship.

To spy on him. His search. Lionel'd failed to earn Rudy's respect or allegiance. He'd come to fear his highly competent captain. Would hide in his cabin rather than face Rudy's obvious contempt—

Esen changed everything. Through her, Paul and Rudy were reunited, the former's ruse explained. Through her, with Rudy's help, Lionel at last discovered his own truth. The monster he'd hunted for fifty long years had been dead the entire time. The subordinate he'd thought betrayed everyone, had instead been wrongfully accused—by him—and lost everything. His fault, all of it.

Evan Gooseberry had asked how Lionel could forgive himself.

He never would.

But he'd found his peace. A second chance, however undeserved, thanks to the generous hearts of Esen and Paul. To Skalet, finding him useful. And Rudy, now working for Joel Largas. Another charmed by their resident little blob.

Who'd taken an extraordinary risk to save him—

Lionel shook off the past. "I hear you've a new ship to show us."

"That I do." With unrestrained glee. "She's a courier, quick as her name on station turnarounds. Can land almost anywhere and barely any time on her engines. Fool owner lost her gambling the Dump."

The unique port city of Minas XII—Paul and Esen's former home, and Largas Freight Lines' current one—the Dump had built itself around debt-grounded starships, the result a maze of connected buildings offering an array of criminal opportunity known well beyond the former Inhaven colony and throughout the Fringe. Its infamy wasn't so much what beings of every species did there but that the Dump hadn't collapsed—again—under its own shoddy construction. *Give it time* was the local saying, the area known for its volcanism and earthquakes.

Paul and Esolesy Ki maintained their business, Cameron & Ki Imports, on Minas XII. Esolesy, especially after one of Lambo's culinary surprises, made sure to share her longing for such Dump specialties as pyati with anyone in earshot who didn't escape in time, making the fiction she'd elected to spend the Botharan winter there entirely reasonable.

And the nature of Minas XII and the Dump? Made it impossible for any authority to confirm she had or hadn't.

"We got the win," Rudy went on. "Joel snapped the ship up for next to nothing."

"Joel's better?" *A relief, on all counts.* A few months ago, the venerable head of the Largas clan and business had suffered a debilitating stroke. Lionel'd worried—they all had—and not just about Joel's ability to keep Esen's secret. "We're going to need him," he said sincerely.

A warm chuckle. "Between us, I swear Joel had a foot in the grave till he got the news Largas Freight was the front-runner to operate out of your new station. Best med ever. Tell Es I've my disguise ready to go."

Thus *Esolesy Ki* would be seen exiting the ship, by the same means she'd left. Lionel grinned. "Esen wanted me to say you weren't sufficiently graceful." Not that grace was a characteristic any non-Lishcyn associated with the species.

An outright laugh. "I'll do my best, but it's tricky walking a ramp in that outfit. Anything else, Lionel? We should be finsdown there in four and a half days local. Joel's having a bit of work done."

"Did Paul mention that Esolesy's in desperate need of clothes? Anything you can pick up." The request, if he had to guess, had to do with Lesy and Esen's closets. "We'll explain when you're here."

"Already done. That it?"

Skalet's orders, for they'd been that, echoed in Lionel's thoughts. *Find a fast, reliable ship.* He wouldn't find a better choice—or captain.

"There is, actually. After you deliver Esolesy, we'll want you to stay finsdown for a while, Rudy. The Library will cover any costs." Which would include, Lionel winced to himself, his time spent placating the captains of those ships not allowed to linger more than a night. Let alone the ire of the Preservation Committee. *There'd be a mountain of memos.*

Skalet told him to prepare. Whatever it took.

The com fell silent. No doubt Rudy sensed something awry, but when he spoke again, his tone held only pleased anticipation. "Sure. Happy to catch up. Summer there yet?"

"Close."

"Winter here. Meony-ro will want to come along, then. He hates the cold."

Meony-ro was in no sense a tourist seeking warmth. The former Kraal—a rarity of itself, a Kraal without affiliation as good as dead— was not only a formidable fighter but had sworn a debt to Paul Ragem, then known as Paul Cameron, on Minas XII, and continued to work for Cameron & Ki. Making the request Rudy's way to ask a question over a communication system they'd all learned not to trust completely. *Trouble ahead?*

He wanted to say yes, but Lionel hesitated. Despite his faded tattoos and new allegiance, Meony-ro wouldn't be welcome on Botharis. The Kraal had tried, often violently, to seize this world for their Confederacy—at least once leaving their sous, noncombatants, behind. Duggs Pouncey was descended from such inadvertent settlers; it hadn't, as far as Lionel could tell, lessened her hate of the rest of their kind. She wasn't alone in that.

And the timing couldn't be worse, with the thumbprints on the agreement between the Confederacy and Botharis prohibiting further Kraal *interest* still wet. More to the point, the Botharan government had Kraal planet-killing missiles and their silos to decommission, a top secret and dangerous project, and a serious sore point with those who were aware.

And opportunity. Lionel nodded to himself. The decommissioning process would benefit from the skills of a former Kraal gunner and munitions expert. An excellent cover. He'd have Paul prepare Nia. "We'd be delighted to have Meony-ro visit."

"I'll have him pack," Rudy replied. "Been hoping to push the *Swift's* drives, as it happens, and there's nothing to stop an earlier lift." Said with slight emphasis. *Message received.*

"Very good. We've missed Esolesy Ki."

Lionel ended the link. He found himself staring at Skalet's wall. At the small deep hole where a knife had plunged deep, then been withdrawn. Next to it was the section where she hung her weapons. A pair of slots were empty; most were not.

Lionel got up to go closer, coolly taking inventory.

With all his being, he hoped none of this, from Rudy's ship to Skalet's deadly gear, would be necessary, but he'd be ready if it was.

First things first.

He sat again at the desk and entered his code, adding a request to access the Kraal portion of the collection, then withdrew his hands as if the pad scorched them.

There was a delay; while it lasted, he grew convinced it wouldn't admit him and he'd need Paul or Esen—

Then, "Access granted. There is new information," the machine stated. "Would you care to review it, Administrator Kearn?"

"Yes." Without a glance at the streams of numbers floating in the air before him, Lionel brought up his Framer model. "Incorporate and process."

Slow, methodical work. Looking into any and all possibilities, sifting through facts, however unrelated they seemed. He knew himself good at it. Knew this was what his friends needed from him.

What Skalet expected of him.

This, he could and would do.

Out There

HE'S out there. I know he's out there.

Veya—

He'll be on a ship. Something unremarkable. Unofficial. A tramp freighter, maybe. It's what I'd do.

Veya, your son is—

Alive. I don't care what you think, Sam. I won't stop looking for him.

When she was alive, she couldn't stop looking.

Now Hell won't let her.

Her eye, *that eye,* seeks and seeks and seeks—

Finds a ship—

Sees it enter translight, wrapped in that telling spectrum. Sees the ship's path as a coruscating ribbon of probability, of hope— *What if it's his?*

Sees the spark of message and answer, the last potent act of the living— *What if it's his?*

Stop now. Stop now.

Veya can't. She's no choice but to see. See Hell open its maw and swallow the ribbon, probability become singular and death.

See the ship impossibly *stopped* once inside, wrapped in what looks like lightning but reaches and binds like filament. They aren't technology but can't be life, for what they do—

She sees the filaments pass through the metal and shielding meant to protect the living. Sees the ship's engines fade and die, their power consumed.

There's worse to come.

Stop now. Stop now.

She can't. She's no choice but to see. See Hell shred what lives—*what if it's him?* —pull it out, *collect it*, bits stuck to glistening filaments, to hang in featureless mist.

She's been in a ship. Been shredded and pulled out. Knows there is no hope.

<u>Mommy, see the drawing I made? It's your starship.</u>
<u>Why does it have all those windows?</u>
<u>So you can see where you're going.</u>
No hope. Only memory, in shards like glass.

Veya adds to it—*wants this, needs this*—what she sees next. For each time Hell opens its door to spit the ship's husk back to normal, life-giving space, a corpse adrift amid uncaring stars?

It gives her a glimpse of real.

Veya cradles the precious image, *HOLDS* it close, encases it.

It isn't hers to keep. That isn't her intention.

Before the door closes she releases the image. Sees it fly outward again, back from whence it came. Most likely a hopeless spark, a futile piece of *her*, lost in the uncaring empty.

But there's a chance—a possibility—this image will find its way.

A chance—a possibility—this one will be seen and understood.

Be afraid . . .

I'm sorry . . .

Hell, ever hungry, bends her gaze outward again, looking for the next ship—

What if it's his—

Driven by her heart's desire.

5: Rooftop Afternoon;
Patio Afternoon

WIND ruffled my fur, what showed outside my tunic and pants, and I pinned back my ears. This me didn't mind heights, but access to the Library roof had meant a ladder. A ladder designed by and for those whose evolutionary predecessors had spent far too much time in trees—granted to elude predators such as myself, but the point was—

This me detested ladders.

To top it off, literally, the roof was smooth and curved, with a lamentable lack of rails. Which would have looked unsightly from the ground, but when I stepped awkwardly outside, I developed a sudden enthusiasm for the concept.

Then I forgot all about sloping rooftops, transfixed by Lesy's impressive effort to adorn this one, though I struggled to decide if gluing on random parts gleaned from, conservatively, three hundred discarded gemmies—many of those originally discarded small appliances or toys—qualified as art. Not only was there no discernible pattern to the mess, but I'd also the distinct impression she'd tossed handfuls of bits in the air to see where they'd drop and roll before acquiring sufficient glue to stop.

A few of the roof vents were thoroughly clogged.

Lesley, confident I'd solve her game, was already there, staring into the distance as if she'd forgotten why. The last of my Lishcyn-self's issa silk caftan and trouser sets billowed around her shapely self, her white hair streamed out against the blue sky, and she looked like a work of art herself.

Then again, she usually did. Ersh would inflict me on Lesy regularly, frustrated with my lack of clothing sense in most forms. Not all, but some species didn't wear anything remotely fun—

Suffice to say, my clothes always looked better on my web-kin, in any form.

All at once, I foresaw a significant problem. If Lesy'd used up my wardrobe, what would Esolesy Ki wear once *returned* to the Library? Notions of fashion on Botharis owed more to a cherished pioneer past than anything remotely suited to that me, let alone the disquieting fact that the only silk I'd found on this world made its way into small scarves.

I supposed I could use a sack. And Rudy would return my precious lantern and bag. He'd worn both as part of his impersonation. *Worry later.* I started easing my way through spirals and blots of disemboweled gemmies, heading for my well-dressed web-kin.

"Ah!" Lesy's abstracted gaze finally found me. Her lashes were coated with purple sparkles, and she'd applied cosmetics to make the right half of her face green. She smiled proudly. "You found it! Such a clever one you are, Youngest."

"Wasn't me," I informed her. "Duggs guessed." Prudent, in Skalet-terms, to remind Lesy not to underestimate the ephemerals around us, but I'd another motive. "She isn't happy to have to remove all this. There could—" I winced at the vents. "—*will* need to be repairs. To prevent leaks."

"Psstp." With a twirl of her fingers, Lesy dismissed such trivial concerns as water dripping in the Library, something she wouldn't do as an Iedemad or any of several other species intolerant of the stuff. Unfortunately, I was stuck with her Human-self. "The glue will dissolve in the next rain, freeing all of this—" With an extravagant wave around the begemmied roof that would have sent a less graceful Human tumbling to the ground.

"Making another mess for others to clean up," I complained. *Why did I try?*

Sure enough, her eyes glinted with displeasure. "You're being very glum today, Esen-alit-Quar. I thought you'd be happy. I thought we were playing." There it was, the tremor in her full lower lip. The hurt.

Knowing it was real, I lifted my ears to a more conciliatory position, the wind trying to bend the tips. "I'm sorry, Lesy," I apologized automatically. "I know you put a great deal of yourself into—" I looked around the roof. "—this. I do appreciate you wanted to play with me. I just—" My temper flared before I could stop it. "I just don't understand you. First you incite Lambo to make holes in the wall and now this? Don't you care you're damaging what we've built here?"

Silk billowed and snapped. Otherwise, she might have been a statue glued to our poor roof, her expression frozen in bewilderment.

That would be no.

I supposed I should be reassured. After all, I'd reassembled Lesy from bits and memories and here she stood, reacting exactly as she would have before. *Which wasn't her fault.* I was the odd one of our little family, having learned to not only value the accomplishments of shorter-lived species but to share in them. To take pride in now, not just bask in forever.

Skalet tolerated the Library and our life here because she'd learned I wouldn't be parted from it. *Not easily.* Ersh would have been horrified.

Or have ignored me, our Eldest having a deeper appreciation of time than any of us. She'd consider the infinitesimal amount I'd spent and would spend with Paul along the lines of briefly toying with a new hobby.

I could hate what I was.

Fortunately, by nature and inclination, I was optimistic to a fault and stubbornly determined to make the Web of Esen function—if only because we'd nothing but each other ahead in our unthinkably long future.

I spoke as gently as the wind allowed. "I'm not angry with you, Lesy. I want you to be happy—"

She swept locks of hair up in one hand and gave the appearance of studying the ends intently. "Then we can leave?"

"Happy," I repeated, choosing to ignore that, "while making sure everyone else is happy too. Isn't that a good thing?"

She squinted at me. "Skalet doesn't know how to be happy."

True, though I'd spot an unsettling glee on our web-kin's face whenever she worked on a stratagem or cleaned a new weapon. *But not the point.* "I'm not talking about Skalet, Lesy. I'm talking about our Human friends—"

She clapped her hands. "Evan's coming?"

She had a favorite?

Fair enough. So did I, content to know Paul Ragem had me as his favorite too. Out of a choice of three, granted, with one mostly Kraal and the other mostly—Lesy.

Who I'd let deflect the conversation and was now dancing close to where the slope of the roof edge made it impossible for feet to stay—

—Lesy disappeared. With a "WHHEEeee-eee!" that faded into the distance as I hurried as close as I dared to look down.

She laughed at me from the collapsed ruin of my trellis. The trellis I'd had built for jamble grapes, which Celiavliet Del had eaten before they could flower, and what stalks had survived the winter were now crushed.

Might be time to give up and order grapes in a basket.

My—her silks were torn, but I was relieved not to see any marks on Lesy's skin. Impressive, to have stayed Human for what had to be a hard, painful landing, but she was my Elder, even if reconstituted. I should expect greater fortitude and strength.

Later, I'd remember that thought.

At the moment, however, my concern was for the Humans I could see running to converge on what must look the site of a terrible accident. "Are you all right?" I shouted loudly.

Lesy's hand came up with a piece of broken trellis. She waved it at me. "I've a wonderful idea for this!"

Of course she did. "Go ahead." I waved back. "She's fine!" Louder, for those approaching. Not that they wouldn't make sure for themselves. Lesley would be the center of attention for a good while and love every minute of it. *Until bored.*

I turned around to regard the roof and the latest of Lesy's wonderful ideas.

Ersh, I was in so much trouble.

Detaching Lesy's masterpiece from the Library roof consumed the rest of the afternoon—even with Duggs' crew pulled from their mud pit—and the work might have spread into tomorrow if those staff free to help, including Paul and me, hadn't lent our hands and paws.

Lesy? She'd let herself be fussed over then conveniently vanished. Paul generously assumed this was to avoid the trauma of seeing her work destroyed, but I knew better. Her mess. Someone else to clean it up. *The habit of centuries.*

One I couldn't see ever changing.

Gemmics filled the recycle bins once more and the roof itself—to everyone's relief—appeared intact after a final hosing to dissolve the remaining globs of glue and test for leaks. That said, I planned to lodge a complaint. The Humans, being hot and sweaty, had encouraged the hose operator, loudly, to spray with wild abandon. Not only did that put water where it had no place being—*on me*—but glue globs and the tiny glittery remnants of gemmies were redistributed as well.

And not a single Human let me shelter behind them. A conspiracy, and if they hadn't all seemed so happy, I'd have snarled. *Might have nipped.*

During this noisy and despicable process, supper appeared as a basket of self-heating tubes. Off went the spray.

Paul nudged my foot with his broom. "Wait for it," he whispered to me, nodding at Duggs.

Our head contractor, who'd been entirely too reasonable and calm throughout the cleanup, and too obviously preoccupied sneaking looks at me as if I'd become Bess again to surprise her—*not happening*—had been first to take a tube. Forewarned, I watched with Paul as Duggs held up the inoffensive object, glared at it, and after ten seconds of glaring, blew up. She turned the air blue, cussing continuously and without repetition until everyone on the roof took notice and several made bets.

Done, she tossed the tube to the nearest of her soaking wet workers, then sent her glare around the rooftop. "I'm going home," Duggs announced, dripping herself. "Where I'm alone. Where it's sane and there's food."

Paul chuckled fondly as she disappeared down the ladder, indicating he shared the same feeling that made me want to wag my tail. Not that I did, in case any remaining Human thought I enjoyed dripping.

But it was nice to have Duggs back to normal.

As if in confirmation, an annoyed bellow echoed up the open ladderway. "No, you can't go on the damn roof. Paul, get down here!"

My turn to nudge my friend. "You expecting anyone?"

Paul handed his broom to Carwyn, running a hand through his hair as he shook his head. The gesture was not only an answer but spread bits and glue, the result less than flattering. I refrained from comment.

The mud might have been worse, but now my fur sparkled with gemmie glitter amid flecks of glue I'd have to cycle to remove. *It was all Lesy's fault.*

After earnestly thanking—and dismissing—those who'd spent their afternoon cleaning the roof, Paul led the way down the ladder. I held back. No matter how curious I was, I wasn't going to be rushed using these paws to climb by a stampede of sopping Humans.

Besides, for some reason they'd left most of the supper tubes in the basket and, being the adept hunter I was?

I'd already noticed a few labeled bacon. *How consoling!*

I abandoned the basket of non-bacon tubes because it was beyond this me to safely carry it down, tucking my empties at the very bottom so they wouldn't attract pests—*my story and I'd stick to it*—before venturing onto the Ladder of Doom. A name I applied on realizing the sopping stampede had left every rung damp and sticky, complete with a puddle at the bottom.

I made it down without slipping, and wiped my poor paws on the inside of my poor shirt. Maintenance wouldn't complain about the mess; they'd contributed their share. Since the mess remained, at a guess, Paul had sent everyone home, being a kind and charitable person.

I wasn't cleaning it.

I surveyed the empty corridor, counting damp footprints. After describing an initial melee that would have done a battalion of Ganthor proud, they vanished in the distance, footwear dried by the leaving of the aforementioned damp footprints. Which would themselves dry, and soon, leaving a semi-permanent glimpse in time to when staff ran free and wild through the hall.

Unless cleaned while damp.

The Humans had done most of the work on Lesy's rooftop and were now busy cleaning themselves.

I supposed it was my turn.

Before I went to the nearby maintenance closet—one of those with equipment, not Esen-supplies—I went to all fours in a bare patch and sniffed out the new arrivals.

After a sneeze or two. *Wet and sweaty Humans, in wet and sweaty clothes. Not a good smell.*

There. I licked my nostrils and sniffed again to be sure. Sam Ragem, Paul's favorite uncle, and Stefan Gahanni, Paul's father. Who I supposed could be a favorite, Paul having only one, but they'd met in person for the first time last fall, so—

Needless to say, the three would have moved outside to the patio we'd set up for family visits and Paul would expect me to take my time joining them, his family not yet inured to my friendly nose in their business. Not that it was—well, yes, it was friendly—*the point being*, I thought cheerfully, as I obtained a mop and bucket, *while it was only Paul's blood around the table, they'd say things to him that mattered.* Maybe propose a larger family gathering. We were due for a party.

He'd tell me any interesting bits later.

Once I arrived, Paul's relatives invariably set aside his Human family concerns to launch the game of *Ask the Alien.* Stefan, more experienced with non-Humans like Lanivarians and afflicted by a comparable level of spacesickness, had created a tidy little story in his head that, like him, I'd come to visit Paul and found myself marooned on Botharis because, like him, I could no longer bring myself to board a starship to leave. We were, in other words, fellow castaways on a rural world and making the best of it, leading Stefan to raise such tantalizing questions as had I found a decent nail clipper yet, and what about this uncontrolled weather?

Sam, who knew all about scruffs but very little about this me, vacillated between a somewhat patronizing view of me as Paul's clever talking *pet* and suspicion. He didn't know what he suspected, only that there must be more to me—and my relationship with his nephew—than cute ears and entertaining conversation. I was careful not to add fuel.

Besides, my ears were *cute.* Shallow Esen was safe Esen.

Sam's questions were aimed at me but often directed to Paul in case I wouldn't understand. Paul, thus far, had gone along patiently. As my friend put it, the more Sam and Stefan experienced Esen-in-the-flesh, the less likely they were to worry.

A turn of phrase I found suspicious, and felt there must be more to it.

Making me happy to mop and rinse, tackle the ladder rungs, and wipe everything dry, postponing the inevitable—

"Es?" Paul came around the corner, eyes flashing. "Why are you still here?"

Tilting my head, I held up a rag in case it wasn't obvious.

"Put that down and come with me."

He was upset. Anger or fear? *The Framers?!* I panted to dump heat and relieve the inconvenient urge to cycle into something—anything—more formidable, not that there was any mass in reach except Paul's. "Has there been word? Another incident?" My voice came out a hoarse whisper, tail heading between my legs.

"Oh. No, nothing like that." He looked remorseful. "I'm sorry, Fang-face. I didn't mean to scare you. I want you to come visit with my family."

"Now?" My ears flattened. "You always want time with your family before I show up—and look at me!" Though Paul did look worse, glue flecks on his clothes and face, and his hair cemented flat which I could attest did not feel nice at all, having a patch or two stuck down myself.

He shook his head. "Jump in a closet first, but make it fast, Es. I need you." With that, he turned and vanished back around the corner.

I tied my rag to the third rung of the ladder to show the night staff where to start wiping, admired my gleaming floor, then bolted for the nearest Esen closet.

If my friend needed me, this wasn't a family visit after all.

In that judgment, I discovered a few moments later, I'd been premature, for glasses and a bottle of local whiskey—a Ragem tradition—sat out on the patio table and had clearly been used.

Then again, Uncle Sam was the one who'd introduced Paul to the ritual sharing of a beverage before any conversation of consequence between adults—defined, as far as I could tell, as any conversation after which those adults could relax, and possibly during, depending on the amount in the bottle provided.

This bottle being close to full, it appeared there'd been a token pour and drink to satisfy Uncle Sam and Ragems past, before Paul came for reinforcements. *Me.*

"Esen," he acknowledged, rising from his seat as I approached. "Thanks for coming."

Formal, were we? I bent an ear the precise amount to suggest *puzzlement,* but for the others, also on their feet, I'd a cheerful grin. "Stefan. Sam. Nice to see you." As they sat, I took the remaining stool, easing my tail to the side, and pointed at the bottle. "Am I too late?" Being family of a sort since fall and included; a courtesy I appreciated. I'd have appreciated it even more had Paul taken my suggestion and inconspicuously switched the local brand for something that didn't make me sputter and cough, but Sam appeared to enjoy that part.

He'd get along with Duggs.

"Not at all." Sam himself poured me a glass. I liked Sam, despite the patronizing and suspicion. He'd Paul's eyes, gray and fiercely intelligent, in a weathered, deeply lined face, and they'd a similar build, slender yet muscular. Like Paul's, when clean, Sam's hair was thick and willful, dropping over a high forehead and aged to an attractive silver. A foretelling, of a sort.

Stefan Gahanni was shorter than either Ragem, solidly built with muscular shoulders. His skin had picked up some healthier color since coming to Botharis but, like Sam, I found Paul in his eyes. Not the color, Stefan's were brown, but the shape. Their lively curiosity and brilliance.

They wore long dark jackets, open in a concession to the warm spring afternoon. I was pleased to see Stefan finally had his own, as Sam's hadn't fit him well, if less by this signal their coming was on serious business.

I lifted my glass, the others did the same, and joined the requisite in-unison sip, holding in most of my flinch. Their smiles had been courtesy only, quickly dropped; Paul's face was clouded. Putting down my glass, I asked bluntly, "What's wrong?"

"My father and uncle disapprove of my lifestyle."

At Paul's unexpectedly withering tone, my ears wanted to flatten. I kept them up with an effort and did my best to look intrigued. "You really should have changed and showered," I pointed out. "I did." And wore a nicely pressed smock over my pants, possibly not appropriate patio wear, but enjoyably loose. *There'd been several bacon-scented tubes.* "Or is it something else?"

"It's not a question of approval," Stefan said, glancing sideways at Sam. "It's—"

"We've invited Paul to live with us," Sam interrupted, his deep voice lower than usual. "Until the addition is finished."

Well, that explained my friend's dour expression. Someone had shared the news we were living in the greenhouse, in tents, but it wouldn't be that alone. Ragems were famous for their love of roughing it and Sam camped for sport.

It would be the we *part.*

"How very thoughtful," I replied comfortably, having centuries' more experience with awkward family than my beleaguered friend. *And his didn't bite.* "It means a great deal that you're willing to be disrupted for his comfort." At their blank looks, I went on, "We can send teams in at once to install the technical hookups. The communication array will probably take an extra day, but Duggs has the machinery on-site."

"'Machinery'?" Stefan echoed.

I caught the tiny flicker in Paul's eyes, but he remained outwardly gloomy. "This isn't about equipment, Esen."

"Their concern is well-founded," I countered. "Your family's aware the director can't simply pack a bag for a sleepover." I widened my smile. "They know one of us must have access to the collection at all times and here we've the most secure connection on this world." *Or many others, more advanced, not that it was the time to brag.* "Shifting an access point off-site is doable—" *We'd several; not the time to mention that either.* "—but will take an effort. The Library will cover your costs, Sam."

"Maybe we should have a list," Paul's father suggested. Catching on, I thought, but then Stefan had never thought of me as a pet. "If Paul's agreeable."

"'Paul' . . . is . . . not."

Oh dear. Not a pretense. He was actually gritting his teeth.

He'd never argued with Ersh. "Paul might be," I corrected smoothly, "if assured his daily responsibilities as director wouldn't be impacted by commuting. The Library is open every day of the year, and Paul is on call at any hour. You do have a landing pad, don't you? For his air-car? You'll need one."

Sam's frown had been growing. At this, his eyebrows collided and he half rose from his chair to roar, "What I need is to talk to my nephew alone!"

Ah. I silenced Paul with a warning dip of my ears.

"That's not what's going to happen. Please sit down, Hom Ragem," I ordered, clear and calm. I'd dreaded this moment. It having arrived, I felt nothing but determination.

Perhaps it showed, even on a face Sam had never learned to read, for he sat. The frown solidified, but to his credit, the Human leaned on his arms, staring every question he had at me.

Some I could answer, and it was time. "You do not understand my presence, either on your world, or in Paul's life. What isn't understood is a threat."

Stefan answered first. "We don't consider you a threat, Esen."

Sam's eyes glittered. "I do."

I watched Paul relax ever-so-slightly, signaling he'd trust this to me, and I flicked a grateful ear tip. "Of course you do," I told Sam. "And when people—when species—fail to understand one another, when they feel threatened, it can be because they lack information. Some key fact to make sense of what appears outlandish, even dangerous behavior. Without it, there are consequences. Stefan's discomfort. Your anger. Paul's offense." I added a hint of scorn to my tone. "Those are mere feelings.

"Out there? The consequence of ignorance are lives. War. Extinction. So here's your key fact, Sam, and you won't find it in any brochure. We created the Library to resolve such misunderstandings because Paul, Esolesy, and I have seen what happens next." I leaned forward, ears flat in emphasis. "We know we can prevent war and extinction because we've done it before."

That, for underestimating what Paul was. What we were. Not that we'd told his family. *Definitely time.*

"We're doing it here, right now," I went on. "We'll keep doing it. My *name*, Sam Ragem, is Esen and my shape doesn't matter. What does is my belief in what we're doing. What does is that I've chosen to come here, with Paul, to build our Library and devote my life to helping him save as many from their own ignorance as we can, any way we can. Including you." Sitting back, I lifted my ears. "And I don't have sex with Humans. Yuck."

"Esen—" Paul choked. Stefan covered his mouth.

Sam continued to regard me with those gray, eerily familiar eyes. No longer staring. Thinking—hard. "I knew something was up," he said at last, his voice no longer thick with resentment.

"You were right. We were keeping the truth from you." *And still were, but such was life.* I showed fangs. "I knew you thought I was Paul's pet."

He'd the grace to blush. "Didn't know what you were." A mumble.

"That's easy, uncle." Paul reached over and lightly tapped the tip of my ear. "We're friends." If there was a husky note to his voice, and if my tail swept from side-to-side, we were, after all, with family.

Perhaps the glimpse of emotion was the last piece of the Paul-Esen puzzle Sam needed, for his face abruptly cleared. He reached for the bottle. "I'm an idiot grounder," he exclaimed as if happy to admit it. *Humans.*

"Often," agreed Paul's father, holding out his glass with a grin I recognized. "Not always."

Glass clinked as Sam topped up all four. An Alini Dove sang in the distance. Before we raised our drinks, Sam spoke. "If you—" waving his glass from Paul to me and back, "—need a night under our roof, door's open."

My ears shot up. "Do you have parties?"

Paul gave me *that* look. I returned my most innocent.

His uncle and father chuckled at us both. Then we toasted one another in the Ragem tradition and when I sputtered at the taste, Paul winked at me.

"I hear Nia's coming for a visit," Sam said next, using that idle tone Humans employed when they'd a non-idle reason for both hearing and speaking.

Though delighted to sense a potential ally, I made sure to keep my ears at neutral. Paul, after an unnecessarily suspicious look at me—*it being mere moments since his uncle considered me an alien scruff and barely sentient, so our conspiring to rekindle their romance was completely out of the question up to this point*—replied, "The Special Envoy's coming at the request of the Preservation Committee."

Stefan snorted. "That lot."

I blinked at him, it being out of character for Paul's father to comment on anything to do with the Hamlet of Hillsview—other than commiserating with me, his fellow offworlder, on the lack of variety in the food market and, always, the weather.

"Hate to speak ill of family, but Lenan's a worse idiot grounder idiot than I am," Sam asserted, thumping his glass on the table to show his disdain for his second cousin. Or was it third? *There were a great many Ragems.* "Old Art follows him like a scruff—no offense, Esen." I let my tongue hang to show none taken. "—And Ruthie's had her nose out of joint since losing the election to Joncee."

Joncee Pershing was a firm friend of the Library. I lowered my ears in dismay, imagining the meetings had Ruth Vaccaro been head of the hamlet's council—if we'd made it to the meeting stage at all. She resented us for putting the Library on this planet, let alone up the road.

Lenan, Art, and Ruth were not only the volunteer heart of the Preservation Committee—and so impossible to remove—they formed the only opposition to the Library and everything associated with it.

Well, other than former reeve Ben Draven who'd wanted to buy the vacant Ragem farm and raise Drattles, the Botharan giant flightless bird native to the southern continent. A toothed and efficient predator, Drattles did produce oversized eggs, tasty meat, and their hide made a sought-after leather, but . . . *there was always a but.* Suffice to say, the phrase "When Drattles roam, best stay home" had its basis.

Draven's ambition to bring the creatures to the lush pastoral hills of Straint had been blocked by every sensible official in the Hamlet, including the Preservation Committee. You'd think Draven would blame his former colleagues—or recognize he'd been a touch premature placing orders for breeding pairs, thus risking a considerable sum—but no. With typical Botharan stubbornness, he blamed Paul Ragem for not being dead and buying back his family property right under his nose— which I'd done, to be precise, so he blamed me, too.

At our one encounter, I'd the impression he'd like to see me in his Drattles' pen.

A pen safely on the other continent, and I'd tried to help Ben Draven out of his predicament by posing as an anonymous collector ready to buy the birds at any price, but he remained stubbornly attached to his dream.

Draven probably had a Ragem ancestor.

While toothy visions of predatory giant birds danced through my head, the Humans had kept talking, as Humans do. Hearing my name, I did my best to look as if I hadn't missed a word.

I didn't fool Paul. "As I was saying, Es," with a meaningful look, "we'd be glad to recommend Stefan's proposed workshop to Nia while she's here. I see no reason it wouldn't fall under her office." At my charmingly attentive, if vague, head tilt, he continued patiently, "Stefan being the only star drive mechanic on this side of the ocean."

I knew that. What I didn't grasp was the part where we were to recommend Stefan to someone who worked on the ocean's other side. I liked Paul's father, quite beyond the fact that Paul did as well and should have his remaining parent close enough to visit. I lowered my ears to woeful and looked at Stefan. "Don't you want to stay here? Near us?"

Sam laughed. "Told you she wasn't listening."

"There was mud," I replied with dignity. "And glue. With glitter," that being an important factor. "So much glitter."

"Tough day." Paul reached over to scratch under my ear.

"I do want to stay," Stefan assured me. "I'd like to build my workshop at the Library landing field. In-ship tune-ups and inspections to start, nothing requiring a tug, but I'd be ready to machine my own drive parts." He sat up, as if prepared to get to work. "The ships I've seen coming here could all use some. 'Cept that beaut last fall." A blissful smile stripped years from his face. "I'd inspect those engines for free, if they'd let me."

Assuming he meant the *Mistral,* they wouldn't, but by now I grasped the situation and why Stefan had snorted, if not why I'd been distracted by Drattles. *Tough day.* "But the Preservation Committee opposes permanent structures near the field."

"They opposed the field," Paul argued, tipping over his hand. "And we have one. A mechanic of Stefan's caliber on-site would be more than an asset. There's safety involved." With a fire in his eye I'd seen before.

"Start ordering what you'll need," I advised Stefan Gahanni. "You'll have your workshop."

His son would make it happen.

Nearby

THE Survey ship *Mistral,* with its contingent of quasi-military security and can't-tell-you-how-fast engines, had been squeaky new when Evan Gooseberry last encountered her, on Botharis of all places. He'd come away believing if ever there was a ship whose mere presence signaled trouble, it was this one.

If there was ever the right ship to be on, going into trouble? *Mistral* was that, too, a remarkable comfort as he wearily entered the bridge behind Eller; Decker, with several bags to stow, had left them at the lift.

Captain Petara Clendon gave Eller a curt nod, reserving a pleasant smile for Evan. "Polit Gooseberry. Welcome back."

Last time, circumstances—in the form of chance and risk-averse seniors—had put him in charge. This time Evan was grateful not to be. "Captain Clendon." He dipped his head a second time, acknowledging the figure shadowing the captain's chair. "Commander Kamaara."

"Polit."

Whatever she'd thought of his query about ShimShree, or any doubts she'd harbored over his right to ask? *Didn't matter now,* he thought, relieved. As far as *Mistral's* officers were concerned, his arrival on their bridge signaled Evan Gooseberry was on sanctioned business for the Commonwealth.

Not that he'd any proof, the datacube having gone into Great Gran's recycler; a point to raise with Eller.

Meanwhile Evan knew not to take Kamaara's frown personally. The deep creases across her broad forehead were permanent as far as he could tell; the present situation wouldn't smooth them. The able head of the *Mistral*'s security detail had no patience for fools, regardless of rank, and detested guests on her ship.

Eller stepped forward, looking as fresh as when he'd arrived at Great Gran's. *Must be spy training*, Evan decided with some envy, feeling as far from fresh after the arduous trip here as could be imagined. "Captain, how soon can we leave orbit?"

The three began a conversation about the departure schedule—according to Clendon as soon as goods were received, who then checked with Snead, the on-duty comm officer. That moved into a back-and-forth about available holds. Kamaara chimed in with a report on—

Locking knees and hips, Evan set down his bag and arranged his face to *attentive but not involved,* drawing on his own training: interminable hours spent in meetings the way furniture occupied space. To stay awake, he focused on what he knew so far. Neither Clendon nor Kamaara appeared surprised to see him, but they wouldn't. The *Mistral* had brought "Eller and Decker Theelen" to Pachen IV in the first place, with retrieving him their goal.

Under whose orders—Eller's *faction* was on board, but who was part of it? Did even Eller know all those involved?

He wasn't to ask questions, any questions; Eller had made that clear. Nor was Evan to volunteer information until he'd met the others brought on board for Mission Passerby. The mission was highly classified. *He couldn't disagree.* They'd no idea what they'd face, be it Eller's malevolence or a peaceful shy species sending well-intended warnings or—most troubling—what Humans couldn't understand.

Restricting information flow wasn't new to Evan. He'd done it routinely since starting as a diplomat, though till this moment his experience had been more along the lines of whisking away menu items depending on guest sensitivities. There'd been the time he'd tactfully not let the Twillex in the waiting room know the Ambassador was late to their meeting because of an intestinal upset, as the being would assume this was a sign of imminent metamorphosis and insist a new ambassador be assigned at once. And once, he'd been put in charge of the ambassador's surprise birthday party. Keeping a secret like that in an embassy hadn't been easy.

Child's play compared to what Eller—the Commonwealth—asked of him now. As he listened to Eller's easy conversation, sprinkled with lies and half-truths, Evan worried his discomfort showed on his face.

Another reason to set it to *attentive but not involved.*

Though he was. Involved and not only as a diplomat, pretend spy, and concerned citizen. As a friend. Reading the datacube, learning the truth about Paul's mother—from the forbidden nav system implant she'd bravely volunteered, *or been forced*, to accept; to the disastrous test of the *Sidereal Pathfinder*; to Veya's tragic loss with the rest of the crew of the *Azimuth Explorer*—not, as recorded, on the *Smokebat*—

Because now Evan knew about Veya's years spent fleeing the faction while hunting her son. About her trip home and her visit to Paul's father, Stefan Gahanni, on Senegal III, if not what she'd left for Paul or said. Knew Stefan now lived on Botharis with Sam Ragem—even that Paul's father recently had applied to set up a star drive shop.

Did they know how closely they were being watched?

Did Skalet? Who'd abandoned the Library and was, as far as Evan knew, back with the Kraal. Who, it was rumored, were massing their fleets under a single leader—

Worse? He had no idea if he'd ever be allowed to tell Paul any of it. *And if he couldn't—how was he to face him again?*

Yet Eller expected Evan to do just that, to secretly contact the All Species' Library of Linguistics and Culture on Botharis and obtain whatever his friends learned about the Passerby, Survey's name for the Unknown Intelligence.

Evan hadn't bothered to explain to Eller that part would be entirely up to Paul, Esen, and Esolesy Ki.

To facilitate his efforts, the spy had slipped Evan an amazingly small pre-encrypted and doubtless top secret translight com. It now rested in the other sleeve of Evan's winter coat, inside the bag at his feet, and couldn't be used without Eller's authorization code. Nor was Evan to tell Paul the truth about why he wanted the information or that he was on the *Mistral*—

Paul being Paul, he'd hear it in his voice. That he'd secrets and was troubled.

With an inner sigh, Evan eased weight from one foot to the other. The ongoing discussion of their imminent departure had yet to hint where the *Mistral* would be heading once departed, but it wouldn't be anywhere safe. A dangerous sector of space, no doubt, space being a hazard at all times, which was why Evan was firmly in favor of landing on a planet. He'd prepared for local weather, having brought his warmest coat, if not boots.

"Polit?"

Startled, Evan blurted out, "I forgot my boots."

Wisely ignoring the nonsensical comment, the captain continued, "We've put you in the same quarters as last time. Steward Colquitts will escort you." Dismissal.

Salvation. Trying not to stagger, Evan left the bridge without another look at Eller.

Feeling Eller watch him.

"Good to have you on the *Missy* again, sir." The steward gave him a sidelong look. "Did you bring any Lishcyns this trip?"

Evan chuckled, almost giddy with exhaustion. "You're safe." After Esolesy Ki's memorable eruption in the guest galley, which this particular steward had had to clean, no wonder she checked. "Evan, please. Betts, isn't it?"

The corner of her wide mouth slid up, producing a dimple. "Aie. Betts it is, sir. Evan. Nice of you to remember."

"I do my best." Usually by making notes each night, but Evan doubted he'd ever forget a moment of that journey, let alone the people he'd met. Betts Colquitt, the steward, unfailingly cheerful and capable, ready to help. Comm Officer Snead less so—he pulled his mind back to the present. "I'll be glad to get some sleep."

"You're sharing with Professor Harpesseon, in case no one's told you." A grimace. "We've been picking up passengers like a liner. You'd best be the last or we'll have to put the next with crew."

"Who else?" Evan stopped in the middle of the guest corridor, weariness falling away as he eyed the four closed doors ahead with interest. The fifth, also closed, they'd just passed; it led to the shared galley.

"Only if you're allowed to tell me, Betts," he qualified. "I don't want to get you in trouble."

The steward grinned. "Can't see why not—you'll be stuck with them once we're on the move." She indicated a door with each set of names. "Cabin one, the Dwelleys. Blue Spider and Wort. You don't want to interrupt their games."

He wouldn't dream of it. Still, Evan hesitated, then had to say it. "Those aren't Dwelley names."

"They're what they told us to use." Betts' casual shrug encompassed all manner of alien oddity. "Something about staying in the moment. Cabin two's you and the professor. Three is the Contriplet, Ionneanus."

Conjoined Humans, especially triplets, were rare. Evan hadn't met any since Tonphiger, his first year at the academy. Trip, that being the preferred pronoun, had made a cheerful, if argumentative, lab partner. A pleasant friend, that too. *So far, so good.* "And in four?"

Her smile faded. "Comp experts. Haula and Poink." Betts lowered her voice. "Fussy as Quebits about their stuff." Louder. "You'll meet them at breakfast."

"Not supper?" He blinked, bemused. "Sorry. I seem to have lost track."

"Happens dirtside."

Easier still when being hustled around a planet. In the interests of speed, Eller and Decker had enlisted Evan's help with *Sparkles,* though they'd proved competent sailors. They'd made the tide and reached the marina before dawn. With Evan out of sight, they'd roused the dockmaster and made arrangements for the return of Great Gran's boat, claiming their rental had had mechanical problems.

A claim Evan judged they'd ensured was true.

What he remembered of the rest was a blur of aircars—three, each larger than the previous—then the shuttle up to orbit. Not from the nearest field, the one Evan had used to arrive, but on the other continent. They'd swapped to a second shuttle through an icy tube, Evan towed like another piece of luggage.

After that, things grew vague. He remembered rations and a stim shot. The clank as they'd docked with the *Mistral*—

A day, at least. Maybe two. He hadn't slept. Evan blinked again, belatedly registering the corridor lights were dimmed and Betts had been talking in a whisper. *Shipnight.* "Do I want to know how late it is?" he asked wearily.

"I doubt it." Betts gave him a sympathetic look. "Get to bed. Don't bother with an alarm. I'm to wake everyone for breakfast."

Evan had a feeling Eller and Decker wouldn't get as much rest. *Yet probably look fresh as a flower.*

They'd reached the door to the third cabin. "Bed sounds wonderful. Thank you, Betts."

She wrinkled her nose suggestively. "Hate to say it, sir—Evan. You might want the fresher first."

He sighed but nodded. "See you at breakfast."

Thanks to Aunt Melan Gooseberry's ample advice on space travel, the hazards of, and required preparations for—*now ingrained as habit*—Evan had packed his essentials in an easy-to-reach pouch. He pulled it out to have ready before slipping inside the cabin, closing the door behind him to stand in the dark. Exhausted as he was, Evan assuredly didn't want to disturb his cabinmate's slumber. There was no telling how old a venerable academic might be. Most Humans continued to work well into their second century, after all, and tenure remained till death. Why, Asukun Sun Gooseberry remained a professor while in a coma—

Listening for snores or wheezing, Evan eased his bag down, then switched on the tiny lamp in his hand, aimed at the floor. The fresher should be right over—

"Lights!"

He flinched, squinting as the room's illumination came on full. "Sorry. I didn't mean—"

"Which idiot are you?"

Evan found himself nose-to-nose with—he wasn't sure with what, at first. The nose appeared Human, if thin and hooked. The eyes were impossible to discern behind huge round lenses, but the mouth?

Pale lips were bared in a full snarl, yellowed teeth sharpened to points that put Esen's fangs to shame. Evan took a hasty step back, finding himself against the closed door. "I'm Polit Evan Gooseberry," he managed to squeak. "Professor Harpesseon?"

"A diplomat?" The professor shoved what Evan now saw were goggles over his—maybe her—head, crushing a wealth of bristling red hair. Green, reassuringly ordinary eyes blinked furiously as if trying to establish focus. "You what we're waiting for?"

"I—" *Was he?* "I don't believe so," Evan hedged, playing it safe. "Sorry, Professor."

"Ah well. You can wait with us. Misery loves company." A hand thrust out. "Call me Harps."

"Evan." Harps' hand had an extra thumb, and the skin was either covered in freckles or some kind of sauce, or both, but Evan reached for it without hesitation.

Only to be startled again as the hand whipped up in his face, fingers and thumbs dancing in air. "Gotcha! Don't touch. First Rule of Harps. Learn it or leave."

"We're on a starship," Evan pointed out, amused. "Where would I go?"

"Don't care. Second Rule of Harps."

Amused but exhausted. The effects of the stim were long gone and his bones *itched*. If he didn't get to stretch out soon on the cot in the corner—which presently looked to Evan like the most comfortable place in the universe—he'd take the floor. "Professor—Harps. I'd like to use the fresher then get some sleep. If you don't mind."

"Don't mind. That's the—"

"Third Rule of Harps?" he hazarded.

A keen look. "Fourth, but who's counting." Lips closed over the teeth, pursed, then deepened at the corners. Evan took it for a smile. "Go ahead. I've work to do."

The goggles came down, and Evan found himself staring into a distorted reflection of himself.

Skin black as space, as Great Gran liked to call it. Hair light reddish brown, twists starting in the short fuzz of her patented *home-for-a-holiday* cut. Pale eyebrows and lashes over eyes as green as Harps'. They'd that much in common, though the other was bone thin and Evan, after a few weeks at home, found himself a little rounder than usual.

"Lights off." With that, Harps and Evan's reflection disappeared, inconveniently turning the room completely dark again.

Instead of activating his palm light, Evan remained still, listening as the other turned and walked away. A rustling, perhaps plas sheets.

A satisfied grunt.

Once his eyes adjusted, Evan realized he could see the table to his left. Small objects on its surface glowed, faint, yellow. The silhouette of a hand with two thumbs moved over them, rearranging their order. Harps, at work.

The glow was sufficient for Evan to locate the door to the fresher stall. He stripped in front of it, leaving his clothes on the floor, too tired to care if the goggles let Harps watch, then stepped inside. No need to see the controls. Setting the spray to hot, he leaned back against the tiles and closed his eyes.

Then slid slowly to the floor and fell asleep.

6: Stone Wall Sunset;
Tent Night

SOMETIME later, slightly aglow from the Ragem family tradition and good feelings, Paul and I sat shoulder to shoulder on the low stone wall behind the Garden to watch the sunset. The wall was behind a field—presently mud sprouting tender green shoots, so we'd had to walk along the outer edge or Rhonda, who farmed it, would have our heads—and behind the barn as well. We might have been alone in the world.

Save for memories of those come before. Towering behind us was the giant misshapen tree fern Botharans insisted on calling an oak, its pot the collapsed rubble of a building left by the first generation of Ragems to live here. Its bark was scarred with the initials of those who'd come after, including Paul's, and inside that hard-to-spot hollow in the trunk?

Veya Ragem had left her son a message.

It sat on Paul's knee, a worn and well-loved little toy with still-bright googly eyes he called Starfield the Very Strange Pony. Web-memory held nothing like it, vaguely horse-shaped and blue with six legs and, Paul told me, dots of glitter on the rump. Veya had wrapped it carefully in a scrap of space suit fabric—admirable protection against the elements, as well as the current inhabitants of the oak.

Fabric from her suit. I'd caught a faint whiff of unfamiliar female Human when Paul first gently opened it. *Not something I'd mentioned at the time or since.* Humans didn't appreciate knowing they left traces of themselves behind. Veya Ragem's scent was stored in my memory, not that I would come across it again, but I relished having this much connection to the mother of my dearest friend.

Veya had taken her son's toy into space with her, without his knowledge, apparently as a memory aid; Humans did cling to physical reminders. We'd learned she'd hidden his toy here on her final visit home, along with a message given to Paul's father on another world entirely. He'd come here to tell Paul and, looking down at the pony, I repeated Veya's last words to her son. "'What we believe is lost simply waits for better eyes to find it.'"

"'Better eyes,'" Paul echoed, low and grim. "Those would help, Old Blob. I wish we knew what we're looking for." He held the pony up against the darkening sky as if it could point.

Unless he showed the toy the Botharan Bats starting to flit overhead. *Humans were capable of perplexing behaviors.*

"We're looking for the Framers," I ventured cautiously. "Aren't we?"

"Are we?" His shoulder bumped mine. "Is there an unknown intelligence out there? We've no proof. Nothing but those images. Even if there are Framers, are these their expression of compassion, to resolve the fate of vanished ships, or gloating over destruction, or even an offer to salvage? We haven't cause, means, or motivation. Only that ships were lost out there—" The pony rose toward space. "—and messages came back. Messages we don't understand." The pony returned to his knee. "It could be we never will, Es."

Doubt. In the words. In his tone. The sort Paul would admit only to me, and that was a trust to treasure. I did, always, but—*admittedly, I fumbled over how best to respond.* If my Human felt a little melancholy, he wanted me to listen.

In case, I angled an ear his way and waited.

Another, firmer, shoulder nudge.

Ah. One of the times Paul needed me to talk as well.

"We will understand," I said at once, going for optimism. Surely reasonable; all I'd need was access to some Framer's bits—hair, slime, skin flakes—in order to assimilate the form and then I'd learn the language.

Not that we'd a clue how to find any of them, whatever they were or where, nor was it ever quite that simple, because there might not be a language as such, and even if there was it would take time, but—no need to list my own doubts. Paul was equally aware what I could, and couldn't, do. "We know something important already," I reminded him. "The messages were sent, translight, to each ship's final contact."

Lionel's connections among the Sacrissee had given us that startling information. Those receiving images of lost ships ranged from traffic control within that system, to warehouses on orbital stations, to a Kraal weapons dealer with a late order. The latter, Lionel had inferred, might be how the Kraal and Sacrissee began to work together on the problem.

An arrangement likely ended as the Kraal withdrew within the boundaries of their Confederacy in what amounted, for them, to full retreat.

The fur on my neck rose and it wasn't the chill night air. The Confederacy lay between Botharis and Sacriss System. Whatever was responsible seemed to have no fear of the Kraal's military might. *No wonder the Sacrissee were remaking themselves as something with poisonous claws.*

Tucking the pony inside his jacket, Paul drew up a knee and stared out over the field. "And based on that, and only that," he said morosely, "we're to assume unknown aliens boarded each ship and successfully accessed their translight com. Or forced the crews of whichever species to do it for them."

His attitude startled me. We'd gone over this with Lionel and Lambo; I'd thought Paul agreed. Technology was standardized across known space-faring civilizations, for obvious reasons. "How else could it be done?"

Apparently it was the obvious troubling Paul, for he drew away and shook a disapproving finger at me. "We don't and can't know. Assumptions blind us to other possibilities. You of all beings should know that."

Scolded, I whined deep in my throat and lowered my ears.

"I'm not mad at you," Paul said immediately, though he'd sounded it—*and shook a finger*—and something definitely was wrong. "Sorry, Es." To complete the apology, his fingers found that spot under my ear and I leaned into the caress, hearing him sigh. "It's only—I can't shake the feeling we're missing something close—something crucial." His hand dropped away. "Ignore me. I'm not making sense."

Well, he wasn't, not really, but Paul's voice had an odd undertone, a rare uncertainty—*or was it dread?* I swallowed another whine and took a precautionary sniff. My friend smelled normal, other than the less-than-memorable whiskey on his breath.

"I trust your instincts," I assured him, abruptly worried. Skalet did as well, not that she'd admit it. She respected Paul Ragem's intellect and judgment, though typically added qualifiers such as formidable and dangerous—while cautioning me endlessly about *attachment and risk*—the point being, my friend often spotted a flaw or made a connection well before anyone else. "If you think we're chasing the wrong trail," I concluded, making my tone firm and forthright, "then we are."

Another shoulder bump, as if he didn't trust himself to answer. I responded with a quick lick of his ear, making Paul duck aside and laugh.

We watched the sun slip away, drawing out long purple shadows. The evening chorus began, quietly at first. It'd grow louder until the moons rose, waking the night hunters.

When Paul spoke again, his voice was closer to normal. "There's Nia's survey. Maybe we'll get some useful data."

"My poor Garden." Paul knew I'd had to postpone several Esen-specific tasks to help with the project, including my annual hunt for new mousel colonies under the hedges. *Possibly reaping benefits later.* Still, I should have fed the Leaping Forsber its duck by now. The plant couldn't bloom until it digested a fresh corpse and obtained certain amino acids. Fortunately, those occurred in most of the poultry species raised on local farms. *Well, fortunately for the shrub.* "Useful data would be nice," I grumbled.

My friend chuckled. "C'mon, Es. You know it's made Lionel happy."

My lip curled over a fang, an expression wasted on Human eyes in this light, but Paul was right, as usual. A tool of Human bureaucracy everywhere—according to Ersh—Nia's proposed survey had been seized upon by Lionel as if he were a shrub starved for duck. Leading me to suspect he'd been waiting his chance to inflict one on our scholars.

The survey's goal was straightforward—in principle. Since dozens of different species arrived at the All Species' Library of Linguistics and Culture every day, Nia proposed we ask them about the Framers.

Indirectly, of course.

Our visiting scholars—a group for the most part accustomed to Ambush by Forms—now completed the Official Botharan Planetary Government Department of Interplanetary Travel Assistance Survey before receiving their response from the collection. While the "Interplanetary Travel" department consisted solely of Nia and her assistant, and *official* was more, in this instance, a state of mind than reality, no one else had to know. Once Paul and Lionel fine-tuned the survey's design, I'd done the hard part. Making the concepts work for our diversity of scholars.

The basic survey document was a promising "How can we better serve your needs?" sort of thing, and under the category: "Present Ease of Travel" were a series of questions to gauge everything from "how worried are you about space travel at this time?" to "by what extent do you believe starships are reliable?"

As everyone had to come via Hixtar Station—until the Botharans built theirs—I'd emphasized the words *space* and *starships* in a likely vain attempt to stop respondents fixating on Hixtar's deplorable plumbing.

As for the Framers? We couldn't ask if any had received or seen a mysterious framed image of a missing ship. Except we could, and I'd suggested it as a time-saver, but my Human friends had looked horrified, refusing to chance inciting panic throughout known space.

Subtle Esen it was.

I'd put a portion of the frame from the image of Veya's ship at the top of the survey, like a logo, had the Library such a thing. *I'd suggested one long ago, but Paul had pointed out how few of our visitors paid attention to blatant signage, let alone a brand, so a logo was a waste.*

It might also have unintended repercussions. Our confident expectation—*mine, anyway*—was that only those who'd seen a Framer image would react. Ideally by immediately telling us, though I was ready to identify hysterics or unusual tension in any form. We should have known better.

I should have.

So far, the only reaction by any species had been from Heezles, who'd done their utmost to hoard and smuggle out as many of our printed survey forms as they could before Henri noticed the piles disappearing and put a stop to it. Upon questioning, a Heezle scholar had blinked moistly, then admitted the patterned strip was highly erotic and could they have more to take home?

Not because they'd seen such before—a detail Lionel'd checked with commendable delicacy. Heezle erotica leaned more toward novelty.

Even more embarrassing? Though they said not a word, I'd no doubt Paul and Lionel knew why I hadn't seen this coming.

Being relatively young in a given form had more disadvantages than I'd realized.

One of the reasons I'd gladly left my friends in charge of their own kind. Human scholars coming to the Library completed their version of our survey, not that we'd many. We'd had three, to be exact, if we didn't count Evan, and two of those proved to be lost.

Why? According to Duggs, Woolies—Humans from Commonwealth systems—were ungrateful snobs who wouldn't believe anything worth having came from an outlying farming planet like Botharis until it was shoved—

I took the rest of her explanation under advisement. Paul's, that the Commonwealth relied on its own first contact expertise, namely Survey, not only made more sense but was anatomically feasible.

As for the rest, Kraal weren't welcome, criminals weren't interested, leaving other colony worlds. Not to be snobs ourselves, but new settlers tended to be preoccupied with survival and construction.

The cooling air carried a fresh scent. *Mousels.* The tasty wee things emerged from their burrows and other hiding places after dusk. I widened my nostrils. By the strength, several were close; I swallowed drool surreptitiously.

Not surreptitiously enough. Paul chuckled. "After all those tubes, Fangface?"

How did he know? Did I have bacon breath?

"Reflex," I admitted. Ersh's stern warning, *don't let biology control you, Youngest* applied to everything about a form. Even the fun parts. *Especially the fun parts.* I dipped my ears in acknowledgment. "I shouldn't hunt mousels." I went on automatically, "Ersh wouldn't—"

Approve.

The unspoken word hung in the air between us, prickly and uncomfortable, like a mousel stuck in my throat. I didn't say it casually anymore. Not since learning Paul had given the phrase to one hundred and ten strangers, his Group, as a password.

Having given me to them as well.

Not literally, of course. He'd told them about me. What I was. Why I deserved to be helped and protected. How to help and protect me. My first, dear friend, knowing I'd outlive him, aware of his relative fragility, hadn't wanted me to be alone. He'd assembled his Group in secret. On the pretext of sharing his past with me, Paul had shown me their faces. I'd been foolishly delighted by his trust.

He'd told me the truth of who they were only when we'd been trapped and he'd been about to die.

I remembered every strained breath, every thud of our burdened hearts—remembered how it felt to hear him gasp out those words even as I'd prepared to accept his ultimate gift, the last of his failing life, and use it to escape—

"Esen."

Just my name, breathed out to hang in the air between us, yet somehow Paul imbued it with affection and a dose of impatience, fully aware why I'd fallen silent.

I'd accepted the Group's presence in our lives, not that I'd much choice. Some had saved us that dreadful day, though later I learned the whole thing had been as much Paul's test of them as theirs of me. *What would a Web-being do if her heart was broken? Would such a powerful being seek revenge? Become the next Death?*

Hearts and revenge being Human concepts, I'd told Paul the truth. Had he died that day, I'd have become something, perhaps an Iberili, able to sleep the next few centuries.

Not that I'd told him why. That I'd planned to sleep until Logan and his evil cohorts, Paul's friends and his Group, the twins and Rudy—until everyone alive that dreadful day was dust and the memory of Paul Ragem, my first friend, mine alone to keep.

Of course, it wasn't long afterward I learned Skalet was alive as well, so my somewhat quixotic plan to eternally mourn in private had a significant flaw.

"Es."

"All right," I said very quietly, before he had to prod again. "I'm thinking about the Group. I haven't met them all."

There'd been a time I'd planned to do just that. Also a time I'd sworn never to go near a single one, then a time—suffice to say, my attitude had matured. Paul's Group existed. They, the members, were helpful. Unfortunately for any personal contact, they were scattered across the Commonwealth and Fringe, and I was busy at the Library.

Besides, I knew about them. More than faces. I'd names. Details. I'd had Rudy Lefebvre investigate each person, discovering—to no surprise—Paul had chosen well. Each had a sincere reason for offering an unusual *last of her kind* alien their help.

Paul and I agreed we were not correcting the *last of* part.

Some had lost loved ones to Death, the wild Web-being I'd—with help—destroyed, and were grateful. They knew I was their best hope should another stray into this life-rich part of the universe. Others simply believed in Paul, passionately dedicating themselves to his cause. All had accepted the risk of anti-truth drug treatments, to preserve the secret of my Web.

One had died for it. Making this unwanted, precious set of Humans my responsibility, if not my Web's. *Fine when it had been Esen the only.*

My ears flattened and fur rose over my spine. *Now it wasn't.*

"Ginny Filer is back on Botharis," Paul announced, as if giving me good news. "We could invite her to—"

Here? "No!" With what might have been a tiny howl.

He turned to stare in my direction, not that his Human eyes could see much more than the reflection of starlight in mine, and waited.

An ominous, *explain yourself,* sort of wait. *Ersh couldn't do it better.*

My tail tried to curl under me. "It's not a good time for visitors, Paul," I said lamely. "Except for Nia. It's a very good time for her to visit. Because it—is." I shut my mouth too late. When I babbled, Paul knew it was to avoid telling him something he wouldn't like. Often that concerned what was left in the greenhouse emergency rations box, or rather wasn't, but this time—

This time was different. As Senior Assimilator for the Web of Esen, I carefully pruned what I'd share with my web-kin. Neither Skalet nor Lesy knew of Paul's Group. Well, Skalet knew he'd forged an excellent network of information collectors, legal and otherwise, and valued that resource herself.

I hadn't shared that Paul had broken Ersh's Prime Law. *Do not reveal our existence to ephemerals.*

Not just a little, either. He'd made a club. With the best of intentions, but as potential for disaster went?

My Elders couldn't know, ever. Overwhelmed with worry, I went to lick the tip of his nose. "Nothing to be concerned about."

"Not so fast." Paul took hold of the loose skin over my upper spine. "I know what you're up to, Old Blob."

He did?

"The dress you left in my tent?" With that distinct *what have you done* note in his voice.

I blinked. *There was a dress?*

Taking the dress as the gift it was, I flattened my ears and let a growl of protest rumble in my chest. "I've no idea what you're talking about," I said truthfully.

Well, unless it was Lesy's *wonderful* idea for Nia and Paul. My web-kin had been mildly intrigued at the notion of assisting my favorite Human in his mating rituals—as long as she didn't have to watch, which I could assure her would most certainly be the case. With Lesy's fickle attention span, I hadn't expected results this soon or without repeated and steadily louder prompting. *How gratifying.*

"What kind of dress?" I asked curiously, as if Paul didn't have me by the scruff of the neck.

He used it to give me a tiny shake, with a growl of his own. "The wrong kind, Esen-alit-Quar."

There were right and wrong kinds?

Humans were so confusing. "I had nothing to do with any dress," I said again, truthfully.

"Huh." The noncommittal syllable suggested my friend wasn't anywhere near to being convinced.

Fortunately, my night sight was superior, letting me spot little blotches of glowing yellow over our heads, under the as-yet-unfurled fronds of the Botharan "oak." I pointed up excitedly, this having been our reason to sit on the stone wall in the first place. "Look, Paul! The Glows are out! The first ones!"

Much as I knew he wanted to press the matter of Nia, dresses, and promises—*and wouldn't forget I'd howled in denial of Ginny Filer's visit*—Paul let me change the topic. Maybe he sought distraction too. "We should have brought a bottle, Fangface."

"Wine?"

He chuckled. "No. Or yes. I meant an empty one. You scrape off some Glows and put them inside. I haven't done it for years. Makes a lamp."

I eyed the dim yellow spots overhead. My dark-fearing Lishcyn-self, soon to return, would not be impressed by a lamp made from disturbed fungi. *There could be panic vomit.*

After we'd admired the Glows for a while, Paul yawned. "Time to head home, Es."

This me had excellent night vision. A Human did not. I hopped down first and, when Paul landed beside me, I found his hand and put it on my shoulder. "I'll lead the way."

Which my friend would do for me once I was again Esolesy Ki, both of us careful of the other, as conscious of respective weakness as strength. And perhaps it was that awareness that made me pause, a shiver running down my spine despite the warm night, to look up at the stars.

My friend saw problems before anyone else—

A while later, having failed to fall asleep, I lay on the floor of my tent to attend to some personal grooming.

Stubborn hunk of mass. Frustrated, I seized the annoying mat of dried mud and barley sprouts—*a single misstep!*—in my front teeth and plucked it from between the tender pads of my foot. To finish, I chewed it to death.

While thinking. I couldn't help it and my thoughts? Were the sort that would keep any being awake at night, especially one who distrusted the ephemeral need to go unconscious at the best of times.

Not that I'd great and grand thoughts racing through my head, which at least would have been productive and I've have loved to wake Paul with an amazing new insight into the Framers.

Instead, mine were petty and personal. *I was*, as Ersh would say, *pointlessly fretting about the inevitable.*

Because of Lambo and Lionel, Rudy was coming. "Esolesy Ki"

would arrive with him, and my life would change. Which shouldn't matter at all. Whatever form I cycled into was me, of course, but—

There'd been a time I'd had to fight to save this me. Skalet had tried to drive me from it, in part because a Lanivarian Esen was a reminder I hadn't budded from Ersh, like the rest of her Web. I'd been born, as this.

Not on purpose, granted, but here I was, and for all my Elders found this me *disturbing,* I found being a Lanivarian both convenient and a comfort. Except when in a starship moving through space.

Not being in space or a starship, I spat out the chewed lump before flopping my chin on my crossed front legs to glower at the wall of my tent, as if I could see Paul through it.

My glower wasn't about him. It was about me.

Over the months spent exclusively as a Lanivarian—*other than a couple of brief adventures to ease the urge to cycle and show Paul the beauty of ShimShree spew*—I'd experienced firsthand how admirably this form worked around Humans. The Library staff considered this me appealing while respecting my teeth. I could give orders. Not that I tended to, being inclined to ask and explain why, but if I were moti-vated, I could be commanding. Sort of. My voice rose.

The point being this me, Esen-alit-Quar, was the Library Curator, a person of responsibilities and importance, someone who made deci-sions and occasionally was called to the Hamlet of Hillsview Preser-vation Committee to explain them.

Not so Esolesy Ki. My Lishcyn-self was a sturdy handsome being, with elegant inlay in my tusks I loved, and—presuming I obtained better clothes than a sack to give me confidence—all the command presence of a mousel.

Mousels would, in fact, chase that me across the Garden, having discovered my scales and hems harbored crumbs after meals and, even better, I'd snacks in my bag. Whenever I stopped to share, they'd swarm over me, whiskers twitching adorably.

Not so this me. My favorite snacks were juicy squirming mousels, and they knew it, though I could go days without a meal if necessary.

That me had to keep all five stomachs busy or suffer the conse-quences. As did anyone in range, Lishcyns having evolved projectile vomiting as a defensive mechanism and never left it behind, being afraid of almost anything. Starting with shady corners and don't get me started about actual dark—

Esolesy Ki had to be indoors after dark. Lesy would have willingly shared the farmhouse with me, or rather ignored my presence after the first hour, but she'd turned every portion of the Ragem farmhouse into her gallery—the portions not crammed to the ceilings with raw materials, including the furniture she didn't like. My sleeping boxes had been demolished weeks ago.

The greenhouse? I pushed my snout outside my tent to confirm that at night, the glass of ceiling and walls seemed to disappear. To either side stood trees and shrubs; my favorite part of the Garden.

To that me, menacing black silhouettes with outreached arms and waiting claws.

Overhead, the night sky glittered. Hope and Destiny, the beautiful— if optimistically named—Botharan moons, were setting to the west, stars rekindled in the velvet black, the perfect time to hunt.

Oh, but to that me? Stark, paralyzing terror as the utter DARK consumed all light and—

I sighed and flopped down again, head and shoulders outside the tent. I'd enjoyed this me as long as I could. The entire winter and the start of spring, in fact, and it was no one's fault but Lesy's—*who was mine*—that without the seclusion of the farmhouse?

Lishcyn I must be, and Lanivarian I must not, once Rudy tottered in disguise down the ramp of his ship in three days' time. Or less. Apparently, he'd a new faster ship and wanted to hurry my—what?

Loss?

I wanted to howl and settled for a soundless whimper, unable to comprehend this sense of impending grief. I'd be me. How could I not?

Had the glimmer of Lesy-taste I hadn't yet excised from my flesh tainted my thinking? The same subtle but real skew from normal terrified Skalet, who otherwise feared nothing—

But she did. Skalet feared being anything but Kraal or her web-self. Feared losing herself to any other form; dreaded having to interact with beings who weren't like her. As if seeing herself reflected in their eyes posed a fundamental threat.

I'd developed some empathy. More than mousels' attitudes toward me changed based on my shape. Evan Gooseberry considered this me a dear friend.

Not that me.

I raised my head, staring in the direction of Paul's tent. The sole person in my life who cared equally for all mes—well, maybe not my Ycl-self, but at least he trusted I wouldn't consume him. Unless starving—*biology posing its risk*—but I knew deep down he'd understand and forgive—

My head hurt. Or was it my heart, as Humans would say?

I could hear Ersh now. *Stop fussing, Youngest.* Knew what Skalet would say, were she here. *Cycle to web-form and cleanse every trace of Lesy.*

But if I did, and still felt the same, what then?

I whimpered after all.

A tiny glow in the other tent. I twitched an ear as Paul unzipped the door but didn't come out. The Human knew there were biters crawling around on the greenhouse floor, it being their home we'd borrowed.

I licked a couple from a paw and crunched, considering his invitation.

Declined it, politely, with an audible *huff* of breath.

While two of us in a tent made it cozy in winter, and I appreciated the offer? On this warm spring night, I'd pant and he'd sweat, then I'd snort—*because Human sweat smelled funny*—then he'd kick—*because I'd snorted in his ear*—

Calm filled me. Peace. Though I'd no idea how contemplating sweat, snorts, and kicking accomplished the feat, the sensation itself was very familiar. *Paul was here. Paul understood.*

We'd work it out.

Pulling out a blanket, I curled beneath the starry sky, tail over my tender nose *in case,* and fell asleep.

Nearby

A S Library Administrator, Lionel Kearn maintained an open-door policy. Staff were welcome in his office at any time, for any reason, and he took it as the compliment it was that some now walked in simply to sit and have tea during their breaks. They'd talk, or not. If they talked, it might be about work, or not.

A far cry from how he'd run the *Russell III,* when he'd used his office as a fortress and distrusted those under his command. Who'd detested him—maybe not all, but most.

Because he'd lied to them. To himself, but to them, oh yes. Had valued secrecy over collaboration. Had begun to jump at shadows as much imagined as real, and another year of it—

There hadn't been. Esen—with Paul and Rudy and Mesa Timri— had saved him from himself. Had encouraged him to be the leader he'd once been, before the lies and fear.

Now? Lionel smiled. Why now he'd become a conductor, waving an invisible wand as he guided the harmonious—*usually*—work of dedicated, experienced people in a symphony of service to the wonderful goals of the Library.

Not that he'd share that image with anyone else, but if he had a wand, it was that of being organized—*with a plethora of detailed lists and color-coded charts, as one must*—and continuously adjusting extensive contingency plans.

Tasks easier to accomplish when he wasn't in his office, interrupted at whim by friendly staff. Paul was amused but understanding, Esen bewildered. She'd asked why he didn't close the door once in a while.

Because he'd closed and locked it for fifty years, and never wanted to again.

Putting aside his flask of juice, the only thing he consumed in Skalet's inner sanctum, Lionel opened his work display. It had soon become his habit, and a saving one, to remain here for the first hour and a half of each day, dealing with those tasks requiring concentration. Safe from interruption.

Now, with his research into the Framers, he relied on this being the most secure location on the grounds, perhaps the entire planet. No one could—

Before the locked and most secure door finished opening, Lesley Delacora stepped inside. "I brought you a cake."

With no protest from Skalet's security system, and, meeting those ancient blue eyes, no protest he dared make.

"A 'cake'?" Lionel echoed weakly. She carried something on a tray, but it was hard to focus past the huge geometric shapes attached to her body. More like fabric barnacles than clothing—

"Hayberry shortcake." She put the tray, and the tall wavering concoction it supported, on the desk, in the midst of his display. Columns of numbers vanished into what he guessed was whipped cream. Purple whipped cream. A frosting? "It's for your breakfast."

"Break—" Lionel shook himself and rose to his feet. "This isn't a good time," he said stiffly. *She shouldn't be here.* Lesley—Lesy's presence, everything about her, even the cake—shattered the serenity of this place, as if she erased Skalet. "Thank you for the cake, but if you'd go—please—I've work—"

"Don't be boring, Lionel." Lesy winked at him. "Skalet let me in before, you know. I came back to find her secrets. Like this." She ran two fingers along the pristine white of a wall, leaving obscene streaks of purple goo.

Violation! He surged to his feet. "Stop—"

Too late. With a muted chime, the streaked wall slid upward into the ceiling, revealing a shallow room filled with green. Reaching in, Lesy tapped a thick leaf. "Duras. Skalet's never without."

Hydroponics. A glance told him the technology was similar to the standard in starships. Probably the design Skalet employed when traveling as a Kraal—if she could.

Lionel refused to fret. Mist was escaping— "Please close it. At once."

Lesy gave an insolent shrug and tapped the floor twice with a sandaled foot. Down came the wall, purple streaks smeared into an offensive band.

He'd clean it. Sterilize it. *Once alone.* Lionel took a breath.

The Web-being slipped close before he could say a word, taking his chin in her firm, cool fingers. "I do love secrets, Lionel." Her face held a disturbing eagerness. "Tell me yours."

He didn't dare pull free, however awkward it was to speak. "None. I've none."

"But you do." Her eyes glittered like ice. "All of you. Skalet. Esen and her Paul. At first, I thought it was about Evan and his, but he left, and it stayed. The silence when I enter. The whispers in the halls. The looks. I notice such things."

Lionel felt a thrill of fear. Esen hadn't said why she kept Lesy in the dark about the Framers, only a cryptic *best not.* "Let me go."

Her grip tightened. "Oh, I don't think so," smiling as if they played a game. A game where he didn't know the rules, only that what held him looked Human. And wasn't.

He couldn't force her to leave. Couldn't wait for interruption or rescue, not when he'd done such a good job of protecting this time and himself from distraction. *No choice.* Lionel braced himself. "Let me go," he managed. "I'll tell you what I can."

Fingers relaxed. Traced along his jaw and pressed feather soft over the pulse hammering in his throat. "The. Secret."

"It's—there's something out there—"

Lesy chuckled. "There's some *thing* right here." Moving away at last, she spun in a slow graceful circle, the patterns fixed to her skin distorting her shape. "What fun! Having you know what I am—part of your brief flicker of existence—I can see why Esen enjoys it." She came to a stop, head tilted. "But I'm not your only secret, Lionel." Her gaze dropped to the cake. "I think it's hiding in there."

Not the cake, he realized with a jolt. What it sat upon—the console with his work display and Lionel didn't need Esen to warn him against granting her strange web-kin any kind of access. "It's the Kraal—" he blurted. "Something's attacked their ships. In response they've consolidated power. There's a risk—"

"Blah. Blah. Blah. Is that all?" She brushed aside air. "Skalet and her pets—here's hoping they finally go extinct. She'll taste better. Being Iftsen would do wonders for her personality."

Lionel stared at her.

"What? Oh, Lionel dear." Lesy pointed her finger at him, shaking her head. "You thought we'd try to save you. How sad. How small. Why would we? There'll be new smart life-forms to assimilate. There always are." The finger stabbed the cake, came out with a glob of purple frosting she put between her full lips, eyes half closed with pleasure. Then they opened, fixed on him in what felt like warning. "Don't worry. When you're less than dust, our Web will remember what you created. That's what matters." She went to the door, glancing back over a shoulder. "But go ahead if you like. Help Skalet play with her Kraal. I certainly won't bother."

She left, the door obeying without code or complaint.

Paul had said it. That Lesy wasn't like Esen. Or Skalet. Lionel'd thought it was because she was fragile. Almost childlike in her whims and fancies. Someone to be humored and protected and—

He couldn't have been more wrong.

Lesy lacked restraint—worse, she lacked empathy or compassion, even for her own kind. She was someone to fear.

The cake had to go. Lacking a recycler—this room sealed from other systems—Lionel emptied his clothes from his bag and put Lesy's offering inside. He'd take it to the Library for disposal. The clothes he set in a neat pile on the cot.

A sock fell. As he bent to retrieve it, the comp system gave a tiny ping.

The model was done.

Lionel hastened to the desk, keying up the results without bothering to sit. He scanned them once, then sank down on the stool.

Impossible.

He checked and rechecked what he'd fed the machines. Paused to call Henri and tell her he'd be late before going carefully through the model's parameters. Had he missed something? Skewed the final result somehow?

By the time his eyes itched with strain and his back was sore, Lionel Kearn was convinced it wasn't a mistake.

The starry backgrounds of the Framer images didn't mark a boundary.

They marked a struggle.

He had to tell Paul.

Out There

MOMMY, I can't find Starfield.
You will. Don't worry. Maybe he's taking a trip, like me.
In space? In a suit? On a ship?
Maybe he's on a wonderful new world. A place where people say hello with stinky farts.
Laughter sweeter than life. You made that up.
Not at all. The stinkier the better. The people are called Iftsen.
Let me . . .

The precious shard turns away, drains everything sweet and joyful. She feels—

Stop now. Stop now. Stop—

She can't. The perilous longing fills her. Her eye leaps to focus on her heart's will, not that she has a heart, and what she sees next—

NO! It will bring Hell closer. Bring it near. *NO!*

Turn away. Turn away. Turn away . . . the cost, she feels it, is pieces of herself drying up, flaking away, dust . . . if she could die that way but she can't. Hell won't let her.

TURN AWAY!

She's done it again. Turned the eye, shifted its focus.

Hell doesn't care what the target looks like, only that she *sees* it, creating the corridor, showing the way. Another starship, as far away from *him* as possible.

Veya can't afford to care about who is inside, so long as what she sees isn't home. *So long as it isn't him.*

It isn't. She's no choice but to see. But what she sees isn't a starship. *Something's gone wrong.*

She sees a world of browns, mauves, and greens. Sees white swirls within a delicate skin of atmosphere.

Stop now. Stop now.

She struggles to turn the eye again, to find a starship entering translight, to find something small. A bearable grief.

STOP NOW!

She has no voice.

Scale is irrelevant. Hell opens its maw from translight, a vile gape into the *real* where it doesn't belong. In its futile attempt to engulf this strange new prey, atmosphere evaporates, the fragile layer of life fries—

Rock and stone are pierced by—pierced by—filaments like lightning—and ripped asunder—

Spat back into the real world as Hell flees to its own. Curls tight. Crushes in. Shudders like agony shake its core. Vibrations like fear course through it. Bits of living matter jerk and dance on their filaments, energy flares, but Veya can see only what her eye sees.

She imagines opening her mouth. Imagines screaming until vomit burns the throat she no longer has—but nothing stops her seeing.

Nothing can.

So she *HOLDS* the image, holds it, holds it, encases it. Forces away the image of the wreckage of a living planet until it becomes a spark and winks away into the uncaring empty.

Knowing she no longer dares turn her eye, *turn Hell*, away.

7: Garden Morning

SPECIAL Envoy Niala Mavis of the Botharan Planetary Government, signatory of the Mavis Peace Accord and the People's Hero, sat cross-legged on a striped blanket in the Garden, shoes set aside, her elegant green-and-gold jacket tossed carelessly over her large portfolio, her eyes unfocused and cast skyward as she chewed the last of the hayberries we'd picked.

I'd gladly given her my share—and couldn't resist giving her Paul's. Observing Nia's bliss, I didn't interrupt to tell her she'd a spot of green berry juice on the tip of her nose, though seeing the line of stinger bugs making a foray toward her bare toes, I'd have to advise her to move to the other end of the blanket sooner than later.

"Mmm. Thank you, Esen." Nia pulled her toes out of danger. She'd long toes and long graceful fingers, and an attractive face able to assume whatever expression she wished. Right now, that was relaxed and happy. Her cap of black hair was tamed in the smooth waves that were the height of fashion on the other side of the ocean; a single lock rebelled, curling over her right eyebrow.

I found the wild little curl reassuring as I met a curious gaze every bit as intense as Paul's, if from blue eyes. "I haven't had fresh picked hayberries since—for a very long time," Nia said. "Did you know they're my favorite?"

Because she reminded me of my friend, and had been his, I shook my head. "I didn't. They're all that's ripe in the Garden."

"The first taste of spring." Her wide mouth curved. "I've missed them."

Mousels tasted better. *Not an opinion to share.* "Aren't there hayberries in Grandine?"

"Not the same. They're—" Nia scrunched her face to illustrate the taste, her eyes disappearing in a delightfully weird expression I'd a feeling she didn't use in the capital. Her features relaxed back into her easy smile. "Besides, it wouldn't do to be caught asking for anything so—ordinary. Ridiculous as it seems, Esen, even what I eat makes the news these days."

Ah. Botharan society was young enough to sneer at the plain country fare that had sustained its founding population. At some point, restaurants would rediscover it as the latest cuisine. *Human culture had its predictabilities.*

But it wasn't right that Nia's new importance to her world deprived her of what gave her bliss. I thought hard, then cheered, ears up. "The crop isn't over. I'll send you a box of hayberries and label it as—as tea leaves. You could eat them in secret. Do you have a closet?" I'd some experience. "Would that work?"

She'd the sort of laugh that invited you to keep it company. "I won't say no. But make it soap and please send to my home, Esen, not the office. It'll be a welcome—" Her laugh stopped as she looked past me, her features settling into a *pleasant anticipation* that wasn't.

I turned, unsurprised to see Paul, and kept my ears at cheerful with an effort. It wasn't right, that a good person like Nia wasn't happy to see him.

And wasn't my problem, I told myself, for what good it did.

My friend came down the narrow, irregular stairs, surveying his surroundings with interest, this being his first time here. He protected the tray of drinks he carried from the tall Cully Grass leaning in from either side and water beaded the glasses and his forehead; today's weather was what locals called a *Touch o'Summer*, hot and intensely humid despite being spring. The sort of weather that made picking the first crop of berries both challenge and reward.

And might bring thunderstorms. *WET!* With a shudder, I kept a wary eye on the horizon.

With a smile at me, Paul set the tray on the blanket and nodded a greeting to our guest. "Hello, Nia. You've got some—" He put a finger to his nose.

Nia rubbed hers with the back of her hand, chuckling at the transferred spot of green. "So I do. Thanks."

The simple exchange somehow eased the tension between them. In romance vids, at least in some Human ones—there being sufficient variation in species' courtship rituals to have kept Ansky entertained for millennia—this would be my cue to make an excuse to leave the potential couple together, which might be all they'd need—

Paul's look pinned me in place before I could make the attempt. *Not that I would.* I twitched my ears as if to dislodge an insect. *We'd serious matters to discuss.*

He brushed the bugs aside and sat, pulling off his shoes, then rolling up his pant legs. "Leave me any berries?"

Nia raised the empty basket. "Sorry."

She didn't appear sorry. On the other hand, Paul didn't appear perturbed to have missed his treat. *I was missing something.* "There'll be more tomorrow," I promised. Hayberry bushes grew in abundance among the rocks early settlers had removed from fields and piled into their first fences, bushes presently full of almost-but-not-ripe berries and the drone of a multitude of pollinators seeking their own harvest from the latest flowers.

My dislike for the smell—let alone the taste—made nosing out mousels trickier than usual. *I suspected the wee things knew it.*

The Humans took up their drinks. Having rumps like cushions, the species enjoyed sitting like this. As for my Lanivarian-self?

With Paul's unspoken *stay, Esen,* I decided there was no need not to make myself equally comfortable. I walked my hands forward until I could ease to my belly, resting my chin on crossed arms to regard my companions. Having chosen my spot on the blanket with care, this put my haunches in the warm sun and the rest of me in partial shade, leading to the logical conclusion that I might close my eyes and thus not be third at the picnic, and wouldn't a nap be wonderful—*not that I was tired*—

Nudge. I opened my eyes to glower at Paul, who withdrew his foot with an unrepentant snort. "No time for napping, Fangface," he said briskly. "Esolesy Ki arrives tomorrow morning. We've matters to discuss."

Which I knew, hence my offering the most private part of the Garden for what was almost a picnic instead of any of its fifteen patios. Not that I'd told Paul this space—enclosed by stone and hidden by hedges of Red-tipped Conchie, with trees arching overhead to form an airy, leafy roof—was where the Web of Esen met to share.

Not that there'd been a meeting or sharing here since Lesy arrived, though I was relieved nothing had been turned into art yet.

Paul would know I'd created it for that purpose. Detect sentiment in the six sides of the mossy stonework beneath our blanket, for the Web of Ersh had held that number, and—

Being Paul and my friend, above all he'd comprehend the gesture I made, inviting two Humans here.

Unwittingly, I'd stared at him as I'd thought all this through. Able to read me in any form, Paul leaned over to scratch under my ear, murmuring, "An honor, Es." In response, I let my tail thump against the blanket.

Only once, hardly noticeable—*unless you were an adult Lanivarian who would and get huffy about manners in public, which we hardly were*—but Nia shifted, almost spilling her drink. Her cheeks were pink.

Paul's gained color too. He snatched his hand back as if my fur burned his fingers, then looked as if he didn't quite know what to do with it.

Humans. I stretched my neck to bring my snout in range of Nia's bare toes, stealing a quick lick before she could move. She started, then laughed. "What was that for?"

Her skin tasted of Nia, pleasantly so, and bruised moss. *Not so much.* "We're alone in my safe place," I said smugly, trying not to obviously spit. "You're welcome to touch me as well, Nia, if you're curious."

To my delight, she didn't hesitate, going on her knees to come close, though I showed a warning fang when her first impulse was to reach for my admittedly fluffy tail.

"Under the ears," Paul suggested quickly.

Much better.

Fortunately, I was well groomed, having thought ahead to her visit. Her fingers sank into the fur of my neck and she let out a small pleased sound. "So soft!"

Of course I was, this me's fur like issa silk compared to the nasty wiry coat of the Botharan canid. Especially there—where—I half-closed my eyes in bliss of my own. *Right there.*

"Tongue." Paul coughed. "Hanging out."

I flipped the opposite ear at him. *Bet he wished he had fur.* Still, I supposed decorum must be reasserted or the afternoon would pass in a dream of excellent scritches and basking in the sun—

A shy pat marked the end of that. Just as well. I rolled my tongue back inside my mouth and gave Nia a bright-eyed look of gratitude, then lowered my ears to a conciliatory angle before turning to Paul.

His eyebrow rose.

I'd sat up, ears erect, before knowing I would. *How did he* do *that?* Maybe I'd been this me too long.

To recover, I leaped into the first topic occurring to me before remembering I'd a tendency when flustered to choose the wrong one. "How was the dress?"

Paul shoved his hand through his hair, giving me what I'm sure he thought was a quelling scowl, but, as it was a little late, I tilted my head in an apologetic shrug.

Nia gave us puzzled looks. "What dress?" she asked.

The one I wasn't to mention, even if I'd glimpsed a filmy red something before Paul shoved it deep into a sack, refusing to show me. *But now that she'd asked—*"I—"

A finger rose to stop me going any further. "Our resident artist, Lesley Delacora, made one for you, Nia. Out of appreciation for your accomplishments, but it's—ah—" Paul hesitated, his cheeks showing pink again.

Couldn't blame him.

"Like her other creations?" she asked warily, eyebrows rising. By her tone, Nia'd heard about the roof.

"Exactly." Paul smiled, at ease again. "I thanked Lesley on your behalf." He took a swallow and put down the glass.

With the motion, his expression turned serious. "Now, to the Framers."

Nia's hand strayed to her portfolio, then returned to her lap as if whatever she'd brought could wait. Like me, had she heard something new in Paul's tone?

I felt a tingle of anticipation. Which, come to think of it, might have been dread.

"Thanks to the Sacrissee and S'kal-ru, we've made progress." Paul didn't look at me, meaning *don't ask* how my web-kin had been in touch.

That Skalet had provided the Kraal data didn't surprise me; she'd taken larger risks, and this was crucial to Lionel's analysis. Though a call to her Senior Assimilator would have been nice.

Or not. My web-kin's evolving relationship with a Human appeared to satisfy them both and, Ersh knew, she'd most likely have found fault with me.

"When analyzed by date," Paul continued, "the star fields in the images produce a path."

Nia sat straighter, tucking a leg under her. "Not a boundary." Her eyes darted from Paul to me. "Is that good news?"

Good or bad, it was news to me. Our Lionel had been busy.

"It's too soon to tell," Paul replied. "There's a pattern." He put a finger to the blanket. "Here's an image of a Kraal ship received over eight years ago." He drew his finger along a stripe toward Nia's toes and stopped, tapping the fabric. "Then another. But the next?" Instead of continuing along the stripe, his finger went zooming across the blanket to me. "Is Sacrissee. The sequence repeats, over and over, as if there's a faction that resists going into the Confederacy," again along the stripe toward Nia, "by choosing the Sacrissee," back to me, "yet is overruled each time." His hand lifted, palm-up to Nia.

Hers gestured to me, then she planted it, fingers spread, on the sunny blanket in front of her as if seeking its warmth. "Kraal space. Do they know about this?"

"They've had the Sacrissee images longer than we have."

"They don't have Lionel," I said bluntly. Skalet had granted him access to her equipment for a reason; none of us, including our scholarly Human, believed it charity. By his diligence and talent she'd gained a potent secret, and I could almost feel her ghoulish delight. *If not appreciate it.* "S'kal-ru won't share this information until—" It gained *particular* value. "—we know more," I finished lamely.

"Anyone—anyone like us," Nia qualified, impressing me further, "would run from the Confederacy. Why continue to approach it?"

Biology rules. I wrinkled my snout at the Ersh-memory. "Living things move toward what they need."

Despite the warmth, she shivered. "I can't imagine needing anything from the Kraal that would be good for the rest of us."

Paul had drawn up his knees. Now he crossed his arms on that support, resting his chin on top to gaze into the distance. "What we need," he said after a long moment, "is more data. Framer images from different sources, if they exist. Especially from the Commonwealth. Without it . . ." his voice trailed away.

"I've brought these." Nia pushed aside her jacket and slid the portfolio into the middle of the blanket, unlocking it with a press of her thumb. "I don't know if they can help."

Opened, the portfolio proved to be full of sheets of paper. *This* was *Botharis.* Paul and I shifted closer to examine them. Star charts, that much I could see, with annotations in code.

Paul gently lifted the edges, leafing through. "Survey hazard maps," he said wonderingly and looked up, finding himself nose-to-nose with Nia.

Who didn't quite scowl as she eased back. *Progress.*

"Copies," she clarified. "Our department buys those pertinent to our system's traffic. We provide a summary to ships leaving Grandine. The latest are two years old." With a hint of defiance. "We can't afford anything newer."

I'd have to see about that. And encourage something more tech-flexible than dried tree pulp though given the stubbornness of the locals, I really shouldn't bother.

"These may be exactly what we need, Nia. Thank you." Paul's smile was dazzling.

"And why do we need these?" I asked, poking the paper curiously.

"Hazard maps are compiled automatically from incoming reports, then released to the public through a tiny division within Survey," my friend said, still smiling. "If anyone higher up is trying to hide information about our mysterious Framers by concealing ship losses, they might have neglected these. How far back do they go?" Without waiting for an answer, my friend carefully slipped the bottommost free, laying it atop the rest. Then stared.

I nudged his shoulder. "Paul?"

"Sorry." He gave himself a tiny shake. "This one's for the year *Smokebat* was lost."

Nia regarded him, her face inscrutable other than the wild curl caught on an eyebrow. Abruptly, her expression softened. "I haven't said what I should to you, Paul. About your mother. What happened to her—"

He shook his head, hair tumbling. "There's nothing to say."

I certainly felt there was. By Nia's stricken look, quickly masked, so did she. Not being Human at the moment, I angled my ears in disapproval, knowing Paul would notice.

Once he finished putting the map away. Which he was taking extra time to do, most likely to avoid looking at my ears. *Humans.*

As befitted a career politician, Nia recovered first. "The maps are all I have. If you need more from the Commonwealth, have you considered your friend Evan Gooseberry?" She gestured upward, as if conjuring Evan from the sky. "I recall he has a rare gift for cutting through levels of bureaucracy."

"Evan's—" I looked at Paul, but he continued to fuss with the portfolio. "—Evan's busy," I finished, finding that wholly unsatisfactory. We should know what our friend was doing, how he was doing it, and where—probably intrusive and possibly unwelcome.

But not knowing at all wasn't a good feeling. Nor was the growing feeling of mistrust. "If you believe Survey has more Framer images they aren't sharing," I said, copying Nia's very proper, *get back to business* tone, "why don't we give them ours?"

Both Humans stared at me as if I'd started to shed and hairs had caught in their teeth. *Which wouldn't happen again for months.*

"They've first contact specialists," I went on. *Maybe being back on his home planet did something to Paul's brain.* "Like you and Lionel."

"That's not all they have," Nia said grimly. "The Commonwealth has battle fleets—they don't like them mentioned, but we all know it."

And what we all knew was wrong. I sighed, lowering my ears as I wondered where best to start. While yes, among the thousand plus

Human systems loosely affiliated under the "Commonwealth," a portion invested to a varied degree in ships with weaponry but since if you had any real problems with a neighbor everyone called in Ganthor—who only needed transport and a purchase order?

There weren't fleets.

There was Survey, and the *Mistral* had been more military-esque than any other such ship in my or Paul's—and even Lionel's—experience, but again, not a fleet. Really, if the Kraal appreciated the might of the Commonwealth was more sheer numbers and a blithe willingness to ignore you while doing business elsewhere? They'd have invaded long ago.

I took a deep breath.

Staving off what would likely be a lengthy explanation—possibly requiring charts—Paul spoke first. "Until we know why Survey has concealed information about the *Sidereal Pathfinder*—which we wouldn't have except for a career criminal's conscience—"

An interesting take on Victory Johnsson's deathbed revelation, but I didn't argue.

"—we don't show our hand."

I blinked. "You think they'll cheat." *Duggs was proving to be a useful exemplar.*

"I think," Nia interjected, "we don't poke the tiger without first knowing if it's hungry."

"Exactly." The two shared one of those annoying *Humans get it* looks.

Glowering wasn't particularly mature, but I indulged myself.

Paul reached out his hand. I huffed, pretending not to see.

"Someone gave Johnsson the image, Fangface. Someone sent her after my father and then here."

Hearing his distress, I stretched my neck the bare amount necessary for him to lightly touch my nose.

"We've an enemy without a face, Esen," Paul went on very quietly. "I refuse to take chances. Not with the Library." The look in his eyes changed *Library* to *you*. My tail thumped the blanket.

Nia sat without a word, fingers following a stinger bug. Paul glanced at her, then frowned. "There's something else."

"Yes."

Amazing how a single word could be ominous. *Might have been the other topic.* "A problem with the station?" I asked, my heart sinking.

"Not at all. That's moving ahead very well, Esen," with a faint smile. "No one's about to turn down an offer of guaranteed funding, especially for an undertaking this immense. Tenders for the project go out this week."

"Good to hear." Stretching out his legs, Paul leaned back on his hands to study his fellow Human. "So what's wrong?"

"I met with the Preservation Committee before coming here." Nia picked up her glass, staring into it as if the contents were engrossing. Or she didn't want to look at us while she spoke. *The latter*, I decided, when she did. "They've insisted I halt your construction project pending a surprise inspection. The request was copied to my superiors in Grandine while I was in the air. I couldn't stop it." Her eyes rose to Paul's face. "I'll have to comply."

My ears flattened and a snarl rumbled in my chest. We were sleeping in tents in the greenhouse, Lionel was in Skalet's hideaway, and Lambo expected an apartment.

Let alone Duggs' reaction. *Wouldn't be me telling her—*

Paul, being the relatively mature one, merely nodded. "We understand."

I snarled louder. "You should have told us before eating Paul's berries." *And scritching.* My fur crawled.

Nia gave me a sorrowful look. "I'm sorry, Esen. If I don't seem to support the committee, I've no reason for being here—and I needed to be." A nod to the portfolio. "Consider it a temporary pause. I'll make a pretense of an inspection. That's all."

It was all they'd need. I knew it. By the slump of Paul's shoulders, so did he. "You can't fool them, Nia," he told her. "You'll be required to produce a report, with vid. They won't believe you otherwise."

"Then I'll keep it to the actual construction site," she promised. "Surely innocuous enough?"

"It would be and, believe me, we appreciate the offer, but the committee will expect to see inside the Library. You'll be asked to inspect plumbing systems and whatever else they can think of . . ." his voice trailed away as his chin lowered to his chest. "This is bad."

I whined. "The worst thing is we don't know what will offend them.

Almost anything here could be against some old rule or other. The committee has books of them." *I should know. They'd stacked them in front of me at every opportunity.*

"Then you know what to do." Nia had long legs and she used one to dig her toes firmly into Paul's lower ribs. "Jig Up."

He bent to cradle his side, staring at her as if flabbergasted. *By the words or ribs?* "What did you say?"

The words. Intrigued, I aimed my ears at Nia.

"You've only been dead five decades. Don't tell me you forgot." Rebuke delivered, Nia curled her leg back under her skirt and gave a little sniff. "Esen, who comes up with the wildest plans at the last minute?"

I liked *this Human.* "Paul does. Sometimes I do, but his are better—mostly," I qualified, unwilling to commit to a future where my friend could remind me every time of what I'd said and overrule *my* plans.

"He always has," she informed me, that intense look in her eyes. "Jig Up we called it. Well, Paul? What do we do about this?"

He kept staring at Nia, his cheeks redder than ever. "I don't—I—"

While entertaining to see my friend at a loss for words in a conversation, we did have a problem to solve. "If we can't alter the vid record," I mused, "what can we change?"

"What did you say? No, don't bother repeating it, Fangface." Paul straightened, eyes flashing. "I've an idea. With your help, Nia."

"Jig Up Paul." If she'd mobile ears, they'd have been perked up as high as mine—*my possibly biased interpretation of a smile happier than any I'd seen, transforming her face.* "Whatever you need."

"First, we get these maps to Lionel. Then?" Paul looked at me, eyes gleaming. "We enlist our resident artist."

I'd have balked at that—my web-kin taking *unreliable* to new depths—except Nia wasn't the only one to recognize that look.

Jig Up Paul. My clever friend had a plan.

Content, I flopped back down on the blanket to listen.

Forgetting to worry about Evan Gooseberry.

Nearby

"EVAN."

No need to respond, Evan thought muzzily. Great Gran checked on him when she made breakfast, in case he was up and hungry, but she knew very well he took a while to become conscious in the morning. If he didn't reply, she'd go away and let him sleep as long as he liked.

He'd like a long long—

"Evan. Polit Gooseberry."

Not Great Gran. He decided it was a dream. Not another horrid *click, click* nightmare of hallways and *click, click* lights but a nice dream for a change, a dream of being back at the embassy, napping at his desk. Not that he made a habit of it, but there were times—

"Sorry about this."

It began to rain in his bed—

No, not rain, needles of ice! Evan groaned a protest, raising his hands to shield his face.

Other hands took hold, pulling him to his feet. *His feet?* "Stand right there, sir."

"Stand—?" he mumbled.

The icy needles transformed into a hot violent wind. Evan could feel the loose skin of his cheeks flapping. By instinct, he leaned into the gale to keep his feet. *Was it a hurricane?* If so—"Great Gran!" He had to wake her up. Close the storm shutters. Hide the goggles.

Goggles?

Evan opened his eyes.

"And there you are, sir. Good morning."

There wasn't much good about it, as far as Evan could tell. He was standing, naked, in a fresher. Someone in a crisp white-and-blue uniform withdrew their arm.

"You're the steward." His tongue felt like a sock, thick and oddly dry. Come to think of it, his brain had a *stuffed-with-socks* feel that was regrettably familiar. "Betts Colquitt."

"Still me, sir," she agreed good-humoredly, urging him out of the stall with a hand under his elbow. "The rest are almost done breakfast. You'd best hurry."

Evan squeezed his eyes shut, then opened them to stare at her. "I fell asleep in the fresher," he said woefully.

"Happens." She picked up the pile of clothes from the floor. "I'll get these cleaned." A small green cylinder dropped out and rolled. Betts bent to retrieve it before he could. To his surprise, she handed Buddy back to Evan without comment.

Maybe everyone carried concealed weapons on board. The thought didn't make him feel less ridiculous. "It's from my Great Gran," he explained. "She worries."

The steward chewed her lower lip, studying his face, then seemed to come to a decision. "She tell you how to use a blister bomb, Evan?"

Great Gran hadn't told him it was a bomb. Holding the thing horizontally in both hands, Evan mimed snapping it in half. "After I close my eyes," he said, feeling foolish. *More foolish.*

"Oh no, that's—just don't do that on the ship, okay? I'll get someone to show you." With that ominous statement, the steward headed for the door with his laundry, glancing over a shoulder. "And get dressed before you head to the galley."

Could he seem less capable? "I will." Evan rubbed a hand over his face, finding stubble, and forced a weak grin. "The galley's where it was?"

Evan was quite sure he deserved Betts' dubious, "I'll wait outside for you, sir."

If Evan had learned anything as a diplomat, it was the inescapable significance of First Impression. Collecting his pouch of essentials, he stepped back in the fresher to quickly wipe the stubble from his face, then rinsed and dried his hair, applying a light pat of stay-put to keep it shaped. Teeth clean and eyes bright, he checked his fingernails before using a touch of cream to soften his palms. Might not be anyone shaking hands, but he'd be ready.

Having donned fresh undergarments, Evan pulled the bottommost packing roll from his bag. A twist and brisk shake freed his suit—jacket, pants, and shirt—wrinkle-free and ready to wear. Footwear came next. Dressed, he tucked a stylo and fresh notebook in an outside pocket, hesitating a moment before putting Buddy into an interior one. *Better the worrisome thing stay with him, than left to be found by his cabinmate.*

As for his private notebooks and the translight com? He couldn't take those to breakfast. Evan sealed up his bag and pushed it under the cot.

Finally, well aware the steward waited outside the door, Evan took a moment for the final, most important step. He stood, eyes half closed in concentration. His breathing slowed and deepened. He pictured the galley as he'd seen it, listed the names Betts had given him, replayed in his mind Eller's briefing and what he'd learned from the datacube. He finished with what had been said on the bridge, and what Harps said last night.

If anyone watched, they'd have seen subtle changes in his posture and expression, detected an air of unmistakable competence and quiet confidence.

Polit Evan Gooseberry, ready to help save the Commonwealth—

His stomach chose that moment to growl.

The last time Evan had been in the *Mistral*'s guest galley, he'd been with Paul and Esolesy Ki. The *generous-for-a-working-ship* room had featured the usual tables and chairs, plus a compact food dispenser on a wall, though their meals had come on trays from the ship's own kitchen.

The only thing that hadn't changed, Evan discovered when he entered, was the plate on the wall identifying the galley as the emergency life-pod for those in guest quarters.

He had to doubt it could safely serve that function now. The tables had been repositioned against three walls, each a workstation of some kind with comps, display screens, and a bewildering clutter of equipment. In front were stools secured to the floor, each with an occupant too busy to notice his arrival—or ignoring it.

Being ignored was fine with him.

As for breakfast? A narrow counter ran down the center of the galley, suspended from the ceiling, and Evan was indeed too late, judging by the litter of used plates and bowls, most with bits of congealed food, as well as the basket of still-fresh and squirming multi-legged Myriapedes—for the Dwelleys but, if that was all there was, maybe they'd share—

"Here, sir." Betts slipped around him, carrying a tray with a steaming mug and covered bowl. With deft movements, she cleared a space for his breakfast, then began filling her tray with the remnants of the rest.

Evan followed her to the counter with a fervent whispered, "Thank you."

She grinned. "I'd hurry, sir."

Removing the cover, Evan smiled back. The bowl held noodles and meat in a dark, savory sauce. The aroma alone woke his senses—and brain. Taking the steward's advice, he ate quickly, cradling the warm bowl in one hand as he studied those around him.

They weren't in uniform, but over their garments all wore a white vest with paired vivid orange stripes down the back, presumably so the *Mistral*'s crew could find their civilians if the ship filled with smoke. Which the ship wouldn't, Evan fervently hoped, so surely they'd another function. He glanced warily at the inconspicuous boxes tucked high in the galley's corners. The vests would make these individuals easy to monitor via the ship's internal surveillance.

Kamaara's idea?

The vest hung loosely on Professor Harpesson's narrow frame. His cabinmate remained hunched over something, oblivious to the rest of the room.

Harps' workstation was to Evan's left, along the short wall at the galley's end. Where the food dispenser had been, to Harps' right, stood a black column covered in flashing little lights and broad dials.

Next to the column and Harps, taking half of the long wall in front of Evan, were the Dwelleys. One appeared to be staring at a screen while picking Myriapede legs from its teeth, the other was—

Evan leaned to see past the creature's rounded shoulder.

—*definitely playing a game.* Hardly what he'd expect a dangerous faction agent to do; then again, he'd no knowledge *what* dangerous agents did, besides being dangerous.

Probably they tried *not* to look dangerous at all, meaning the Dwelley could be—

Betts approached with her tray and Evan added his now-empty bowl and spoon to the others, toasting her with his mug of marfle tea, a spice-thick drink Esolesy'd requested when on this ship that Evan enjoyed. *He'd an ally.*

The workstation being used by the Contriplet was beside the Dwelleys' and took up the remaining half of the long wall. From what Evan could see of trip from the back, Ionneanus had opted to retain five arms and three legs, with a torso twice the width of Evan's to accommodate a multiplicity of organs. Two heads, one with short brown hair, the other black, merged into a single wide skull; the third rose from a slender neck slightly ahead of the others, with blond hair caught up in a net.

Three of trip's hands were flying over an elongated console, fingers a blur. Another held a mug, while the fifth rolled a stylo back and forth on the tabletop.

Evan casually looked to his right, to find he wasn't being ignored after all. Two Humans had turned on their stools to watch him. Behind the pair were more typical comp stations, like any at a desk in the embassy, but their displays were blank, as if to keep their work secret.

Both were female, possibly older than Great Gran, and—he wasn't sure what made his shoulders straighten and stomach clench, unless it was something in their silent combined stare, as if he were being assessed. They must be Haula and Poink.

Evan adjusted his face to its pleasant *here to assist, not be trouble* expression, telling at a glance these were exactly that, trouble. Senior-most. If not in charge, they felt they should be, and while they wore casual attire under their vests? If they weren't officers, he'd no instincts at all.

Then he spotted the patches affixed to the upper left of their vests. The design was unfamiliar: a black star-filled space overlain by a golden dragon—*Great Gran had an excellent library*—bat-like wings outstretched, its claws supporting a starship that might be the image of *Mistral*. Beneath was written "Intrepid Few" in red script.

His initial reaction was to freeze, thinking of what Eller had told him of the faction. His next was the somewhat embarrassed realization that even if the pair in front of him were ruthless agents, they'd hardly attack him. *And probably not wear patches.*

As for the attitude he sensed? The Intrepid Few drew its members from ranking officers, active or retired. *Active,* Evan judged the pair. Mug in hand, the breakfast counter now raised to the ceiling, he walked up and stopped a respectful distance away. "Polit Evan Gooseberry," he announced as if reporting for duty.

Which he was, if not entirely clear what that duty entailed. *If no one asked, he wouldn't have to lie.*

Ionneanus spun on trip's stool. "A polit?/ You why we're stuck here?/ We could use someone with tact."

"Greetings." Evan faced trip, bowing once, careful to keep his focus somewhere between the heads. The earlobes of both bore small open circles in black ink or paint, indicating the Contriplet considered trip-self gender-free, a not uncommon choice. The conjoined head had otherwise average Human faces side-by-side, sharing cheeks and forehead, but their features were offset and those leftmost were larger.

The solitary head had been the one to snap *"You why we're stuck here?"* in a deep baritone. Obviously being merged didn't mean they were of one mind or voice but, as Tonphiger would stress, often, any combined Human was a single entity who'd undergone a difficult and strenuous procedure to become one. Whatever had drawn these formerly separate individuals to spend the rest of their lives glued together was intensely private, and it was the height of insensitivity to address any portion as if still apart.

An Intrepid patch was pinned loosely to the leftmost arm. Evan began to feel outnumbered.

Courteously focused on trip's earlobes, Evan added a tactful, "I expect there'll be a briefing."

"There's always a briefing," a voice at his elbow agreed dolefully. Evan looked down into a pair of huge-pupiled eyes, set in a round, finely scaled face. Large cheeks puffed politely. "Hello, Polit Gooseberry." The Dwelley offered a limb hand, exhibiting a nice grasp of Commonwealth protocols. "Call me Blue Spider."

"And me, Wort!" The other of the two. Neither wore patches. *Not that a real spy necessarily would*, Evan reminded himself. "We're running a *Turn of Shadow's Edge* campaign—after work, that is," Wort specified. "Do you play?"

"I haven't yet," Evan replied. Trili, his best friend at the embassy, had been waiting months in the borrow queue for a copy. *And might have it now, given how long he'd been away.* He pushed the thought aside. "Is it tough?"

"We'll teach you." Wort's hand reached out.

"Thank you." Charmed—and well aware of disapproving looks from the nearby Humans—Evan touched the offered hands but didn't enclose them in his unpleasant-to-Dwelley drier ones.

His care was for naught as Blue Spider seized his hand by finger and thumb, pressing the palm to the small slits that served the species for olfaction and inhaling deeply. "Ah." Releasing Evan's hand, the alien beckoned the Human closer. "You've an emollient moisturizer," in a loud whisper. "We've run out."

Their generous bosoms, four each, did seem unusually flat for healthy adults and lacked the glisten Evan had come to expect. He puffed his cheeks, let the air out again, and replied, also in a whisper, "You're welcome to mine. Shall I ask the steward to—"

The Dwelleys bolted, waddling back to their workstations in haste.

Straightening, Evan turned to see Eller and Decker standing in the doorway. Both wore Survey uniforms with First Contact Specialist bars on chest. Eller had dispensed with his beard and tourist tan, but he wasn't the reserved administrator from Dokeci Na, or the amiable boat buyer who'd chatted with Great Gran, or even the earnest spy on a mission.

This version had a commanding presence—as if Eller had staged a mutiny in the early hours. No need to wonder for what—who—everyone here had been waiting.

A slight nod acknowledged his attention. "I see you've met the other members of Passerby, Polit Gooseberry."

"Who are you supposed to be?/Crew?/When do we get moving?" demanded Ionneanus, now on trip's feet. Two hands pushed Evan aside. "No more delay!/We're ready!/What good's a diplomat?"

As Evan tried to catch his balance, striving at the same time not to spill his remaining tea, someone took hold of his arm and steadied him, fingers like clamps. It was the shorter of the Human females. "Don't be annoying, Ionneanus," she said sharply. "The polit's our connection to Ragem's son. Glad you're here, Commander." The fingers let go.

Evan's arm throbbed in time with his thudding heart. He took a slow deep breath in through his nostrils, let it out, waiting for his pulse to slow and steady. Poor manners. Upset strangers. Nothing to trigger fear. *He'd gone through worse at concerts.* Deliberately he moved his free arm to sip tea, eyes watching over the rim of his cup, aware Decker's stare hadn't left him since hearing "connection to Ragem's son." *So much for Eller's keeping* that *under wraps,* he thought with some sympathy.

"Who?/Who?/Who?" the Contriplet demanded again.

"Commander Dane Strevelor," said the person who'd been Petham Erilton, then Eller Theelen, and Evan seriously doubted this name was any more real. "My aide, Lieutenant Kelce Decker. I'm in charge. You'll find our credentials have been sent to your comps, along with my authority." That penetrating gaze found Evan again. *Was there sympathy in their depths?* "Thank you for your extreme patience. I know you've been ready to begin for some time."

"Damn right!/Bureaucratic nonsense./What are we waiting for?"

"Nothing. I'm pleased to announce *Mistral* has left orbit."

Murmurs from all around, punctuated by an anxious burp from one of the Dwelleys.

"Captain Clendon is standing by for the translight course. I assume you have it?" That piercing blue gaze traveled the room. "Well?"

The Dwelleys' eyes popped outward with stress. Ionneanus snapped all three mouths closed as Haula exchanged looks with her counterpart, who shrugged.

"Ayup." Evan turned with the rest to see Harps, still hunched over and seemingly oblivious, wave a cheery two-thumbed hand in the air. "Pathfinder X23-42-6. Echosymm confirmed. Trace locked. Been good to go for seventy-three hours, four minutes. Correction. Five minutes."

Pathfinder X23-42-6! Shocked, Evan quickly lowered his eyes to his cup, schooling his expression to neutral. It had been in the datacube; the number referred to the implant the faction had put into Veya Ragem. He'd flinched at the thought of Paul's mother giving up an eye, then grown ill reading the rest. Her implant, unlike medical ocular protheses, had sent tendrils throughout the brain and upper spine, hardware designed to integrate a Human nervous system with the machine senses and translight capabilities of a starship.

Hardware that couldn't be removed from living tissue and ultimately drove its host insane, making its use forbidden in the Commonwealth and beyond. Had the faction warned Veya? Or had she learned the awful truth for herself, that there was no going back. Was that why she'd run?

Veya no longer suffered, Evan consoled himself. He wished she could have known that one day her implant would be crucial. That by it, she'd left them a key to finding whatever, whoever, had sent a framed image of her ship—of so many ships.

Paul had to know, he vowed.

Meanwhile, Harps' announcement drew everyone else to his end of the galley. Evan stayed back. He'd a clear view, thanks to the shorter Dwelleys in front of him, and didn't try to pull sense from the more technical questions being fired at Harps. He did notice Poink's concern was why Harps hadn't come forward sooner, while Ionneanus and Haula seemed upset the professor hadn't confided in them first.

Harps appeared unfazed by the attention, leaning on an elbow, sweaty goggles dangling from a neck strap. "Ran the probs again last night. Pings solid as it gets. Got your course."

Those thin lips continued to work for a second more; Evan guessed the unspoken part was *so let's go already.*

Blue Spider's eyes hadn't fully retracted, giving the Dwelley a dazed look, but he addressed those gathered in a loud firm voice. "We were essential. We designed the tagalong." A limp hand gestured to Wort.

Who puffed cheeks to confirm. "We did. But it took a major stinky genius like Harps to tune the search parameters. A genius who doesn't give up. Don't Fail!"

"Fifth Rule of Harps." That pursed-lips smile. "Sixth Rule is work with the best."

As the Dwelleys hummed their pleasure, Evan wanted these three to be what they appeared to be. Earnest, quirky scientists without a secret between them. He stomped a foot to approximate Dwelley applause and smiled at Harps, then risked a glance at Commander Dane Strevelor.

Meeting a look and tiny headshake that made his heart sink. *Trust no one.*

Strevelor returned his full attention to Harps. He held out his hand. "The course."

The Dwelleys groaned to one another. Harps leaned back, a casual head jerk indicating the black column. "There. Bridge calls it up, punches it in. Who're you again?"

"Commander Strevelor." A pleasant smile. "The one you've been waiting for. It's my job to direct the effort to communicate with our new friends once we find them. And to tell the captain of this ship whether or not to trust you can do just that." Strevelor scanned the gathering. "Before I do, does anyone here need to confer or review the professor's claim?"

The room fell silent, other than the exchange of looks.

"Very well." A slow nod. "Exemplary, Professor Harpesseon. Blue Spider. Wort. I ask you remain here while I speak with Captain Clendon. The rest of you? Prepare for translight. Once underway, we'll go over your preparations for contact." Then, without a look or warning, "Decker, escort the polit to his quarters. I believe he has some work of his own."

Having no idea what Strevelor expected him to do—other than leave a place where he'd nothing to contribute—Evan set his face to *on an urgent task ahead, let me through,* and followed the security officer out.

He kept his mug, there being no obvious place to leave it and the feel of something within his control?

Felt like a lifeline.

8: Library Afternoon; Bedroom Afternoon

OF all the times for Lesy, as Lesley Delacora, to be engrossed in the job she supposedly held but rarely performed, I should have known it would be now, when we needed her not to be.

"I must finish the response for the Dwelley," she informed me for the second time, not bothering to look up.

"That's coming along well, Esen. Don't you think?" Ally Orman gestured wildly at me from behind Lesley.

Humans. She might have been chasing biters from her ears, and I angled mine to show I'd no clue what she was trying urgently to convey. Except that "well" wasn't how I'd describe the three-dimensional object my web-kin's long fingers were busy constructing. An animal of some kind?

No, more like a tiny servo cleaner—and why Lesley was building it out of sticks and wadded gum when the Response Room fabricator stood waiting—

Ally dropped her arms in exasperation and whirled to her desk. "I'll get you the question." Lesley gave her a sidelong look through her hair. "So Esen can see how special your response is," the real Human added quickly, pressing her noteplas into my paw. Reassured, my web-kin focused on whatever it was.

I might have missed what the waving meant, but when Ally used *how special,* it was her code for *that can't be right.* Which she'd said fairly regularly early in our acquaintance and still whispered to herself at times, unaware of the sensitivity of this me's hearing. Not as often anymore. Overall, Ally'd come to believe I was curator for a reason and not just cute.

It'd be Esolesy Ki here tomorrow, meaning more "how specials" and "why don't we show that to Lionel or Paul firsts." Fortunately, my Lishcyn-self had a thicker hide. And scales.

Not what mattered now. I read the Dwelley's question aloud, hoping to accelerate the process. "What binds the ancient Treaty of Chweci, Spat 238 BD, Dwellalish Singular?"

Dwellalish Singular was their homeworld. The "spat" was, well, mouth secretions, Dwelley possessed of exceptional tastebuds. Spit had been used on official documents of import since Dwelley had imports to document. "BD" was commonly believed to refer to "Before Dry" with the year zero assigned to when the first Dwelley strode onto land and true civilization could begin.

As the amphibious species more cautiously tiptoed back and forth for a few millennia, according to Ersh, developing a perfectly accept-able civilization within the wetter edge of tidal mud flats, this was a case of history rewritten by mutual consent. For "BD" originally meant "Before Drought," a cataclysmic climate event that baked away most of Dwelley culture, along with those Dwelley unable to endure being out of water for long periods. A point of pride, now, to do so, later generations serenely unaware it had once meant survival.

Ally had written: *The collection has nothing on this treaty.* Meaning an alarm should have notified me and Paul, except that Lesley had been here. She'd known the answer.

As for how she'd convey it? I pulled up a stool, moving my tail out of the way, and sat where I could watch my web-kin. With context, I realized what she was making for our Dwelley scholar.

A spawn catapult.

When water became the limiting resource on their world, those Dwelley survivors forced farthest from it resorted to flinging their fer-tilized eggs over the heads of those hoarding the last suitable pools. By so doing, according to Ersh, the catapulters ensured their species would continue.

In my opinion, something ephemerals most often accomplished without thinking much about it.

What Paul wanted me to accomplish had to be done the instant our Dwelley scholar and the rest got on the final train, so I gave Ally a confident nod and snatched the miniature catapult from under Lesley's nose. "It's perfect," I exclaimed.

"I'm not done! The Chweci Sigil!" Surging to her feet, my web-kin tried to snatch it back.

I dodged behind Ally, who outmassed Lesley and stood her ground. "Better without," I said glibly. "Irrelevant and confusing. The response is that the treaty is forever bound by the transfer of eggs by those who spat and as such cannot be—" Lesley's hand snaked around and almost had it, but I jumped aside. "—cannot be broken without calamity to their descendants. The Dwelley can't wiggle out of it, sorry."

As I said "sorry," I tossed the spawn catapult to Ally who slipped it into its case and dropped it into the delivery tube.

Panting, Lesley pushed back her hair and gave me a Very Disappointed Look.

I grinned, unrepentant. *I knew how to make her happy again.*

"Like to make something bigger?"

Paul's plan, he later told me, was inspired by something he'd witnessed on Urgia Prime during the 300th Festival of Funchess the Unrestrained and Gloriously Joyful, when Evan and I, with Prela, were being kidnapped by an odious Hurn. Not that my friend would have willingly paused to enjoy a spectacle during our plight, especially had he known the particulars of this one, but he and Rudy had been trapped by the seething crowd.

Suffice to say, they were trapped in the right place to see one of Kateen's famed performing mechanicals—enormous, fanciful creations operated by dozens of multi-tentacled Urgians in steadily worsening stages of inebriation and exhaustion—walk off the street and right through a brick building, reappearing on the other side to enthused applause. Knowing his insatiable curiosity, I wasn't surprised Paul had wanted to find how they tricked the audience.

Only that he had. Kateen's street artists were notoriously proud of their secrets. *Then again, Paul could charm anything.*

His idea?

To permit—as demanded by the Hamlet of Hillsview's Preservation Committee, and they'd sneakily sent Lionel a memo on it mere moments ago—Special Envoy Niala Mavis and her assistant Onlee Naston to roam at will through the Library and its grounds, Onlee with vid in tow and activated throughout. Nothing would be off-limits, should Nia deem it pertinent to her inspection, nor could any agency alter or edit the resulting official record.

When I'd heard that part, even knowing he'd a plan, I'd whined. The only positive in any of it was they'd wait for the train to leave before getting started, to protect the privacy of our scholars. *At least the record wouldn't include any Heezles.*

Then Paul told us the rest.

"Hurry up. Careful!"

Ally, holding the heavy end of what Lesley called her "masterpiece," muttered something uncomplimentary. I snuck her a quick lick of sympathy, a Lanivarian not the ideal form to be lifting either heavy or wide. She tasted of Human sweat and paint.

And fabrication plas, making me sneeze repeatedly. All three of us were coated in a floury dust of the stuff, courtesy of Lesley's thorough approach to her art. When we'd realized why she wanted the grinder, there'd been no time to don whatever protective gear might be in maintenance or Duggs' aircar.

My lick was rewarded with a grimace. "Little gritty, Es."

"Sor—"

"We're here. Stop," Lesley commanded. "Ease it down. More left. Down. More right and gently! Down. There. Put it there. No, over—"

"It only fits one way," Ally told her. "Esen, move your toes."

Hastily I scampered back, not wanting to risk my tail either.

"Esen."

At the sound of my name, I waved the bag of adhesive patches to prove I hadn't left them in the Response Room. *Elders.* "Ready!"

"You're on the wrong side." Ally sounded muffled.

I blinked, discovering I was alone in the corridor. *Not that I was—* "It works!" I yelped, quickly shutting my mouth in case someone overheard.

But it did. Work, that is. Paul's plan. By the evidence of my eyes, the admin corridor stopped just past Lionel's office, the length I knew continued beyond—and the door to the Response Room—seemingly erased.

The wall turned like magic to reveal Lesley's impatiently beckoning arm. "Hurry up. We need to secure it."

"It works," I repeated numbly. *I hadn't believed the Urgians had given my friend their secret.*

"Of course it works." Lesley's face poked around the wall, laughing silently. "My masterpiece is flawless. Except for that." Her fingers wiggled at my feet. "Hurry. Ally says they'll be here in five minutes."

I looked down to find a distinct line of dust prints, my prints, broken by a jump, right to the wall, appearing to come *from* it. I looked up in time to receive a cloth in the snout. "Tidy your mess," my helpful webkin ordered.

The rest of the afternoon passed in a blur of moving walls—more accurately, moving *a* wall. Lionel, who'd been thrilled to hear there was a plan, used Skalet's snoops to tell Ally where the small convoy of Nia, Onlee with her recorder, Paul, and—trailing well behind, Duggs— would arrive next. I'd have loved to be part of it, especially as it seemed Paul's plan might actually work.

Not that I'd still doubts, but the phrase "too good to be true" had been a favorite of Ersh's.

But my place was peeling and sticking adhesive patches because I wasn't, at present, Human. That was a key part of the plan, not to draw attention to why the Library existed in the first place, namely the incredible diversity of intelligent life beyond Botharis who came to us. We'd lull the Preservation Committee to sleep with the plain, Human, and uninteresting, hoping they'd turn their full attention back to the post office porch.

Poor Duggs. I couldn't help but be disappointed for her. The creativity and craft she'd lavished on our non-Human zones, unique on this world and worthy of awards on most others, would not be part of Onlee's recording. On the other hand, given where we'd set up our "wall" and where we hadn't, the record should do justice to her plumbing and airducts—

"They're about to leave the Chow," Ally whispered, lurching to her feet. "C'mon. Last one and done."

Lesley stroked the back of her masterpiece lovingly. "Good job," she told it, then grabbed the center support with both hands and pulled with all her might.

Our precious wall snapped in two, falling with a final puff of plas dust.

So much for the plan. Ally and I exchanged looks of horror. I shifted mine to my web-kin, who was aglow with satisfaction. "What have you done?!"

A flicker of confusion. "Ally said done."

The real Human smacked her palm against her forehead, then spoke quickly into her com. "Change of plan, Lionel. We can't block the Iftsen Habitat Zone." A glare at Lesley. "Don't ask." She listened for a second, then turned to me. "Es, he says you'll have to provide a distraction, but how—"

The Iftsen Habitat Zone, starting with its airlock filled with green smog. "Meet us in the Lobby—what will you need?" I asked my web-kin.

If I'd thought Lesy glowed before, this expression was incandescent joy. "You want more art?"

Not in the least, but— "The Library needs its Artiste in Residence to put on a show." What would Paul say? I tried not to wince. "One they'll never forget."

Lesley pursed her lovely lips, then nodded. "Ally, bring the spray guns, all the spatulas, and the bottle of soap." She waved her hands in a shooing motion. "Go! Go! Go!" Ally managed to shake her head even as she set out at a run.

Drawing herself to her full height, my web-kin regarded me with impressive dignity. "All shall be astonished."

Just this once, I hoped so.

"They didn't make it to the Iftsen Habitat Zone." If my tone had an anxious whine to it, I felt entitled. Paul hadn't said a word since Niala and Onlee fled the Lobby.

Duggs hadn't stopped laughing, while Lionel sat on a bench shaking his head, making it more difficult than usual for me to interpret my Human companions' reaction to Lesy's creative distraction.

I quite liked it, *a response admittedly having something to do with being out of range when it activated.*

Lesley Delacora, who wasn't Human, was reacting precisely as I'd expect. Carefree. Triumphant. Singing and dancing in the midst of it all, skin and hair changing color each time she moved through another giant floating bubble of paint and it burst. Lesy, become her art.

Astonishing covered it.

More bubbles, of varied sizes and thus loads, drifted and jiggled through the air. The majority had burst and the Lobby floor resembled either a kaleidoscope or—I tilted my head—a serious chemical spill. A bubble contacted the overhead walkway, spattering it with yellow.

"It's water soluble," Ally offered, eyeing Paul warily. "There's already soap."

A bubble of blue had caught my friend on his right shoulder. Red from the one that had smacked into Nia's face had sprayed over his head as well, resulting in fetching streaks of purple. He'd clawed the stuff from his eyes and mouth, but not bothered with the rest.

I'd a sneaking suspicion he'd left it so I wouldn't lick him.

Lionel, mostly yellow, complemented Duggs' combination of greens. Ally wore most of her color on her arms, a consequence of discovering she could waft a bubble away if she stroked through the air vigorously, if not the ones arriving from behind.

Duggs ran out of laughs, or realized she was the only one finding this funny. *Which it was*, I thought, lowering my ears in annoyance. It had worked, no one was hurt, there hadn't been property damage—*color didn't count*—and Lesy was happy.

Not that the last was a major factor, but opportunities to productively gratify my web-kin were becoming rare.

Paul nodded, as if to himself. With a start, I realized he'd been silent because he was listening to something not here.

Sure enough, catching the angle of my ears, he beckoned me over. If Paul wanted the petty satisfaction of seeing my beautiful fur doused with paint—

I was not *going under wet nasty bubbles.* To emphasize the point, I stayed put, safely seated beneath the wide leaves of the plants in one of the Lobby's planters. My fur had been through too much yesterday, between two coats of mud and sticky gemmie glitter. With water!

As if hearing the thought, or feeling some reasonable level of contrition, Paul stopped beckoning and started coming to me. Before he got too close, I rose to all fours, ready to spring should he attempt contact. Even his clothes were dripping blue—*and water soluble with soap didn't make that any more appealing—*

He halted a reassuring distance short of me. "Excellent job."

Words to make my tail thump, except for what I could see of his face beneath the paint. *Consternation. Worry.* "What's wrong?" I'd a horrible thought. "Are Nia or Onlee allergic to paint? Is that why they moved so fast?"

The quirk of his lips vanished almost at once. "They're fine, Es. This is fine. Lionel," louder. "Duggs. Ally."

As the other Humans approached, watching for bubbles, a large one sank down overhead. Duggs dodged one way, Ally the other, and Lionel walked straight through it, immediately turning from mostly yellow to mainly brown. I hadn't known our administrator used that sort of language. Duggs gave him a wet slap on the shoulder.

Lesy continued to dance and sing, reinforcing my observation she'd lifted self-absorption to an art form of its own.

"Something's come up," Paul said. The crisp edge in his voice brought me to my feet. "Duggs and Ally, please coordinate the cleanup with the night crew. Best you can," he temporized. "If we need to lay down mats—"

"We'll get it done," Ally promised.

"Almost a shame to stop her." Duggs jerked a thumb at our delirious artist.

"You can't," I assured her. *Unless—* "Pop the rest of the bubbles. She'll get bored and leave."

"That's cruel." Wiping paint from her cheek, Ally frowned at me. "Lesley's work is a remarkable achievement, from her knowledge of chemistry to modifying the sprayers to generate the bubbles—and so quickly."

Practice helped. I flicked an ear. "It's on the vid." Everything before a bubble burst on the recorder, ending the inspection.

Giving up on me, Ally turned to Paul and pleaded, "They'll finish on their own in a few minutes."

"I leave it in your hands," he said. "Lionel? With us." Paul set off without looking to see if we followed.

"What's wrong?" Lionel asked me as we hurried to keep up.

I shrugged to show I'd no idea and moved faster.

Something certainly was.

The showers were deserted, staff having left for the day, not that I participated. From a prudent distance, I listened while the Humans cleansed themselves of paint.

Lionel was protesting. "I haven't had time to scan Nia's maps—"

"We can't wait." At this, my heart gave an odd little skip of dismay. Something had changed. Something big. *Sure enough,* "Es and I are leaving tomorrow on Rudy's ship. As fast as he can do the turnaround. Let everyone know Esen has a family emergency."

A pause, then, from Lionel, "Are you coming back?"

The grim question shocked through me, followed by a close-to-hysterical babble of my own. *Was this it? The moment we were no longer safe on Botharis? Had we lost the Library? How?*

And a possibly pertinent, *which family?*

Paul's brisk, "Nothing like that," let me breathe again. "Esen was right."

I was? I felt even better and waited impatiently to know what I'd been right about—not that I wasn't right often, but lately it hadn't seemed *as* often—

"We're not the only ones looking for the Framers. The *Mistral* just picked up Evan Gooseberry, and her cabins are crowded with experts in several fields. Wherever she's going, we need to be. It's time to work together." With that, Paul stepped from the stall, wrapping a towel around his lean middle.

"'Evan'?" I echoed weakly. I shouldn't have been surprised; our young diplomat's knack for landing in the thick of things rivaled my own. "He's got his ship back?" *That would be a surprise. Likely to Evan, too.*

"No, he's a passenger. I don't know why." Anticipating my next question. "But Evan was here, Old Blob. That might be the reason."

Here during both Victory Johnsson's incursion and the Sacrissees'. *We had to work on our timing.*

Paul's gray eyes found me, a question in their depths.

Much as this me loathed space travel, I deliberately lifted my ears, tongue lolling to one side. *Ready when you are!* After all, we'd an Evan to find.

Paul went to one knee. Understanding what he asked—*shuddering inwardly at the damp*—I dropped to all fours and came to where he could wrap his arms around me, resisting the urge to stick my cold nose in his ear. He whispered in mine, "Can Lesy take Esolesy's place while we're gone?"

I squirmed, gawking at him in disbelief. "Paul, she's *old.*"

He stopped the hugging, which was awkward and Human—and damp—in favor of rubbing under my ears, which was pleasant but *cheating.* "We've no time for finesse, Fangface. You can't be in two places at once."

"OLD," I growled warningly. *It was ridiculous. No one would mistake us—*

Paul dared chuckle, right in my face. "C'mon, Es. How old a Lishcyn does she appear? Comparatively speaking."

Despite the laugh, his breath held a tang of *anxious*, not that I'd tell him. Reluctantly I made myself consider the question. "She has more . . ." the last word came out a mumble.

He took hold and shook my head gently. "More what? Hair in her ears?"

Come to think of it, Lesy would. And have a greater girth. And—

"Last time I saw her Lishcyn-self, Lesy had more inlays," I admitted. "In her tusks," in case my friend forgot where that telling accessory belonged. "They were stunning." And grown into each tusk, making them part of form-memory. *Hers, not mine.*

"Then when this is over, you'll need even more—equally stunning—to keep anyone from noticing the switch."

Also cheating, because I couldn't believe even Humans would fail to see the difference between Esolesy Ki's callow youth and Lesyole's statuesque maturity—let alone that my web-kin had missed the entire Lishcyn fascination with all things Dokecian and lacked a "Ki"—*not as important.*

Against my better judgment, *and that me certain to lust after more inlays regardless if deserved*, I found myself warming to the idea. "I'll have to convince her," I warned. "She's not fond of the stomachs." *Few were.*

Paul grinned and stood. "If anyone can, it's you."

Lionel came out of his shower stall, combing his mostly paint-free hair back with his fingers. "Can what?"

"Convince Lesy to impersonate Esen's Lishcyn-self while we're gone."

"What?!" He stood dripping on the floor as if transfixed.

"Exactly," I said approvingly. "Sounds impossible, but Paul says no one will be able to tell us apart, especially since we'll be apart." *Not that I doubted Paul, especially when it came to his own species, but this?* "What do you think?"

Lionel finally moved, if slowly, to obtain a towel. He shot us a sober look. "I think Duggs has to be warned. We can't risk—she can't afford a mistake."

Paul's eyes flicked my way then back. "Where's this coming from?"

My heart sank. "It's about Lesy." I didn't need Lionel's tiny flinch, his cautious breath as he looked at me, to be sure. "I'm guessing she's shown you her—" I searched for a word and went with, "—not-nice side, hasn't she." *Family.*

The brave Human managed a wan smile. "Let's say I no longer consider her fragile or childlike."

Paul carefully didn't look at me. We'd discussed Lesy; he knew I felt—I was—responsible for her despite our ages. *It hadn't seemed the complete reassurance I'd hoped.* "Did Lesy threaten you?" There was an edge to his voice, meant for me. *It'd be my fault.*

"No. Not at all." Lionel appeared to gather himself. "It was more—I found it disturbing, to be frank, hearing her speak openly of time. Of us as flickers in it."

"Well, now you see what I had to put up with, growing up." I gave an annoyed huff. "Lesy's not just our Elder, she's *OLD*." At Paul's *be serious* look, I lifted my ears in defiance. "She is. With *OLD* habits. Among them, surviving." *Admittedly, she hadn't escaped Death, but neither had Ersh.*

As I'd intended, Lionel's expression grew thoughtful as he absorbed this. "By remaining secret. But Esen, because of you, she accepts Paul. And me. Surely the safest approach would be to tell Lesy about Duggs—"

My "No" came out a yelp.

At Paul's grim nod of agreement, I continued more normally, "It wouldn't work. Lesy accepts you because I've shared years of my memories of you with her—how you've earned my trust. Duggs and I—don't have that history. Not yet."

And what we did have? Duggs surprising me while I cycled. Duggs letting me fall into the pit. *Blobbie.*

I shuddered. "Duggs is smart. She guessed my other form and Skalet's true nature at once." No need to go into my admitting to the Human we'd a third web-kin at the Library. *Not my finest moment as Senior Assimilator.* "That's what Lesy would get from me, and she'd—she'd panic." And if she couldn't escape, she'd eat Duggs, then I'd have to—

Whatever happened, it wouldn't end well.

"Duggs can do it if anyone can," I said firmly, hoping I was right. "We just have to explain to her she has to convince Lesy she believes her to be me."

Assuming I could convince Lesy to be just that. My head wanted to spin. There were so many ways this could go sideways—*and it wasn't even my plan.*

I looked at Paul, seeing determination in the set of his jaw, a burning anticipation in those eloquent gray eyes, and knew we were committed. "It'll help," I told him resignedly, "if Rudy's brought very nice clothes."

And if my web-kin had done sufficient art today to satisfy that strange *need to change* itch of hers.

So many ways . . .

The race to be ready, on every front, began immediately. Lionel went to draw Duggs aside for a now-urgent conversation, and Paul would follow up with her later to be sure. First, though, my friend would be busy. He was to contact Rudy to tell him that, while he was to bring a "Lishcyn" passenger to the Library as arranged, he'd be leaving with us, and quickly. That done, Paul would dash to the Hamlet of Hillsview Pub, where Nia and Onlee were spending the night, to explain why the Library's director and curator were heading into space when they should be trembling under beds—or equivalent—to await the Preservation Committee's response to the Special Envoy's inspection. As for any questions, we'd do what we could over coms, but what couldn't be deferred until we came back—*a thought I clung to while doing my own racing*—would fall into Lionel's lap.

Because, as Paul said, I'd a family emergency on Lanivar. Plausible, in a sense. Conceivably this me had living relatives on that world—if my sire had continued his winsome ways and if his lineage had survived down through, conservatively, twenty-two generations of Lanivarians—suffice to say it was the sort of drop-everything commitment Humans, being family-inclined, should believe.

As for why Paul would accompany me?

Everyone—even on Botharis—knew Lanivarians were terrible spacefarers. I'd need his help. And anti-nausea meds, a dark corner, a bucket—

Not looking forward to that part of it.

Our fabrication should convince Duggs as well, though no doubt she'd assume any "family" emergency I had involved Skalet and the Kraal and not be happy about it. *Poor Lionel.*

Meanwhile, Henri was coming back to the Library and Ally asked to linger, so Paul and Lionel could meet with our seniormost staff and dump everything we wouldn't be here to do on their capable shoulders. The All Species' Library of Linguistics and Culture must stay open and function.

On the bright side, this made an excellent dry run to let us take a vacation offworld more than the once—maybe to Minas XII, or with Evan. Not that I mentioned that out loud.

What mattered most was we'd a chance to learn what Survey was hiding about the Framers—knowledge being the essential step before "hello" led to understanding and, hopefully, conversation—ideally before any more dead ships showed up in frames and crews disappeared. Which was why Paul sent us scrambling to complete our separate vital errands.

But as I ran to find Lesy, it occurred to me my friend challenged Skalet herself when it came to layers of motivation and outright cunning. *Paul was never obvious.*

Suggesting another, not mutually exclusive, reason Paul had us dashing around like newly spawned Carasians. To postpone an explanation of how, suddenly, he knew where we had to go. More to the point, who'd told him about Evan and the *Mistral*.

Leading to a suspicion that made me run faster.

Was his Group involved?

I found Lesy where I'd thought I would, naked and draped languorously over the lounge chair—*formerly Paul's*—in her bedroom—*formerly Paul's*—humming contentedly to herself. My Elders did smug better than any ephemeral I'd met. The warm colors of sunset filled the room, bathing her flawless skin in light. Flawless but for a stylish new blue question mark peeking over a shoulder at me and what was that about?

Focus, I reminded myself. "Lesy?"

A finger's twitch invited me closer.

Confront or coax? Perhaps a combination—*No, with Lesy it'd have to be coaxing.* I sidled up beside the chair. "Paul said your art in the Lobby was excellent. And it was. You saved the day for the Library, Lesy. Thank you." Because it was true, I licked the side of her wrist, then laid my head on her arm.

Her other hand stroked my dappled snout from nose to the top of my head. "And were all astonished, Youngest, as I said they would be?"

"No doubt about it." I chose not to tell my web-kin the vid record might make Lesley Delacora famous, should the Botharans see fit to share her portion of it and likely they would, this world barely past a fixation on once-useful craft pieces and large items made from string. That was more Esolesy Ki's opinion; Grandine had several respectable galleries, and the southern half of Lowesland boasted a healthy community of painters and glass blowers, inspired by vineyards and the products thereof. *But they'd never have seen anything like our Lobby and Lesley's bubbles before.*

A vain hope, that she'd satisfied her disturbing *itch* to change things and could pause her art while impersonating me. That me. *Explain later,* I decided. There'd be a great deal of that going around once our mission to the planet or system of the Framers was done.

Back to coaxing. "Lesy, we need your help—eep!" I yelped as her hand clenched on my snout, the arm beneath gone rigid. "A different kind of help—a not-art help—"

"No." She withdrew her appendages, almost dropping my tender snout on the chair arm. "I'm exhausted." Her yawn struck me as contrived, but I hadn't been the one dancing through paint bubbles.

"There'll be new clothes." *Ersh, I was shameless.*

"I've some arriving tomorrow." Another fake yawn, this time with graceful stretching. Lesy closed her eyes, waving me away. "Go play with your Human."

Any other word and I might not have snapped, teeth closing on a finger. Unless deep inside, I'd known a little confrontation would be required.

As we cycled into web-form, mouths gaping open, all I had to say for myself was she'd started it.

Nearby

BREATHTAKING skill and unique beauty. Paint bubbles and glued gemmies. A child's innocence, an adult's mystery, and the contradictions inherent in Esen's sister were part of an entity so long-lived the sum of Human history was a minor note and their future a passing curiosity.

Lionel Kearn had no idea if his next encounter with Lesy would send him to his knees or in search of another shower.

Regardless, he had to prepare Duggs Pouncey for hers. Since Lesy had walked into Skalet's sanctuary as easily as he'd enter his office, he had to assume she'd access to Skalet's surveillance systems as well, leaving few secure choices for a meeting. The greenhouse was snoop-free, but Paul and Esen needed their privacy. Likely the Garden was safe, but Lesy might be hiding behind a bush.

Leaving him with one.

When Lionel returned to the Lobby, he discovered the cleanup had turned into a party of sorts. Henri, summoned for her briefing with Paul and it being decidedly after hours, had brought beer as well as supper. She waved a bottle cheerily at him. Smiling, he shook his head and looked for Duggs.

Finding her on the floor against one wall, a beer in hand, her arm resting on a raised knee. Despite the dried green paint streaks from her short once-black hair to her boots—though at some point she'd wiped her face—their head contractor looked decidedly pleased with the world. After all, the inspection was over and from this side, a success.

He walked up.

"There's beer," she offered generously, patting the floor beside her.

"Perhaps later. I need you to come with me for a moment. Some changes to the blueprints. They can't wait."

She regarded him dubiously, but got to her feet, bottle in hand. "Your office—"

"No. This way."

Duggs followed him outside without a word, until she saw their destination. She stopped dead, squinting at the tall, long train car, agleam in the hot sun. "You left the blueprints in there? What were you thinking?"

Of prudence. The car had been shunted to the side track, out of sight of the Library entrance, windows opaqued. The stack of buckets and gear in its shadow suggested maintenance were on a break, as Lionel knew they would be, as he knew Lambo had ripped out Skalet's snoops and they hadn't been replaced.

"This won't take long. Come." He led the way up the ramp and through the open door.

The air inside hit like a stifling wall, hot and rank with whatever was being used to clean the car—or more likely whatever needed to be cleaned from the car—and as Duggs stomped her opinion behind him she muttered a few choice words about Lionel's ancestry.

Her mutter became louder as she looked around to find no blueprints waiting. "What the hells?"

"We need to talk." Despite the heat and smell, Lionel closed the door and switched on the interior lights. "In private."

"So talk." Duggs dropped on a bench, stretched the arm without a beer in hand along the back, and scowled. "But if this is about some dung spit follow-up to that inspection, I'll be damned if I'm going to sit back and let those—"

"It's not," Lionel broke in. "It's about Esen."

Eyes brightening, she gave an interested grunt.

He took the seat opposite the bench, balancing across slats designed for posteriors with additional limbs. "You know about tomorrow's plan, where Rudy will pretend to arrive as Esolesy Ki."

The beer lifted in a toast. "Fooled me last time."

"People see what they expect." Lionel leaned his arms on his knees, easing his backside off the rear slat, and wished he'd thought to grab a bottle for himself. *No time.* "The plan's changed. When the *Largas Swift* lifts, Paul and Esen will be on board. Until their return, I'll be in charge of the Library and Esolesy Ki will resume her work in the Response Room."

Duggs' lips formed a perfect "O" then spread in a gleeful grin. "Dances-with-Bubbles Lesy. Our mess-maker."

Impressive. And a perfect example of potential trouble for, like now, Duggs' mouth was often as quick as her mind. *A trait Skalet detested.*

"That's right," Lionel confirmed. "Lesy's to assume Esen's Lishcyn persona. Lesley Delacora will have left the Library to attend an artist's retreat."

"Solid, if their weird works as advertised." Duggs eyed him, then jerked her head at their surroundings. "Why the sweat box?"

"To discuss how you'll behave around her. Lesy mustn't suspect you know about her or Esen."

A casual shrug. "I get it. She isn't like Blobbie." The bottle lifted to her lips and she poured a generous amount down her throat.

He shifted back and up, gripping the stanchion to ease the pressure below, but it wasn't just a seat made for aliens making Lionel uncomfortable. It was his abrupt realization Duggs wasn't ready for the whole truth about Web-beings, not their longevity and most certainly not their attitude toward ephemerals; in that respect, her first having met earnest, caring "Blobbie" became a significant handicap.

"No. She isn't anything like Esen." With asperity. "You'd better lock that in."

Duggs lowered the bottle. "You sound as if Bubble Girl scares you."

"What's Lesy's capable of, should she feel threatened? Yes, that scares me and it better scare you."

She stretched out her legs, crossing her ankles with a deliberate thump of boot heel to metal floor. "Relax, Lionel." With a lift of the bottle. "As I said, I get it. 'She's not a tame cat.'"

"This isn't a game." Lionel frowned.

A wicked unrepentant grin. "It's from a book. Botharan; doubt you'd know it. A child's followed home by a tiger. Wants to keep it for a pet, but her grandmother warns her it's not a tame cat and has to go back to the mountains. Her parents tell her the same and all her friends, but the sweet young thing refuses to believe anyone till the tiger gobbles her baby brother. By then, it's a little late. Oh, and the tiger eats her next. Great book. See?" The grin disappeared. "I am taking you seriously."

Lesy as tiger, not pet. *Add the eating part and the metaphor was*, Lionel judged queasily, *more apt than Duggs realized.*

"Good, because I made the mistake of underestimating Lesy, of thinking her simple and, yes, a little foolish at times but charming. I couldn't have been more wrong. She's capable. Intelligent. Dangerous. I'm convinced Lesy can access the Library's security feeds at whim— and will if she becomes suspicious. That's why we're meeting here— and why, once 'Esolesy Ki' arrives, we can't risk any further discussion she could overhear.

"Lesy's different because she's older than Esen," he continued. *How had the dear little Blob put it?* "To Lesy, secrecy about what they are isn't a choice, it's the basic tenet of survival. And if you've any inkling Lesy's onto you? Don't stop to tell me. Don't be alone with her. Run."

Duggs took it in; thought it over. A muscle worked along her jaw, but she gave no other reaction he could read. All at once, she set the bottle on the bench beside her. "Why? She like Skalet, a blaster up her butt?"

This, he decided, *she had to know.* "Web-beings don't need weapons. They take any living mass they contact and assimilate it into more of their own."

"Those damn trees. So that's how Es did it!" Duggs waved away whatever he might have asked. "All right, Lionel. Don't poke the tiger. Don't get eaten."

"It's not that simple—"

"We make it simple," she countered brusquely. "Everyone in the Library knows I don't stick around Esolesy. Nothing against her personally, but you never know when she'll spew lunch and, to be honest, she isn't really in charge, is she? And her incessant requests for those ridiculous slides—" A low whistle and a look of surprise. "You know, Blobbie's damn convincing."

"As Lesy will be. Must be. If you keep away from her—without being obvious—that'll help." *He'd breathe easier, that's for sure.* Lionel sighed. "I do fear it's going to be awkward."

A bark of a laugh. "Oh, she's going to play you, Lionel."

He winced. "I'm afraid so, but whatever it takes to support her. Lesy will want to succeed in fooling everyone else."

"Can she do it?"

"As the only Lishcyn on Botharis, with Esolesy gone these past months? Yes." If anything, Esen would find returning to the role more of a challenge, though, as Lionel understood such matters, she'd share Lesy's memories of what happened in her absence. "Esen and Paul won't be gone long," he said without thinking.

"Why are they going again?"

"Esen has a family emergency—"

"Elk Balls!" Duggs swept up her beer. Eyes on him, she drained the bottle, then wiped her lips with the back of her hand. "I'm in this with you, Beetle Eyes. Don't lie to me."

"I'm not telling you everything you want to know. There's a diff—"

Boots slammed on the floor. "Elk balls on toast and you're holding back the mustard?!"

Lionel blinked. If an authentic Botharan crudity, he'd have to add it to the collection. "I don't—"

Duggs scowled. "Means part of anything's no damn good. What's the rush to send them offworld? What's got you all burning the night oil?"

He leaned back, easing his sore backside onto the larger of the slats, and clamped his mouth shut.

"Let me guess. It's her. Ska-let the Sneak-y. And—oh ho," she crowed softly, studying his face. "There it is."

Lionel frowned. "There what is? Duggs Pouncey, if you can't hold a normal conversation—"

A slow smile. "She know you've got it this bad?"

"I've no idea what you're talking about," he retorted stiffly. First lewd suggestions about Lambo, now—the sweat dripping down the sides of his face was from the stifling heat, nothing more. He rose to his feet. "This has— Skalet doesn't— You're insufferable."

Duggs sat. Her eyebrows lifted, her expectant silence grating along his nerves.

"Very well." Lionel stared down at her. "They're leaving to conduct an urgent investigation on behalf of a visitor to the Library. The subject is dire. Lives may be at stake. This is what they do, and I trust Paul and Esen to know how to do it. As should you."

"So they sail off on a grand adventure while we sit on our thumbs and play nice with Bubbles." She slouched and glowered at him. "Can't even work."

An adventure, yes. He only hoped they survived it. Lionel shook off the sense of foreboding. "Ah, but you can." He pulled a memo from his pocket and held it up. "I've confirmed only the new addition to the Library is under contention. We've every right to maintain and repair."

Her eyes rolled. "Don't tell me—"

"You get to finish Lambo's patio and door while we await clearance to restart."

"You're just full of gifts today." She didn't sound displeased.

Lionel could guess why. Duggs hired the best, exceptionally skilled tradespeople other contractors would pounce on if she left them idle. Even this relatively small project would keep most of her crew employed. He let himself relax.

She got to her feet, throwing a sweaty arm around his shoulders. "Let's get more beer, Lionel my lad, and discuss your appalling taste in females."

So much for relaxing.

Out There

THE techs have no idea what they'd made. Of the ship. Of me.
What do you mean, Veya?
They were after faster response—
They've got it. Your reflexes are off the charts—

The memory spins away. Another appears and oh, it's her ship, her magnificent ship, twisted and bent and broken, still beautiful against the stars. She sees it because she broke it, dropping it back to real, and those with her in the lifepod pressed her face against the view port to make her look, unknowing she'd saved them.

Now she dooms them.

It's not reflex, Mar. This is—since the latest connection, I see. In my head. I see.
What?
All of it. Too much. Spectra. Bends in space. Waves of gravity. I see starships flicker in and out of reality. If I think of a place, a destination, everything I see warps into a single irresistible ribbon and I'm pulled along, unable to escape—I need to stop it. Mar, stop it.

<u>You know better, Veya. This is the tough part. Give it time. It'll
stabilize. You will.</u>
Another ship.

Another.

Another . . . she's lost count. All she can do is snatch its final image
against the uncaring reality of stars and space. Hold it, then send its
spark away.

Be afraid . . . I'm sorry . . .

All she is, is what she sees. If only she could go blind. Lose her
mind. Become oblivious. Why hasn't she? Why can't she?

Because this is truly Hell?

Stop now. Stop now—

<u>I'll miss you, Mommy.</u>
<u>Think of all the new stories I'll have for you when I'm back.</u>
<u>You'll come back, won't you, Mommy?</u>
<u>I always do.</u>

Or is it because she made that promise, to *see* her son again—

And Hell is coming with her.

9: Bedroom Night

WITH the optimism central to my personal worldview, I'd looked forward fondly to my next sharing with Lesy and Skalet, envisioning us under the arching trees of the Garden, within the stones of our private place.

Not so much on the carpet in Paul's old room.

Still, I'd managed—granted, in haste and probable disarray—to sort the memories Lesy tore from my flesh before she struck. If she assimilated something that caused her distress, well, she shouldn't have told me to "play with my Human," should she?

A thought I'd remember later.

While she huddled in a corner—predictably Human again—absorbing everything I'd fed her about Esolesy Ki and her time in the Library, I remained on the carpet, doing my best not to leave a permanent stain. Much of the web-flesh I'd snatched in return held *smug* and odd views of faces I knew, including my own. With unsettling extra versions, as if whatever caught Lesy's eye—mostly faces, with occasional pots—were somehow modified by her attention.

More than unsettling, disturbing. When I came across Paul's face amended to have a long white braided beard and plucked eyebrows, I hurriedly began excising everything *weird*. Hence the potential for water stains. I could afford to shed mass; Lesy had brought up plants—in pots—to the room, though I wasn't convinced she'd done it so much to supply prudent emergency mass for herself and guests as for an excuse to decorate more pots.

I kept her side of the interaction with Lionel Kearn, Lesy, as usual, delighted by her own cleverness in bypassing Skalet's security systems. No wonder our other web-kin fretted. At least Lesy'd baked Lionel a cake. Though by the look on his face?

The Human had been too terrified to eat it. We'd a problem, and while I hated adding more to Paul's lengthy pre-departure list? A reassuring *how to live with your Web-being* talk with Lionel had to be on it.

Unless it should be me. I'd some useful tips. Starting with *let Lesy shop*, a guaranteed way to distract my web-kin, and the infallible *Lesy likes tickles—*

No, better it be Paul, I decided, feeling again that reluctance to betray my own. *Ersh.*

Before taking hold of my molecular structure and expending energy to force it back into a Lanivarian, similar in concept to winding a spring as tightly as possible, I indulged in a fleeting moment of being myself. A teardrop of blue wasn't a responsible thing to be around anyone but Paul; even with my dearest first friend, as a Web-being my ability to communicate with a planet-evolved life-form consisted of jauntily waving a pseudopod or two.

And to expose our true form was forbidden.

Where had that—? Ah, Lesy-taste, with a nauseating undertone of Elder righteousness. Ersh's Rules. Lesy would have received the same stern message every time she'd shared with Ersh. *I certainly had.* Meaning she'd received it, over and over, for millennia before I was born, permeating every part of her—except for the purely Esen bits.

I took comfort that my latest sharing had included a fair amount of stomachs' upset and vomit, then oozed over to the nearest pot for some mass.

Time to convince my web-kin to be me.

In hindsight, I should have known that'd be the easy part.

"What a splendid game, Youngest!" Human Lesy clapped her hands and spun around. "I'll trick them all, you'll see." She paused her celebration to fix me with a look. "There'll be new clothes? You promise? Beautiful silks? I'll need those. And a jeweled bag. With blue jewels. I must have blue."

"You'll have new clothes, Lesy, but you have to carry my bag. Everyone here has seen me with it. It's nice," I defended, all at once protective.

"That thing?" Her eyebrow lifted. "You kept it? Why?"

I gave in, partly because I stood to inherit whatever my fashion-conscious web-kin picked, Lesy typically done with anything she'd used once. "Fine, order a new bag, but you must make sure everyone sees you with mine first or they'll guess you aren't Esolesy. It's important."

She planted a kiss on my nose. "Fear not. My impersonation shall be flawless! Oh, this shall be such epic fun—and here I thought I was done on this little world."

"Pardon?" I'd tasted *restlessness*, but that was Lesy's normal and Our Plan—*technically Paul's, since he'd come up with it, but I wasn't about to say that to my web-kin*—point being, I'd told Lesy moments ago we were to say Lesley Delacora had slipped away in the night to recharge her artistic well in a remote mountain retreat.

And nowhere in Our Plan did it say Lesley wasn't coming back. More significantly, that Lesy wasn't.

"My art from today cannot be surpassed, even by me," Lesy responded, eyes glittering with pride. "To continue to create, I must have new vistas to inspire me." Her hand rose to the sky. "I've found the perfect place. Wait till you see the view."

Her smile held that troubling hunger.

While potentially reassured "Esolesy Ki" wouldn't be lumbering around artfully defacing property in my absence, *this* I had to nip in the bud. "But you must stay with our Web—" *She'd only come back from the dead last fall.*

"Silly Youngest." Her other hand rose, as if to launch her Humanself. "Our Web meets on Picco's Moon, with Ersh."

I'd allowed her that fantasy, kept from her the end of Ersh's Web because she'd pleaded with me to spare her from the truth. *Had it been a mistake?*

"I know what you're going to say, Es."

Good. I didn't. I lifted my ears to indicate interest.

"You're going to say I mustn't leave and go anywhere fun without you." Lesy touched my ear tip tenderly.

She was half right. I swallowed, glad to be sitting on my betraying tail, and ventured, "So you'll be here when I get back."

"Why? You don't need to bother coming back either. Come where I've planned, or I'll meet you wherever you say. Though if it's boring, Youngest—" a tap on my nose, "—we simply won't stay."

Centuries we'd traveled together, those sporadic trips with Lesy highlights of my life, and for less than a beat of this me's heart, I was willing. Despite the tidying up, fetching, carrying, and interminable *Youngest, would you be a dear . . .* , being with Lesy offered giggles and joy and freedom from responsibility, other than caring for her.

And nothing more. No watching for another destructive Web-being. No protecting the innocent from ignorance, theirs or others'. No Library. No chips from the pub or fudge from Henri. No mousel hunts around Duggs' cabin on card nights.

No Paul.

I don't know what she saw in my face, but Lesy took a step back, her eyes wide.

"It's all right," I said softly, rising to two feet. I held out my paws. "When I return, we'll talk about this. I'll understand if you don't want to stay. I'll come with you and help you make your life where you want but—this is my home, Lesy."

"For how long?" she demanded, her voice thin and strained. "Until he dies? They do, you know. They all do. They fall like raindrops into an ocean."

"I know." I let the words fill the air between us, the way they occupied the space within the atoms of my flesh. Then, as calmly as if I were the Elder, I continued, "For now, this is where I belong. And right now?" Easing forward, I caught her hands in mine, squeezing gently. "I need you to stay, Lesy, to be me while I go hunting. There's an unknown life-form out there. A potentially dangerous one. For years, it's been leaving empty starships adrift along a path— What is it?"

Her lips were working as if trying to speak. All at once, a word dropped out. "Null."

I stared at her. "What did you say?"

Lesy whimpered and tried to pull free, her face gone white. "The Null. The Null."

She knew? Aghast, I held onto her. "What are you saying? What are the 'Null'?"

"No, Esen. No. No. No. Null aren't real. Ersh told me so. She promised. They're just my dreams. Bad horrible dreams. Ersh told me not to think about them." With a rising note of accusation, "You shouldn't have made me think about them!"

There'd been nothing like this in her sharing with me but—I hadn't assimilated all of Lesy. *If I had, there'd be nothing left of her—and little of me.*

Words would have to do. Releasing her hands, I grabbed her by the shoulders. "Tell me what you know!"

"If you hadn't said . . . I'd almost forgotten . . . you shouldn't have said . . . Ersh said to forget them . . . bad dreams . . . horrible—" Without warning Lesy began to thrash, hair whipping into my face, words spilling in a barely coherent flood. "Bad—Dream—Bad—Null hide behind their door—Null wait inside their hole—" A crescendo close to a scream, spittle hitting my face. "ARMS OF LIGHTNING FIRE— GRABBING—PULLING—STAY AWAY OR DIE—GET AWAY OR DIE—"

Lesy broke my grip but didn't run. Wrapping her arms around herself, she sank to the floor. Hair obscured her face as she began to chant, over and over, in a chilling monotone. "Just a dream. Just a dream. Just a dream."

Then why was I afraid?

Nearby

"THIS is me," Evan said unnecessarily, stopping outside the door. The affable "Decker" might have never existed. The tousled brown hair had been trimmed, the blunt features set in a professional mask, and, as Lieutenant Kelce Decker, somehow the other Human took up more space, shoulders broader, his bulk no longer that of someone who enjoyed his beer. *Not just the uniform.* This was a person able to change his appearance and manner at will, and Evan knew better than underestimate him.

"I'm to come inside with you, Polit."

"Very well." Opening the door, Evan stepped through. "Lights." The room was more of a disaster than he remembered. *Not a disaster—effort.* He gave himself a stern inward shake, thinking of the galley, and explained with a hint of pride, "Professor Harpesseon worked through the night." While he'd slept in the fresher.

Evan refused to feel remorse. He'd needed that deep nightmare-free sleep.

Chairs, table, the bed—the only surface free of what Evan took for meaningful and important clutter was his yet-to-be-used cot. A lump of clothing in a corner suggested Harps wasn't interested in having his laundry done.

"I'll stand, sir." Decker spread his legs and cupped his hands behind his back, a daunting point of order in the mess.

About to sit on his cot, Evan stayed on his feet. He tried for friendly. After all, they'd shared a meal at Great Gran's—and a trip on her boat. "Evan, please. What do I call you now? Lieutenant?"

"That'd be best, *sir*," with stress. "Or Decker. *Mistral*'s a tight ship."

And perhaps the newcomers weren't receiving the warmest of welcomes. Evan nodded in sympathy. "They put you with the crew?"

"Commander Kamaara gave us her quarters."

Evan highly doubted there'd been any *giving* involved. It did reinforce Strevelor's claim to be in charge, leading him to consider his own instructions. "I've left—" about to say *translight com,* Evan switched to, "—the item in my bag." For all he knew, someone was listening. Though if someone listened, and he no longer had the authority to make them stop, how was he to use the com without being overheard?

Being secretive was more difficult than he'd imagined. Evan gestured vaguely to the cot, the edge of his luggage showing. "Should I get it out?"

"I'm not authorized to know what you're referring to, sir," Decker responded, his expression bland. *Which would be no.* "The commander will stop by shortly. I'm here to answer your questions regarding the mission—those I can," he qualified.

Evan let his relief show. "That's excellent news. Let's get you a seat, Lieutenant." Picking the chair with the fewest articles, he carefully set those on the floor in the same orientation, then turned the chair to face the cot. "Please sit. I've a few."

A real smile. "I'm sure. Thanks for this." A little of the former Decker showed as he dropped into the chair, stretching out his legs with a stifled groan. He frowned at his feet. "I want you to know—" He looked up, brown eyes troubled. "I want you to know I'm sorry for my part. Lying to Celonee, taking her food, her boat. Not what I signed up for, sir, treating good people like that."

And not what Decker was supposed to say to him, Evan guessed, touched. He found himself grinning. "Great Gran got you with the Bloat Flies, didn't she."

"That she did," with a wry chuckle. "Now, sir, what do you want to know?"

Where to start. Evan sat on the cot, pulling his still-blank notebook from its pocket.

"You can't make a record, sir."

"Oh. Sorry." Chagrined, *not a spy,* Evan put away the notebook. "Are the two of you really first contact specialists?"

"Yes, sir." Decker brushed his fingers over the bars affectionately. "My last service was with Captain Lawrenk Jen, of the *Vigilant.* Captains Haula and Poink teach at the academy. Between them, they've conducted over twenty first contacts. Captain Ionneanus may have retired, but trip's applied codebreaking technology to the study of nonverbal languages. We do know what we're doing, Polit."

He hadn't confirmed Strevelor's credentials, but Evan had read them for himself. As for their combined knowledge?

"I certainly hope so," Evan replied, then realized how that sounded. "Sorry—"

"No need to be, sir," with welcome frankness. "We've met species oblivious to any Human-tech signal before. The Passerby are the first to ignore us while using each lost ships' final translight communication to send their own messages. I'm told Survey considered a machine intelligence, but there's a contradictory pattern to the image star fields suggesting biological minds, perhaps groups in disagreement." Decker rolled his shoulders, tipping his head from side to side. "I won't deny it's a puzzle."

Fascinated, Evan leaned forward, elbows resting on his thighs. "Say we find the Passerby. What's the approach?"

"Up to me? Standard first protocol. Stay well back and don't provoke. Observe. Let them start the conversation."

"They have started it," he countered. "By sending the images."

A thin smile. "You sound like the commander. He's pushing for a modified second, where we'll reflect what they've sent back to them while testing their tolerance for a closer approach. It offers some tactical advantages." The smile disappeared. "No matter the approach, Polit, we stay the course until convinced the Passerby pose no further danger to ships. Our orders don't include retreat."

He'd told Great Gran the truth. *They might not come home.* "Understood," Evan replied, quiet and firm. "But we've already engaged with them, haven't we?"

"What do you mean?"

He had to be careful. Eller—Strevelor had warned him not to tell his aide about the faction or their efforts to thwart them. Despite his reaction to Decker, the feeling the other would make a good friend?

For all Evan knew, Decker was the faction agent Strevelor hunted. *Distrust was part of the game,* he told himself sadly.

"This mission," Evan said at last, "is based on the assumption that when Veya Ragem's implant activated to navigate her ship in translight, it somehow caught the attention of the Passerby. Twice in *Sidereal Pathfinder,* the final time, the *Azimuth Explorer.*"

"Lacking an image, we can't be sure the *Azimuth Explorer* met the same fate, but that's the working hypothesis." Decker folded his arms behind his head. "Since part of the implant remains active—leave it to the techs to explain that—we've coordinates for it. And thus for the Passerby."

They were talking about a dead person's eye, artificial or not, and Evan's skin crawled. "We can't know they kept it."

"Ah, but we do. The Echosymm Harps mentioned? That's a lagged correspondence between the implant remnant and the star fields in the images." Seeing Evan's face, Decker half smiled. "Means we can prove the implant moves in sync with the Passerby, more than by coincidence. Not that we've a clue why they have it." A snort. "Heezles collect erotic geometry and don't get me started on Ervickian hoarders. Call it Passerby curiosity." A pensive, "That would help."

Curiosity being a commonality of those who left their worlds for space, as often as not, a shared starting point. Evan frowned. *Nothing about this felt like sharing.*

"What is it?" Eyes no longer sleepy in any way regarded him. "You said we've already engaged with them. What did you mean?"

"If the Passerby reacted to the implant's activity, what's to say they haven't to whatever Harps is doing to locate it? And if they have? We've told them we've made the connection. That we know how to find them."

"And we're coming." Decker sat up, no longer looking relaxed. "Contaminates the approach, even if the Passerby take it calmly. Damn."

"I'm sure it's occurred to the others," Evan said quickly. "It's too obvious—"

"It's the obvious that sneaks around to sting." The officer shook his head. "You saw that group, Polit." He grimaced. "Look to you as if they've been comparing notes?" He got to his feet. "The commander needs to hear this."

After the door closed behind the lieutenant, Evan remained sitting, hands loose on his knees, Decker's final words echoing through his mind over and over with one change: *Paul needs to hear this.*

And he couldn't tell him. Everything concerning Paul's mother was classified so far above his pay grade Evan Gooseberry grew nauseous contemplating it.

That didn't stop him worrying at the problem. Paul deserved to know. If there was any justice, he'd be here, now, as what Veya died for came to fruition and, quite possibly, helped humanity through a first encounter chancier than most.

Paul had to know.

Evan pulled his bag from under the cot, setting it beside him. Inside was a translight com. One he couldn't use without Strevelor and, when he did, Strevelor would be standing right there, listening, so that wouldn't work.

He sighed, opening the bag. Might as well be productive, and jot down what notes he could in his private notebook before his next visitor. Nothing of what Decker had told him of course, or secrets, but he should record his observations of the experts. Their names.

Evan's fingers touched his winter coat. He opened it, reaching in—

The sleeve was empty.

He took a slow, deep breath, determined not to panic. He felt the left sleeve. The translight com was there.

He'd been in a rush. His notebooks must have slipped out when he removed his suit roll.

But even as he dumped the contents of the bag on the cot, even as he worked through socks and the spare shirts and the night clothes he'd yet to wear, Evan Gooseberry knew they hadn't slipped. Knew he'd secured his precious, private notebooks inside the sleeve, inside the coat.

And now they were gone.

"Lost something, Polit?"

What Evan didn't know was how long Commander Ne-Sa Kamaara had been watching his desperate search. She stepped inside, closed the door behind her, then locked it.

"Oh no. I'm just unpacking," Evan said warily. "Is there something I can do for you, Commander Kamaara?"

She held out her hand, palm up. "If you haven't lost it, then give it to me." Her fingers closed and opened. "The blister bomb."

"Buddy?" He gaped at her. "That's why you're here? But you're the commander—"

One corner of her lips deepened. "And the most experienced weapons officer on the *Mistral*. Unless you want someone else to instruct you, Polit?"

The steward. "Betts sent—reported to you," Evan corrected.

Her hand moved impatiently.

He took out the green cylinder. "Buddy—This belongs to a relative of mine. I promised to return it to her."

"Did you?" she murmured, her keen gaze locked on the device. "How long has your relative had 'Buddy' around the house?"

"I've no idea."

"Looks antique to me. Polit?" Kamaara gestured again and this time Evan carefully put Buddy in her hand. In the midst of examining it, she glanced up at him. "What made you bring a weapon on my ship?"

"It was my relative's idea. Things were—I had to leave quickly and couldn't explain why. She was afraid for me."

"Because of who you left with. Yes, we know," with a grim smile at whatever she read on his face. "Operatives have a particular stench."

Evan held back a protest he wasn't sure was sincere. "About Buddy?"

"Buy your caring relative a replacement, Polit. A new one. Betts did us all a service—this is long past expiry. I'll dispose of it before it blows us up." As Evan shuddered, Kamaara wrapped the cylinder in a piece of foil material she produced from a pocket, then tucked the thing away. "Here." A small black disk appeared in the palm of her free hand. "Single use stun. The effective radius is about the width of this cabin. Firm press in the center, like so. You'll be unaffected, but it'll slow any theta-class species and knocks out Humans for up to ten minutes, depending on mass. Leaves a wicked headache." As Evan gingerly accepted it, she patted his shoulder. "More importantly, it won't damage my ship."

From his shoulder, her hand slipped down his upper arm, stopping above his elbow. "The steward said it looked as if you'd had a stim shot. Here." A finger pressed.

Evan winced. "That's the spot. I was getting pretty groggy. Commander Strevelor said it would help."

"Bet he did. I need to see your arm, Polit. Now."

"He and the lieutenant took the shots, too." But it was an order and Evan put the stun disk down with care, then hurried to remove his jacket, then shirt, feeling a chill inside. "What's the matter?"

"Our observant steward belongs in security." Kamaara squeezed a fold of his skin, over the sore spot. "This. See it?"

Evan stretched to look at the outside of his arm. Where she squeezed a foreign lump protruded, like the tip of a stylo.

"Subcutaneous tracker. Someone doesn't want you wandering off, Polit. Which of them administered the shot?"

He closed his mouth, only then realizing it had dropped open in shock. "Decker—Lieutenant Decker, I mean. It stung at the time. I—I remember saying it was revenge for the Bloat Flies."

She studied him, then nodded. "Get dressed."

"You're leaving it there?" he protested, hand hovering over his violated arm.

"Removal would take a trip to medbay—and won't answer any questions, starting with why. Why are you on my ship, Evan Gooseberry? Because I don't believe it has anything to do with a ShimShree on Botharis or finding the Passerby aliens."

Her ship. Kamaara had made her priorities crystal clear from their first meeting. After shrugging on his shirt, Evan met her intense gaze.

Coming to a quick decision, hoping it was the right one, he sat on the cot and pulled his coat from the tangle of his belongings. He removed the translight com from the sleeve, resting the device on his lap, then looked up again. "Commander Strevelor gave me this in secret before we boarded. To contact the All Species' Library—Paul Ragem and Esolesy Ki. About Passerby," he added.

"An unauthorized translight message was sent from the *Missy* last night. Was it yours, Polit?"

Evan shook his head. "I can't use this without the commander. He has the code."

"Could Strevelor have used it without your knowledge?"

"It's possible—I fell asleep in the fresher," he confessed. "But Harps was here working."

"The professor could have used it."

By the same token, Harps could have taken his notebooks. Evan refused to believe it.

Trust no one. He shook his head again, this time in denial of that inner voice. Fine advice for a spy, but trust was at the heart of what he was. More than that, trust—knowing who to trust and when—was crucial to his function as a diplomat at the interface of humanity with everyone else.

"I trust you," Evan declared quietly. "I trust Harps and the Dwelleys are what they seem to be. I came here to help, not point suspicion at the innocent."

Her eyebrows rose, erasing some of her habitual scowl. "Strevelor. He show you credentials?"

"Yes, but he had me destroy them."

"Why am I not surprised."

"They appeared in order," Evan protested. "There was even a note from my—the ambassador at Dokeci Na approving my time on the mission."

"Passerby."

He hesitated.

Kamaara squatted in front of him, balanced on her booted heels as if ready to stay that way for hours. "Evan, there are a hundred and four innocent people on this ship, give or take a few passengers I'd be happy to spit out in a lifepod. I don't need to tell you how dangerous this situation might become, and it's essential I know everything that might tip the scales one way or the other. Why did he bring you here? What's in those bags he brought? What's Strevelor really after?"

Great Gran had told him . . . *trust those who've earned yours.* Though it wasn't easy to come to attention on a cot, Evan Gooseberry stiffened his spine and shoulders, decision made. "He told me there's a faction within the Intrepid Few who've funded illegal research for decades, including *Pathfinder.* That some of them are here, using Mission

Passerby as a cover to find and destroy evidence of what they did to Veya Ragem. He's been posing as one in order to find them."

"Your role?"

At the question, *at her belief,* he let out a shuddering breath. "To be a witness for him if anything goes wrong but—mostly I'm here because Strevelor believes Paul Ragem trusts me. Enough to answer questions about his mother and to learn what the Library has about the Passerby."

Kamaara reached out to tap the translight com. "Why not use the ship's?"

"Because—" Their eyes were on the same level and Evan found himself staring into hers. The pupils were large and dark, surrounded by brown irises, striated in honey tones. The whites were yellowed and bloodshot, as if she'd hadn't slept well of late, and what he had to say wouldn't help. "Strevelor said Paul doesn't trust Survey. And he doesn't know who else on board is in the faction yet. They're dangerous, Commander. They intend to eliminate anyone who knows about Pathfinder, including Paul. They've tried on Botharis. The kidnapping?" For she'd been involved in the resolution.

"Strevelor told you all that." Kamaara shook her head. "Evan. Evan. Evan." Her hand reached again, this time to deliver a stinging snap to his ear.

He cupped it, eyes watering. "What was that for?"

"For being you." Rebuke delivered, Kamaara collected the translight com and rose to her feet.

Evan knew better than risk trying to reclaim it. He stood, taking a deliberate step to put distance between them. "I don't understand."

"I know." All at once Kamaara seemed more distracted than angry. "And we're out of time. You said Strevelor's coming here, soon?"

"Yes, but—"

"Tell him you opened your bag and the com wasn't there." She shot a look around the room, pouncing on a box full of tools. Before he could argue they were Harps' and shouldn't be moved, she'd buried the com inside and tucked the box under her arm. With her free hand, she tossed him his jacket. "Get that back on. Don't forget the stun."

She'd believed him. *She didn't believe Strevelor.* Heart beginning to pound, Evan obeyed wordlessly, slipping the small black disk into an inner pocket and standing for inspection.

"Good." Kamaara's scowl deepened. "We didn't have this conversation, Polit. I came for this." She tapped the box. "Clear?" She spun, heading for the door.

"Wait." Evan caught up to her in two strides. "You think Strevelor lied to me."

A sidelong look. "No, Polit. I think everything he told you was true. Other than the part about being a *Survey* operative."

Stunned, he watched her unlock and open the door. "What—what should I do?"

"Stay here. I'll send the steward for you in ten minutes. Till then—" Kamaara gave him an almost sympathetic look. "Pretend you still believe him."

With that, she stepped into the hall, walking away briskly. Evan retained the sense to close the door behind her.

He didn't bother locking it. Neither codes nor keys seemed to matter much on the *Mistral*. Someone had stolen his notebooks. Maybe the same someone who'd used the "secret" translight com he no longer had.

And Strevelor wasn't posing as a faction agent. He was one. *He* was the danger to Paul. Had planned to trick him—*he deserved worse than a stinging ear*—into harming his friend. It all fit. Hadn't Great Gran suspected? She hadn't trusted "Eller" for an instant.

Strevelor could be here at any moment.

Pretend.

Ten minutes till Betts came to interrupt. If he could attend a meeting of honest Dokeci, with their WRINKLES and TENTACLE ARMS, pretending not to feel FEAR even when he did?

He could do this. Evan brushed his lapels and tugged his cuffs. He ran a hand down his left sleeve, pausing over the tracer implanted in his arm, distressed to know it meant the pleasant Lieutenant Decker must be faction as well.

Evan pulled out the stun disk, going over Kamaara's instructions before returning it to his pocket.

Ready as he could be, he picked up a sock and methodically looked for its match—

The door opened and he braced himself.

But it wasn't Strevelor.

The Dwelleys waddled in, holding the dazed-looking professor by an arm each, thrumming in stress. "Dire news!" exclaimed Wort as Blue Spider moaned "Dreadful!" at the top of substantial lungs.

Evan stood staring, a sock in each hand. "What's wrong?"

"Did my job. Traced them," Harps mumbled, then looked up, eyes full of horror. "They've killed a world."

10: Office Evening; Greenhouse Night

PAUL regarded me silently. He'd been doing it since I'd burst into his office to tell him about the Null. Not the reaction I'd expected, having solved our mystery.

"Well?" I prompted, ears up.

"An extradimensional space monster with lightning tentacles."

I hadn't put what Lesy told me of the Null together in quite those terms, but Paul had a talent. "So we warn the *Mistral*."

"*About an extradimensional space monster with lightning tentacles*," he repeated, each syllable distinct as if I'd missed some point he'd tried to make. "That Lesy told you was a dream."

Could my first best friend possibly doubt me?

"We don't dream," I countered testily, ears going flat. *Well, Lesy did, or claimed to, and I really hoped the smidge of her I'd assimilated contained no instructions on how.* "If you'd been there, you'd have seen. She wasn't playing a game or trick. And what if the Null are real?" I asked him. "What if there is something in space able to capture ships, then drain the power and life from them?" *Which sounded like Death.* "Something that attacks Web-beings." *Which also sounded like Death.* "But isn't one of us," I finished hastily. It wasn't easy to explain being something that practiced cannibalism. Ask any Queeb.

"What about . . ." Paul made a square from his index fingers and thumbs, then peered at me through the opening.

"If the Null are real," I insisted, wondering when I'd become the stubborn one of us, "then the Framers must be a mysterious new sentient species, sending us warnings we'd no context to understand before. And now we do. Not bad things at all."

"Because of a dream." Paul lowered his hands to his lap, shaking his head. "A dream told to you—spoken, not shared—by someone you've said isn't always truthful or stable."

Reputations were a problem. Fortunately, I'd someone with an impeccable one to consult.

"If you won't believe Lesy," I told my friend, "come with me."

"Where?"

"To ask Ersh."

When you hide something, it helps if others leave your hiding place alone. *Not my experience.* Lesy was forever finding my things, not that I'd much to hide on Picco's Moon. Ersh? Well, until I'd figured out how to hide within myself, my soul was hers to scour at whim.

But when I'd hidden my latest something in a wall of our farmhouse, I hadn't expected a Carasian to get stuck in the staircase, necessitating repairs. I'd nipped in before those repairs to rescue my something, hiding it in the greenhouse.

Where all at once I'd had to hide New-Lesy, so out the something came again, back to the farmhouse.

Where it might have remained except that Lesy, once herself, added herself to the farmhouse with no warning at all and busied herself searching every nook and cranny. Back to the greenhouse my something went, safely out of sight.

Until now. I sat beside Paul, both of us staring into the hole I'd just re-dug in the floor. In it was a cryosac.

It held frozen web-flesh. More specifically, Ersh's flesh, mined from her mountain by Pa-Admiral Mocktap, a Kraal who'd believed it a weapon. She'd revealed a flask of achingly perfect blue during her final confrontation with S'kal-ru. The flask had smashed, its contents lost once more within rock, and I'd thought that was the last of Ersh I'd ever see.

But no. Mocktap had had more and it followed us to Botharis courtesy of Joel Largas, who'd received it from his old friend Alphonsus Lundrigen of Picco's Moon's Port Authority. Alphonsus, being a member of Paul's Group, had taken charge of clearing the last traces of Kraal from Ersh's home and found the cryosac stashed inside some mining equipment.

How Skalet and I failed to detect it was a moot point, since we hadn't—*she'd been stabbed and I'd been, in my defense, distracted.* If I'd known in time, I'd have asked Alphonsus to thaw the stuff and pour it out on the floor like the rest. Instead, our helpful friends, guessing the significance of what they'd found, sent me the cryosac and what it contained as a gift.

Ersh-memory was many things. *A gift none of them.*

"Are you sure it's here?" my friend asked quietly.

My ears wouldn't lift. "I'm sure I've nowhere else to look."

Paul knew what I meant. I'd told him the nuggets of Ersh-memory already in my flesh, her uncomfortable legacy, hadn't stirred when Lesy spoke of her "bad dreams." Of this mysterious, deadly Null. Of—

—what we both desperately hoped wasn't real, because then what we faced was an ancient threat to my kind and in no sense was "hello" a wise approach. *Running would be.*

Back to my first name choice. *Bad Thing.* Hence the dirt under my blunt clawtips. *And on Paul's pants.*

Those Ersh-memories inside me had arrived in leather-wrapped bundles. The ancestors of that leather's source hadn't crawled on land when the Eldest of us started nipping off bits to save. *Oh, not for me.* That regrettable notion occurred to Ersh a mere five hundred years or so ago, with my birth. No, initially what she'd set out to accomplish was a cleansing, of sorts. To be rid of the worst of her past, easing her conscience.

And to remove the temptation to do it all again.

That temptation resided over Paul Ragem's heart, in my gift. A silver medallion, suspended as a pendant from a chain, containing a speck of me in a miniature cryounit. The speck was my introduction to any Web-being he might meet without me. It had been a sharing, too, making us truly of one Web. He'd been deeply touched.

What I hadn't told my dear first friend, not yet, maybe not ever?

After the events on a certain asteroid, when I'd almost lost Paul, I'd added a smidge more: part of the memory Ersh had left me of what we'd been, for Web-beings had begun as space dwellers, adapted to vacuum and cold, feasting on the decay of stars, and able to soar through translight more easily than any ephemeral starship.

All it took was mass.

Which was why, when Ersh wandered far from her origin, starved by barren stretches of space, to arrive here, in a portion of the universe teeming not only with radiation, but life?

Why, when she discovered, having tasted intelligent life and assimilated it into herself, no other mass would do?

Civilizations ended. All so Ersh could continue to be what she was, and fly.

I'd done it. Spent the mass of an enormous tree simply to leave orbit and hang for a moment in space, an experience proving to me Ersh had been right to forbid herself—and us—this. The cost was unsustainable. Ultimately, I'd excised the knowledge from my flesh, to keep it from Skalet.

To keep it from me.

What did it say that I'd lied to Paul, telling him I'd destroyed it? That like Ersh, I'd kept that terrible, dark temptation secret and safe—by putting it around his neck?

Unaware of my silent turmoil, Paul reached down, his arms longer, to retrieve the cryosac. He rested it on his knee. "How do you want to do this?"

Ersh had been right. Biology always won.

"Esen?"

I blinked at him. "Sorry. How to do this? Good question." I poked morosely at the sac. "Our way's messy. I like your way. Lists. Databases. Labels. Tidy tables. Chairs."

His fingers found the spot under my ear. "I wish I could do this for you."

"You're here." I found I could lift my ears after all. "Besides," I told him, attempting to lighten the moment, "it's probably nothing but Tumbler debates. Ersh loved those."

"Might be useful."

I almost laughed. "Spoken like a being who's never sat through one."

My preparations went too quickly. I stripped, handing Paul my clothes. He folded them neatly, despite my no longer needing them; I wouldn't be Lanivarian any longer than it took Rudy to see us to our cabin on his shiny new ship. "Are there cabins?" I asked abruptly.

"On the *Swift*?" The dim glow from the light on the floor left his eyes in shadow. "Rudy said to tell you he's got it covered."

Remembering my last trip with Rudy Lefebvre, I wrinkled my snout in a frown. "Not being a Quebit." *Even if Rudy let me putter on his shiny new ship—* "Absolutely not."

Paul leaned back, hands around a knee. "I believe his exact words were: 'Tell my *niece* I've got it covered.'"

I'd be going as Bess? Or rather Grace, that being the name Rudy'd used for my Human-self, but names weren't the problem. *Well, they could be because Humans fixated on*—the point being, "I can't be. His crew expects a Lanivarian." And thus likely worrying about the consequences of a spacesick alien in their very small ship.

"His crew's going to watch their captain pretend to be a Lishcyn, again. I think they can handle the idea of our Lanivarian sneaking off the ship while Grace sneaks aboard."

While I had to hope Lesy pulled herself together to be a Lishcyn for me—our list had too many variables. It was as if we ventured out on a bridge of fragile sticks and I'd no idea which would fail us first.

I dropped on my haunches in front of the one who started all this in motion. "Paul, what do you know about the *Mistral* and Evan?" I stopped, then went on very softly, resting my chin on his knee. "If you can't tell me yet, I understand. I'm just—" I swallowed a whimper, "—a little scared to go out there." *Extradimensional space monsters with lightning tentacles* covered it.

He went still, barely breathing.

Instinct made me wait for whatever was going on in my friend's head, even though I was about to assimilate an unknown batch of Ersh— *never pleasant and this would likely be worse than usual*—and getting it over with before I lost the rest of my nerve might be a good idea.

"So am I, Dear Old Blob," he admitted finally.

Not helping! I lifted my chin and whined, loudly, to tell him so.

"None of that." But the admonishment was gentle, and Paul offered me fingers to lick, which I did. "We should be a 'little scared.' Even terrified. Best scenario, all of this leads to first contact—something we know how to approach but always chancy. Worst? We meet what we can't communicate with, something able to terrify your Elder and strip crews from starships, and then—" My friend let the rest hang in empty air.

Because how could we have an approach for that? *Other than turn and run.* Which we couldn't do.

"We stopped Death," I stated at last, to remind us of victory, though I'd had a significant advantage over a barely sentient Web-being. Or Ersh had, it being her memories suggesting what to do, namely feed it to a crisis of mass. *As it was me it gobbled—which* hurt—*not helping.* I lifted my head, ears half down. "I'd prefer not to be eaten this time."

"I concur." He hesitated.

"What is it?"

"You asked what more I know. The *Mistral*'s tracking whatever's behind all this."

"If Lesy's right, they'll find the Null." *And have their bodies pulled into the bulkheads—* "We have to stop them!"

"Easy, Es," soothingly. "We'll get there first."

How was that *a better idea?* But I'd had this sinking feeling before, when my dear first friend knew what he shouldn't. "How can we do that?"

"I've *Mistral*'s next destination and we're closer. That's the rush to launch. If Rudy can—"

Paul stopped because I'd jumped to two feet. "Who told you all this?"

He eyed me warily. "We've a friend on the *Mistral.*"

My sinking feeling grew stronger. "You don't mean Evan."

"No."

"From the Group," I concluded, tail between my legs. "Is it one of the ones who know about me? What I am? Who I am?" *At least for a few mes.* Too many mes. "Is it?"

A grave nod. "You haven't met in person." A pause. "Do you want to know who it is?" By his tone, Paul preferred I didn't.

I found I agreed. Faceless and nameless let me not worry. Worry less. *Worry in a nonspecific, can't-let-the-name-slip-out, way.* Doubtless Paul was worrying for both of us, but still— "I don't, but—" I swallowed. "How do we have someone on the *Mistral* when we didn't know about the *Mistral* being involved before—unless we did," I finished, a tad out of breath and confusing myself.

"We didn't," my friend confirmed. "Call it luck."

Ephemeral folly. I flattened my ears. "There's no such thing."

"Then give credit to our friend, who spotted an opportunity and took it."

This stranger was no friend of mine. I regretted the churlish thought instantly, lifting my ears partway. "Is our *friend* in danger?"

"No more than anyone else heading for the Framers."

Framers. Not, I noted, the Null, and I wished I could be as confident as Paul there wasn't a monster. *I certainly didn't* want *one.* "No less," I said.

"No less," Paul concurred, looking up at me. "I'm worried about Evan too. I still don't know what he's doing on the *Mistral*, Es. I can't ask."

"I understand." Sending a message you weren't supposed to, from a government ship on a secret mission you weren't supposed to be on, had its difficulties; receiving one would be tantamount to tossing our mysterious "friend" under a herd of stampeding Ganthor.

Besides, however worried I was about our young diplomat, it was time to focus on my own part in this before I lost my nerve completely.

"Move back," I told Paul, waving the paw without the cryosac of Ersh.

He stood and, contrarily, took a step nearer. "Old Blob, you know if I've any reason to suspect a risk to you—to your Web—I send someone from the Group to follow up."

An expectant pause, implying this was one of those times Paul wasn't being as obvious as I thought he was, so I nodded to show I was paying attention. *Even though I'd Ersh in my other paw.*

"And even if their inquiries turn up nothing of concern, there are some I keep active, no matter how long or tedious, because I've a feeling we should. It lets me sleep at night and my guess? That's what this is." With "this," Paul's finger aimed ceilingward.

I stared upward, earnestly searching for whatever "this" was through the greenhouse glass. Stars. The moons rising. A bat—

"Esen." In his *you've missed the point* voice, so I resumed staring earnestly at him. "When I said a Group member found themselves on the *Mistral,* it has to be because they were following a line of inquiry I started. The message burst didn't include which or when."

"And not Evan?" I dared ask. "Aren't you having someone follow him?"

A frustrated, under his breath, "I should have." Louder, "No. After my call to the embassy, I tried his Great Gran again. She told me Evan was there but resting and couldn't be disturbed."

While I hadn't met Evan's Great Gran, I'd developed a sense of her. By this, it was flawed. "She lied."

"If so, it'd be because Evan asked her to."

I'd the sudden urge to nip someone. *Ideally Evan Gooseberry.* "What's he got himself into this time?"

"I don't know, Old Blob." With shared exasperation. "As I said before, Evan was here. That links him to my mother and her ship—*and* he saw the Sacrissee Framer images brought by the Kraal." Paul ran a hand through his hair. "No wonder he left here in such a hurry." This with remorse. "I should have asked him to stay. Talked to him. This is my fault."

I failed to see his logic, but as that happened regularly when Humans—even my friend—were upset, I didn't try very hard. *Besides, it was never Paul's fault.* "You can talk to Evan when we get wherever we're going that he's about to go," I declared. "Right now I need to—" I waved the cryosac at him. *Eat Ersh.*

Paul ducked his head and peered up at me from that odd and uncomfortable posture. "I'm forgiven?"

Silly Human. I flicked an ear. "For finding us our first real clue? Or, wait, for telling me what you obviously would have told me *and* Rudy once together in a more secure location than a greenhouse? No, I have it, you're sorry you took the last—or was it the snoring? You do snore. Wait, it's—"

His laugh stopped a list I was ready to continue for some time. "I surrender."

"Good. Because I've work to do. Move. Please."

I released my hold on this shape as slowly as possible, easier since I'd cycled within the hour.

Yet harder, because this time I had to resist instinct. The cohesive blob of warm living mass within reach—*Paul*—wasn't tempting. *Well, a little.* The speck of web-flesh glowing on his breast was.

Both eclipsed by the lure of what lay nearest me. I didn't form a mouth. The cryosac couldn't escape. *More importantly, the appearance of a gaping mouth might set off my friend's own instincts and he mustn't run.*

There being Ersh-memory of such chases in me.

In less than a blink of Paul's eyes, I oozed sideways to cover the cryosac, discarding what wasn't living, and took in what still was.

It wasn't Ersh.

BAD IDEA—BAD IDEA—BAD IDEA—

"Esen, if you're all right, twitch an ear—"

Wasn't. Didn't.

"I should have known better." Bitter and low. "What Mocktap mined—Old Blob, I'm sorry. I should have realized it had to come from near the surface. She'd no time to drill deep—"

The outermost were the newest.

The last.

"Es, cycle again. Spit it out—"

No. I had to live it . . .

Death raced in along the elliptic, hit atmosphere as a ball of primal flame, drove over the land below in a supersonic scream. Over clusters of life. Life it would take later, at whim. The best of all—the *OLDEST*—waited ahead with no more need to defer satiation.

APPETITE! APPETITE!

There! She would be there! The memories Death retained from the flesh of the others assured it. Mixs-taste, Lesy-taste, Skalet-taste—not enough of Skalet, a tease of Esen. A trick. A cheat! There'd been danger. Death had fled. Had fled—*fear*—

No. Death would remember them. Death would hunt and find them—

AFTER.

No chance to cheat today. No way to escape. Triumphant, *HUNGRY,* Death plunged down to the mountain, *HER* mountain, landing with precision.

This was where they'd shared their flesh, exchanging tiny futile bites. *The FOOLS.* All flesh belonged to the one who claimed it. Could take it. *MINE!*

Where was the Oldest hiding? In what crevice did *ERSH* quiver with fear?

. . . SHARE . . .

The command—the *ACQUIESCENCE*—came through the air, coating Death in a tonic, driving it to a frenzy. Mouth open, it oozed up the diffusion gradient, plopping without grace across stone polished by feet. Feet were lies.

There was only the true shape.

. . . HERE . . .

There it was. There *she* was. The Oldest. The ERSH. Magnificent. Pure. Ageless and ancient.

Death found itself stopped. Insignificant.

. . . Share and join my Web . . .

Death found itself troubled. Almost . . . tempted.

Hunger won.

. . . I pulled free, gasping. Choked on drool.

I was— *Oh, no!* I scrambled from Paul's lap, heedless of the scratches left by my claws. "Stay away!" I warned him, backing in urgent clumsy haste as he rose to his feet, concern on his dear face, in his outreached hand.

"Es—"

HUNGRY—

If he wouldn't get out of range, I must. With a snarl, I spun and leaped for the door, barreling through it into the dark.

I ran, each curl and extension longer and more desperate.

Death-memory was faster . . .

A game. Delicious and daring, the Oldest kept just ahead, almost in reach, shedding irresistible molecules of WEB-FLESH. There were no thoughts beyond *HUNT* and *CONSUME*. No hesitation.

The Oldest didn't fly. The Oldest stayed on rock, as Mixs had stayed inside her walls, and Lesy clung to her metal shell, and Skalet/Esen had—

Almost killed it.

Death remembered *fear.* Recalled cunning and stealth. Slowed and tried to anticipate where the Oldest led. But there was only this rock, this mountain. *There was nowhere to go!*

The Oldest, as if waiting for this moment, came to a stop. Held out a portion of her perfect blue flesh as if in offering.

As if that could satisfy! Death surged forward, mouth agape.

To its surprise, the Oldest surged forward at the same instant. Their flesh *merged.*

So much to know, so much to know . . . Death convulsed, trying to bite and swallow as quickly as possible.

While the Oldest choked her with flesh, distracted her with eons of pointless knowledge— Why know that legs filled with fluid curl upon death and desiccation? That eggs need warmth for the life inside to mature and hatch? That what Ganthor clicked and Urgians sang made poetry. Why speak at all?

Why be able to list the overlapping ages and shapes of civilization—

And why, upon why, *care*?

Esen does. A sharpened focus. *Attack!* The Oldest summoned memory after memory of the Youngest, the trickster, the elusive—

Esen the wondrous and new.

A mistake! Death knew Esen-taste. *LONGED FOR IT.* Wanted more and more—was winning—

But the Oldest was despicably clever. All at once, the only memory, the *everywhere-everything-everwas* memory, filled with crackling lightning. REACHING from their hole in the depths of empty space. GRABBING! DRAINING!

IMPOSSIBLE! Death had fled. Death had made it across dreary barren space to this safe place, with its young stars and their fierce cleansing winds. *There could be no Null lurking here!*

Death closed its mouth, refused the taste, refused to believe—

WAS GRABBED! Not by the Null. By what was remained of the Oldest, thinning, sinking down into rock, drawing Death with her into unthinking solid oblivion.

Trapped, survival became the imperative. Death frantically sorted its flesh, sacrificed what couldn't be freed, at the last possible moment pulling free!

Spending mass to flee, howling its disappointment. *Never go back. Never never never.*

CHEATED! CHEATED! CHEATED!

. . . I shook free of Death, swallowing a howl of my own.

Branches arched overhead, leaves limned in moons' light. My flight from Paul hadn't just saved his life. It had brought me back to where the Web of Esen met.

I stretched out on cold stone. Had I stayed in web-form to assimilate Death's memories of Picco's Moon, had Paul—*living mass*—been in reach—

As Ersh would say, *Don't fuss, Youngest.*

The peril was over. I was back in control of my urgings—*and any I'd assimilated, no thanks to Death*—though I'd prefer not to repeat the experience. Or tell Paul.

But I would. First, though, I'd something of my own to digest.

Ersh, calling me "wondrous and new."

Which was predictably when Ersh-memory seized me and the present vanished behind the past . . .

. . . alone is instinct. Alone preserves self. *Avoid the same path. Avoid where others had gone.*

For where Null had fed, Null wait to feed again, having one simple strategy. Ambush. Ersh-I would not be prey.

Ersh-I soar through and between, following radiation gradients, bathing in what sustains us.

Without warning—lightning strikes! Writhing filaments of energy seize Ersh-I. Steal. Tear and pull, drawing Ersh-I closer and closer to where everything ends.

Ersh-I *divide*. Sacrifice flesh in an unthinkable sacrifice—

In the daze of pain and fear, what's left goes anywhere that's *AWAY*—

I stood outside the greenhouse door, absorbing the scents and sounds of the warm spring night. A busy night, full of life doing what it must; feeling new empathy, I didn't flick the biter from my ear, letting my blood nourish her next generation. Ephemerals like the biter—like my Human friend, waiting on the other side of the door—were part of a larger community of life. Co-evolved, mutually dependent, insepa-rable.

How had I believed us different?

Ersh's constant—and, at times, admittedly ignored—exhortations to me to beware the trap presented by a form's biology? Included our own, not that any of us but Lesy had the least inkling. However unique Web-beings might be—and I cherished the hope for the sake of ephemeral species we were—we weren't the only life to exist in space.

I lifted my paw to push the door open.

It swung gently inward without help, Paul standing there, a deeper shadow in the dark, and all at once what I needed, as desperately as if my Lishcyn-self, was light.

"Let's go inside," I said faintly, pushing by my friend.

We sat in Paul's tent, the glows along its supports set to max. He didn't ask why I wanted it bright, nor did he offer to touch or comfort me. My friend remained still, brilliant eyes locked on me, listening. He stirred only once, when at the start I told him whose memories I'd assimilated.

And whose had stirred within me, for Ersh-memory, buried deep, had surged upward in response. The first of our Web had known the

Null and barely escaped their clutches, leaving behind flesh *numbed* by contact with filaments made of energy, hungry for all of hers.

I'd been much happier not knowing what that felt like.

At least now I could be certain. Lesy hadn't imagined the Null. She'd fragments of Ersh-memory manifesting as horror-filled dreams. After this, if she'd forgiven me, I planned to spend the coming months making her forget them and be happy.

I wished I could.

"There are Botharan analogues," I concluded. "The giant ocean swimmers who filter the smallest of prey from the water as they swim. Whales, you call them." *Which they weren't, but this was hardly the time for precision in nomenclature.* "They have predators who know where and when they're most vulnerable." I wrinkled my snout, not satisfied. "We are—we were—like whales in space, but what preys on us—" and I was proud to be able to spit that out without a shudder, though my ears were plastered flat to my skull, so likely my feelings were obvious, "—is more like a trapdoor spider." The Botharan equivalent, there not being—*not the point.* "The Null hide, filaments of energy spread out from their core to set the trap and wait. If a Webbeing—or starship—happens to touch a filament, a sort of door opens and more filaments spring out to take hold and pull their prey inside— I don't know into what." Presumably a stomach, but given we were beings as much of energy as mass, I supposed web-flesh might not need digesting—

And how that was more horrible than our predilection for eating one another, I'd no idea, but it was.

"Hells, Es."

I nodded and went on because this was the part that mattered. "Null exist outside of real space, setting their traps within translight corridors. Web-beings are rare, Paul. It's possible the Null had to wait eons between—catches." Even to me, such patience was appalling.

Ersh had forbidden herself and us to fly. *Had it been about more than its cost in ephemeral life?* I carefully didn't drop my gaze to Paul's medallion as I continued, "I think Ersh and Death fled to this part of space because it was free of the Null. I don't think it is anymore." *On the bright side, we might not need to worry about another wild Webbeing anytime soon.*

"And now they hunt starships and their crews."

"Their engines," I qualified. "The energy in them. I've no idea what a Null would want with—people bits."

"Singular," Paul replied thoughtfully. "You think we're dealing with one organism."

"Or a single colony of untold billions. Which doesn't matter." I didn't try to lift my ears. "The only hope I see is the pattern of disappearances suggests one Null, choosing to open its trap along different translight corridors."

"Hunting."

I swallowed, but if our conjectures—the dread inside me—were right? "The *Mistral*—Rudy's ship and crew. We can't let them get near the Null. What can we do?"

Paul considered the question, his dear face morphing from thoughtful to an abrupt and most welcome determination. He stood. "We wake up Lionel, Old Blob, and give him the news.

"Then you and I are going down to the pub."

Nearby

"THERE'S a request to enter, Lionel," the door panel announced in its uncanny mimicry of Skalet's deep voice. "Shall I terminate the fools?"

Mimicry right to her appalling sense of humor. "Do not terminate," Lionel ordered in haste, rolling off the cot he'd brought in to use. He squinted in the room lights, now on full. "Who is it?"

It wasn't Lesy. *She didn't knock.*

"Idents confirmed: Director Ragem and Esen."

"Let them in. My authority." He snatched the clothes he'd dropped on the floor, pulling on pants.

There wasn't time for more. Paul and Esen came through, not waiting for the door to fully open, and Lionel's heart sank as he saw their faces. "What's happened?"

"We need the translight com—and your help," Paul told him.

Esen nodded, her expressive ears hovering between panic and resolve. "I've found out what we're up against."

Then they took turns telling him about the Null.

And what they needed him to do.

Once finsdown, the *Largas Swift* wouldn't lift as quickly as previously planned, despite the dire urgency of the situation, and Lionel had his part to play first. Once Paul and Esen left, he finished dressing. There'd be no more sleep for any of them tonight.

Taking a seat in front of Skalet's translight com, Lionel took a calming breath, then activated the device. The first call was simplicity itself, Captain Lefebvre being on the bridge of the *Swift,* and Lionel quickly had the answers they needed about the status of the *Swift*'s cargo hold. There'd be room.

The next call took preparation. Forewarned Paul had someone working undercover on the *Mistral,* Lionel elected to use his own contacts rather than risk more exposure of the Group. Patiently, methodically, he worked his way through the labyrinth bureaucracy that was Survey, putting the right words in carefully chosen ears until, two hours plus later, he'd reached the ears that mattered.

Lionel Kearn made a request, using up decades' worth of cautious preparation and indebtedness. *If not for this,* he reminded himself, *for what?*

As a result, Evan Gooseberry would receive a message—wherever he might be—urging him to contact the All Species Library of Linguistics and Culture immediately regarding "his inquiry." The com address supplied would shunt Evan's response to Paul and Esen wherever they were, even on the *Largas Swift,* while sending a confirmation alert to Lionel.

Finger on the button to shut down the com, Lionel hesitated. Esen and Paul hadn't asked him to reach out to Skalet.

They hadn't needed to. If he'd ever had anything she must know, and now, it was the presence of a predator of her kind.

He pressed the button, shutting down the com, then leaned back in his chair. "I've urgent information to convey," the Human told the white and empty room, with its weapons' wall and hidden plants.

No telling how long it would be until Skalet—S'kal-ru—could find a secure moment to respond. Instead of wasting time, Lionel pulled the hazard maps from Nia's portfolio and set up the scanner. Done, he sent the data to the model, asking it to process.

His mind on Skalet and monsters, he started when the comp signaled completion of its task. Lionel opened the display out of a sense of diligence, not because he expected any change—

Only to stop and stare in dismay.

Nia's data, the only data they had for the disappearance of non-Kraal Human ships, had indeed changed the model.

By the pattern, every other path taken by the—by the monster? Had been reduced to a single highest probability destination.

Here.

Lionel reached for the com.

Lionel poured himself some juice and leaned back, contemplating with a modicum of personal satisfaction the neat folder of memos he'd brought from his office yesterday, having dealt with each as was appropriate. He'd even done next month's payroll—

"Botharis. Impressive," praised that voice like deep dark velvet.

It most certainly was—to access his model in real time—

But what happened next was even more so. Lionel half rose from his seat in astonishment as a shape—*her shape*—formed from the air to stand before him. "Skalet."

She wore Kraal battle armor, with only her hands and, at this moment, for him, her head exposed; not the latest style, nor new. There were blaster burns, a patch to a knee. This armor not only made her a threat, being a potent weapon itself, but was a statement: *I have achieved glory; affiliate with me and achieve it as well.*

Thin lips almost smiled. "A mere tool, Lionel. The means to show my face to those who need to remember it and to those about to—" Her strong graceful hand stroked the air.

She might downplay it, but this was unlike any projection he'd seen, or heard of, before. Flawless, the tech reading and compensating for the room's ambient light to draw shadows under arm and jaw, adding a subtle glint here and there to the black of her armor and over her shaved head. While her eyes—

Told him to get to work. Lionel sat back down.

"We've identified the threat," he told her projection, gratified his voice was steady. "It's an energy-seeking predator, non-sentient, that hunts by ambushing what enters translight. We've a name. The Null. It was known to your—ancestor." He'd observed Esen's discomfort at hearing "Ersh" spoken by one of them.

"*She* confirmed this?"

By avoiding Esen's name, Skalet signaled this contact had its risks. "Yes," Lionel said promptly. "This new information challenges our assumptions about whomever is sending the images."

"Indeed." A fraught expressionless pause.

Lionel felt the urge to rub his hand over his scalp, a habit he'd thought he'd left behind, and stopped himself. *Could Skalet see him?*

Then, "No doubt *she* now considers them warnings. Some act prompted by benevolence."

Detecting scorn in the curve of her mouth, he frowned. "You do not?"

"I consider it more likely they are *!!*mementos*!!* shared to instill panic."

In Ganthor click speech, the word meant nothing so benign as the Human version. It referred to proof-of-kill trophies particular clients required of the mercenaries before payment. *Trophies such as body parts.*

Skalet put the Framers and Null together as a combined enemy. Lionel shuddered. *If she was right—*

"I've arranged a gift," Skalet continued, after granting him a heartbeat's grace. "When it arrives, you'll understand why I choose not to follow *her* down the path of compassion, but instead shall promote extreme efforts against this declared foe. And Lionel?"

He steeled himself. "Yes."

"It is no longer safe where you are. Be on that starship with *her*. Leave the system as soon as possible."

Not because of some extradimensional space monster with lightning tentacles. Because, *he could see it as clearly as if the war charts were in front of him*, the "extreme effort" Skalet alluded to must be a plan to ambush the Null in the Botharan System, with the full might of the Kraal's combined fleet. A victory to resound across space and species—

And the consequence of that victory? Would be to elevate the leader of that fleet—a person, not a House and its trusted affiliates, not the Great Houses with their checks and balances, *a person*—over the entire Confederacy. Botharis would be the first world to suffer. It would not be the last.

And that couldn't be Skalet's intention—not the full extent of it.

Lionel thought abruptly of her book, the one she'd let him translate, detailing her intricate, careful, calculated plan to establish a House of her own. No. Not of her own, not right now.

Lesy'd taught him Web-beings thought in terms of time beyond what he or any ephemeral would. Wasn't it possible—even probable—Skalet, who was the ultimate strategist, planned for a future Human generations from now when she could again be S'kal-ru and thrive?

To do that required the Kraal Confederacy endure—with checks and balances—

To do that, Skalet would act to preserve them.

He saw it, felt it, believed it. *Believed in her.* "You won't let the—" about to say, "Fleet Commander," he caught himself, "—the effort succeed."

"Careful, Lionel," she warned in a voice so soft and dire it raised the hairs on the back of his neck in an atavistic response to a predator.

She acted over generations yet urged him—a single Human—to save himself. Lionel met her gaze with his own, unafraid, utterly sure of her. "I can't be on that ship. She won't let me. It's too dangerous," Lionel replied, rather enjoying the irony. "She's going to intercept the Null."

He could forget Skalet was a projection, seeing her reaction in the tautness of her body, the tense angle of head and neck. When the ensuing silence grew impossible to bear, Lionel offered a lame, "They have a plan."

"She always does." *Was that a sigh?* Skalet's projection walked away from him, then back again. "Tell me everything, Lionel," she ordered. "Including what she wouldn't want me to know."

An extradimensional space monster with lightning tentacles . . .

Mementos of the grisly kind . . .

Lionel sat back, steepling his fingers. "Evan Gooseberry is on the *Mistral*," he began, choosing each word with the greatest of care.

Knowing if he failed the trust of either Skalet or Esen?

A world could fall.

Out There

'VE a message for you to give Paul.
Stop this, Veya. He's dead. You know he's dead.
I know he's not. Our son's hiding, like I am. He'll come out one
day and you'll tell him this: 'What we believe is lost simply waits
for better eyes to find it.' Repeat it to me. Those words exactly.
Why must you hide? Why must you run?
Those words, Stefan. Please.

More bits. More limbs. More bone. More flesh and organs hang.

More eyes stare outward, beyond reach.

None see as she does. Her eye, the one that isn't hers but is, is Hell's
favorite. Hell's prize. Veya hangs within the growing obscene bundle
of flesh, part of it, core of it, and cannot weep. Her eye saw them first.

Her eye found them.

Her eye brought Hell to them.

Even now, her eye sees—

How did this happen?
Acid. It splashed—the eye's lost, isn't it? I can't see.
Don't worry. I've had to reconstruct the orbital bone and graft a
new lid, but the eye itself wasn't harmed. You'll see again once—

<u>Take it out.</u>
<u>What—</u>
<u>Damn you. The eye. Take it out!</u>
<u>I can't—</u>
A heart orbits, beating still.
    Is it hers?

11: Pub Night; Balmy Morning

WE took Paul's aircar to the Hamlet of Hillsview, lights off and engine set to hush. As this was precisely the sort of activity most feared by our doubters on the Preservation Committee—namely an unannounced, uninvited alien skulking about after everyone was snug in their beds—Paul set us down neatly on top of Samgo's vegetable patch. Where, true, we wouldn't be seen, but we'd need to reimburse or replace whatever we'd crushed, or the menu would suffer.

We exited as quietly and quickly as possible. Paul wore black, his ability to skulk on demand most impressive, while I went on all fours, the better to be mistaken for what wasn't me, a scruff. To our knowledge, the pub didn't employ one of the annoying canids to keep aircars out of the vegetables and raise the alarm for aliens on the property, but I sniffed cautiously before signaling my nefarious partner to proceed.

The Highview Pub and Eatery—as named on the hanging sign out front but everyone called it the Hillsview Pub, it being the sole such establishment—had been a village fixture for four generations. As I'd come to expect from this part of Botharis, ownership hadn't changed in that time either. Samgo was the fifteenth Cameron to run the place, had no choice in the matter—I'd heard he'd wanted to be a beekeeper— and one day I hoped to introduce him to Evan as a fellow example of someone afflicted by lineage.

The point being, a young Paul Ragem had had the run of the place, and the present-day version led us directly to a never-locked door and up the secondary stairs—cautioning me about the squeak in the fourth tread—to the floor with rooms for paying guests.

Almost too easy.

A thought I regretted an instant later as Paul froze on the stairs, his hand over his ear in that ominous *incoming call* pose. I regretted it even more when his other hand sought the support of the wall.

That wasn't good.

He dropped his hands, but instead of offering a hopefully reassuring explanation, he hurried up the rest of the stairs, then eased open the narrow wooden door at the top. The hinges were well greased, possibly to make it easier for sneaking—*this me loved sneaking*—though more likely it was to let the pub staff come and go without disturbing the paying customers. As planned, I went first, ears up and tongue lolling, on the premise if we bumped into a stranger, best they think me a friendly local.

The guest floor had a grander staircase in the middle, with rails around three sides. Rooms were arranged in the outer rectangle, except for the large window overlooking the village square. There were antique wall sconces throwing a soft warm glow, except for the far one which had gone out and two that sputtered but, considering they appeared original to the historic-for-Botharis building, could be forgiven. The carpet underfoot was newer, if not its pattern of giant roses, but the doors to each room were vintage as well, slabs of solid wood carved with fanciful images of Botharan wildlife, posed looking back over what they had for shoulders in abject terror.

Might have been my interpretation.

I caught the scent of a stranger—Human, male, and, I wrinkled my snout, must work at the brewery—under the door featuring a regal, if terrified, Botharan Elk and ignored it. Paul had been here this afternoon and knew Nia and Onlee had the largest room, to the front of the pub, so that's where I headed.

Once at their door, with its striking display of weasling flexibility, I crouched to sniff the crack at the bottom.

Paul nudged me out of the way, tapping a weasling with a finger. Once, twice, then two more quickly.

They'd a secret signal? Perhaps my daydream of reconciliation had potential after all.

Or this was a remnant of a past both Humans wanted to leave there. *Such a complex species.*

The door opened for Paul and me to slip through together—with token bumping because I may have rushed. Nia's assistant, Onlee Naston, closed it behind us. She was shorter than average for a Botharan female, with short curly brown hair and brown eyes tilted up at the ends. Her hair stood out in all directions and she wore a night dress printed with what Botharans called "palm trees." Which were more colonial lichens than plants, and self-digested their stalks every winter leaving a gooey mess, but Humans liked the shade and shape of the things and encouraged them to grow around seaside resorts.

Not important at the moment, I reminded myself, catching Onlee's yawn.

The room had a second door, open a crack, that I assumed led to the bedroom. In this portion of the suite—not a word I'd thought to apply to a pub—there was an overstuffed couch, two chairs at a small table, and an armchair. There were more dim wall sconces, keeping the theme alive, but also a modern bright light on the table, illuminating a closed comp and stacks of plas notes.

Nia sat in the armchair, a blue silk coat tied over whatever she wore to bed. When she went to speak, Paul put a finger to his lips. Pulling out a palm-sized detector, he began to methodically sweep the room.

Onlee and Nia exchanged looks, but neither objected. While the village pub was the last place I'd expect surveillance equipment, the highest ranking government official presently on this continent made a tempting target.

And Paul didn't take chances.

"Clean," he announced at last, putting away the device.

There was the usual brief shuffle as the Humans worked out seating for our small gathering. I left them to it, jumping up on the couch. Finding the cushions exceptionally comfy, I curled in—

Receiving *that* look from Paul, I struggled up to a sitting position; while not as comfortable, I refused to relinquish this fine piece of furniture simply to be professional. *I'd have to ask Samgo where he'd bought it.* Not that we'd an apartment to furnish yet, or really more than a muddy hole in the ground with the potential to one day be an apartment if—

"I'm sorry to disturb you both again," Paul said. "But this can't wait." He'd taken his chair to where he could sit and see the rest of us; Onlee sat at the table, a notebook and stylo at the ready.

Nia'd either brushed her hair or not yet been in bed; by the work strewn over the small table, I assumed the latter. "So your message said." Her face was set and pale, but resolute. "Has there been another disaster?"

I angled my ears at Paul, expecting him to relate whatever he'd learned in the stairwell. Instead, he nodded at me.

So I answered, my friend and I having discussed who would say what on the way here. *Before crushing vegetables.* "We found information in the collection after all," I announced, being the curator as well as the part of the collection in question. "We're dealing with a mindless force of nature known as the Null. Think of it as an interstellar spider, lurking just outside normal space."

Onlee gasped.

Nia's reaction was a slight nod, her eyes hooded. *Acceptance of what I'd said or waiting on proof?* "And the messages?"

"That we still don't know," from Paul. "Our best guess? Someone's trying to warn us about the Null the only way they can, making our supposition about an unknown species, the Framers, still valid." The lines at the corners of his mouth and eyes deepened. "And there's a new development, based on your maps, Nia." Something in his voice made me tense. "The Null attacks haven't been switching between Sacrissee space and the Confederacy—they've been switched between Sacriss and us."

Her mouth formed the word without sound, so I supplied it, just to be sure. "Botharis?"

A nod, then Paul went on as if he hadn't lowered the temperature in the room and raised the hair over my spine. "It doesn't change anything. We have to stop the Null before it takes more life. For that, we need a weapon."

I tilted my head, counting under my breath. I'd gotten to two before Nia tensed and shook her head. *She was quick.* "Impossible. You can't be serious."

She knew he was. No one could miss the fire in his eyes, the intensity in his voice, but it was a very big favor we were about to ask and, as Paul'd told me, she'd every right to protest.

Nia sat back, meeting Paul's level gaze with her own. "I see you are. You want one of the decommissioned Kraal missiles."

"Not all of it," I countered helpfully. "Just the boom."

Her gaze went from me to Paul, and her lips twitched. "We've seen this vid. Remember, Paul? It didn't end well."

He gave a little huff of acknowledgment, then leaned forward. "This isn't fiction. The Null has a core hidden from normal space. We're confident we can get it to pull the explosive inside—"

By coating it with irresistible web-flesh, otherwise known as me, not that anyone but Paul and I would know. *Not my favorite part of the plan.*

"—then we detonate it."

"BOOM!" I contributed, waving my paws dramatically.

Onlee pushed her notebook aside, deciding on her own this wasn't a meeting to record.

Nia stared at Paul, who continued doggedly, "You don't have to be involved—other than to let us in. We'll have the expertise to dismantle an intact missile without anyone knowing."

"Lionel told me. A *former* Kraal." Her brow arched. "Is there such a thing?"

"I trust Meony-ro with my life."

"You trusted your head of security and look where she's gone."

Into danger. Ignorant of the true nature of the threat, but if anyone could reach Skalet with that information it would be Lionel. *She'd her favorite too.* I was counting on it.

I snapped back to attention. "Skalet serves us still."

Nia ignored me, her focus on Paul, her voice gone low and hard. "This is beyond *jig up*, Paul. You're what—going to load an antique planet-killing missile on poor Rudy's ship, then blast off like cosmic vigilantes to toss it in this Null's mouth? Do you even hear yourselves?"

My friend half smiled. "I believe we saw that vid too."

"Why you?" Nia rose to her feet. So did Paul. "Why does it *always* have to be you?"

I wrinkled my snout to express displeasure at not being included in her fierce concern, but Nia wasn't looking at me. *Humans.*

"I didn't come back to stay safe, Nia. We—" Paul's warm glance at me brought up my ears. "—didn't create the Library to hide behind. We're here to help."

"Even if it's a boom," I added, again being helpful.

Nia glared at me, at Paul, then threw up her hands. "If you die again, I won't care."

For some reason known only to Humans, her warning made my friend duck his head to hide a smile.

But on the way back to the Library, our mood in the aircar was somber. Nia had agreed, reluctantly, to find out what it would take to get what we'd asked. She didn't promise to give it to us, a lack I noticed, but Paul had been willing to leave it at that.

What kept us quiet? Thinking what might be happening out there now. To the *Mistral*. To any ship that might be grabbed by the Null and it didn't make me any happier to know I might have a connection to it, that the monster might have been lured into this life-filled region of space after a Web-being.

Death wasn't done causing harm.

We were in sight of the Library when Paul spoke. "If Lionel's contacts don't reach Evan soon, we'll warn the *Mistral* ourselves."

And if we did, we'd attract the worst sort of attention. "How will we explain knowing about their mission when we shouldn't?"

"Our friend will confess to being a Kraal spy, passing information from the *Mistral* to S'kal-ru who in turn shared it with the Library to save a Commonwealth vessel from a monster."

Clever, devious. *Skalet would approve.*

I didn't. "Our friend will be arrested!"

"Better that than dead," Paul pointed out, his tone cool. "The Group accepts the risks. You know that."

Knowing wasn't the same as facing the consequences. "Evan will be in touch. You'll see."

Instead of answering, my friend reached over and tugged gently on my ear.

Meaning Paul wasn't hopeful, and I should resign myself to another sacrifice to keep our secret—my secret.

I wasn't good at that. *I didn't ever want to be.* Then and there, I came to a decision—one I'd tell Paul after we'd defeated the Null and survived to argue. His Group had to change. I'd no idea how, yet, but change it would.

Paul yawned, so I did. Morning was coming at us faster than a train from the landing field—*or a monster from space*—but neither of us would sleep. It'd be breakfast, finish packing, deal with administration—and Lesy—board the ship—get the boom—*or should that come before packing?*

To stop the list, I turned to my companion. "What vid was Nia talking about? Where did you see it?" Most importantly, "Would I like it?"

"*The Evil from Planet XX,*" Paul answered patiently. "Uncle Sam showed vids in his barn in the summer. All the kids went. I don't think we should watch that one till this is over, Old Blob."

"Why?" I liked scary vids. *If I had a blanket.*

A sidelong look. "The monster wins."

The night ending with nefarious trips and talk of scary monsters—*one of them all too real*—I approached the day's start braced for the next unpleasant shock and could tell Paul felt the same. Our mood wasn't improved by the prospect of another round of supper tubes for breakfast. *Lacking bacon.* Which might have been my fault, not that I'd admit it.

We'd underestimated the news network of the Hamlet of Hillsview. On hearing the Anytime Chow was closed, the ever-enterprising Samgo took a day to prepare, then loaded up his truck and arrived at the Library door bright and early with sample hot breakfasts for staff and special handwritten menus from the Highview Pub. A double bounty of eggs, sausage, still-hot fried chips, and other edible stuff was waiting for us in Paul's office and, in the interests of community spirit, we sat down to thoroughly test the offering. *A shame we wouldn't be here for tomorrow's.*

A short while later, delighted by this turn of events, but seeing room for improvement, I stealthily swapped my fruit bowl for Paul's box of chips.

He crooked a finger without looking up from whatever he was read-ing. "Not so fast."

I returned his chips and began licking my empty box suggestively.

Still without looking, Paul slid the fruit bowl back to me. "Eat that."

A Lanivarian had its omnivorous side. This me liked jamble grapes. And chips. This me emphatically did not like those round green—

"There are hayberries," I informed him with disgust.

"They're in season." A smile tugged at his lips, but Paul held firm. "Eat around them."

I would not. Merely being in the same container for the trip to the Library tainted the other fruit with the bitter/musty/nasty of hayberry. Nia might love them, but how Humans tolerated the things was a mys-tery and no, I wasn't about to test the taste as Bess.

Besides, by now I'd noticed that Paul was ignoring his sausage, leav-ing it all alone. I uncurled the fingers of my paw and quivered in my seat, ready to pounce.

Beep . . . beepbeepbeep . . . Beep . . . beepbeepbeep . . . Through the com in my jacket pocket, echoing from Paul's desk, came what we'd heard previously only in tests. The alarm for *Inquiry With Risk Poten-tial Received.*

Otherwise known as "Esen-Urgent."

Our eyes met across the desk, remembering monsters.

I surged to my feet, hair rising on my spine even as my tail tried to slip between my legs, this me stuck between fight or flinch. "What's the question?"

Paul was already accessing the collection, keying in the code reserved for the two of us. "Not the question. The alert's for submitted info."

My tail stopped, but my heart kept thumping. "That's better, isn't it?"

"Maybe not." His eyebrows drew together. With a finger flick Paul sent what he'd read to hover between us. "Well, Old Blob? New to you?"

Which should have been exciting, the Library having yet to receive much that was new to me beyond updated language forms and fashion, but—what I read made no sense. What the block of text, entered by Henri Steves at the Assessment Counter within the last minute, said was: *The Ervickian Primacy has licensed the establishment of crèches in seven Human systems, effective immediately.*

"New to me—and Ersh-memory," I replied, knowing what he asked. "Ervickians reproduce within the Primacy." A boundary including the species' homeworld, three other habitable planets within the Ervicki System—and their barely livable moons—and, at last count, three hundred orbital stations and one asteroid mine, the point being Ervickians confined their reproduction to where they were majority stakeholders, to the relief of everyone else.

"Seems that's about to change." Paul indicated the list of systems affixed to the text. "Those are deep in the Commonwealth."

If the Commonwealth was the intestine of this section of space, Ervicki was a bunion on its toe, well beyond other space-faring civilizations and on the far side of the Kraal Confederacy. A large and prolific bunion, adults setting forth to seek out commerce and crime wherever they could with a laudable lack of prejudice and deplorable enthusiasm, but still—any species with its reproduction tied to a single star was vulnerable.

My tail went decisively between my legs. "And the question?"

"We don't have it yet. The scholar's waiting in the Lobby, requesting assistance, but Rudy's on approach and I should finish here." Paul gave me *that* look. "Es—?"

"I know," I told him, encompassing all the delays and digressions my dear friend could imagine—*and remember*—including the time I'd hidden in a closet, but I wouldn't. *Not this time.* "I'll go straight there," I promised, in case he'd lingering doubt of me, then went so far as to touch the com button on my jacket. "If you like, I'll leave it on." *I was reasonably sure I remembered how.*

His eyes lit up. "Thank you."

Now I'd have to check. I lifted my ears in acknowledgment.

But as I left Paul's office, I spared a moment to be grateful I wasn't yet Lishcyn.

This me wouldn't lose my delightful breakfast.

"His name's Pretty Bill," Henri Steves informed me when I arrived a moment later at her counter. "He's waiting for you outside the Median Theta Habitat Zone." Which she and other staff—in reference to its environment being set to a lovely local summer morning and having a conveniently Human-suited accommodation—called the "Balmy," but Henri's usually twinkling blue eyes were somber and her tone business-like. "Can't miss him, Es." She shook her head in emphasis, curls bouncing. "He's—you'll see. Unbelievable."

I resisted the urge to point out incredulity was the default Human response to any Ervickian met in person, let alone on Botharis, where you'd only encounter one here or at our landing field. Possibly regurgitating. Beyond doubt running a con of some kind and petty theft was a species' trait. They could tuck non-food items in their secondary mouth—

I noticed Henri was giving me her *patient* look and lifted my ears in a friendly acknowledgment. *Esen to work.* "Thank you, Henri."

"Before you go—" She leaned forward over the counter to whisper confidingly. "Don't listen to the rest of them. I like the paint. Brightens the place."

My wince was involuntary. Maintenance had done their best, but the walkway over the Lobby would have yellow amorphous blops on it until they could bring in a sander—and the floor? "Glad you do," I replied. *Maybe our scholars would consider it the local fashion.*

Henri's face turned serious. "Really sorry to hear about your family, Es. Hope everything works out for them."

It took me two heartbeats longer than it should to remember Paul and I were supposedly rushing offworld to Lanivar, with Henri among those shouldering our duties here. Her eyes began to narrow.

I let my ears droop. "I'll share your kind words with my loved ones," being the truth if exaggerated—*love* not particularly web-like; Lesy would smile and Skalet grumble—adding a woeful and sincere, "I just hope I survive the trip."

Her cheerful smile returned. "Take your anti-nausea meds, keep a bag handy, and you'll be fine. Paul'll take good care of you."

Paul and the com! I smiled back at this very capable Human and held out my com button in an outstretched paw. "Thanks for the reminder. Would you set it so Paul can listen in?" This last a whisper, it occurring to me that bringing Paul's ears along with mine was something to either tell this Pretty Bill or keep secret. For now.

Secret seemed prudent.

As I was me in any form—if rarely a convenient relative age and don't get me started on those with metamorphic stages which presented a whole other level of complication if I failed to keep track and mistakenly cycled into a dormant pupa or worse, an egg—I understood variation within a species in a way only a Web-being could. *Or so I thought.* Meaning I walked through the Lobby in search of Pretty Bill, secure in my assumption this must be a particularly noxious individual for Henri to comment and I shouldn't inhale through my sensitive nostrils. Ervickians at the best of times wore the remnants of their previous meals as smears on their clothing and their breath?

I owed Henri an apology.

When I spotted the Ervickian standing by the entrance to the Median Theta Habitat Zone, I came to a sudden halt, almost stepping on a Dwelley who hooted in disapproval and popped eyes at me.

In my defense, Pretty Bill wore a suit.

A suit not scavenged from a waste container, ill-fitting and crusty, but new and clean. More than that, it was tailored to a perfection of style and fit that would have made my Lishcyn-self swoon. The fabric was soft green, complementing the polished yellow of his bald head, the delicate brown mottling over the large non-mobile ears indicating early wis-morph. Old enough to sire a litter or two and, by first impression, likely had three.

The jacket had elegant black piping at the collar and hems. More piping bordered the neat opening mid-chest for his secondary mouth, a tidy, pursed round with lips rouged the same tasteful pale orange as the primary.

Whether the outfit, rouge, or something in his bearing—*maybe all of it*—Pretty Bill's four eyes, below neatly trimmed eyebrows, sparkled with intelligence. As previously I'd have described an Ervickian's eyes as beady, if I felt charitable, and shifty if not. *Who* was *this being?*

Both mouths formed an oval smile, my reaction noticed and found amusing.

Time to be professional.

And find out why Ervickians were leaving their Primacy.

The Balmy Zone wasn't the largest in the Library. That label belonged to the wing for aquatic species, housing not only the areas available to our scholars and requisite air/liquid portals to reach them, but also the wealth of unseen equipment required for them to function, from its own power source to multiple distinct plumbing fixtures—there being no one material right for all the possibilities, delighting Duggs with the challenge.

Balmy required nothing of the sort. The zone shared its air with the administrative portion of the Library and Lobby, though had its own temperature and humidity controls. It was a little dark and damp for Esolesy Ki, a touch warm for Esen, but Bess had loved it during my brief clandestine test of the facility. The interior design was, well, efficient. We weren't, as I'd tried—*failing repeatedly*—to explain to Lesy, and innumerable Queebs, running a spa.

It was a single spacious room, long and curved, without windows and with a floor reminiscent of a decent station corridor, offering traction while easily cleaned. Separated consoles lined the walls and marched down the middle, each with an optional persona-field that could be opaqued against whatever sensory intrusion the scholar using it decided was necessary. Or to avoid being distracted by the more excitable of our users.

A scholar ready to pose a question selected the console best suited to their body structure. Not all bothered to do so, having made do with Humanocentric facilities on the trip here and typically in a hurry to get their answer and leave. We'd provided a variety of input methods as well but, to my chagrin, in Balmy most simply vocalized in comspeak for the same reason. *When on Botharis . . .*

If the Preservation Committee observed how accommodating our alien scholars actually were, they might feel more comfortable letting them move around the Hamlet. *Then again*—I watched a Heezle get a little too happy with its console while verbalizing and made a note to put the machine on a deep clean cycle before maintenance saw it.

Other than the rapturous Heezle, Balmy was deserted when I entered with Pretty Bill. Successful scholars from the first train of the day had come and gone, to await their responses in the Lobby before heading to the landing field. Once the second train arrived, it would start to fill again.

As he didn't aim for a shorter-than-most console, I did it for him, determined *someone* appreciate the effort I, as tester, had put into the layout. A tall Ervickian was shorter than me as Bess and the average found themselves hopping to see over the Assessment Counter.

"Would you like me to demonstrate the console?" I asked.

In response, his four eyes blinked in sequence at me.

A wink?

What did it mean? Obviously the inner workings of Pretty Bill weren't like those other Ervickians I'd known either. *Paul should have come instead.* The instant I thought it, my ears lowered in dismay.

"Oh, my apologies, Curator," Pretty Bill exclaimed, reading my expression with deplorable ease. "I assumed you were making a little joke. A clever one."

Humor. Always tricky. If I had made a joke, I'd no idea about what. I narrowed my eyes at him. Ervickians had two brains as well as two mouths. Though Ervickians pitied those of one brain, they didn't technically have twice the thinking power. The brain in Pretty Bill's rump performed similarly to a Human's, or this me's. The larger brain in his skull hosted social skills, an adaptation to a rigorous childhood.

Ervickians were born in massive litters, each litter confined until maturity within a competitive crèche. Survival through the euphemistically called "settling" stage—when the little monsters ate one another, or at least toes, if they could—depended on a quick assessment of risk and even quicker grasp of the slightest opportunity to advance at the expense of their peers.

Explaining an Ervickian motto for success: *Gobble the weak.*

By ept-morph, able to leave the confines of their crèche, they'd stop eating one another—*unless threatened*—and would remain loyal—*unless threatened*—to their crèchemates for life. Ervickians had no concept of the idea outside of it. It was crèche against crèche forever.

And everyone else. According to Ersh, Ervickian hard-wiring made adhering to a fixed moral code inconceivable, and they deeply distrusted those who claimed to do so, a handicap when comprehending other sapients. Offworld, Ervickians were thus in a constant heightened state of suspicion. *Where's the threat? Who's about to take advantage?* Most of all, *why is*—insert anyone else—*being nice to me?*

Which was why Ervickians who left their world to work with other species were considered by their own kind to be borderline insane and, by others, untrustworthy at best.

Not, I suspected, *this individual.* "What did you take as a joke?" I ventured.

"In your survey, I listed my occupation." When I continued to regard him blankly, Pretty Bill winked again. "I make these." A slim arm lifted toward the console, eight fingers spread wide.

A reminder the term "scholar" we used in the Library for our visitors was, in fact, a polite generalization covering every possible occupation. Also that I really should, in future, read completed survey forms before engaging in one-on-one.

And now we had to worry about Ervickian morality in our console design? *Leaving that to Paul.*

I left my ears at their unsettled angle. "Then your request for assistance was a joke. On me." With a touch of snarl.

The Ervickian raised his hands in an appeasing gesture. Or defensive. "A ploy, Huntress. Let us speak openly before others come. You're here, not a junior member of your staff, because you saw the information I provided in trade and found it troubling." Four eyes made for a most effective stare. "As all should."

This was an important person. A decision maker. *Why was he here?* I lowered my voice to a whisper, though the Heezle had oozed away and we were alone. "What would you ask the Library?"

Pretty Bill produced a glove from a pocket, put it on his left hand, then opened his secondary mouth. Reaching deep inside, he retrieved a fist-sized bulb, a container, unscathed by however long it had been exposed to the Ervickian digestive juices now dripping on the Balmy's floor.

Which should be able to take it, I assured myself, eyeing the sizzling drops with some dismay.

"This is my question. What could do this?" Squeezed in his gloved hand, the container changed shape, a slit opening in the top, and from that projected an image. It showed an ordinary-seeming planet, with blue oceans and continents covered in verdant living purple. A storm swirled out to sea. A polar ice cap made a jaunty hat.

Something of an anticlimax. This time, I was ready with a joke. "Geologic time and a sweet orbit."

"That was before this," Pretty Bill said, changing the image.

The frame. A backdrop of stars. Those were familiar. *Framers.*

What sent my tail between my legs even as I whined?

The image wasn't of a derelict ship.

It was of a shattered world.

While I remained frozen in horror, Pretty Bill began flipping between the images. That verdant world, continents coated with life. The Framers version: shattered rock, set in a frame. Flip. Flip. Flip.

Ephemerals had no patience. Not that I was known for mine, but in that moment, I'd nothing worthwhile to say. Ships were one thing—

If this represented a Null attack, I'd no idea how it was remotely possible. If the Framers were responsible, perhaps in a failed attempt to stop the Null? The weapons in my memory left signs of destruction. Altered atmospheres. Sullied water. Melted ice and stone. Craters. Even nudged asteroids left clouds of orbiting dust post impact.

Ersh at her most ferocious took years to decimate the life on a world. Even then, she'd stuck to the thinking-screaming kind, and left the rest alone. *Not, mind you, out of charity.* Web-beings couldn't assimilate non-sentient life and remain thinkers themselves. I shuddered, my tail sliding between my legs.

Understandably, the Ervickian mistook why. The images mercifully vanished as he released his grip on the bulb. "Terrifying, indeed," he said. "This is—was—Noam, orbiting the star known as Bry-Mis-Wed. My question for your famed collection, Curator. What killed this world?"

"Come with me," I ordered and wheeled around, walking as quickly as this me could without hopping. Thanks to Henri's work on my com, Paul had heard.

He had to see for himself. Now.

Pretty Bill hurried behind me. "You know something."

"Not here," I told him, and sped up. Though my pace forced him into an undignified trot, his fancy shoes tap-tapping, the Ervickian didn't protest.

Because "terrifying" didn't cover it. I started to pant, dumping heat.

As we rushed through the Lobby, heading for Paul's office, there might have been a hop or two.

Paul opened his door before I could hit the control, proof he'd over-heard and gauged our progress by my breaths and Pretty Bill's tapping. He closed and locked it behind us.

Lionel stood waiting by Paul's desk, my clever friend saving time and repetition by gathering our little group. By the look on both their faces, there was more upsetting news from Skalet.

Mine first. I didn't bother with introductions. "Show them."

Pretty Bill held out his bulb projector—fortunately, he hadn't put it back in his stomach, Paul having replaced his carpet not that long ago—and activated it. "Noam as it should be." The living world. "Noam as it is."

The dead one.

I watched a muscle jump along Paul's jaw; otherwise, his look of intense attention didn't change. Lionel let out an audible gasp, attracting the Ervickian's gaze.

"What killed this world?" Pretty Bill repeated for his new audience, lowering the bulb. The projection disappeared into Paul's desk. "How is this possible?"

Gray eyes flashed at me. I angled my ears the precise amount to mean *at a loss.* Paul tightened his lips. *Understood.* To the Ervickian. "In order to answer, we'll need to ask our own questions first, Hom Bill. Is that agreeable?"

"You're Director Ragem." Four eyes regarded Lionel next. "Administrator Kearn. Curator Esen alit Quar. The three who run this place." He closed his fingers over the bulb, giving another jarring wink. "I find that agreeable."

"Thank you. Please take a seat, Hom Bill." Paul, again proving himself the thoughtful one. *Or worried about his carpet.* "I can offer tea."

Beverages? I bit back my protest, knowing I shouldn't have been surprised these particular ephemerals had more patience than a

Web-being—not that I was known for mine—but time wasn't a friend. *Our monster had just grown.*

"Pleal juice?"

The Ervickian intoxicant. "I don't believe we have any." Paul looked at me, lifting an eyebrow.

One time—besides even if I had some juice, or the Chow was running, he knew as well as I did that we assuredly didn't want an inebriated Ervickian around. I flicked an ear. "Sorry."

"Tea will do," Pretty Bill said, graciously smacking both sets of lips. His back to the indicated chair, he bent slightly at the knees, then sprang up into the seat and composed himself, the bulb still in one hand.

I'd have to try that trick. Not that I planned to be Ervickian for another six centuries unless I found a way to hide in a crèche without being eaten. *The woes of the young.*

Pretty Bill's secondary mouth opened, preparatory to the bulb being returned to it.

"May I?" Lionel asked at once. "You did bring it in trade, did you not?" By his tone, it wasn't a request, and I angled a curious ear at Paul.

Who gave that tiny *not-now-Esen* shake of his head.

For the first time I saw something close to a more *normal-for-the-species* suspicion cross the Ervickian's face, but he offered the bulb without argument. The Human picked up a sheet of plas and used it to protect his hand from any lingering enzymes—and there'd be some—taking the bulb gingerly. "Thank you."

There was a momentary delay as Paul found a tall glass better suited to Pretty Bill's anatomy and filled it with tea, while Lionel copied the image and sent it to Paul's desk. He didn't return the bulb, putting that safely inside a spare mug.

Lionel didn't look himself. Planet destruction could do that, but I suspected Skalet of saying something to him that put his tail between his legs, had he been Lanivarian. *I could wait to find out.*

Paul, demonstrating a superb grasp of current culture, and the high status of our visitor, took three sips from the glass, then turned it to offer the Ervickian the opportunity to put his lips where the Human's had touched. Thus sharing both the risk of poison and offering the antidote, should Paul have one in his mouth.

Pretty Bill did his utmost not to be impressed, but was, I could tell, because after taking the glass, he turned it once more. *The intention to trust, if not the reality.* He poured the remaining tea, quite neatly, into his waiting mouth, belched once, and returned the glass. "A pleasant beverage. Your questions?"

"Yes." Duties done, Paul went to sit behind his desk. Lionel remained standing beside it. So I wouldn't pace, I took the second chair, moving my tail aside at the last second. "Where did you obtain the image, Hom Bill?"

"Is that relevant?" Four eyes narrowed. "What's shown has been authenticated. The disaster—whatever it was—that stripped Noam clean took place within the last four planet days. I would think that rates some urgency."

"It does."

"Wait." Lionel put a finger to Paul's desk. "Noam. In the Bry-Mis-Wed System?" When Pretty Bill grunted an assent, the Human continued in an expressionless voice, "According to the annals of House Noitci, that's a former Kraal outpost."

News to me. It wouldn't be to Skalet, busy being S'kal-ru the Courier and plucking the strings of empire. She'd have wanted us to have this news.

Had sent it, I concluded, via this Ervickian and a multiplicity of pawns, before learning of the Null.

I just knew she'd manage to leverage a planet-level destructive event to solidify her position with the Kraal, who'd be terrified. And now, with what Lionel had told her?

If she *had a plan, we had a problem.* Glancing at Paul, I tilted my head and showed teeth. A barely perceptible nod signaled he'd the same thought.

Pretty Bill snapped his secondary mouth shut in a firm line but didn't try to deny it. "Excellent clients."

I really wanted our consoles checked . . .

"I cannot speak to the original message recipient," the Ervickian continued. "Only that the framed image came translight."

"And you were told what to do with it." Paul leaned forward, palms flat on the desk.

"To bring it here, to us." It wasn't a question.

Beads of sweat appeared on the Ervickian's polished head. "My question is what matters." Evasion.

To my surprise, Paul allowed it. "As is the safety of your crèches. Those are *your* crèches being relocated, are they not?" Cold and flat.

It was as if the air had been sucked from Pretty Bill's quadruple lungs. He collapsed in the chair, his tailored jacket sagging in the middle. Distracted, he fussed with the fabric, trying to free one mouth as the other gasped for breath.

"That's a yes," I deduced, doing my utmost not to judge. By looking out for his own offspring and mates at the expense of all others, Pretty Bill was only being true to his nature. *Didn't mean I approved.*

Paul and Lionel exchanged *informative only to Humans* looks, then my friend leaned back, steepling his fingers. "What question were you told to ask the Library?"

Quite sure my "look" was utterly blank at this—though by now you'd think I'd be used to Paul Ragem's ability to take a flying leap to the side and pounce on whatever he suspected—I turned to Pretty Bill.

Who'd straightened to glare most unpleasantly at Paul, all four eyes wide open as was his secondary mouth, exposing gore-dripping teeth. "This is ridiculous! What other question could there possibly be? What else matters?"

Not being a lesser status Ervickian—who'd interpret Pretty Bill's display as a dire promise of *going to eat your toes unless . . .*—my friend merely raised an eyebrow. "You're here because Kraal sent you. I'd ask their question, Hom Bill, or you may find relocating your kin insufficient."

Clever, clever Paul. Skalet would be impressed. Or expect nothing less. I restrained the urge to thump my tail, letting the admiring lift of my ears speak for me.

No one did sullen like an Ervickian caught, as the expression went, smirking with the wrong lips. "Don't you care what killed that world? What it will do next?"

"The Kraal question."

How did he do that? Those words, spoken with quiet composure, sent a shiver down my spine, and I wasn't the target.

Pretty Bill looked like a being who ardently wished to be anywhere else, and quickly. His gaze slid my way. In case he wondered if he could outrun this me, I wrinkled my snout and showed my much cleaner teeth in anticipation.

Flinching, he looked back at Paul. "I was to ask for manifests and staffing lists from the Dresnet Shipyards related to the building of Stellar Explorer Class vessels ordered by the Commonwealth between ten and thirty standard years ago. How can any of that help save us?" with sincere indignation.

I'd no idea. It was as convoluted a way of sending a clue—*unless it was a message, or even a warning*—as could be imagined.

Typical Skalet.

Her use of an Ervickian—in particular this one? That, I understood. Despite there being no resemblance whatsoever, I was willing to bet Pretty Bill's crèche included Able Joe, who'd revealed S'kal-ru's stash of illicit Kraal relics, hidden in an Ervickian warehouse, to her enemy, Admiral Mocktap, exposing our secret. Ultimately ending Mocktap's life. *I could almost feel Skalet's satisfaction.*

Of course, by sending Pretty Bill the image of a devastated planet, my web-kin had, in a single stroke, done more than enlist his urgent participation. Unwittingly, Skalet had inspired his plan to preserve his lineage—a truly remarkable exhibition of forward thinking, for an Ervickian.

Not a consequence she needed to know, I decided, feeling some sympathy for the species in question.

"I don't know, Hom Bill," Paul replied. "Unfortunately, the Library does not contain such information." He glanced at me.

I nodded. The collection didn't, but Lambo Reomattatii had worked at Dresnet Shipyards before coming to the All Species' Library of Linguistics and Culture in search of Veya Ragem's secret, and it couldn't be a coincidence that Veya's ship, the *Sidereal Pathfinder,* had been of that class.

The question I could see building behind Paul's eyes as he looked at me was neither simple nor safe, but could be crucial.

Had they made more?

We'd someone to ask.

Nearby

A world couldn't just break. The evidence hung in front of him, a globe smashed into jagged pieces displayed in the center of the *Mistral*'s galley, yet Evan Gooseberry's mind refused to accept it.

He wasn't the only one struggling. The Dwelleys huddled together in the hall, refusing to enter so long as the display was up. Breaking the First Rule, Harps stood close to Evan, a hand on his shoulder as if needing support. For some reason, that helped Evan stay standing when what he'd have vastly preferred to do was find a cupboard and cower for the rest of his life.

A world . . .

Haula's cough to clear her throat was startling in the hush. "Noam. That was its name. In the Bry-Mis-Wed System. Theta-suitable, but not settled."

"Had a Kraal outpost, long ago," Poink said. "This came from a prospect servo passing through the system. No lives lost."

A lie, Evan told himself. They'd been shown a before-destruction image of Noam. There'd been life on it. The vital components that made life possible on it. All smeared along the orbital plane, chased by an orphaned moon.

"Harps. Professor Harpesseon," Strevelor said quietly. "We haven't seen a framed image. Are you certain the implant was in this system at the time of—of—" His voice failed and he ran a hand over his face.

Whatever Evan thought of him, there was no denying the faction agent was struggling like the rest of them to grasp the scale of this tragedy.

He felt Harps' grip tighten. "Yeah. Confirmed. Passerby there, when."

"They did it." Three sets of eyes locked on the display. The Contriplet's three voices spoke as one. "They did it."

Captain Clendon and Kamaara stood to the side, both grim. The captain let out a breath. "There's a probe on its way. Until it arrives, we don't know what happened. My orders are to stay on mission. Is there a new course?"

No one moved.

Evan looked down at Harps. "I think that's you," he whispered.

Green eyes looked up, unfocused and awash in unshed tears.

He gently took Harps' hand from his shoulder, keeping it in his. The extra thumb was curious; the chill of palm and fingers no surprise. He walked Harps through the ruin of Noam to the workstation, helped the professor sit, then pulled up an extra stool for himself without once letting go.

"When you're ready," Evan told him, feeling the expectations of the captain and the others as a pressure against his neck. *And how much worse was that pressure on Harps, tasked with sending them after what had destroyed a world?*

"Third Rule of Harps," the other said faintly, free hand creeping toward a low console, the motion reluctant, almost furtive.

Evan raised their joined hands to the tabletop, opening his fingers as if releasing a bird. "Don't ask?" he guessed.

A sad little chuckle. "Smart guy." But both hands set to work, flying across the console and screens for what Evan judged less than a minute before stopping. "Got it. Trace locked." A nod to the large black cylinder. "Flipped again."

"Back to the other side of the Confederacy," someone murmured in Evan's ear. *Strevelor.*

He didn't start. Managed, Evan thought with some pride, not to show any outward reaction, the prickle of sweat and sickening sway of his stomach surely common in the room. "Is that the pattern?"

"Flips to Sacriss System. Flips back to fringe past Kraal. Flip flip flip." With each "flip" Harps pounded clenched fists against the table.

Evan captured them. He held firm against unexpected strength until Harps gave it up. When he released his grip, Harps pulled loose with a fretful, "First Rule. You know the First Rule."

Don't touch.

With a nod, Evan stood and moved away. To his relief, the display had been stopped. Commander Kamaara remained where she'd been. If she paid any special attention to Strevelor, Evan couldn't tell. Instead of rushing to the bridge to input the new course, the captain was still with Haula and Poink, going over something on the latter's screen while Ionneanus loomed nearby. They appeared to be arguing—

"How's your stellar cartography, Polit?"

This time Evan did start, covering it with a grimace at Strevelor. "Not good."

"There's a difference of opinion over how best to proceed." The other lowered his voice. "One that might be resolved by consulting the Library. In private."

"I'd call at once if I could." Evan set his face to *indignant resolve.* "I was robbed."

Strevelor's blue eyes turned to ice. "On the *Mistral?*"

"Must have been on the way up." To keep Strevelor from suspecting Betts or any other innocent crew, Evan switched to *remorseful subordinate.* "I wasn't paying attention to my bag." A lie. Groggy or not, he'd kept a foot or elbow on it—Aunt Melan's good advice—except when Decker ferried all the luggage between transports, the one person with no reason to steal from him, meaning Strevelor was right. The thief was on the ship.

With his notebooks.

"I'll let you know when I've made other arrangements," Strevelor was saying. "There's time. We're not moving till they resolve this."

But they had a course— "What's the difficulty?"

"Professor Harpesseon identifies a temporary fixed point, one we need to reach before the Passerby moves again. This time?" A fleeting frown. "The most direct route goes through the Confederacy and our good captain is understandably unwilling to take it. If we skirt their space, choosing the right path could become critical. Haula's pointed out the Kraal may not be the next target. The Passerby have headed for the fringe worlds before. This time, if they don't flip back again? There's a possibility they could reach Hixtar—maybe even Botharis."

Evan's stomach lurched. "What?"

A humorless smile. "Interesting, isn't it, Polit—how so much revolves around that backwater planet. No wonder you go there so often."

He knew. Evan wasn't sure what gave him that sinking conviction, but something in Strevelor's demeanor toward him had changed. Had what had been put in his arm eavesdropped? Did it show in his face?

It didn't matter. *He wouldn't let it.*

Evan straightened, unaware of the fire in his eyes, only that he'd seconds to convince the faction agent before they were interrupted. "Whatever our differences, Commander, we've a common purpose. Contact with the Passerby—stopping this," with a gesture to where the display had been. "Do you agree?" The gesture ended in an outthrust hand.

Strevelor met it with his own, an indecipherable expression on his face. "We must protect humanity."

Was that the faction's ultimate goal? To promote Human interests in space by whatever means? *It wasn't*, Evan thought morosely, *even original*. Though his skin crawled, he shook Strevelor's hand and even gave a tiny nod the other could take as he wanted.

They had to work together.

A disturbance at the door caught Evan's eye. The steward had entered and was speaking to Commander Kamaara who pointed his way. With a nod, Betts came toward them. "We're busy," Strevelor snapped when she arrived.

"My business is with Polit Gooseberry, sir." Betts looked at him. "Polit? Message for you on the bridge. Marked urgent."

Kamaara had drifted close behind the steward. Now she swept in, taking Evan's arm in an irresistible grip. "I'll take care of it. You stay here and manage all this, Commander," she said briskly. "I'll see the polit gets his message."

Harps looked around, alarmed. Evan gave a helpless shrug. "I'll be back as soon as I can," he promised.

When they were in the hall, he shook off Kamaara's hand. "You told me to pretend. I was. You didn't have to pull me out."

"I'm not." Her scowl deepened. "Come along." She led the way down the hall to the lift; he had to half run to keep up. "There really is a message. Don't ask me how it found you on my ship."

Was something wrong at home? *Gods, not Great Gran.* Evan swallowed. "Is it—" His voice failed.

"You're to contact the All Species' Library of Linguistics and Culture at once about your inquiry." Pushing the button to open the lift doors, the *Mistral's* security chief raised an eyebrow. "Someone's in serious trouble if this *inquiry* isn't relevant to our situation—"

"It is," Evan assured her, almost giddy with relief. A shattered world? *They needed Paul and Esen.*

Now, like a gift, he had them.

12: Basement Morning; Creekside Morning

WHILE Paul and Lionel continued to interrogate Pretty Bill—the saying "an Ervickian in hand is the only one you'll catch" particularly appropriate, given he'd a starship waiting to take him beyond reach and we'd one on approach—I took the lift and went looking for Lambo on the lowermost floor of the Library basement. For reasons he hadn't explained, he'd taken over two rooms down there, the doors marked with caution tags courtesy of Zel and Travis, who did night maintenance and preferred to avoid a surprise encounter with the surly giant.

I found our Carasian behind the second tag, in a storeroom recently switched from its original purpose of housing seasonal furnishings from the Garden to hold more new-to-the-collection artifacts.

Lambo hadn't so much moved in as trashed the place. Correa's snow blowing machine had been shoved into a corner. Broken and dismembered artifacts—his habit with worthless gemmies, though he hadn't explained his reasons for that either—formed a pile halfway up one wall. But the destruction of what we'd thought to keep paled next to the sight before my astonished eyes.

Lambo was on a shelf.

He shouldn't have fit, despite the badly bent metal of the shelf above, but there he was, looking like some monstrous growth of machine bits ready to break forth and conquer the planet. *I'd watched that vid with*

Paul. Once he awoke, for the Carasian's head plates were almost closed, barely pulsing, the row of black beady eyes withdrawn into the gap. Asleep?

Pretending. What gave Lambo away wasn't so much that he'd left on the room lights, but the creaks as the shelf holding his mass reacted to uneasy shifts. He was fidgeting.

Carasians, by predilection and anatomy, weren't fond of heights, though able to leap tidal rocks and clamber short cliffs. I supposed ours, having enjoyed perching in menace from our walkway, then on the train car shelf, might have picked up a new hobby. *A disturbing one.*

Conscious of the great claw hanging in midair like the functional end of a crane, and about the same size, I stepped close. "I know you're awake." Stretching up, I aimed the words at his nearest elbow, that being where auditory organs were found in the species. There were a number of other adaptations to this terrestrial phase of their life cycle and—

Before I distracted myself, I tapped the claw gently with the pad of my knuckle. "Lam—"

He erupted from the shelf, hitting the floor like a bin full of loose pots. I jumped, hair sticking out wildly in all directions, ready to run.

He came to rest in a smug, *gotcha,* posture.

Growling under my breath, I composed myself. First Duggs, now Lambo. *What was I, a play toy?* "That was unnecessary," I informed him stiffly.

"You should knock," Lambo countered, eyestalks in a coy wave.

"Knocking doesn't work with you. You don't answer."

"Because I don't want to be disturbed." Eyestalks bent to converge on me. "This is my private place. Why are you disturbing me?"

I pointed at the artifacts he'd taken apart. "Those are—were—the Library's."

"This is my room," he stated, giving a settling shake. "Therefore everything in it is mine."

It certainly wasn't, and we'd have to do something to make sure Lambo didn't continue through the basements, claiming space at whim. At least he hadn't destroyed the snow blower. Yet.

"Why did you break them?"

"Why do you keep them?"

I'd need a Human to answer that. "Why are you down here anyway?"

"So I won't be disturbed."

Ersh. I should know better than debate with an almost-female Carasian, especially one plainly enjoying the process. Putting aside my morbid curiosity about Lambo's personal habits, *not the priority,* I refocused. "What can you tell me about Dresnet Shipyards?"

"Contact them. They also have stupid pamphlets. Go away." A claw snapped near my nose.

To my chagrin, I flinched before controlling the reflex. *Biology.* I composed myself. "I'll be more specific. Did Dresnet build the *Sidereal Pathfinder*?"

A disquieting pause. A surly, "I discuss such matters with the admirable Lionel, not you."

Revealing, if unhelpful. I eyed the adhesive dispenser clamped to the wall, envisioning gluing Lambo's head plates together—briefly, of course. *Maturity being overrated.*

"Lionel's busy," I said at last. And, we'd decided for our friend's sake, busy he'd remain till Esolesy Ki arrived to take over the touchier aspects of Carasian relations. "Paul needs this information. He's busy too," I said to forestall Lambo's logical comeback, then went on. "There's been an important new development. Regarding the Framers—"

I stopped.

A trick I'd learned from Paul. *Who'd use it shamelessly to keep me asking questions*—the point being intelligent minds—and, despite his habits, Lambo had one of the better ones—craved input as ravenously as an Ycl craved living flesh. My hint would be irresistible. I waited expectantly.

Lambo shook as if ridding himself of a pest and lumbered around to present his back.

Well, that was annoying.

I could be annoying too. Thanks to his molt, I could see my reflection in his shiny nethers, at least where there weren't streaks of dried condiments. Watching myself, I began to flip my ears up and down. Up. Down. Up. Down. This me had such excellent ears, tall and tufted. Much better ears than a Lishcyn's—

An eyestalk peered over his carapace, aimed at me. "What are you doing?" Suspiciously.

"Nothing." Up. Down. Up. Down.

Lambo clattered back around, catching me mid-Up. "Stop that."

I paused, then resumed. Down. Up. Down. Up.

"You are a dreadful mannerless creature. Yes. Yes, *Pathfinder* was built there. All Stellar Explorers were. Stop! Along with fifteen other classes of Survey starships. STOP!"

I halted my ears at *perked with interest.* "How many Explorer Class were built since *Pathfinder?*"

Lambo's eyestalks shifted evasively, as if he couldn't decide if the ceiling or floor was more fascinating. I began, slowly, to dip my ears. All eyes converged on me again. "Please. They're so—so—bendy. Stop."

I felt a rush of shame. *What was I thinking?* Well, yes, that this was the most fun I'd had in a while—and a pleasant change not to be the brunt of someone else's teasing—but I'd come on the most serious business imaginable. Why was I fooling around?

Classic Esen. I did it to avoid what was terrifying to contemplate, and I'd plenty of that, thank you, from an ancestral predator in the neighborhood to a shattered world, let along mysterious Framers and poor Evan and being a spacesick Lanivarian in a starship even if Rudy promised I could be Bess/Grace—

I could almost hear Ersh's scathing, *Where's your courage, Youngest?* At the time, referring to my continued inability to hold form without exploding, but applicable now. *Though exploding had its appeal.*

"A scholar brought us that question, Lambo, along with—" I paused to swallow. "—a Framer image of a planet, recently destroyed. We need to—"

"A world?" All at once, Lambo's posture altered, slumping into a limp *you have my attention, so I'll get comfy.* Carasians were refreshingly non-subtle. "Curator, I request access to the image and all data pertaining."

"You'll have it as soon as Paul and Lionel are done," I promised. "About the ships?"

"Only one thing matters now, the Passerby. I must contact the *Mistral* with this information. We're tracking the *Pathfinder* implant—"

"Stop." My ears flattened. "What are you talking about?" *The* Mistral? *Pathfinder implant?* "Start with who's 'we'? It isn't us, is it?" Hairs rose on my neck. "Making you someone else."

"Yes." Lambo gave himself a dainty shake, resting his great claws on the floor in a confusingly conciliatory posture. When he replied, his voice had dropped, reverberating inside this me's chest cavity. *Not the most pleasant sensation.* "Curator, given the increased urgency to the situation, we must work together. It is time I told the truth."

His eyestalks sagged and he heaved a melodramatic clatter. "I am not a qualified food dispenser operator."

Hardly a revelation, but— I sat abruptly, staring at the giant being. "Or a stardrive engineer?"

"I am that, Curator, which is why I was selected." As abruptly as I'd sat, the Carasian's vocal patterns altered almost unrecognizably. "What will seem egregious transgressions to you, given our perceived relationship, were functions of my duty, yet I am despondent to have deceived such extraordinary beings as yourself, Lionel, and Paul." To demonstrate, not only did his eyestalks resume sagging, but a great claw rolled over, limp, as if Lambo had no strength left to hold it.

"Deceived us how?"

"I'm a Commonwealth operative, working for Survey. A spy, in the Human vernacular."

I blinked. "In the All Species Library of Linguistics and Culture. On Botharis." It was ridiculous.

Unless it made too much sense.

"Not only here. My original assignment was on Dresnet, where I investigated a splinter group channeling Survey funds into forbidden research, research used in the *Sidereal Pathfinder*."

It was as if Paul whispered in my ear. "The Intrepid Few."

"That's classified at the highest level." Lambo tensed which for the species involved a spasm ending in rigid eyestalks and open claws. "How did you know?" said in a dramatic whisper.

"I didn't. Not till now." Either Lambo wasn't a particularly good spy, or his kind faced serious disadvantages in the role. *Focus.* "Lionel showed me their invitation before he tossed it."

"Lionel Kearn." Eyestalks flexed. "A person of interest."

Part of me was ready to leap to all fours and show serious teeth in

Lionel's defense, which wasn't as futile a threat as it might seem since I could grab an eyestalk before Lambo crushed me in a claw. *Maybe.*

Of course, if there was imminent crushing I'd cycle—or explode— *Not helpful.* I'd stick to words.

"We know you're interested in Lionel," I retorted. "You want him to build a pool. For the female you."

Claws hit the floor. "What? With a—a *squishy SNACK*—? Never!"

Though I'd a certain empathy, I didn't let it show. "He'll be disappointed."

"And you are deliberately evasive." Lambo's eyestalks formed a skeptical row. "The splinter group is a dangerous faction within the Intrepid Few, unknown to the rest. With Kearn's Survey record—what is it, Curator?"

I lowered the paw I'd raised to interrupt. "Lionel's record—" *was my fault,* "—is that of an officer seeking the truth, and I assure you the only contact he's had is to refuse their overtures." *I was starting to talk like our spy.* "Lionel Kearn has my complete trust." And, more impressively, Skalet's.

An eyestalk bent. "He named a monster after you."

"A mistake, rectified." *People kept bringing that up.* "Back to Paul's mother's ship. So you did come for her logbook."

"I did not. We already had it." A dismissive rumble. "With the coordinates Veya had been supplied by her captain, but not her implant-driven translight course to get there, a course she was, upon recapture by the faction, ordered to repeat on the *Azimuth Explorer.* Which is what provoked the Passerby."

"Provoked who?" I held up my paw again. "Wait. Let's start with what's not possible—Veya died on the *Smokebat.*" Lionel'd looked into the accident reports. Rudy and Paul's Group had searched for evidence, understandably minimal when ships collided in orbit, the remnants burning up in atmosphere. *Paul had gone quiet. The unhappy quiet I couldn't fix—*

"Veya Ragem sold her ident years before the accident."

And the only surprise was we hadn't seen it, though now I had to suspect Skalet had and failed to share. *Family.* We'd some excuse. "Veya" had left behind a spotty but clear trail, supported by what Stefan had told her son.

Based on what the real Veya told Stefan two years after *Pathfinder*'s accident. Hadn't he described her as afraid, desperate, and angry?

Meaning she'd been running from the faction while we'd been safe and happy on Minas XII. *How did I tell my friend?*

"How did they find her?" I asked numbly. But I knew, didn't I. Veya had kept searching for Paul. Had risked leaving her message for him where those hunting her—as I'd hunt a mousel—had lain in wait.

"It doesn't matter." A claw snapped, making an ominous low ring. "To hide what they'd done, the faction intercepted incoming Passerby messages from the authorities as long as they could." Eyestalks focused on me. "By the way, referring to them as Framers? Silly name. Too obvious."

Bad Thing. Still the best. I waved him past it.

"When at last those images were leaked to Survey, we learned the first Passerby message—an image of the *Sidereal Pathfinder*—had come to the faction at Dresnet's research facility after the *Azimuth Explorer* entered translight. That ship was never seen again and is presumed lost. That's when my mission—all missions—changed from a focus on the faction's activities to learning what—who—they'd disturbed."

The Null. Not the moment to introduce our *extradimensional space monster with lightning tentacles* to Lambo.

Who hadn't stopped talking anyway. "Others undertook different avenues of investigation. I was tasked with clarifying Veya Ragem's history and her connection to those two ships. The *Azimuth*'s mission didn't take place until she was found, confirming the importance of her implant to the faction. When the person most important to Veya in life reappeared, I came here to find out."

"Paul." There might have been the hint of a snarl.

"I wasn't the only one," Lambo rumbled righteously. "Lionel Kearn arrived—whom you say you trust—followed by the Johnsson criminal sent by the faction's cleaner."

"Their what?" *I needed more spy terms.* Not that I wanted them.

"One or more individuals charged with preemptively destroying evidence. I see you require proof, Curator."

Lionel would. I didn't. I believed Lambo because he'd answered our most troubling question: why the Commonwealth, that conglomeration of disparate Human interests, had stayed silent about the images sent by the Framers—the Passerby. They hadn't known.

Because a tiny self-absorbed *faction* had decided to hide the truth to protect their petty interests.

Ersh-memory held an abundance of small groups of nasty-minded Humans who hid in plain sight within organizations and governments until caught with digits where they didn't belong. Not to say Humans were the only species infested with conspiracies, selfish behaviors, or poor manners—*just visit a Queeb spa*—but according to the Eldest of us, who should know, Humans had maintained an exceptional talent for it since rising to balance on two feet.

At least now Survey was on to them, though I wasn't impressed their first move had been to plant a spy in our Library.

Whatever were we to do with him?

Meanwhile, the Carasian had lumbered to the broken gemmies for my "proof." He began disassembling the pile by rapidly tossing gemmies over his carapace with all four claws.

To avoid being buried under a rain of plas and metal pieces, I jumped onto the shelf he'd vacated. The door out of reach, this also gave me some distance from those claws if Lambo had, as his actions suggested, gone berserk. *Safety first.*

Then I glimpsed what the pile had been hiding. A console of the Skalet-variety, black and ominous, with a thick pipe leading into a jagged hole in the wall that looked regrettably familiar. "Better fix that before Duggs finds out," I warned.

A terse rattle answered, Lambo preoccupied with tapping controls. Controls he wasn't letting me see, positioning himself in front. Two eyestalks bent to watch me in case I tried sneaking up for a peek.

Professional paranoia.

If Lambo thought to remain the Chow's operator and our sometime head of security—*which was beyond ironic*—we'd have to treat him as before, but Paul knew I wasn't very good at—

Lambo spun on the spot, crushing gemmie bits, and thrust out a handling claw. "Here. Take this." Pinned between his clawtips was a flexible sheet of plas.

I stayed on the shelf. "Does it blow up?"

"I'm not that kind of operative," he said stiffly. "Take it."

There were kinds? I wondered if Lionel knew anything about spies, knew Skalet did, then decided I'd better run the question by Paul first. Along with everything else.

I jumped down, landing without a sound to demonstrate it was possible, and rose to take the sheet, expecting another dreadful Framer image.

It was an image, but unframed and unposed: an instant captured as a Human female looked back from within a group of similarly uniformed individuals, moving up a dockside gangway. Older than the rest, the right side of her face bubbled with scars from midcheek to hairline, the eye covered in a patch, lips thin and twisted.

I wouldn't have recognized her but for her left eye. It was the gray of her son's and stared out at me, its expression so bleak and hopeless I whined.

Veya Ragem.

"Lambo, go to Lionel's office and wait for him there," I ordered with commendable calm. "You'll apologize when you see him and report everything you know."

He rattled into an aggressive stance, claws out. "I must contact the *Mistral!*"

I flattened my ears in threat at the enormous, armored creature. "Either you work for us, or you work for them. I suggest you choose who you think can stop another planet being destroyed, because that's what's at stake, Lambo. Not Human squabbles."

Ears still flat, mostly because I wasn't sure I could lift them but also to add dignity, I stalked around him and left.

I figured the odds were fifty-to-fifty he'd choose us.

But Lionel could tip the scale.

Paul spotted me across the bustling Lobby, head lifting as he read *trouble* in what he saw. I didn't waste time trying to come to him. After a quick word to Lionel, who couldn't help but glance in my direction before returning his attention to our Ervickian, my friend headed for me.

I wished I could be glad he was. Wished I'd anything but the news

I brought, but such wistful thinking, as Ersh would say, was because I was Youngest.

As I'd be forever unless I budded in some unimaginable future. I certainly didn't see Lesy or Skalet giving it a try—

"I'm here," Paul said, interrupting my inner babble.

Instead of speaking, I angled my ears in a *follow me* and led him from the crowd.

The first Ragems, either inordinately fond of their name or feeling the vast aloneness of a new planet, had bestowed it upon a number of local landmarks. Most notably, there was Ragem Farm, but also a Ragem Hill, Ragem's Last Valley—named after an adventurer who'd gone into the nearby mountains only to die of starvation—and, running cheerfully alongside the Library, the delightful little Ragem Creek.

During snowmelt, Ragem Creek gained pretensions of riverhood, snarling at its banks and generally misbehaving. Before the Library opened, I'd had its surging waters to myself. Not this me. Another me altogether, and Lesy wasn't wrong to want to swim as a Rrabi'sk. The pure joy of it—

—wasn't worth the risk, now that we'd busy foot and groundcar traffic on Ragem Road, which ran alongside the creek, as well as people lingering on Ragem Bridge to admire the sparkling water. Awkward enough to explain a pair of aliens gamboling in it, without those being of a species gone extinct before there were Ragems at all.

Where the creek curled around the edge of the Garden, however, was a place no one casually roamed—mostly because of lurid signs warning of the perils of approaching the Library's bio-eliminator field. It was to protect the Garden's residents from spreading over Botharis and vice versa, and we'd told Skalet to set it not to fry stray livestock or children. In case she'd thought we were joking, Duggs erected a fence to mark its outer limit.

You had to walk along the fence, past more dire signs, to reach the spot where Ragem Creek widened and slowed into a pond. There'd been a mill here once, and on part of its stone ruin perched an ominous gray metal box. Those who didn't know assumed it was part of the field generator and thus even more reason to avoid the spot entirely, but the box, despite appearances, was harmless. Other than its contents, for inside were stored the nets and sticks and shoes with knife edges and whatever else Humans required for the game of hockey, this portion of Ragem Creek, when safely frozen, being claimed for that purpose by our staff. And Paul.

Today, in the sultry warmth of late spring, the banks were soggy with the remnants of flooding and the air full of what liked to bite anything with blood. Paul followed me without a word, but his concern was palpable, knowing how much this me detested both damp and biters—unless I could catch them in my teeth. To bring him here meant I'd something to say I didn't want anyone to overhear or record.

I hoped that was true, that this place, with its memories of stone and water, was truly private. My only other choice had been to go under the barn into the collection, which had all the pleasant atmosphere of a giant comp bank, being one.

Reaching the first foundation stone, I jumped lightly to the next, and sat.

Paul stood on the soft ground in front of me, putting our eyes on the same level. *He was thoughtful like that.* Or wanted a good view of my expression. *Also likely.* He was framed in soft greens and browns, the pond behind him reflecting the leaves and branches arched overhead, and looked no longer as much worried as patient. Kind.

Meaning he'd concluded this was about me and my unwieldy family, and was ready to comfort and offer help.

Sure enough. "Lionel heard from Skalet. She's all right, Old Blob," Paul assured me. "Her place among the Kraal remains strong. She's in a position to influence fleet movements and plans to mount a defense against the Null. Who she believes is working with the Framers." He clapped, *!!*mementos*!!*

Trust my cynical web-kin to leap immediately to the conclusion that everything was out to get us. *Might not be wrong.* We'd have to deal with what Skalet meant by "mount a defense" later.

"Skalet's not why I brought you here." I lowered my ears.

Paul tensed. "Why did you?"

"Your mother," I said. "I know what happened to her. Most of it, anyway. Lambo told me. He's a spy."

"I was right?" Incredulously.

"You knew?" With the same note in my voice.

Paul shook his head. "No. I—I was talking to Lionel—go on. Tell me about Lambo the spy."

"It doesn't matter—well, it does, but you need to hear this first." And rather than drag it out bit by painful bit, as Lambo had, I told my friend what I'd learned from the Carasian. Should Paul decide to check aspects of the story later, he could do so. For me, what mattered was telling Paul what might finally be the truth.

Whatever went wrong, the crew did abandon the *Pathfinder,* the ship was lost—until the Framers/Passerby/Bad Thing found it—and Veya?

What we hadn't known, what Paul hadn't until I sat on a stone to tell him, was that his mother had been a fugitive. Whether she'd fled because she discovered she was working for an illegal faction or not, we couldn't know.

From the scars on her face, she'd been desperate to remove their implant and, when she couldn't, decided to vanish. *Not a speculation I shared.* Paul could reach his own.

I told Paul how Veya had put her ident and credentials on the black market. Comprehension flashed across his dear face: it hadn't been his mother who died on the ill-fated *Smokebat.* It wasn't a comfort, given the rest I had to say.

At some point, the real Veya came to Botharis to leave Starfield the Very Strange Pony, wrapped in her space fabric, in the family oak for her son, left a message with his father, then prepared to vanish again.

The middle of the story—where else she'd gone, who else she'd been—was missing, but we'd the end. Veya was found, her implant intact, and forced on board the *Azimuth Explorer,* a ship identical to the *Pathfinder.*

A ship never seen again, lost with all hands.

Paul didn't interrupt, his expression changing from dismay to hope to horror.

He didn't speak when I finished and gave him her picture.

I kept still to wait for him to process it all—which wasn't easy as various annoying small things took advantage to dig through my fur and *bite*—knowing the last thing my friend needed right now was me twitching. Or scratching. Or rotating a hip—

He folded the plas sheet, slipping it inside his shirt. "Someone gave the order to chase her down." His hands folded into fists. "I want that name."

I'd been prepared for anguish and grief, even a deserved amount of anger at our Carasian, who'd taken his sweet time telling us what was Paul's right to know. *This*—I struggled to hold form, seeing in my dearest friend's face what I'd never seen there before. Hate.

It didn't belong. Rising to all fours, I curled my lips and flattened my ears at him, ready to bite if necessary. "No."

"Esen—"

"Don't you growl at me," I snapped, ears still flat. "People behaved badly and your mother suffered. Ersh knows, people are always behaving badly and others suffer for it. Not just Human people," I added, to be fair and having Skalet in my Web. "What's rare and precious are those who help. Who care. People like you."

His hands stayed fists, his face in harsh strange lines, but he was listening. After a too-long pause, he gritted out, "We can't let them get away with this."

The "we" eased some of the tension from my spine. "We don't know they have," I pointed out. "Everyone on the *Azimuth Explorer* was lost."

"Because they made her do it again—follow *Pathfinder's* course—straight to the Null—" All at once, his voice changed. "Gods, Es, how did I miss it . . ."

Ears less flat, I tilted my head. "Miss what?"

Paul staggered forward, his feet having sunk into the mud, and buried his fingers deep in my neck ruff, using that less than comfortable grip to bring our noses close. His eyes were wild. "Why *Pathfinder?* Why that image first? Why the struggle between this way and Sacriss—don't you see, Es? It's my mother!"

"It's her eyeball," I said, as cautiously as I'd step on the first fragile skin of ice on the pond behind him. *Not that I would, but the awareness of imminent disaster was distressingly the same.*

"No. Listen to me. Skalet's wrong. When the Null caught their ship, the crew could have been rescued by the Passerby. That could be why they've sent the images—to tell us there are survivors! Es—what if—what if she's alive?"

So now we were using Survey's word? Did Paul think it somehow made what was out there more reasonable? *Body bits in bulkheads*—I stifled a whine in my throat.

One thing I did know. My friend wasn't thinking clearly and it was my turn to help him. "If they'd saved the crews," I said gently but firmly, "why not send images of people instead of ships?"

His grip eased. He pressed his forehead to mine and the eye I could see was squeezed shut. His voice was almost too quiet for even my ears. "You think I'm a fool, wishing for the impossible."

"You're Human," I reminded him. "It's a species' trait." Then I stretched my tongue to lick his chin. "We won't learn the truth here. Lambo told me the *Mistral* has a way to track the Passerby, so that's where we'll go, together."

An eye opened, gray and shining. "Dear Old Blob. How do you do it?"

Paul being overwrought, I didn't try to puzzle out what I'd done this time. *It didn't appear to be wrong.*

"We're friends." I poked my cold nose into his neck to make him jump.

Failing to remember what poor comfort the truth could be.

Pretty Bill was on the train back to the landing field, Lionel reported by com sometime later, along with one of Skalet's minuscule tracking devices firmly stuck inside a neck crease should we need to find him again. I'd a feeling he'd done it more so my web-kin could find him again, but we'd each had our loyalties.

Mine was clear. I followed Paul to his office—where I watched him do things at his desk he didn't explain—and followed him out again, determined to keep following until convinced my friend was over the shock and himself again.

To be thwarted by his turn into the staff accommodation. Undaunted, I tried to sneak through the door only to meet his hip, strategically blocking the opening. "I can manage on my own," Paul informed me. "Why don't you check on the Response Room?"

As if we hadn't learned terrible things and drawn dreadful conclusions. I regarded him suspiciously. "What will you be doing?"

A finger tapped my nose gently. "Don't worry, Fangface. I've set some things in motion ahead of us. We'll be ready." About to close the door, Paul hesitated, glancing around as if to be sure we were alone.

That never boded well. "What is it?"

"The *Largas Swift* has landed. We'll lift as soon as Nia can get the cargo to the field. Tonight, with luck. Esen—"

I stepped back, unsure why, unless it was because we'd run out of time. Esolesy Ki's arrival. Our journey *out there.* All to start within hours. "I'd better check on Lesy."

"I'm sorry there won't be a goodbye party."

It was like Paul, to think of such things. "I didn't enjoy the last one," I confessed. "Don't tell Henri," I added hastily. Having staff celebrate one me being replaced by another me had brought a decidedly pleasant opportunity to indulge in treats, but the event had been deeply confusing. As before, I'd still be here.

Just not as the me some of them, being Human, liked better, making it a goodbye to their confidences and affection, even trust.

Paul nodded. "I understand."

I knew he did, as I knew something else. I stepped close again to lick his chin. "I'm glad you don't have a favorite me." *Even if I did.*

"Es—" He stopped, looking past me. "What is it, Henri?"

She stopped so fast curls bounced on her forehead, grinning joyfully. "Our Evan's on the com! It's shunted to your office."

I looked at Paul, he looked at me.

We both set off at a run.

Having four legs, I'd get there first.

Nearby

PAUL and Esen knew what he'd decided to tell them. Skalet knew what he'd decided to tell her. Then her "gift" to them all proved to be the image of ruined Noam and a clue, and Esen, after meeting with Lambo, had shown up wild-eyed and grim to take Paul aside.

Lionel Kearn found the floor—*or was it his moral compass?*—remarkably unsteady as he made his way to his office, having seen Pretty Bill to the train.

He'd never imagine he'd filter communications between Esen and her sister, much less become the nexus of their secrets, but there were times—*this certainly one*—when someone had to protect them from one another. *Someone thoroughly expendable.* The thought came with its own grim gratification.

Had Skalet learned Paul and Esen planned to bring a Kraal missile warhead to their meeting with the Null, she'd interfere to extricate her web-kin, with possibly disastrous consequences to everyone else.

Had Esen known Skalet warned them off Botharis in order for her Kraal to take any and all measures against the Null without regard for Paul's home and those living on it, she'd blow S'kal-ru's cover and make her run for her life.

Then there was Lesy—

He'd done the right thing, Lionel told himself, giving Skalet other information to digest. Evan Gooseberry and the *Mistral*. As he didn't know what the young diplomat was doing on board, nor how Survey was tracking the Null, these were things she'd need to discover. Unsaid, but hopefully implied? That being on the same side, against the Null, should—*might*—keep the Kraal from an unfortunate reaction should *Mistral* stray too close after its target.

At least delay the orders.

Duggs, coming toward Lionel down the corridor, glanced into his office as she passed the open door. She missed a step, a hand going to her mouth, then continued on by him not saying a word.

Her eyes were suspiciously gleeful.

What now? Lionel wondered.

He heard the sound of crashing furniture and broke into a run.

Lionel Kearn closed his door and activated the lock for the first time since— *It didn't matter.* He waited for the next crash of furniture behind him to subside before turning to face his visitor.

Lambo Reomattatii crouched, caught with a chair dangling from a great claw, outstretched as if to move the item to a safer distance. The second chair in front of the administrator's desk was in pieces beneath a balloon-shaped foot. *Had he tried to* sit *in it?*

When Lionel didn't move, the Carasian very slowly set the intact chair down. It teetered, almost stilled, then toppled with a bang.

Lambo reached for it again.

"Leave it," the Human ordered, going to stand behind his desk.

With a barely audible clatter, and a loud *crack* of breaking wood, his visitor shuffled his bulk around to face him. "The curator sent me to confess to you." Claws drooped to rest on the floor. There was barely a gleam to his eyes; even his carapace lacked shine.

"I do hope you haven't damaged another part of the Library," Lionel said fatalistically, nodding to his stack of complaints.

"No. Well, yes, technically, I suppose, but that's not why I'm here. I'm to tell you the truth. I'm a Survey operative—"

Lionel sat rather hastily.

"—sent to investigate the clandestine faction within the Intrepid Few." A pause punctuated by a delicate *chime* from a handling claw. "And your connection to the faction, if any."

The social club? Lionel collected himself. "I've none." Though if they posed a risk, in future perhaps he should.

Eyestalks sagged. "As the curator assured me. I'm to apologize for my suspicions, Administrator Kearn, and hereby do so." A claw came almost timidly over his desk, a disk between its tips. "I've prepared a report for you of my actions and findings regarding what happened to the *Sidereal Pathfinder* and Veya Ragem and the resulting provocation by the faction of the unknown dangerous species Survey refers to as the Passerby, a better name than *Framers*. Everything's there."

Lionel took it as if it might explode. *Given the contents, the result might be equally messy.* "Thank you. I'll review this—I'll have questions."

"They must wait. First I must choose—" Lambo rumbled abruptly, eyestalks chaotic, "—between loyalty to Survey or the Library. Human squabbles don't matter when planets are being destroyed."

Exceptional. Esen was behind this. She'd a gift for reducing problems to their crux. Careful to keep his expression neutral, Lionel leaned back, putting the disk on his desk despite his burning desire to view its contents. Four eyestalks lowered to follow the disk, then returned to his face. When Lambo remained silent, Lionel prodded quietly, "And have you? Chosen?"

"I seek your advice on the matter, Administrator Kearn. You are the most rational individual available to me. That," with a claw snap, "is the sum basis of my appreciation for you. Any suggestion I might retain interest in any squishy beyond future value as a snack is puerile and unwelcome."

"Of course." Lionel hid his relief. He touched the disk. "If I access the materials in here, doubtless classified, and Survey found out, your decision is made for you, is it not? You'd be finished as an operative. Probably charged."

"They would not find out. I am too intelligent." Lambo gave a smug little shake. "But if they did, I would claim you found my datafiles and stole them."

"I could claim you sold them to me—but what matters to Survey is the exposure of their secrets. Trust me, they don't forgive that." He pushed the disk back to the Carasian.

Eyestalks bent to stare at it in seeming disbelief.

Lionel coughed delicately, regaining Lambo's attention. "Let's start fresh, shall we? I propose to give you information I believe you do not possess, relevant to the situation facing us. Based on its value, you shall decide where to put your allegiance. With them or us."

"The primary goal is to stop the depredations of the Passerby, one that transcends mere Human politics." Great claws rose into the air. Opened and closed. Lowered. "I accept. Provide this information."

The wording had to be precise—*and ideally avoid terms like monster*, Lionel thought ruefully. Lambo would know his history.

"We have learned through the collection that there are two forces involved in the current situation. One, and deadly, is the Null. The Null disrupt a starship's passage through translight, then steal the energy from a ship's drives and destroy any life on board. The Sacrissee," he elaborated, "were the first we know to suffer such attacks. The second is whomever is sending framed images of those ships, presumably to warn us of the Null." *Or not.* "Your Passerby. A species yet to make contact in any other way. Unless Survey knows differently?"

"If so, I am not informed." Eyestalks lined up, all staring at Lionel in obvious astonishment. "This is new and critical information. I underestimated the resources of the Library. I choose to work with you."

"Not so fast." Lionel steepled his fingertips under his chin. "The question is, do we want you? You've lied to us, Lambo."

"I was a spy."

Was, not is. Promising. Lionel pinned the disk to his desk with a finger's tip. His free hand brought forth the small needler he'd collected from Skalet's wall that morning, leveling it at the Carasian. A solitary eyestalk bent to study it and Lionel thumbed the control.

Red light limned the outermost edge of the bulky torso and head plates, indicating the extent of the beam's coverage should he press the trigger, prompting the rest of Lambo's eyestalks to bend and twist in alarm. "Administrator, I feel you are overreacting—"

"I have concerns," Lionel said evenly. "Foremost among them, what if Survey and the Library—Paul and Esen—find themselves at odds?

You make a choice today. What's to stop you making a different one in future?"

Lambo appeared to swell. "I will swear my allegiance to you by the Never Sandy Third Armpit of Ramki the Enormous. If I ever fail you or the Library, I will be unable to procreate and be cast out to die in shame."

That would definitely do, especially as he'd activated the recording in this room. Lionel thumbed off the needler and tucked it away. "Do you so swear?"

"I—"

There was a polite knock on the door. Lambo's eyestalks bent backwards. "The door—"

"Ignore it," Lionel ordered after a look at the time. Teatime. Whoever it was on staff intending to take their break here would come back later. "Swear, Lambo Reomattatii."

The Carasian stretched to his full height, great claws open and aimed at an acute angle, pulled in his eyestalks within his head plates, and spun around. Deafened by the clang and clatter, the Human jumped back as the first spin demolished the remaining guest chair and the next ripped out the front half of his desk.

"Is this necessary?" Lionel shouted.

A third spin, and Lambo came to a stop, teetering wildly. To Lionel's consternation, as eyestalks reappeared, they split and the Carasian's usually hidden jaws protruded, glistening. Before he had to worry about the wisdom of accepting what looked like the intimate gesture by offering his hand to a dizzy giant, the jaws retracted and Lambo lifted his great claws, now reassuringly closed, and touched them tip to tip. "I swear by the Never Sandy Third Armpit of Ramki the Enormous to be loyal to Administrator Lionel Kearn and the All Species' Library of Linguistics and Culture until death," he intoned in a voice like thunder.

With an embarrassed-seeming rattle, he tidied his bulk and sat. "Satisfied?"

He'd need new office furniture and, from the renewed knocking on his door, would have to explain the ruckus to now-alarmed staff, but they'd gained a Survey operative with connections.

Admirable. Lionel smiled and nodded. "Welcome to the Library."

"I won't work at the Anytime Chow, of course," Lambo the former spy informed him. "That contract was obtained through Survey. I'll need a new job."

That Duggs burst through his once-locked door at that moment, hammer raised and swearing, seemed, to Lionel Kearn, like poetry.

"I've got just the thing," he assured the Carasian. "If you'll wait outside for a moment please? I need to talk to our head contractor."

Once sure they were alone, Lionel let out a long, shaky breath.

Duggs raised an eyebrow. "Do I want know what that was?"

"Not really." He went to a cupboard to pull out a bottle and two glasses, holding them up in invitation.

"Do I want to know how Nia's going to keep those Preservation Pups at bay without Paul and Esen here?" She grunted unhappily. "There's stuff in this place that gives me the shakes."

Lionel poured, leaving the bottle on what remained of his desk. *They might need it.* "We'll deal with them," he said, offering her a glass. The dark liquid within caught the light.

"Huh." Duggs set her hammer on the floor, took the glass, and tossed back the contents in a single gulp. Holding it out for a refill, she pointed an accusing finger at him. "You let those Pups glimpse that crazy Carasian and we're good as done."

He chuckled as he poured her another.

She scowled. "Not funny."

"Lambo's kept his skulking after hours off the snoops since arriving. Not even—" About to say Skalet, he changed to the safer, "—Paul's figured out how. I think we can trust him to keep out of sight."

"Nope." Duggs shook her head at him. "Not trusting that angry excuse for a crab. Never did." She toed a piece of chair. "What's this about? I allowed to know that?"

"If you wish." Lionel felt his face harden. "Lambo lied to us. He came under false pretenses. He's confessed he was here hunting information about Paul's mother—classified projects she'd done for Survey."

"Confessed, did he." Putting the drink down, Duggs crossed her arms across her middle, resting her chin on her chest. Her eyes half closed. "A bit out of character."

"A change of heart. Hearts," Lionel corrected. *Esen had given the Carasian his reason: a world laid waste.* She'd known. The species thought in terms of legacy and morality. Though with Lambo? For all he knew, there was even a degree of empathy between those head plates. Or healthy self-preservation.

He considered for a long moment before speaking again. "Shipping Lambo out is a last resort. I'd prefer to find a better solution. One that offers a chance at redemption—and to prove it—while keeping our Carasian under observation."

"Luck with that," Duggs asserted affably. "Don't care how handy those claws are—with that temper, he's a damn menace."

Handy, indeed. "And they're powerful," Lionel responded. "Precise. Did you know Lambo can pick up a spoon with his great claws?"

"I can open a bottle with my elbow. So what?" With a challenging glare.

She knew what he hinted at—*knew and, typical Duggs, made him work for it.* "You cheat at cards," Lionel accused, playing along.

Her arms unfolded, and she blew dismissively across the fingertips of one hand. "I repeat. So what."

"I find it highly unlikely anyone could trick you."

A jab of her finger. "Don't butter me up, Beetle Eyes. I am not putting your problem on my crew."

Unless . . . the word not spoken aloud, but her eyelids had cracked open. Most significantly, her outrage was verbal. Duggs wasn't storming from his office.

Lionel leaned a hip on an intact edge of his desk. "One more?"

Time to negotiate.

Out There

ALL hardware is classified and the property of Survey. The installation is for the trial period only. Your eye will be stored and reattached upon your return. Is that understood?
What if I break it, sir?
You can't. But if you happen to expire before the end of the trial, the hardware will be retrieved, your remains analyzed and discarded, and your next-of-kin provided with a credible cover story. Is that understood?
Good to know, sir.
Last chance—

The memory shard spins away. The next spins into view, filled with his face. Gray eyes. Black hair, tumbling over a high forehead. A lip between teeth. He's concentrating—on what Veya can't tell, can't remember, should know—but none of that matters. She tries to turn it away, knowing it's the trap.

Destination acquired. But—there's something in the way again—
I swear it—
You've warned us. We've proximity alerts, Navigator, and the crew's prepared. Engage translight drive on my go. Three—

How Hell learns, if it does learn or inanely repeats similar actions, she's unable to comprehend. All she knows is where it aims her eye, what it makes her see—

<u>Two—</u>

—is where it goes—

<u>One—Engage.</u>

13: Library Morning; Farmhouse Afternoon

W E passed Duggs hurrying along the corridor with a hammer in hand, for reasons I hoped had to do with construction and not expressing her opinion, went by Lionel's surprisingly closed door—hearing sounds inside suggestive of construction, or perhaps its opposite, not that I was aware of any work needing to be done—and arrived at Paul's office.

My friend rushed to his desk. I hovered at his shoulder, quivering. Our eyes met. "The *Mistral*'s translight com is on the bridge," Paul reminded me, finger paused over the com button.

I took a breath and calmed myself. "So others will be listening." Others being the captain and bridge crew. "Saves time."

My friend's lips quirked to the side. "That it will. First, though. Lionel's played it that Evan's posed a question to the Library. What would it be?"

He asked me? "You're the Human."

"You're his friend."

"He likes you better."

Paul actually blushed. "That doesn't count, Es. C'mon. You know how Evan thinks."

We might share a predilection or two, our Evan and me. Paul didn't have to say it. "Evan saw the framed images," I responded, thinking hard. "And he knows the Sacrissee are afraid. He'd ask—" *Suddenly, I was sure.* "—what in the Vast Out scared them so much they blended a carnivore's genome into their next generation."

My friend's eyes lit up. "Yes. That's his question. And now we've the answer, don't we?"

"An extradimensional space monster with lightning tentacles?"

His lips tightened, then he surprised me with a curt nod. "Put it out there, Es. They're chasing a monster. They have to know it."

This wasn't going to go well.

Giving me what I'm sure he thought was an encouraging look, Paul pressed the com button. "Director Ragem and Curator Esen-alit-Quar here."

"Paul. Esen! Is Esolesy with you?" Evan's voice, but the relief in it was stronger than I'd expected. I slanted my ears. *He was in trouble.*

Hearing it too, Paul frowned. "Esolesy's returning shortly." Much as we wanted to know if Evan was all right, my friend wisely kept it professional. "Esen has the response to your inquiry: what in the Vast Out scared the Sacrissee so much they hired Molancor Genomics to blend a carnivore's genome into their next generation?"

"Yes. That was it." Perhaps the com distorted the words; they had an unfamiliar edge.

Paul gestured to me. I wrinkled my snout in futile protest. He gestured again, raising his eyebrows.

Fine. "Hello, Evan," I said. "The Sacrissee were frightened by an attack that happened fifty-two years ago. Ship engines were drained of energy and—" I looked to my friend. He nodded encouragement. "—and they found the bodies of the crews embedded in the bulkheads, as if something had tried to pull them out through the metal."

A gasp came through the com.

"We know what it was," I continued—no point in stopping now. "A rare space creature called a Null. The Null exist within translight corridors and trap—" *Web-beings* "—their prey with filaments of energy. This one has learned to trap ships."

"You're saying—are you saying . . ." Evan's voice trailed away, then came back in a rush. "That's there's a monster out there. An extradimensional monster with—with lightning tentacles."

I shot a look at Paul, who gave a *wasn't me* shrug. I suppose the description couldn't be avoided.

"Yes, Evan," my friend stated in an emphatic, *here be monsters* tone. "What's left ships derelict isn't an undiscovered intelligent species. It's a force of nature and as such can't be reasoned with. Warn the captain against approaching the Null until we know more. In the strongest terms."

"Commander Kamaara is listening." Evan went on, sounding like a person standing on a precipice. "How powerful are these Null? Can they destroy a planet?"

This time I gave the *wasn't me* ear flip; the day I was consulted on Skalet's decisions who to inform I'd explode from shock.

"If you know about Noam," Paul replied with care, "you understand the importance of taking the Null and the risk they pose with the utmost seriousness."

Which wasn't a yes but wasn't a no and certainly gave away that we already knew what they knew. *That we hadn't known they knew till now.* I blinked wistfully at Paul, relying on him to keep all this straight.

I heard Evan's heavy, stressed breaths, then couldn't, indicating he'd hit the mute to consult with someone else.

All at once, he was back. "If the Null are non-sentient, who sent the images?"

"We're pursuing that line of inquiry offplanet," my friend said with enviable smoothness. "I propose we meet, Evan, to combine our efforts. This is a threat beyond the norm."

There was an understatement. I flipped an ear at him, startled by his wink. *Was Paul enjoying this?* I supposed, to a Human, there was something positive about finally making progress.

As the one whose flesh was at stake, I could wait.

I might know Evan, but Paul Ragem understood how those in command of ships thought, because the next voice wasn't Evan's yet was very familiar indeed.

"Agreed. This is Commander Kamaara. On my authority I'm sending coordinates for our rendezvous, Director. Respond with your arrival estimate as soon as you have it. Do yourselves a favor and don't share with anyone."

Translight. *Trapdoors.*

My tail slipped between my legs. "Keep us away from the Null," I broke in, not keeping *anxious* from my voice.

When she replied, her tone had changed. "Understood, Curator. *Mistral* out."

I shook my head in protest so vigorously it sent my ears flapping. "I wanted to talk to Evan."

Paul came around his desk, eyes alight. "No time to chat, Fangface. We'll be seeing him as soon as we can.

"It's time to get out there."

Before we left Botharis to meet the *Mistral* and together hunt the Null— which sounded even more like the plot of a vid than tossing it a *missile-plus-me* snack—we had to begin Lesy's impersonation of Esolesy Ki.

So we could jump into a starship and enter a translight corridor, a corridor where above all we had to hope the Null wasn't lurking in wait to gobble us all.

Including Evan, who had monsters of his own. I whined to myself.

"Stop fussing," my first friend advised, his tone kind but firm.

Meaning the whine had been audible. I wrinkled my snout. "I'm considering, not fussing," I informed him, inclined to be offended. "Fussing would be asking you to call Nia again, because there's no point going wherever it is we must without a boom."

"My mistake. Stop considering." He closed his bag. "Ready?"

Not in the least. "I will be."

He'd know what I meant. My Human-self was braver than most mes. In fact, as Bess, I'd proved to be daring and even bold on occasion, if not always sufficiently concerned with the consequences of my actions— this according to Paul, who tended to go over past events with an eye to improvement.

And could read any me. "We won't do anything reckless, Es. I promise."

This from the one who'd come up with a plan straight from a monster vid? Rather than comment, I flipped an ear and picked up my own travel bag. Inside were Duras plants, that useful, hard-to-kill living mass, and more Duras filled Paul's second and larger bag. I'd have brought several trunks of the stuff—being confined in a starship was

risky of itself, without the only other source of mass being my friends—
but more wouldn't fit in Paul's aircar.

Not and leave room for Lesley Delacora. Paul, capable of bold and
daring himself when the time called for it, had decided we'd whisk
Lesy's Human-self away from the farmhouse before her triumphant,
albeit incognito, return as a Lishcyn toddling down the ramp of the
Largas Swift and onto the train to the Library.

In other words, he shared my doubt of my web-kin's full adherence
to our plan and wanted her where we could ensure her help by grabbing
if necessary.

No more nipping. That hadn't ended well the last time.

Bags stowed, we walked up the path to the farmhouse together. The
air was fresher than yesterday's, the sky bright blue with fluffy clouds.
Ideal Confront Monster weather, I thought gloomily, inclined to be
annoyed how every bird in the area was trying to outsing its neighbor,
punctuated by the drone of eager pollinators. Farther away, beyond
Human ears, but not mine, the rumble of the construction truck coming
up from the village was a reminder work on the patio continued while
we awaited the committee's reaction to Nia's inspection.

Not that we'd be here for it.

Little cone-like webs dotted the turf, their threads heavy with dew.
I saw Paul notice them. Saw the shudder he tried to hide and understood. *Not comfortable, was it, thinking of oneself as supper?*

If the Null ate what they pulled inside.

I'd a strong personal aversion to finding out. Just as well the plan
was to feed it a little bit of me.

As if that was easier to contemplate. I shuddered and walked faster.

Lionel was waiting on the porch swing when we arrived. He got up
without smiling, eyes bruised from a sleepless night but alert as always.
His endurance was slightly terrifying. "Glad I caught you before you
headed for the landing field. I can't see you off—I have to stay in case
we've a delegation from the Preservation Committee."

I glanced at Paul, seeing the same guilt writ on his face. My friend put down his bags, resting a hand briefly on Lionel's shoulder. "Thank you," he said simply.

Because goodbyes by com weren't enough, not when we went after a monster. Resisting the urge to lick—*not Lionel's preference*—I let my tail drift from side to side, happy to see a smile flicker across his lips.

Then Lionel gave his little cough, resetting the conversation. "Esen, Lambo chose the Library—and me." I'd come prepared to apologize, but he went on without blaming me for a Carasian-sized hunk of trouble. "I'm convinced of his sincerity, but I've arranged for Duggs to keep an eye on him—not that she knows Lambo was a Survey operative. He'll work on her crew." His voice lowered, though we were alone other than the noisy birds. "I put Lambo's report into the private part of the collection for you both, but this is urgent—I spotted something during my own scan of it. You've a problem on the *Mistral*."

"Space monster," I said archly.

"What is it?" Paul asked, not bothering to quell me.

"Survey suspects one or more faction agents are on board. There were no names, but Lambo was ordered to record any communications with the ship if they occurred." A gleam in his eyes. "Don't worry. I've put a dampener on his equipment."

"You think the faction's cleaner is on the ship." *I knew some spy jargon.*

Raising an eyebrow at me, Lionel nodded, then gave Paul a concerned look. "And I fear you remain a target of those intent on eliminating any and all trace of Veya Ragem's past."

A ghost of that dreadful *hate* crossed Paul's face, disappearing behind a reassuring smile I didn't believe for an instant. "Again, thank you, Lionel. I'll be careful."

"Because I'll be watching," I vowed, bristling. *Might have been a growl.*

A better smile from my friend, who lifted his bag and mine. "Rudy's ready to lift. We'll stay in touch, Lionel."

My ears shot up. "I'll get Lesy—what is it?"

Lionel had grimaced. Now he winced. "About that. I don't think she's at all ready to go, Es."

Of course she wasn't. I sighed.

Family.

"You don't need to pack," I told Lesy for the third time. *Holding in the snarl.* "You're not leaving."

She stood, clutching an armload of shirts—Paul's, not that we'd been able to pry them loose—and her lower lip came out in a pout. "Lesley's leaving."

Predictably, my web-kin showed no sign of last night's turmoil or the revelations that had cost Paul and me both sleep and peace of mind. I'd found her halfway up the staircase, busy painting the risers so the stairs themselves vanished into an illusion of giant mushrooms. She'd painted a blue question mark on the back of her pants, having dressed this morning, twisted her hair into a topknot full of paint brushes, and appeared happily surprised to see me. Which was when I'd reminded her of The Plan, and that she was to come with me at once.

Prompting this frenzy of meaningless packing.

Taking the shirts, I tossed them on the bed with everything else she'd wanted to bring. "Yes. Lesley's leaving, and you're coming right back here as Esolesy Ki. Remember, Lesy, you've promised to stay Lishcyn until I return." I gentled my tone. "I won't be gone for long."

Not something I should promise, but this was Lesy. Skalet could know the risks and face them in her own inimitable way. Lesy would abandon us to save herself. She'd run from Picco's Moon if Ersh was in a temper—most often at me but just as often because of one of Lesy's games. In which I'd participated willingly, granted, but not fair. She'd run to Picco's Moon as well, fleeing real or perceived threats to an identity—or a bad review—and it'd be my job to incite more games to cheer her up.

Suffice to say I'd an interesting childhood.

As Senior Assimilator for our tiny Web, however, I accepted that reality, as Ersh had before me, and found a smile. "It'll be a wonderful game to play on the Humans. If you can pull it off," I added off-handedly.

Blue eyes glittered. "If? IF? Youngest?" Lesy tugged her hair out of its knot. "Check your memories. None of the others pretend as well as me. None."

Since what Lesy meant by *pretend* had more in common with how I'd played with Paul's twins when they were young—a Lishcyn on the floor making an excellent dragon to attack with tiny blunt swords—and nothing at all with what Skalet was doing at this moment to stay alive and function within Kraal society, I bowed my head. "It's true. You are the best."

"Exactly. Let's go." She headed for the door.

Her latest question mark flexed with every step. "Wait," I said, even though Paul had gone to the roof for the aircar while I fetched Lesy and in all likelihood was tapping a finger on the dash. *As if that ever worked.*

Lesy paused, twisting at the waist to regard me solemnly. Her hair drifted over a shoulder. Waiting.

I pointed at her backside. "Why are you wearing a question mark?"

She twisted a little more in order to gaze down. "Well, look at that. I am." Her hips wiggled. "It's quite evocative, don't you think? I wonder how it got there."

I should have known.

I reached up to the ceiling, pressing where Paul had shown me. The previously hidden staircase to the roof dropped down without a sound, and I set a grateful foot on it.

"I found that the first night," my web-kin assured me. "I found this today." She reached inside her shirt and produced Starfield the Very Strange Pony, which she shouldn't have.

"Give that back!" I half-shouted, lunging for Paul's precious keepsake.

Lesy let me take it, a puzzled look on her face. "Oh, that isn't what I found. Well it is, but it isn't. Not really."

Later I'd think over this moment and wonder what made me close the staircase on my waiting Human friend and turn to face my web-kin. Unless it was knowing no one found things like Lesy did.

"I'd like to know else what you found, Lesy," I said, keeping my ears up and my voice pleasant with an effort.

"Would you?" She flashed a smile of rapturous delight before taking quick strides to Paul's easi-rest by the window. Bending over, my perplexing web-kin tossed aside handfuls of plas sheets.

As I joined her, stepping through a veritable blizzard of sheets, I realized with a jolt that the ones drifting past me held familiar images.

Except that Lesy had cut off the frame around the stars and ships—and presumably around the planet as well if she'd stolen the latest and I'd no doubt she could. *But why?*

"What have you found?" I heard myself ask.

She snatched one up and fanned herself with it. "Can't you guess, Youngest?"

Ersh save me. "I need you," I said very very gently, "to tell me. Please."

"I solved the puzzle. Here, I'll show you." Lesy, on her knees, tossed aside a final sheet. "See?"

Avoiding the paintbrushes in her hair, I bent over her shoulder to stare.

Here were the frames—or rather the symbols on each, for these had been printed to show only those. Cut into strips. Tacked to Paul's carpet. Some overlapped, others touched in varied orientations, and whatever in Lesy led her to find *this* within what we'd thought were indecipherable symbols was beyond my ability to grasp.

For I was staring at an incomplete but unmistakable representation of the toy still in my paw. *Starfield the Very Strange Pony.* There was only one mind in the universe from which it could have come—

"Would Paul like to see it?" Lesy asked, all innocence and joyful expectation.

"NO!" I snapped, making her recoil. My insides churning, I managed to reach out a trembling hand to stroke her hair. "No, Lesy. It would make him—" *Ersh, I'd no words.* "This is so special, let's keep this our secret. Promise?"

She studied my face as if I'd grown an extra nose—or she planned to draw me one. Somehow I raised my ears and grinned. "Once you promise, we'll go to the ship and you'll get your new clothes. They're beautiful."

"I promise! I promise!" Clapping her hands, Lesy jumped up, her feet tearing a patch from Veya's message to her son.

Until I knew what had sent it and why—

Until I knew what Veya Ragem had become?

Following behind Lesy, I took a moment to carefully scuff the rest of the frames from the carpet.

This secret I would keep.

Nearby

" "   *MISTRAL* out."

The bridge fell eerily silent, the crew motionless at their curved stations, eyes locked on them. Evan, with Kamaara at the com, had the sense of a storm about to burst, unleashing a cacophony of questions, challenges, and outright disbelief for which he'd no answers, none.

Only his own doubt, for despite the relief of hearing Paul and Esen's voices, what they'd had to say—*surely it was impossible.*

The commander nodded to the com officer to resume his seat. "Get the captain up here," she ordered. "He'll want to verify our course change," this to Evan, as calmly as if space monsters were a normal occurrence, then shocked him with a laugh. "Should have seen it coming. Your friends have quite the reputation in Survey."

Acutely conscious of the crew, Evan lowered his voice. "You—you believe this?"

"What I believe, Polit—" knife-sharp and confident, "—is the *Missy* isn't going to suffer the fate of those other ships and crews. Not on my watch. If we're to guard ourselves against a monster, that's what we do. Captain," she greeted as Clendon stepped from the lift. "There's been a development." Her hand clamped on Evan's shoulder, pulling him with her. "You're gonna love this."

Without pause to consult with the experts safely, as Kamaara put it, minding themselves, the ship was on a new heading, one that would boldly clip the edge of the Confederacy. They'd adjourned to the captain's cabin to discuss the ramifications.

No guest quarter luxury here. Storage cupboards lined the walls and the bed folded out of the way. The three of them sat, knees almost touching, at a table bolted to the floor.

Captain Clendon wasted no time. "We can't dampen our ident squeal. You'll see to it the Kraal don't object to our presence in their space, Polit Gooseberry."

"Me, sir?"

"You're our diplomat." A tight smile. "Be diplomatic."

"With the Kraal?" Kamaara shook her head. "Good luck with that."

Evan heartily agreed, not that he'd say so. Direct contact between the Commonwealth and the Confederacy was done at the ambassadorial level, if at all. The sum of his experience with the Kraal themselves consisted of encounters with the terrifying Skalet, now returned to her kind as S'kal-ru, and the equally intimidating Virul-ru, courier for his House. Neither of whom personages a mere polit could simply call up, let alone where did he start? *Don't mind us, just passing through on a monster hunt—*

Captain Clendon pointed a finger at his security chief. "Leave this with the polit, Ne-sa. Keep our other guests in their section. Give the polit a direct link to coms and a secure spot to work."

A glower. "I'm open to suggestions. Ship's jammed to the bulkheads."

The captain rapped the table with a knuckle. "Here, then. We'll hit the current border within the hour. Need anything from your quarters, Polit?"

Rousing himself, Evan shook his head. "No, sir." He could have used his notebooks. *At least he'd the blank one in his pocket.* This was a job better suited to Paul and Esen and the Library—presently on the far side of the Confederacy. Or to Niala Mavis—also beyond—

Leaving him. "How much latitude do I have, Captain?"

"We're on our own out here, Polit," the captain told him as he stood, the others doing the same. "You're free to do whatever it takes to get us safe passage." He paused, giving Evan a speculative look. "I don't need to know."

Plausible deniability. "Understood, sir," Evan replied. Far from the first time any failure would be his alone and, to be honest, he hadn't climbed so high to make a fall more than a relaxing of duties.

Provided the Kraal didn't blast the ship apart.

"I'll set up the link," Commander Kamaara said.

The captain left. Before Kamaara could, Evan gestured to get her attention, then touched his arm where the tracer sat under his skin. He raised his hand to cup his ear, eyebrows raised in question. *Does it listen?*

In answer, she pointed to a small cube where the wall met the ceiling. *Everything does.* Aloud, "Stay your course, Polit. I'm on it." Kamaara's feral grin lacked only fangs.

He could almost feel sorry for Strevelor.

Sitting down again, Evan pulled out his notebook and stylo, arranging both where he could use them if he thought of a reason. He brought out his holocube, turning it over wistfully in his hands. When connected to a public com system, it sent and received messages to and from Great Gran, and a very few special members of his family. Not something to try and use on the *Mistral.*

Evan thumbed the control to bring up images of home, flipping until he found his most recent of Great Gran. She stood knee-deep in the ocean, hands supporting a Sharp-fin she'd caught and wanted to release. The creature was thrashing in the water, intent on sinking its teeth into her. Seabirds circled overhead and Great Gran was laughing—

Wait—he lifted the cube. "S'kal-ru," he whispered to it, hope dawning. "*S'kal-ru and the Great Serpent of House Adana!*"

Seizing his stylo, he began to write down everything he could recall of the ancient fable Great Gran had told him after he'd shared his adventures with S'kàl-ru in the Library—with the *might-have-died* parts removed.

In the fable, S'kal-ru was a Kraal hunter who pursued a great serpent onto the lands of House Adana. Instead of killing S'kal-ru for her trespass, as was proper for Kraal, the head of that House let her continue her hunt, expecting to watch her die for her folly. Instead, S'kal-ru lured the serpent into the House to dispatch all who opposed her, ruling Adana for the rest of her life.

While the serpent's description came close to triggering Evan's *SNAKE* fear—and he was *not* going to think about space monster *TENTACLES*—the fable suggested an approach the present-day S'kal-ru might approve.

The truth. A lone Commonwealth ship hunting what could kill them. If it did, a spectacle Kraal would appreciate.

When Kamaara returned with the link, setting it on the table, she found Evan muttering to himself over his notebook and didn't interrupt.

14: Aircar Afternoon; Landing Field Afternoon

PAUL smiled at Lesy, waiting until we were both seated and secure before setting the aircar in motion as if time wasn't running away from us, but something had changed while I'd struggled with my web-kin over shirts and gained a dreadful secret. There was a muscle jumping along his jaw and, once in the air, he gripped the controls as if willing the machine to fly faster. Catching my scrutiny, he gave me a tiny nod. *Later,* that meant, so I sat back and kept my worry to myself.

Lesy wasn't a peaceful passenger. She shifted eagerly from side to side, exclaiming as if she'd never seen a landscape from the air before—*which*, I realized with sudden compassion, *she hadn't*. Not this one. After all, she'd arrived in a cryosac of bits and stayed on the Library grounds since. "Would you like Paul to fly lower?" I asked, as the aircar swooped to follow the train tracks into the hills.

"I like this height," she said, pressing both hands and her nose to the transparent shield. "It's like being a Skyfolk."

To forestall Lesy becoming one, I hastily dug into the box of snacks I'd prepared. They were for Lesy's Lishcyn-self but should work as a distraction for a Human. "Fudge?" I offered, ignoring Paul's little cough. *Fine for him to be amused.* I, as Senior Assimilator, had to ensure we didn't crash or cause a Lamentable Incident, while keeping Lesy happy.

Minding his twins had been easier. Until Laura and Tomas discovered my Lishcyn-self's aversion to the dark, adding a smidge of personal terror to my side of the popular *where, oh where are we hiding?* game.

Lesy relaxed, taking dainty little nibbles of the fudge as she continued to press her nose to the side shield.

Our games, hindsight my view of the moment, had contained not only a significant amount of *scare Esen* but also inconvenience and occasional, albeit minor, bodily harm. There'd been a bout of near starvation when she'd put puzzle locks on the food cupboards. Then the time she'd tricked me into inhaling Urgian pepper powder—the point being, as Youngest I hadn't minded, enjoying attention that wasn't scolding.

Unfortunately, now that I'd others to protect, I saw all this in a different light. My Elder was fun and passionate, but consequences to others simply didn't matter to her. Those around Lesy learned to take care of themselves, as I had, because Ersh hadn't given Lesy empathy or remorse.

Add that to Ersh's Laws, and Lesy was as perilous as she was undeniably brilliant. *Hadn't she found what no one else could?*

As if it had waited for this peaceful moment to pounce, it was as if the significance of what Lesy'd found in the frames suddenly grabbed me by the neck and shook me, hard.

The Null. The pattern of hither-and-yon destruction. Images of derelicts framed by fragments of a child's beloved toy. The continual stubborn inexplicable return to a path leading to Botharis. Lesy had called it a puzzle—

All at once, the pieces fit together.

There was no mysterious unknown species sending out warnings or threats. No Passerby or Framers. Only the monster that had ripped Veya Ragem through the bulkhead of her starship, preserving her navigation implant and enough of her mind to use it.

The part with her longing to return home to her son.

Assuming there existed some part of a Human that allowed the transfer or holding of memories, as in a Web-being. I'd the urge to nip someone to find out and caught myself speculatively eying the lobe of Paul's ear. *Not that I should.* Unless I'd permission—

All at once it wasn't a puzzle or a curiosity. All at once I felt lost and alone, even as my first and dearest friend banked the aircar through hills that should have been familiar. How did I tell Paul the Bad Thing might be a remnant of his mother? That her ghost, for I had no better term, might be guiding a planet-destroying Null to this lovely living world?

That to stop it, I might have to end all that remained of her—

I let out a yip, rubbing *my* assaulted ear, and snarled at my web-kin. "What was that for?"

"You were huffing." Rebuke for revealing my justified agitation delivered, my Elder smiled beatifically and resumed nibbling her fudge, watching the forest below.

Paul half turned around to look at me. "Something wrong?"

What wasn't? I tipped my head meaningfully at Lesy, then gave a shrug. *Family.*

"Won't be long," he promised with a sympathetic grimace.

I resumed huffing, albeit more quietly.

By midday, the Library landing field—the only one on this continent—was full of starships. Most were small shabby freighters, the type to offer passage to a scholar or two if the price was right. A couple were larger, less shabby for-hires. Some of our scholars were very well funded, not that they'd admit it.

Closest to the train station, an unusual shape caught the sunlight, reflecting it back with almost blinding brightness. Sleek and narrow, with outsized engines and even larger landing feet splayed out to three sides, one containing a ramp. *Our ride.* A wheeled truck was pulled up to its shady side, ostensibly delivering supplies.

Its actual purpose was to provide a plausible means for a couple of important players in our game of *shuffle-the-aliens* to have boarded the *Swift* unremarked. As Paul said, no one noticed the ordinary.

Being not the least ordinary by Botharan standards, the *Largas Swift* had drawn the rapt notice of what looked to be everyone who worked at the landing field, a ragged crowd surrounding her ramp at a distance hardly respectful of how soon we planned to lift.

If Nia showed up with our boom, I'd no idea how we'd disperse them to load it. Botharans were stubborn about being told what to do at the best of times. Now, with a clear duty to welcome one of their own, Rudy, in his shiny new ship—with Esolesy Ki in the bargain?

Not that I *knew* these Humans had come to say hello to that me and goodbye to this one, but I enjoyed thinking it.

Needless to say, Lesy's reaction to the gathering was altogether different. Her eyes sparkled with anticipation. "I shall make a grand entrance."

"Followed by another, as Esolesy Ki," Paul reminded her with a bow. "Thank you again for your help. It's essential."

Lesy glowed as he assisted her from the aircar. I was left to jump out, not that I complained. It was something this me was exceptionally good at, provided someone else took the luggage.

Paul had eased the aircar down, granting those beneath time to shout, complain, then grudgingly move aside. The instant we landed and everyone could see who'd so rudely demanded space to land, there were cheers and a few bawdy suggestions directed at Paul and Rudy implying the beer tent had been open and busy since dawn with most of the clients their cousins.

It was a wonder any of our scholars made it through to the train. At least today our presence, and the *Swift*'s, helped; I could see a stealthy trickle of non-Humans evading the mob. They'd still have to pass through the "port village" and be afflicted with gemmie dealers—

"What a busy happy place," my web-kin exclaimed. "You should have brought me here sooner—Esen—" she gasped. "ARE THOSE SHOPS?"

Paul adroitly stepped between Lesy and the alluring cluster of tents. "Time for your grand entrance, Lesley Delacora."

The *Swift*'s ramp stood waiting within the shadow of the landing support, a couple of crew in coveralls at its base and a sturdy form I recognized at the top. Paul waved and Captain Rudy Lefebvre waved in response, then opened his mouth. "Largas Transport is honored by the presence of the Famous Lesley Delacora!" Augmented by tech, Lesy's Human name soared across the landing field. I flattened my ears to protect them.

Lesy moved forward as if transported to some higher plane, her every step a lesson in what the Human form could attain if you gave it a few millennia to practice. The crowd created a corridor, everyone craning for a glimpse of exactly *who* was famous before she departed Botharis.

"Es—" Paul stopped there, stunned to silence like the rest of those witnessing that departure.

I'd let Lesy change out of her question mark pants. It was that, or back to the *I must pack* issue, and I hadn't paid attention to what she'd elected for the exit of her Human-self, other than to notice it looked like clothing and to be glad she'd been quick.

It wasn't clothing—not Botharan clothing. *Which, to be frank, tended to boring.*

This was not. My web-kin had wrapped her Human-self in veils shaped like leaves. Together, they'd formed an ordinary-seeming green dress, but there was nothing ordinary about this.

With each step, another "leaf" drifted down to the landing field and more of Lesy's admittedly magnificent form showed.

By my quick calculation, she'd enter the airlock of the *Largas Swift* veil-less.

If only we'd had Nia's boom handy, I thought with some regret. No one here would notice us loading twenty of the things, especially once the first few began dashing from the crowd to collect a leaf and the rest realized they'd better hop to it or lose out.

Paul gave a start and began to move, a bag in each hand. I followed.

I caught a faint "Esen!" Angling my ears, I obtained direction and turned my head, spotting Paul's father and uncle struggling through the masses toward me, though I supposed it was equally likely they were struggling to reach their son and nephew, but they were calling my name as well so I let my tail drift a bit with pleasure.

Then I saw Henri and Ally coming behind, followed by Carwyn and what looked to be the entire staff of the All Species' Library of Linguistics and Culture.

Bells began to ring. Each person shook one, it being the custom in Norrsland for family to make as much joyful noise as possible to send off a far traveler. Paul had told me.

I'd never experienced it, there not having been such a glad farewell for either of us since his return.

My tail, wagging uncontrollably, smacked Paul as he whirled around to stare. "Lionel—" he breathed. "He must have put them all on the train before we left. I don't believe it."

Like mine, his surprise held delight though, at a guess, this left upward of sixty aliens roaming the Library unsupervised; maintenance—also here with bells—would face the result. *Let alone chasing the strays—*

I found I couldn't worry, not when bathed in smiles and waves and good wishes being energetically rung by so many we knew. Including a couple of elderly females I realized belatedly to be Paul's great aunts, who hadn't set foot near anything alien, especially me, before today.

What had Lionel done?

He'd arranged this warmest of Botharan farewells for Paul and me before we headed into danger, and a solid greeting for "Esolesy Ki" to support Lesy's impersonation—which my web-kin was welcome to consider *all for her* and probably did—and my tail refused to behave, so I didn't bother to try.

Paul dropped our bags and ran to embrace his family, and I might have let out an exuberant *howl* that startled those nearest who then laughed, which was fine too.

A leafy piece of veil waved near my snout. Lesy, reminding me our time was short—or that she was running out of veils—smiling as only she could smile.

I grinned back, for an instant forgetting what she was—what I was. "Such bright little raindrops, Youngest," she whispered in my ear. "Don't fret. We'll remember them always."

Trust my Elder to remind me.

She'd her viewpoint. I'd my own. These precious lives should last as long as their nature permitted. I would not allow them to be cut short by something that didn't belong here.

My grin must have developed some fang, for Lesy abruptly gave me space as did those Humans closest. "Time to board, Paul!" I grabbed the smaller bag, nodding vaguely at the crew as I dashed for the ramp.

My nose, however, didn't stop gathering information about my surroundings. Even as I climbed, I knew I hadn't met the Human female on the left, and she'd had sombay spiced with cinnamon a short while ago.

The Human male on my right, angular features shadowed within a hood, was Meony-ro, disguised as crew. To make room for us—and keep out of our way—they'd both stay on Botharis until our return.

Meony-ro, if necessary, would go with Nia to separate the boom from the nearest Kraal missile. She hadn't shared the locations of the other four with us, possibly to prevent a moment like this where we might have been tempted to leave her completely out of the loop and obtain it for ourselves, Nia knowing Paul that well.

I hoped not. Lingering instead of dramatically launching into the air was the sort of thing Humans noticed. They'd get bored, then curious. Concern was likely.

Whatever the pair at the ramp thought of their role in tricking the local population into believing Esolesy Ki had been offworld for months—while they believed she waited in the truck to sneak on board—their loyalty was to Cameron & Ki and Largas Freight, not some backwater planet.

Though I was reasonably sure Meony-ro—however much he'd prefer to be part of something clandestine and important, ideally armed and flying an aircar—knew Esolesy Ki well enough to be suspect I'd abandoned my duties to shop.

Hopefully, our former Kraal didn't know that me well enough to see through Lesy's version, but—as I'd remind Paul—*every plan had its hopeful bits.*

Though each time he'd give me that *your plans* look. *Might be accurate.*

Our plan was to go straight in, have Lesley Delacora disappear into the ship's accommodation—there to cycle into Esolesy Ki and don the outfit Rudy'd left for her there, Paul passing along my advice not to leave her an array of choices or we'd be lucky to lift by nightfall even with the boom. The Lishcyn, with her new luggage, would exit the ship gracefully and be escorted to the Library by the *Swift*'s crewmembers.

As if merely thinking about the plan made the Cosmic Gods pay attention, Lesy, drunk on the crowd's adulation, spun about with a joyful jiggle to wave and blow kisses, instead of entering the ship. Paul moved out of her way, taking the moment to hand a bag to Rudy and put an arm around his cousin.

Then they turned to wave too.

Not the plan!

Normally, I enjoyed improvising, from the giddy *will it work* to the—usually—triumphant *it did!* There'd been occasional *next time, let's not* moments.

Not this time. I wanted inside the ship. All of us in, following the plan.

Because if I looked out again, saw all those faces, my resolve to keep my terrible secret would crumble and it mustn't. Not until I knew what to do about it. About Veya.

Picking up the bag Paul left on the ramp, dodging the others even as I flinched at another cheery ringing of bells, I entered the *Largas Swift* alone.

The relatively dim lighting revealed a pinched low-ceilinged space, redolent of metal and, yes, that was polish, not that I could see anything worth buffing. I assumed the upper portion of the ship would be less cramped, for this had to store the landing supports. There were two tubes leading up, each with doors clipped open. I hooked our bags on the waiting conveyor cable inside the leftmost. The one to the right contained a ladder.

I was too upset to care.

In some starship designs, such tubes could be set to zero-g once in space, convenient for Humans and highly unfriendly to this me. *Again, didn't care.*

There wouldn't be room for the others in this antechamber with me here. Resignedly, I stuck my snout in the tube and looked up, then sniffed. *Wait. That wasn't polish.*

My nostrils widened as I inhaled what shouldn't be here.

Who shouldn't!

Unrolling my fingers, I began to climb, snarling deep in my chest. The scent grew stronger, fresher—as if I needed proof this wasn't a trace from an earlier visit, but a living presence.

Special Envoy Niala Mavis was on the *Largas Swift*. If she'd brought the boom, our plan against the Null had a slight chance of success.

If I couldn't get rid of her before Lesy came on board?

I snarled louder, the sound echoing up the tube.

It had none.

Nearby

B^E *on that starship . . .*

BE on that starship . . .
    About to reenter the Library through the Garden portal, Lionel deliberately paused and turned to face the sun. Its radiance shone red through his closed eyelids and warmed his skin. With each breath, the fragrance of living air, impossible to replicate on a ship, filled his lungs, and despite Skalet's concern?

He wasn't leaving this place, ever.

Surprised by the depth of that conviction, Lionel gave a self-conscious little cough as he went inside, only to squeeze himself quickly against the corridor wall to let a cluster of chittering Rands tumble by.

Scholars, where they shouldn't be. He'd a sudden sinking feeling. *How many staff members had taken him up on his offer to take their bells to the landing field?*

Moments later, Lionel had his answer. *All of them.* The Assessment Counter gate was down, with a firm *Back by Lunch* note on it, but scholars who'd wait patiently—or not—in the queue under Henri's watchful gaze had apparently taken her absence for permission to mark their place in line with their artifact or gemmie and wander.

Where they were wandering, Lionel could only guess, but by the slime on the counter and beneath it, more than Rands had decided to check out the off-limits administration section. *Curiosity about the forbidden definitely crossed species' lines.*

Hearing a loud roar, Lionel sighed as he set off for the Chow at a brisk, *no panic here,* pace.

A Heezle, a Carasian, and four Humans stood—the former leaning quite fetchingly—in the gutted remnants of the Chow.

He needed a punch line. Lionel made sure his amusement didn't show. "May I be of assistance?"

Two eyestalks snapped his way. Duggs took a step, stopping as the Heezle, half a meter taller, swayed in her direction. "What's this *guest* doing here?" the Human asked through gritted teeth.

The remaining Humans, having paused in the midst of spraying the food dispenser with protective foam, looked more interested than alarmed.

Lambo, on the other hand, had backed himself into the partial hole in the wall that would become the patio entrance, claws up in a defensive posture.

From the rosy skin spots on its ventral side, the Heezle was more entertained than aroused. The beings had an excellent sense of the ridiculous, especially when it came to the reactions of non-Heezles to their overtures, and rarely took offense. *Just as well.*

"This is an area under renovation, *Oimett*," Lionel told their wandering guest, using the honorific for *one-who-seeks-enlightment.* "Be aware there could be desiccants in—"

Condensing to a thick pillar, the Heezle ejected a startling quantity of yellow slime and skidded oimett's mass along it right out the door.

Anticipating a flight response—desiccants a serious threat to a Heezle's integument—Lionel dodged aside. *Almost in time.* He shook a glob of glistening yellow from his shoe; more coated the floor as far as he could see into the corridor.

"Who's cleaning that guck?" Duggs grumbled.

Lionel gave a rueful chuckle. "I'll get a mop." After all, he'd frightened the poor Heezle, not to mention sent away the rest of the staff.

He only hoped the accommodations weren't plugged—

After opening his second closet to find neither mop, bucket, nor any recognizable slime removal device, Lionel Kearn came to the reluctant conclusion that being Library Administrator hadn't prepared him to clean up after a Heezle. Let alone what else might be going on. There'd been a suddenly hushed series of chirps when he passed the staff accommodation, and something *unusual* was in the air wafting from the Lobby.

Slime first. Determined to resolve at least one problem before the staff—and "Esolesy Ki"—returned, Lionel quickened his pace.

He broke into a jog when he realized the door to the Response Room was ajar. Who—what—was in there? More importantly, what might they do with the fabricator—?

Grasping the door frame, Lionel pulled himself to a stop and straightened, smoothing his jacket before stepping inside.

Ally Orman looked up from her table. "Hello, Lionel."

"What are you doing here?" He made an apologetic gesture, dropping on a stool across from her. "Sorry. You surprised me. I thought you'd gone with the rest."

"I'm here getting this done." After nodding to the pile of oddments on the table, Ally gave him a keen look. "I said my goodbyes, Lionel. I want to clear as much as I can before—before Esolesy jumps in." Her nose scrunched. "She has the oddest ideas sometimes."

"I understand." Staff preferences distressed Esen but, in Lionel's opinion, they couldn't be helped. Her personality changed with her species—and not always in subtle ways—altering the responses of those interacting with her. Still. "Call on me whenever you wish," he offered. "To, ah, mediate. I've fudge in my desk," with a wink.

Ally's answering smile dimpled her cheeks. "I'll hold you to that."

Lionel smiled back, rising to his feet. "Do you have a mop?" He gazed around the room, looking for one, and spotted a neat stack of travel bags under the coat rack; surely not a response from the collection, though there'd been some unusual ones. He raised a questioning eyebrow.

She dropped her tools with a clatter, her honest face struggling. "I wanted to tell you properly. You, Paul, and Esen. I—I ran out of time."

"You're leaving?" Ally was more than senior staff; she was arguably the most essential after Esen herself. Lionel sat, searching for the right words. "If it's about pay or working conditions—or Lesley—" because Ally had borne the brunt of their artiste's irresponsibility.

Her eyes lit up. "It's because of Lesley I know it's time for me to move on. We talk every lunchtime. She's very wise, you know, and seeing her joy in being creative—it's been too long since I've felt that for myself."

"There must be some way to do that here, Ally." Lionel leaned forward. "Tell me what you need. Anything."

"Water. Waves." Ally tipped her head, as if listening to what only she could hear. "When Lesley heard I'd stopped swimming because of the pressure to win, she convinced me I mustn't abandon a vital part of who I am. That I owed it to myself to swim again, this time for the love of it."

For an instant, Lionel actually contemplated putting a suitable pool in the Garden, then remembered Lambo. Mixing Human swimmers with a predator was not, he shuddered inwardly, a good idea. He ran through his Botharan geography. "Where would you go, Ally? South Lowesland?"

"If working at the Library's taught me anything, it's that there's more to the universe than this planet. I want to see some of it for myself." Ally grinned at him. "Don't look so worried, Lionel. I plan to start simple. Lesley's helped me book passage to Pachen IV. It's Human—and in the Commonwealth." Said with the nigh-religious fervor of someone from a world that wasn't. "I'll be fine. Lesley's friend owns a beach house."

According to Paul, Lesy hadn't been alive, not technically, for the past fifty-two years, making it unlikely she'd any Human friends left—if the word *friend* even applied.

The stack of bags abruptly seemed ominous. "How soon are you going? Surely not before Paul and Esen are back."

"As soon as I'm done here," Ally announced, dashing that hope. "Samgo's got a transport heading to Neanerton this afternoon to pick up fresh fish, and he'll drop me at the airport. I've a spot on tomorrow's first flight to Grandine. Then it's off I go." She fluttered her fingers in the air.

It had all the drastic impulsion of a Lesy spectacular. Lionel took a breath. "Ally, can I convince you to delay your departure until—" *We know if the Null or Kraal will destroy the world?* "—we can train your successor? I promise we'll cover any fees and pay for new tickets."

Ally shook her head. "I don't want to desert you, Lionel, but I can't wait. Lesley's left already, you see, and asked me to meet her there. It's all arranged. She needs someone to travel with. Someone who understands her."

And who hadn't the remotest idea what "Lesley" was.

Skalet planned ahead; he should have realized Lesy would as well. Was this Esen's blind spot, being unable to predict her more volatile Elder? He couldn't blame her. From what he'd learned—surmised—it was Ersh who'd kept a firm grip on the members of her Web.

Yet hadn't stopped Esen befriending a Human. *A thought for later.*

Lionel waved at the busy table. "By this," he said with forced good cheer, "we have you for a couple of hours yet."

"I won't change my mind," Ally warned him, a determined glint in her eyes.

"I wouldn't dream of trying to make you," Lionel replied.

He'd settle for changing Lesy's.

Out There

KLAXONS. Lights flash. Red Alert! Proximity Alarm—
Sir! It's happening!
Report, Navigator. Specifics. What's happening?
The Something—it's reacting to our presence, sir. We have to
abandon ship—
Calm yourself, Ragem. We expected this. First contact—
If only she could pick the shard to hear, the moment to see and relive.

If only she had hands to push away the worst, but this is Hell and she
has none.

Listen to me—it's closer than the last time. If you want to live, we
have to get—too late.
What do you mean?
You've doomed us all. I see them. They've taken hold. The fila-
ments. They have the ship.
They're coming for us—
In the real, light is everywhere. In the real, spectra blossom, opening
every possibility; she's only to see to find the way.

Only one spectrum amid the uncountable number of stars shines on
his dear face, welcomes her home after every journey, and now, more

than any wish, if only she could erase it from her mind—if only she could die before—

Her eye finds it.

Hell finds it.

If only she could die . . .

15: Starship Afternoon

PARTWAY up the *Swift*'s access ladder, clutching the next rung with already aching paws, I froze, Ersh's admonishing *Do you* ever *think before you leap, Youngest?* ringing in my ears. Not that I heard her voice, but the memory was there to stay and cropped up every so often.

I preferred remembering Paul's *Let's take a moment, Es.* With a similar meaning but far more soothing and occasionally came with a snack.

Nia was somewhere above me. I angled an ear. By the sounds, Paul, Rudy, and Lesy had entered the ship below me. No one could use the ladder to go up or down while I was on it and, for a brief moment, I contemplated hooking an arm and leg around a rung and staying here for the duration of the trip, simply to avoid the problem.

Which wouldn't work, if only because the ship couldn't lift without its captain on the bridge punching the right buttons. Then there was the whole issue of those not secured and strapped down for lift slamming into bulkheads—

With an inner sigh, I pulled myself up a rung and, grudgingly, reached for the next.

The other advice Paul would give me was *One thing at a time, Es.* I might have a slight tendency to fuss over everything simultaneously— under the circumstances, not useful. So, what was the first thing?

Get an Esolesy Ki back to the Library.

A thing having attached to it an improbable sequence of other things, given Nia's presence, starting with Lesy presently being her Human-self. I pulled myself up another rung.

I might be fussing over nothing. Lesy would cycle unseen some-where, Nia leave with a Lishcyn—I'd let Paul explain about the truck delivering an alien—then Paul, Rudy, and I would lift bravely into the sky and all would be fine. Other than the *chasing monsters with a boom* part.

One thing at a time, I reminded myself.

Even if dozens of people had watched Lesley get on the ship in mem-orable fashion, or rather lack of, and not get off again, surely Nia would accept our explanation that our artiste had ducked into a cabin to clothe herself or meditate.

I began climbing with renewed optimism.

Four rungs later, feeling the vibration as a larger being took hold below and began the climb, I thrust my head through the opening at the top and found myself looking at a pair of legs. Legs in spacer coveralls ending in mag boots and for a fraction of a heartbeat I let myself pre-tend it was just a final member of the crew ready to leave.

"Why were you growling, Esen?" Nia Mavis demanded in a worried whisper, easing back to let me climb out. "Is something wrong?

"Ladders," I muttered, forcing my ears up as I looked past her.

But yes, something was wrong, and from what I could see? It was far more than Nia's unexpected presence and disguise. Our plan had a serious flaw—one I sincerely believed should have been anticipated by my Human friends.

The *Largas Swift* wasn't small, it was ludicrously tiny.

All there was at the top of this ladder was a roughly circular room, barely larger than the antechamber below and packed with inflated seats making it exceedingly difficult to spot any operation stations to prove this was the bridge. An opened door on the wall led to another tube, with its ladder, leading up.

"Where's the accommodation?" I blurted.

Nia pointed up. "In the crew quarters. That's where I've been. When I heard the bells—I thought it was time I came out," with a hint of bel-ligerence, as if I should know all this.

Because I didn't, I blinked woefully. "But—why are you here, Nia?"

"To bring what you and Paul asked for." She placed a possessive hand on the bag hanging from a strap over her shoulder. Her eyes flashed. "It's my responsibility as a representative of the Botharan Planetary Government and isn't leaving my possession."

I wasn't sure what was more unsettling, that planet-destroying ordinance—at least the *boom* part—could be carried around in a bag—

Or that Nia was determined to stay with it.

No, what had my tail curling between my legs was the thought of Lesy entering the *Swift* when it held the boom *and* Nia. I managed not to nip with an effort, but a growl deepened my voice. "Does Paul know about this?"

An uneasy look. *Probably the growl.* "He set it up. The truck. The rear ladder and open port. For you—in case you decide not to risk space travel—"

A deeper growl.

"Mostly for me," she modified. "To sneak this on board if I got it before the truck left the hamlet." A disquietingly careless pat of her bag, then Nia plucked the sleeve of her coveralls. "I'm a surprise."

Not one we needed—

Rudy's head and wide shoulders filled the hole in the bridge floor. His eyes widened as he saw who was with me and he opened his mouth—

It's not entirely fair to say I panicked.

Still, there might not have been an abundance of reasoned thought involved as I frantically waved both paws at Rudy before I pushed Nia—and the boom—ahead of me into the next tube. Hopefully Paul's cousin would guess I wanted him to plug access to the bridge so I could get Nia out of sight before mostly naked Lesley Delacora arrived—

And Paul discovered we'd too many Humans on board.

Halfway, Nia stopped, twisting to give me a clear *what are we doing* look.

Having no idea yet, I put my mouth around her ankle and let her feel my fangs through her boot.

She hurriedly resumed climbing. I tongued out *boot-taste* and bent an ear, hearing Paul's voice and Rudy's deeper one, along with a cheerful giggle announcing my web-kin had reached the bridge and was likely trying the seats for bounce.

What was I to do?

First and foremost, Lesy mustn't suspect Rudy's knowledge of Webbeings. While I couldn't be sure what she'd do? Cooperate would not be remotely part of it.

My paw grasped the next rung. Fortunately, my Elder would never cycle in front of a stranger. I'd doubts she could make herself do it in front of our Human friends, unless planning to take their mass. *Not happening.*

Unfortunately, the *Largas Swift* was the size of a closet and Paul needed, somehow, to arrange privacy for Lesy to become me and Lesley to stay—and that clearly wasn't going to be in the accommodation we'd planned to use for Lesy because we'd Nia, who'd been hiding in it already—

I felt I'd been climbing ladders forever.

—plus whisk Esolesy Ki to the landing field and on the train before the crowd grew restive.

Not to mention my own conundrum. My sole job before liftoff was to reassure my web-kin I hadn't let another *raindrop* know what we were.

Whining to myself, I followed Nia out the hole in the top, unsurprised by this point to find myself in a third sparse circular space with a series of curtains tied against the outer walls. The *Swift*'s version of cabins, no doubt. There were three more inflatable seats, these collapsed in rolls, and, yes, the predictable opened door on a tube going up. The conveyor tube had obligingly stopped here, our luggage still secured on their hooks.

What I couldn't see was— "Where's the accommodation?!" I whispered rather desperately.

Nia reached for a handle on the wall I'd overlooked and pulled. An opaque bag oozed from a slit, expanding with a hiss into a firm, adult-Human-sized column. *Oh good*, I noted almost hysterically. *Has a zipper.* With the requisite efficient little connectors and unpleasant suction things inside.

Meaning it wasn't the tubes that would be gravity-free for our journey, but the entire ship. Explaining the handles and cupboards on the ceiling I'd been too preoccupied to notice until now.

As a Lanivarian, I felt I'd a perfect right to feel the onset of spacesickness at the mere thought. *I'd bite Rudy some place tender for this.*

Still, if not for Nia's unexpected presence, we'd have managed. My dear friend was a wonderful improviser—a skill Paul claimed I'd encouraged him to develop—and I was confident he'd have thought of something.

Maybe.

Unaware she'd single-handedly demolished an *unlikely-but-all-we'd-had* plan, Nia sat gingerly on one of the seats, easing her bag onto her lap, only to get up again to move a buckle out of her way. During this, her face went through an interesting sequence of expressions from frustration to discomfort to—when she realized I was watching her—a calculated calm I didn't believe for an instant.

"You haven't been to space."

"I most certainly have," Nia countered. Her gaze traveled around, lingered on curtains and bare metal, the hatch waiting to cover the hole in the floor, and she caught her lower lip between her teeth. Her eyes met mine. "Not in something like this," she admitted sheepishly.

"Where you aren't supposed to be," I told her, my brain finally working. We should have stayed on the bridge. Let the others see her, let her exit down the ramp like the crew she pretended to be—

It wasn't too late. A thought I'd remember later.

"Nia, you have to leave."

Her wide mouth curved down. "I'm afraid I can't, Es." She held up the bag. "I knew I'd never get authorization, so I jigged up. After you left last night, I took it from Mal's safe."

She stole the boom?! On Paul's word and mine, Nia risked her career. Risked everything and I sat, unable to hold back a whimper of dismay. "Nia—what have you done?"

"What I had to." Her eyes held a fierce and remarkably familiar determination. "We're all in danger if we don't stop the Null."

If there were Cosmic Gods, they had to be laughing. To stop the Null, this ship had to leave Botharis.

To leave, I had to convince Lesy everything was going to plan, so she'd do her part.

And to do that? I had to be Human. In front of Esolesy Ki, Bess—supposedly arrived on the truck that actually brought Nia—was to tell Captain Rudy Lefebvre that Esen the Lanivarian had snuck down the rear ladder and left on the truck, and explain to him that Lesley Delacora was indisposed and wouldn't be seen for the remainder of the journey.

Only then, as far as Lesy was concerned, would all entities be accounted for and the security of our Web preserved—

Skalet wouldn't fall for it. Lesy, on the other hand, merely needed an excuse not to be bothered and to check out her new clothes sooner than later.

I went to the tube and stared up wistfully.

"It's packed with cargo," Nia said in a small voice. "I thought about hiding there—but there wasn't room."

And she'd have died during lift, a dreadful consequence I'd let others explain, having my own to worry about. Someone was coming up the ladder from the bridge.

I was out of time.

Paul wasn't going to like this.

I reached inside my jacket and pulled out a child's garment, dropping it on the deck by my feet. "Nia—"

At her quizzical look, I fell silent, resigned to my fate. Either she'd be like Duggs and accept me—

Or not.

I loosened my grip on this me, shedding excess mass and what had been a favorite outfit as a small puddle of water.

And stood before Niala Mavis as Bess.

I did up the fastenings of my coveralls—a garment that mimicked the adult version—just as Rudy, doubtless prodded by Paul, heaved himself into the crew quarters. I smiled up at him. "Hello, Rudy."

"Welcome to the *Swift*. Paul said you'd be up here—Bess." The big Human actually winked before returning to script. "Where's our Lanivarian?" He looked around, getting no help from Nia.

Who'd raised her fist to her mouth when I'd cycled and had yet to move. She wasn't in shock, that much I could tell, for after her eyes flicked to Rudy, they returned to me, brimming with unasked questions and the beginnings of what I thought might be comprehension.

Yes, I wanted to tell her. *I'm Paul's secret. I'm why he stayed away. I'm why he's back.*

But now wasn't the time. "Esen left," I told Rudy in this me's soft, higher-pitched voice. Listening, Nia gradually lowered her fist. "She gets really spacesick, you know. She decided to stay home. But I'm here!" I added a little twirl to distribute my clothes properly. And because this me liked spinning and hadn't for quite some time.

"That you are." The corners of Rudy's eyes crinkled with amusement. Then again, he enjoyed this version of me for reasons more to do with being a Human without a family than sense. "Nia."

"Rudy."

They knew each other. How could they not, she Paul's former love, and Rudy the one cousin who'd rushed to welcome Paul home between adventures and sat raptly to hear his stories? His blunt features were composed and I refused to guess what he was thinking. From her slight frown, I was reasonably sure Nia grasped she wasn't the only one to know about me.

Later. I stamped my foot impatiently, that being something my Human-self did. "Nia's brought the boom." I didn't give her title.

She gave me a different, considering look, then she lifted the strap over her head and passed the bag to Rudy. "I'm told it's stable."

His grunt was unconvinced as he took the thing with greater care than she'd carried it, keeping the bag tight to his body with an arm. "I think we'll all feel better once this is locked in."

With the dexterity of a primate, Rudy stepped into the next ladder tube, pausing to swing the door closed behind him.

Nia, who'd started to follow, stopped and turned to me. "I—I wanted to keep it in sight."

"I'm much happier not seeing it, thank you," I confessed. "If it helps, there's nowhere else for it to go." *And we'd blow up with it.*

She gave a numb little nod, likely catching what I didn't say.

All things considered, Nia Mavis was doing very well for her first exposure to a Web-being. *No screaming being a bonus.* I put a finger to my lips. "Stay here."

With that, I went down the ladder much more easily than I'd climbed it, intent on seeing how Paul was coping with his difficulty. Who was also mine.

Lesy.

Paul was in the tube, an arm hooked around a rung. I came down as far as I could, and he grinned up at me, pointing to the closed door to the bridge. *My clever friend.*

A light taptap and he opened it, stepping out. My oft-contrary web-kin was, to my relief, her Lishcyn-self. She didn't look up, busy adjusting the strap of my—her bag to fall correctly. A tidy ear flicked my way. *Aware,* that was.

Though slightly paler than usual, Paul stood aside to give me room. His eyes bored into mine as if trying to see through my skull, his grin somewhat fixed. *Tell me you've done it,* that was.

"Rudy's using the accommodation," I said promptly. "I told him Esen left. The back hatch to the truck," in case anyone forgot the story we'd prepared.

Lesy swiveled at the hips to regard me, a Lishcyn's neck built more for strength than mobility. She was every bit as gorgeous and mature as I'd remembered, with glorious thick tufts of hair out each ear. "And when the captain is finished with his biology, you can tell him, *Bess,* that Lesley Delacora took one look at this—this inadequate bucket of bolts—and left with her." A disdainful sniff. "So true. You couldn't pay me to travel in such a ship."

Paul closed his eyes briefly—which might have been in thanks or to restrain himself—then my first dear friend picked up an elegant piece of luggage by its carry strap and smiled warmly at Lesy. "Time for your grand entrance, Esolesy Ki."

Recognizing the abrupt distraction on her face as an ominous flutter in either stomach two or five—or both, given Lishcyn anatomy and reflex—I clambered over seats to where our bags now rested and reached in, pulling out a good-sized protein bar. "There's fudge in it."

Lesy shoved it in her mouth without removing the wrapper, chewed and swallowed, then flashed me a grateful tusk, its glamorous inlay of precious shell catching the light to send sparkles around the *Swift*'s cluttered bridge. "Delicious."

"Shall we?" Paul urged, gesturing to the ladder.

"Of course." She stepped into the hole and dropped, landing with a heavy thud that reverberated the plating beneath our feet. An airy, "Do bring my clothes!" followed.

Paul and I exchanged identical looks, both being Human at the moment.

We'd done it!

Nearby

"*S'KAL-RU and the Great Serpent of House*— What drivel is this?"
The Kraal on the com knew. The rudeness was a tactic, one
Evan ignored. "*House Adana,* Admiral Nadaneo. Unlike the hero of
the tale, our intention is to pursue a hunt of benefit to all, including the
Confederacy. May we have your leave to pass?"

No ordinary Kraal, this; confirmation they'd matched his com signal
to the ident squeal of the *Mistral*—bringing forward someone with the
authority to blast a Commonwealth stray from Confederacy space.

Where they'd be in a few minutes. Evan licked dry lips.

"Your pursuit is as unnecessary as your force is pathetically inadequate. Great House Virul leads the Confederacy to destroy the ship-
eater. Reverse course before you trespass and we do the same to you!"

Historically, Kraal Houses hadn't cooperated. A threat like the Null
could change that—had changed it, Evan judged suddenly, thinking of
the rumors of a new leader.

And if they'd taken their hunt to the predicted final goal of the Null?

Despite what he'd told Strevelor, every diplomat knew a great deal
about stellar cartography—in particular where the Commonwealth was
and wasn't. To reach the Botharan System, the Kraal fleet had to cross
a sensitive sliver of what was Commonwealth space.

Evan sat back with an unconscious smile, folding his hands on his
lap. "In that case, the Commonwealth will consider forgiving *your*

trespass, Admiral," he proposed smoothly, "in return for leave to pass. *Mistral* out."

"Diplomacy, huh?"

Evan gave a start, only then realizing he wasn't alone. He sat up straight. "I—ah—" He closed his mouth.

She leaned back to call into the bridge, "Good to go when ready, Captain."

Clapping her hands soundlessly, Kamaara peeled herself from the frame of the open door and sank into the seat across from Evan. "Good instincts, Polit. Sensors—and we've the best—show no Kraal warships in range of the *Missy*. In fact, we've detected no shipping as far as we can reach."

He felt something tight inside let go; it wasn't relief. "They've sent everything to Botharan space. A combined fleet."

"Still think we should meet your friends beforehand?" A finger tapped his notebook. "We could," with a sober look, "change course. I'd take that recommendation to the captain."

A test. Evan didn't hesitate. "We can't leave the Null to the Kraal. If they fail, we're no better off. If they succeed, it will be a victory that cements every affiliation to the new leadership and there'll be nothing to stop them." A new invasion of Botharis would be the least of it. "We have to get there first, Commander. *With* Paul and Esen and what they know."

"So be it." The security chief rose to her feet, gesturing for Evan to do the same. "We've received confirmation from the *Largas Swift*. She's a fast one. We'll meet on the other side of the Confederacy in under three hours. If—" a humorless grin, "—the Kraal haven't updated their stealth tech or left a surprise in our way."

Imagining what could go wrong was her specialty. His? *Preventing it.* "That's good news. Please thank the captain for the use of his quarters," Evan said, hoping he'd done just that as he methodically tucked away his holocube, notebook, and stylo—

"Oh, you're not done, Polit."

He paused in the midst of tidying his jacket. "I'm not?"

"Moment we enter Kraal space, *Mistral* goes to battle stations—and we've a faction agent on board of unknown capabilities and goals. I want eyes on Strevelor. Yours. Here. It's set to mine." She handed him an intraship com button identical to the one on her collar, stopping him when he went to attach it to his. "You aren't crew. Somewhere less noticeable, Polit."

Under her impatient and judgmental gaze, Evan quickly patted his pockets—notebook, stylo, holocube, *stun disk*—and started to put the button into the left upper one, that being the only one empty.

"Oh, for—not there." Taking his wrist, Kamaara folded up the cuff of his sleeve. When he put the button on the fabric, it stayed in place, out of sight with the cuff restored to normal. "Good," she decided. "Try it. First touch on, second off."

Had she noticed he'd a habit of tugging down his sleeves? *Probably,* Evan thought, more intrigued than embarrassed. Pressing the button while holding the cuff was as easy and natural as could be imagined. He made sure to deactivate it with a second press before letting go. "Thank you, Commander." Evan smiled ruefully. "I've a great deal to learn about this sort of thing."

Her perpetual scowl deepened as if he'd said something wrong, her mouth a grim line. Then, sharply, "Bulkheads close, make sure you're with Strevelor. You're no good to us locked in with the experts."

"Shouldn't be a problem," Evan replied, trying to sound confident however much he'd have preferred to be with Harps and the Dwelleys. "He'll want to know why I was called to the bridge. I'll use that."

Though he'd a sinking feeling Strevelor would be the one making sure they stayed together.

The bridge hummed with activity, all of it centered on displays and none of it involving Evan Gooseberry, so he made his way to the lift feeling invisible. *Plausible deniability,* Evan reminded himself.

But before the doors closed, Captain Clendon glanced up and gave the young diplomat a short approving nod.

It was more gratifying than a glowing monthly review from the ambassador. More, Evan decided, smiling in the privacy of the lift, than any of the *you-can't-tell-anyone* commendations he'd earned. Not that he could tell anyone about dealing with the Kraal either, but he'd take the regard of a person like the *Mistral*'s captain any day.

When the lift doors opened and he found himself face-to-face with Commander Dane Strevelor, Evan lost his smile. Regardless, he'd a job to do. He collected his wits. "Commander. I've been in touch with—"

"Not here," Strevelor cautioned, and indeed the corridor swarmed with crew, including now-armored security, helmets in hand. Every face was intent and serious. "The captain's going to battle stations— we've minutes. But you already know that," he added slowly, blue eyes gone cold. "Come with me, Polit."

Feeling alone despite those around him, Evan nodded.

"Polit!" Lieutenant Decker appeared, pushing his way to them. "I'm here to escort you to your quarters."

"That won't be necessary," Strevelor informed him. "The polit is with me, Lieutenant."

To Evan's surprise, Decker stepped close and took hold of his elbow. "Captain's orders, sir."

"And mine," the words snapped and crisp, but low, "are to release the polit and leave us. He's under *my* command—as are you." Strevelor frowned. "Unless you're attempting to interfere with our mission, the goal of which supersedes Captain Clendon and every officer on this ship."

Decker shot a look at Evan, as if for guidance. *Or for a reason to keep him from Strevelor.*

Though sorely tempted, the young diplomat swallowed what he might have said and pulled his arm from the other's unresisting grip. "The mission comes first. I'm staying with the commander."

Something changed in Decker's eyes. Hardened. "As you wish, Polit. Commander. I'll return to the rest of the team." With that, he wheeled around and walked away.

Evan watched him head in the direction of the guest quarters, knowing he'd lost his chance at sanctuary.

Strevelor didn't wait, going left, crew stepping smartly aside to let them pass. Following numbly behind, Evan recognized the access to the ship's medbay, now closed. Their goal was beyond it, the corridor growing empty as they reached the officers' quarters. Strevelor stopped in front of a door to enter a code, waving Evan through when it opened.

Commander Kamaara's cabin. Larger than the captain's, but not by much, and the walls were oddly bare except for the bed set into one wall and a fresher. A folded cot was secured in a corner, Decker's presumably, and the bags Evan had watched being shuffled from aircar to shuttle formed a tidy pile near a half table. There were two comfortable-looking chairs but otherwise no sense of personality to the place—because Kamaara lived that way?

More likely, Evan decided, she'd stripped out everything personal before giving up her space.

As Strevelor closed the door, the lights dimmed then flashed orange before resuming their usual hue. A voice filled the air, calm but stern. "This is your captain. Battle stations in three minutes. Crew to your posts. Guests, please go to your quarters. Doors and bulkheads will remain sealed until we stand down. I repeat. Battle stations in three minutes. This is not a drill."

Not a drill. Evan's stomach tried to climb up his throat. Crossing the Confederacy no longer scared him. Where they were going in this fragile bit of metal did. To where Harps had found the implant—to where the might of the Kraal would be waiting—to where a monster—a *ship-eater*—waited for what traveled translight—

With a slight deviation to meet Paul's ship. It made no sense, none whatsoever, to find that a comfort, but Evan did.

"Get comfortable, Polit," Strevelor advised, taking one of the chairs. "We're stuck here till it's over. Whatever it is."

Evan sat, resisting the urge to perch on the edge of the seat. There was nowhere to run even if he tried, and that wasn't, he reminded himself, why he was here. Composing his features into *earnest subordinate,* he tugged his cuffs casually as he eased back, pressing the hidden com button.

"We're at battle stations while transiting the Confederacy," Evan said, making the words a report. "I obtained permission from the Kraal." *Pushing it,* but they needed Strevelor to talk, so before the other could do more than raise an eyebrow, he continued, "The message on the bridge was from the Library. Paul and Esen wanted me to contact them. I did."

"And?"

"They're on their way. Their ship will dock with the *Mistral* before we approach Harps' next fixed point."

"They're coming to us?" Strevelor's smile was dazzling. "Evan, that's better than I'd dared hope. Every piece of the *Pathfinder* puzzle brought together at the same time. We can't fail. You'll get a medal for this."

Captain Clendon's nod had been real; this praise wasn't.

"Thank you, sir." Evan gave the words the right layers of humility and pride. "We'll need all the help we can get against the Null."

"The 'Null'?"

Expression shifting to *subordinate bearing bad news,* Evan nodded. "Paul and Esen discovered what's been attacking ships—and destroyed Noam. It's a mindless creature able to set traps in translight."

Strevelor's lean features seemed to become almost gaunt as he digested this, his eyes fixed beyond Evan at what only he could see. "Then I was right," less than a whisper, more than a breath. "The images were warnings. Warnings everyone had to se—" He snapped back to himself. "Did they say how to kill it?"

"No, sir." Had Kamaara caught those faint words? In his bedroom, the erstwhile Eller had said *the images were leaked to Survey by someone in the faction who recognized what they implied* . . . Had Strevelor just admitted to being that someone?

If so, Evan decided with a rush of hope, they'd common cause after all. "Sir, the Kraal have sent their—"

The lights dimmed then flashed red, a klaxon sounding. Strevelor rose to his feet, the light driving the humanity from his face. "That cursed navigator brought this down on us all," he half shouted over the din.

Before Evan could move, the faction agent seized a bag and opened it, spilling the contents on the floor. They weren't clothes. They were weapons. Other things. Devices.

None of them harmless.

The klaxon died off but the lights glowed a warning red along their rims, as did the door, now locked. "Why do you have weapons?" Evan said as loudly as he dared. "What are you doing?" The stun disk was in his inner pocket. He couldn't reach for it, not without Strevelor growing suspicious.

"What I came to do." A sharp look. "You aren't stupid, Polit Gooseberry. You know governments clean up their dirty little secrets. That's my job. To clean up."

"You're faction."

"It doesn't matter what I am. I made sure Haula and Poink stumbled over the *Pathfinder* data—they were coming close anyway, as was trip. Let them do the work of gathering everyone with restricted knowledge on this ship, a ship the Intrepid Few—and yes, those with greater vision and guts—helped create. Did you know that, Polit?"

He didn't wait for Evan to answer. "Now, thanks to you, Paul Ragem will be here, where none of his friends can save him. All that's left?" He lifted a narrow white box. "Is have Veya's monster finish the job. Ironic, you warning Decker what was out there might react to Harps' device."

He'd pushed the button. Kamaara must be hearing this. Evan refused to think of the alternative, that he'd failed and by that doomed them all—and Paul. Esen.

The only chance was to keep Strevelor talking—give Kamaara time to get here. "What's ironic about it?"

A finger tapped the box. "Because I guarantee you this will get its attention. Think of it as a summoner, keyed to call Veya's implant home."

"Then you can lure the Null away from ships." *Words.* They were all he had. He had to try and reach the other. "You cared about Noam. I saw it. You told me we have to save lives. Protect humanity. Don't you see—to do that, Strevelor, we must work together. We can stop the Null!"

An unwelcome hand found his shoulder. Pressed down as Strevelor bent to bring their faces too close. "I've a better idea," the agent said, his breath filling Evan's nostrils with a tinge of sour. "After feeding it this one last treat, I'll stop it harming Human ships. If it chooses to hunt what's in the way of humanity's next great expansion, well, Evan. You said it yourself. It's a mindless creature. Nature will be on our side this time."

Green eyes glared into blue. "They've heard you. Every word," Evan said in a strange hard voice that had never been his before. "They've heard and we're locked in here, Strevelor. You're finished."

"Thank you for your service, Polit." The hand shifted to the back of Evan's head. Cold dry lips pressed against his forehead.

Instead of trying to free himself from the loathsome contact, Evan used the moment to slip his hand inside his jacket and pull out the stun disk.

Only to have it stripped from his grasp. "None of that," Strevelor said, shaking his head as he stepped back. "I've places to go." Putting down the box, he emptied a second bag.

A ship's security uniform, complete with armor and helmet.

Evan gripped the arms of the chair. Opened his mouth to shout a warning as Strevelor raised the stun disk and pressed—

"Goosebumpies. You there or not?"

The voice wasn't Human. Evan fought through waves of pain, clinging to that, though it felt wrong, being sure not-Human meant safety. *His head hadn't hurt like this—ever.*

"I'm—I'm here," he gasped. Sitting, no, lying in a chair. In Kamaara's cabin. Stunned by his own weapon.

Mortified, Evan pulled himself upright and squinted around the room. He was alone. "Where are you?"

"Pocket pocket."

The com? He reached down frantically, only then realizing he no longer wore his jacket. It was on the floor. A glittering spot marked what had to have been the button. His notebook and stylo had been tossed aside.

His holocube with its image of Great Gran and the Sharp-fin stood on the table. Had Strevelor thought to leave him some comfort? Evan wanted to spit; his mouth was too dry.

"Goosebumpies, we're ready to start. You in?"

The voice—it was Wort's—came from the cube? *Pocket pocket!* They'd known he had a personal holocube and tapped into it. *Those smart, wonderful*—Evan lurched to his feet and staggered to the table. He picked up the cube. "Is Harps with you?"

"Yup. Eighth Rule of Harps. Be in the game."

"Wait," Evan ordered. Holding the cube, he made it to the door. Fused shut. The wall com panel had been melted.

Strevelor, buying time. How long? Ten minutes for a Human to recover from the stun—but he wasn't totally Human. Maybe he'd recovered faster. Before Kamaara could get someone to him past sealed bulkheads—

Had Strevelor known they'd go to battle stations or seized an opportunity—

Evan's breath caught.

The faction agent had opened a door locked by the bridge.

He'd claimed the faction helped design the ship. That he'd chosen the *Mistral* for his closing act of sabotage and murder.

If true, the faction agent could move freely during the alert. Add that he was disguised as those searching for him, would he be spotted in time?

There was nothing Evan could do about that.

Maybe he could do something else. Evan gripped the holocube in both hands. "Listen to me carefully. What you've been tracing is the implant. What has the implant isn't an intelligent species but an extra-dimensional space monster—"

"Did you show him the game?" "I didn't. Must have been Wort." "I didn't—"

"STOP!" Evan shouted. "Please. This is real," he went on in a more normal voice, hoping the silence from the cube didn't mean they'd abandoned him. *Please not that.* "The monster's real, I promise you, and we're in danger. Strevelor lied to us. He has a device—a summoner, he called it—to attract the implant. It'll bring the monster right to this ship. If that happens, we'll all die."

Harps' voice. "Not fun, Evan."

"No. It's not." He closed his eyes; it did nothing for the drumming in his head. "I've no com. Contact the bridge. Tell them what I've told you, but there's no time, Harps. You have to keep Strevelor's device from working." *What did he know?* "He said it was ironic I'd suggested the Null—the monster—might react to your tracer, since it reacted to Veya's implant. That's when he claimed his device could call it. Does that help?"

"Harps is busy doing it," said a Dwelley. "Wort calls the bridge." Making the voice Blue Spider's. "Are you hurt?"

He wasn't alone.

Evan turned to lean his shoulders and aching head against the wall. "I'll be fine," he replied and dared hope for the first time. "Thank you. Thank you all."

"Sixth Rule of Harps, work with the best. But next time we play the game, Goosebumpies. Deal?"

"Deal."

16: Starship Afternoon

LESY'S boisterous landing on the plates of the antechamber was echoed by an echoing lighter *clank* from above—Rudy, closing the hatch to the crew quarters before climbing down the ladder. Then a series of *tickticks* as he secured it.

Which might have been standard pre-lift protocol on a courier ship like the *Swift* but was more likely what Rudy had decided to do about Nia in the short term. She was coming with us, and whether she'd leave the ship again might be a decision Rudy felt was his to make as well.

If so, I'd news for our protector. Nia wasn't going to pay for my improvising.

Paul, meanwhile, had followed Lesy. I dropped to my stomach to peer down the tube, wisps of hair tickling my cheeks. I didn't need the ears of a Lanivarian to catch the low roar of what would otherwise have been a gratifying cheer from those outside the ship as the fake me appeared.

One of these days—

My friend had to hurry to keep up with her. Certainly it wasn't more than a moment before I heard the airlock door close and felt a rumble through the floor that must signify the withdrawal of the ramp, the *Swift* apparently more like a bucket than was comfortable even for me, and I sincerely hoped those cheering would notice the ship was preparing for lift.

A dark-haired head appeared in the tube below me. The light caught the fine chain around his neck, though he'd tucked the medallion inside his shirt. *As if that would prevent Lesy sensing the bit of Esen inside.*

I'd shared with Lesy what it was—a small medallion inscribed with the logo for Cameron & Ki, our company, the names Paul Cameron and Esolesy Ki entwined about a starship, with the date below. I'd shared with her why it held my flesh in a cryounit—being an introduction to any strange Web-being Paul might meet.

She'd been amused and offered to make Paul something less boring to wear.

Paul looked up with a relieved grin, beginning to climb. "Tell Rudy we're ready, Old Blob."

He used the nickname because he believed it was just the three of us, my safe little Human Web, and I backed away not only to give him room but to hide a face Paul read better than any other.

Rudy was in the bridge, busy collapsing the seats we wouldn't need. He'd closed the door to the tube leading up. I touched his arm, then pointed to it anxiously. He scowled to show he wasn't impressed with my latest indiscretion and There Would Be Consequences—even for a Human, he'd remarkably expressive features—then sighed, knowing it was hopeless. "All stowed and safe for lift."

I gave him my best Bess smile.

Rudy tried valiantly to hold his scowl against it, giving up as Paul arrived. "I'm venting the engines," he muttered, tucking away the last extra seat.

My first friend chuckled. "That ought to clear the field." Space on the bridge being minimal even with the removal of some seats, Paul had no trouble reaching over to tug a lock of my hair. "Thought for a moment there we weren't going to make it. Good job."

Praise I didn't entirely deserve. About to confess, I saw Rudy, behind Paul, shake his head.

He didn't want Paul to know about Nia. Not until we were off the ground and there was no option to leave her behind. *Fine.*

I still stuck out my tongue at him, that being a thing this me could do to express an opinion, then jumped on the nearest inflated seat to check its bounce. Paul laughed.

There were times, I thought cagily, *being Youngest had advantages.*

And there were times it had none. I lay back, wishing I could growl as Rudy checked the straps securing me to the seat, then Paul had to—*not because he didn't trust his cousin but because this me brought out instincts even my oldest friend couldn't deny*—regardless of my having done them up perfectly myself.

Humans. Mind you, once Rudy input the lift sequence, I'd have liked to check their straps and Nia's, because the *Largas Swift* began to rattle and clank like a stampeding herd of Carasians—not that they moved in herds, but the comparison sounded about right.

"Is something broken?" I shouted, gripping the seat with both hands as the universe shook with heavier and heavier vibrations as if ready to explode.

"Hang on!"

As I was doing just that, to the limit of this me's strength, Rudy's cheerful advice didn't help. On the next seat, Paul rolled his head to face me; I was gratified to see he didn't look particularly happy either. *And was holding on.* "B-be smo-ooth-er when we—we're up," he gasped, though I'd no reason to think my friend was any more experienced with this category of starship than I was.

I tried not to think of Nia, alone above us. Or, for that matter, the boom above her. *If we survived this, I wouldn't complain about Duggs' piloting again.*

"WHOOOOO!!"

I thought that was what Rudy shouted but as the engines—obviously too close to our part of the ship—roared, it was more a guess. I gritted my flat primate teeth and endured, grateful I'd cycled so recently I shouldn't explode from stress.

Around the time I'd changed my mind about stress and exploding, beginning to grow exceedingly warm, the ship stopped.

Not that it did. We were still hurtling along, but the cessation of engine noise came at the same instant I felt very strange.

Very . . . light.

I did my utmost to ignore the confusion of my inner ear, this me reacting to weightlessness. Rudy freed himself and pushed up to the ceiling, which was now a wall as, I supposed, was the floor. While he was busy doing whatever a captain did when he'd no real crew, I undid my straps.

And floated. Up and up until I bumped into Rudy, who reached around without looking to gently push me away.

It was almost as much fun as being a Blimmit, a species that lived in the middle atmosphere of their gas giant and propelled themselves along by passing gas out of the requisite orifice. *Oh, could this me do that?*

Before I could try, a hand snagged my foot and pulled me down, not that there was down except that Paul was, in fact, standing on what had been a wall. An oddity explained by his new footwear, I realized as he held out a Bess-sized pair of magboots. Adrift like a balloon on a string, I folded in half to gaze at him pleadingly, if upside-down. Something this me did very well. "Do I have to?"

His thick hair swayed as if underwater, also fun, and his lips quirked, but I knew that look. *Safety before somersaults in midair.* "Rudy needs us to stay in place, Old Blob."

Implying Paul had his own wish to float thwarted, so I took the boots, managing three complete revolutions before getting them on my feet—where they fit nicely—and aimed myself for the nearest surface before clicking the heels together.

Down I went, or up, since I'd aimed myself for a blank space beside the panel that had Rudy's attention, that being the fastest way to transfix him with what he called my irresistible stare, hopefully still effective given we were oriented in opposite directions. "I need to pee."

His eyes didn't leave the panel. "No, you don't."

True. What I needed was to check on Nia, but I'd noticed adult Humans frequently underestimated the speed with which such biological urges could affect their offspring. At the same time, they obsessed over the potential for accidents, not that I was *that* young anymore. Though there'd been the time—

Not important now. "But Rudy—" Was that a thump from underfoot?

"What's going on?"

And that would be Paul. *Who noticed everything.*

Rudy and I exchanged glances. His eyebrow rose. *Your fault, you tell him,* that was. Aloud, "I've confirmed our departure with the *Mistral.* We go translight in fifteen minutes."

Where the Null could catch us. Not thinking about it.

I walked to the right-angled junction between former ceiling and wall, paused to remember which of my Elders had the better technique— Mixs—then turned my left foot toe in to free the boot from the metal. Stretching the exact amount to connect to the wall, while leaning way back was ideal.

Stretching less than that while loosening the right boot accidentally being not, I drifted haplessly into the air again.

Paul caught my outstretched hand and drew me to where I could click heels and attach beside him, then regarded me with a most unreasonable level of suspicion. Since I'd a guilty conscience, that might have worked; fortunately, I'd news to distract him. *Hopefully.*

"What's gone on," I said primly, "is that Nia brought us the boom and Rudy's put it away." I pointed up before checking my directions, then quickly angled my arm to the left, adding, "In the cargo hold." To cover my mistake.

His suspicion didn't fade so much as solidify. "And?"

And I'd let Nia see me cycle—and—

"'And?'" I echoed innocently.

"Tell me you were expecting Kraal warships," Rudy interrupted. "Because two just matched our course and velocity."

Saved by my web-kin. Well, unless we were doomed by the misdeeds of her favorite sort of Human.

I preferred to go with saved, under the circumstances.

The voice was deep and velvet smooth. The tone, impatient. "Where are you going?"

Paul and Rudy kept silent, this being a conversation between me and my testy Elder. Who was, apparently, the next best thing to second in command not of two paltry warships but the largest fleet in Kraal history, presently hovering at the outskirts of Botharan space to give the planetary government fits.

How Skalet explained her need to intercept a shabby little courier ship I didn't bother to ask, and this wasn't so much a conversation as tedious repetition. *At least they hadn't ordered us to stop moving.* "We're going—" I said again, "—where we're supposed to be going. Why are you here?"

To this point, Skalet had replied with variations on *you answer first.* Maybe I'd worn her down. More likely, she'd hadn't much time either. "We offer the protection of the Confederacy to Botharis."

"You can't mean to attack the Null within the system," I countered.

An ominous silence. *Like that, was it?* I looked at Paul, understanding the worry on his dear face. Sharing it.

We'd just have to deal with the Null first. Rather, second, my webkin presently in the way. I attempted to deepen what wasn't the most effective voice for negotiating. "Skalet—"

"Your clever Evan talked an admiral into letting a Survey ship pass unchallenged through the Confederacy." *Amusement.* Her voice sharpened. "If you're planning to join forces against our mutual foe, I suggest reconsidering your choice of allies. Stay."

Ersh, it was almost sentimental.

Rudy nodded vigorously. Gray eyes somber, Paul shook his head.

So be it. "Can't do that. We promised Evan we'd pop in," I said, switching to the carefree childish voice I knew would irritate her the most.

"*Unacceptable.*"

After three seconds I started breathing again. Skalet had to be alone and on a secure channel. Otherwise, that word in that tone? Gunners on both ships would have opened fire to eradicate the object of their glorious leader's scorn. Me.

"There could be an outstanding chance for glory, you know. You could come along," I said, half closing my eyes to better picture her face. There'd be fury. Scorn. Even outrage.

Followed by speculation. *What was I up to?*

Then, "Agreed. The *Centos Pa* will accompany you to relay information and coordinates. If you locate the ship-eater first, the fleet will follow and destroy it."

Paul stirred. Knowing what he'd want, I held up a finger for patience and he subsided. "And the fleet stays where it is until you hear from the *Centos Pa*. Your word on it." *Knowing Skalet too.*

Another pause, this one worse than the first. I'd no idea what it would take for her to seize control of the fleet, if that's what it took. No idea if her identity as S'kal-ru and all it meant to her would survive it.

No idea if she *could.*

We were all taking risks today, those of us able to, and I took it as a mark of maturity that I waited for her. Even when Rudy flashed five digits in warning that was all the time we had to spare.

"Given." The com went dead.

Paul, understanding Skalet as well as anyone could, ran a hand through his hair and shook his head at me with a wry smile. I wasn't entirely sure if he meant to convey approval or commiseration. *Conceivably both.* "Rudy," Paul said, "time to send our arrival confirmation to the *Centos Pa*. And warn the *Mistral* we're bringing a friend."

"Done." Rudy released his boots and soared across the bridge to the tube door. "I'm going to check our cargo." Meaning Nia, who should have been part of any decision about her world and the Kraal, and shouldn't be riding up there alone, but hadn't been and must. *I owed her a great many hayberries.* "You two strap in. *Swift* tends to shimmy a little going in and out of translight. A partner makes things interesting."

"And there could be a monster waiting," I reminded them, not because they'd forgotten, but because they were brave and—all of a sudden—I wasn't, not at all.

"Evan and the *Mistral*." With that presumed reassurance, Paul guided me through the air to my seat. His medallion floated by its chain and I curled my fingers to keep from reaching for it.

Not yet.

Nearby

THE message from Rudy had been terse and to the point: missile on board, the *Largas Swift* on her way to find and fight a monster. *His friends were beyond his help.*

Of more immediate import to Lionel Kearn was the arrival of not one but two full trainloads of staff and scholars, the latter somewhat perturbed to share seats with the people supposed to be greeting them, though as it happened Henri had set up an impromptu assessment counter and dealt with a fair number before her train pulled up to the Library's platform.

First off was a Lishcyn, snout up to the sunlight, followed by two of the *Swift*'s crew struggling with luggage. Though he'd thought himself prepared for a difference between Esen and Lesy's version of the form, Lionel found himself awestruck. This Esolesy Ki wasn't just more mature, with rougher scales and hairier ears, she moved with a restrained elegance that made Esen's Lishcyn as clumsy as an elk calf.

Which she was, to be blunt—adorably so, provided you removed any breakables in advance—and Lionel realized in that instant Esen couldn't resume this form at the Library. *A problem for another time.*

"Welcome home, Esolesy Ki," he said, stepping aside to let the larger being into the Library.

"I most certainly am *NOT* Esolesy Ki," bellowed with the distressing volume of Lishcyn lungs. Those exiting the train with auditory organs paused to stare, those without moving along. "First those HUMANS at the FIELD and now THIS?! I expected BETTER from staff here. Imagine confusing us. IMAGINE!"

"Your pardon, Lesyole." Henri hurried up, appearing unusually flustered. "Administrator Kearn, Es—Esolesy Ki had to change her plans and visit her homeworld." Her half-bow to the Lishcyn also let her catch her breath. "Let me introduce the distinguished Lesyole, Founder of the famed Lesyole Kilns, who graciously consented to travel across the wilds of space to bring us word."

"IN person, as you can see." Those deep-set Lishcyn eyes twinkled, Lesy waiting with wicked glee for him to process her ambush of Esen's plan, and Lionel's first reaction was that Duggs had been right. *She was playing him.*

His next? That Esen's Elder had known from the start the imposture couldn't work and played them all, her web-kin included. Lionel bowed with sincere appreciation. "Greetings, Lesyole. We are truly honored by your presence."

She flashed both tusks at him, touching the tips of her forked tongue to inlays the like of which he'd personally never seen outside of a museum collection. *And must have cost a fortune.* "I'm thrilled to visit YOUR famous Library," this as she walked into the Lobby and aimed her huge head to gaze around like a tourist. "Esolesy Ki has told me ALL about it." She came to a sudden stop, looking down at him, a hand clutching her bag—Esolesy's. "The poor young thing gave me this trinket to show you. I simply must tell you of her situation—but first—" The hand let go to fling outward, the sweep of her thick powerful arm almost decapitating a careless Queeb. "—travel is SO arduous. Take my bags to the house," to the *Swift*'s crew. "Lionel—may I call you Lionel? I feel we're old acquaintances already. I'm famished. FAMISHED!"

Her stomachs growled and burbled in alarming audible confirmation, causing some of those walking past to give her more room.

"Fudge?" Lionel offered promptly, holding out the bag he'd brought. She took it, ears flicking with delight. "I'll send up your luggage. In the meantime, if it pleases you, Lesyole, I've a supper waiting for you in my office. I'll be—right there," he called after her rapidly retreating back.

Lionel turned and raised a hand to halt the burdened crewmembers, who promptly set down what looked to be heavy bags with relief. "Thank you." He waved to bring up two from Library maintenance. "Use the cart," he advised. Rudy had exceeded expectation on his shopping.

Next, Lionel settled the female crewmember, Daisi Largas, with Carwyn, who'd agreed to house their visitor. The pair wandered away, Carwyn asking questions about Minas XII and space travel, Daisi craning her neck to see everything she could of the Library. *They'd be fine.*

The male crewmember stood turned so his hood shadowed jaw and cheek, eyes glinting as they measured, assessed. *You could remove the tattoos*, Lionel thought. *That didn't make Meony-ro any less Kraal.*

"One last item," Lionel told him. Greeters and other staff, many with bells tucked into pockets or belts adding a festive chime to their steps, were sorting the new arrivals from the scholars who'd more or less patiently been waiting since the morning, giving the latter precedence. He caught the attention of Brooks Louza, one of the seniormost. When she approached, he beckoned her close to whisper in her ear, pressing a list into her hand.

Giving him—and the list—an amused look, Brooks headed off, collecting two more staff as she went.

If anyone could round up the rest of their strayed guests, Lionel thought with some relief, it'd be the retired poultry farmer.

"Thank you for your patience. This way please," he said to Meony-ro. Speed was the key. It wouldn't appear odd to have the administrator whisk a Human visitor from the Lobby into the admin corridor and few non-Humans would be able to tell the difference between this visitor and any of the other Humans in the building.

It was their Botharan staff who concerned Lionel. Years of intermittent Kraal rule had left its scars, and the promise to stay away from the planet far too new for most to believe.

Then there was Ally, eager to leave it—

"We gave them a great send-off, Lionel," Henri said as she raised the counter and held it for Meony-ro to pass. "Poor Esen was overcome—you should have seen her scamper up the ramp. You saw, didn't you?" Her bright eyes fixed on the Kraal.

"I did. An emotional celebration," he confirmed in a low, pleasant voice, ducking his head in acknowledgment.

"I'm glad—though I regret you now face all this, Henri." Lionel nodded to the restive line of scholars. A Dwelley bumped an Iterod who stepped on the toes of something that squealed and he hesitated.

"Go," she ordered, dropping the counter behind them. "I had my break this morning. You there! No spitting. Do it again and you're at the back of the line."

Around the corner, out of sight and alone, if briefly, Lionel turned to Meony-ro. They were the same height, but the former Kraal outmassed and outmuscled him. *Let alone whatever was concealed about his person,* a thought Lionel found unexpectedly reassuring. "Thank you for coming."

"Captain Lefebvre said you'd need of my skills," with anticipation. "I can get to work at once."

"The situation has evolved. Follow me." Lionel led the way to Paul's office, unlocking the door with a card he passed to Meony-ro. "There's a cot, fresher, food, and a change of clothes. You'll find a datacube on the desk detailing everything we have on a task you're uniquely qualified to handle. If you need anything more, call me on the com by name. We'll meet again in the morning."

"Agreeable."

Succinct. Reminded of Skalet, Lionel offered his hand. The one that took it was callused and strong, scarred across the palm.

Meony-ro drew him forward by that grip, drilling him with a cold stare. "The honor I seek, Lionel Kearn, is to die for Paul Ragem."

Hopefully not on Botharis. "I swear to you," Lionel said solemnly, "this task is extremely dangerous, and failure would pose a direct threat to Paul." And to the rest of Botharis, should any of the missiles go off during decommissioning, but he saw no reason to quibble with someone of such clarity.

Though when Constable Mal Lefebvre arrived in the morning to meet his new bomb expert, it should be an interesting encounter.

Meony-ro wasn't done. "Esolesy Ki—she is unharmed? The stranger Lishcyn refused to speak to me on the train." Lips twisted. "Other than orders. I do not trust her."

"Esolesy Ki," Lionel stated, certain of this much, "is where she needs to be."

Lionel waited after the door closed behind Meony-ro, hearing the door lock. *Good.* Another item on his list if not safe, then at least put somewhere for the night.

He strode down the corridor to his office, determined to resolve the next. After a perfunctory knock, Lionel opened the door and quickly stepped inside, closing it behind him. "I want to—" His voice died in his throat.

"Hello Lionel."

"Hello Lionel."

There wasn't one Lishcyn in his office.

There were two.

Out There

NTREPID Few? I've heard of them. Old has-been officers, dreaming of their glory days.

Some of them are more. They've sponsored a project. Classified, high tech. Nav system like no one's seen before. They want you for it, Veya.

The shard spins. Mistakes. Wrong turns. Errors. She spent her life striving for perfection. Now to end it, seeing every way she'd failed.

But this is Hell, after all.

There are risks. Others play it safe.

Others stay home. That's not for me.

Glad to hear it.

Home. She still fights. Still tugs the eye off its goal. Slightly. Slightly. There are ships ahead and Hell is hungry.

There are ships and one could be his. There are worlds ahead and one will be.

She mustn't stop fighting. Won't stop.

Momma, can't you stay a little longer? Till the hayberries are ripe. Stay till then, and we'll pick them and—

<u>Hush. You know I can't. My ship needs me.</u>
<u>I need you.</u>

Veya watches what might have been an arm or intestine drift past, broken free from its filament. More and more such lonesome bits pass in and out of sight; Hell's damage or Hell's waste. If only she could gather them, build with them, regain a shape. Fight with it. Die with it.

Her eye has found another ship.

And Hell is hungry.

17: Starship Night

TIME spent traveling in space was transitory. A chrono on a control panel of the *Largas Swift* counted down to when we'd finish moving through the translight corridor. Two hours. A handful of minutes.

To cross what took light itself centuries.

Human measurement to soothe fleshy brains.

I found myself drawn more and more to Paul's medallion, with its memories of how a Web-being—perhaps the Null as well—moved through the void. Eons spent along gradients of gas. When the mood or need struck, and energy abundant, slipping out of normal space to soar—

Rudy rapped his knuckles on the door to the tube leading up. I started and stared at him, receiving a grim, "It's time, Bess."

I snuck a look at Paul. He put down the e-ration pack he'd been consuming, securing it in a pocket. Having forgotten that rule, mine floated out of reach, and I'd been about to launch myself in pursuit until spotting the chrono and having thoughts.

I couldn't interpret the particular expression building on the face of my first and dearest friend, but it wouldn't have surprised me if *what has Esen done now* was involved somewhere.

The door swung slowly open. Rudy, nearby, hooked it in place and offered a hand to the person floating out, headfirst.

With an expert spin and click of her heels Nia gracefully attached herself to what had been the floor—and was again, it being the one with seats—and I couldn't help but blurt out, "You know how to do that?"

Though her eyes were locked on Paul, who didn't seem to be breathing, her smile was for me. "I've been to the moons, Bess. Standard training." The smile disappeared. "Paul."

His name snapped him back from wherever he'd gone. "You can't be here." An illogical statement since Nia clearly was here, but I'd noticed Paul tended to be less coherent in her presence.

Was it a good sign?

"It's my choice."

"She stole the boom," I contributed to speed this up. Two hours wasn't that long.

Rudy said something rude in an approving tone. Paul went pale, but his eyes suddenly softened. "Nia."

She made that odd little grimace that squeezed her eyes shut for a second. "You don't get to have all the fun."

For some reason this made Paul and Rudy grin. The latter actually laughed, with Nia joining in as I looked from one to the other, at a loss. *What was happening?*

My friend caught my look. "It's—we're in this together, Bess."

Of course we were, being on the same ship. But he hadn't meant that. "I don't understand."

He put an arm around my shoulders. "I'm glad Nia's here," he explained. "So is Rudy."

I frowned up at him. "Where she could be gobbled by a space monster."

For some reason, this made all them chuckle.

"Yes," Paul agreed. "And I'd never have asked you, Nia, to put yourself in danger."

She smiled at him.

"But together, Bess," with a gentle squeeze for emphasis, "we're stronger. Isn't that why you helped her hide?"

Rudy had the grace to look uncomfortable; I said it for him. "Not exactly. We locked her in until it was too late for her to leave. She's seen—" a wave at me, "—you know."

My friend turned me, a hand on each shoulder, and crouched to bring our faces to the same level—which would have been easier if I'd known he wanted to do that and released my magboots to float.

It made a tiny space of us, as I'm sure he intended, one in which I couldn't evade him if I tried. His brilliant gray eyes scanned my face, reading it with the ease of long practice. "You chose to protect Rudy," he said, the words spaced out and gentle. "You made sure we could leave Botharis."

"I had to."

"I know." The slow warm smile that meant I wasn't in any trouble at all and I missed having a tail to wag. He put his forehead to mine—actually easier without a snout—to whisper very very quietly, because we weren't really alone, "I dreamed of sharing you with Nia, Old Blob. You made it come true."

To be precise, she'd forced me into cycling by being where and who she was, but I grasped the essential. "You're not mad at me?"

"Never." He gathered me into his arms, that Human embrace. It worked best for this me, though wasn't too bad when I was a Lishcyn. Well, Paul got bruises if that me hugged him back and—

The point being, a hug meant I was more than forgiven. I'd made Paul happy, bizarre as it seemed, so I twisted my feet and launched into the air with a happy laugh.

Having done so without due care, I'd have bounced off the ceiling and possibly struck some controls. Fortunately, Nia set herself free as well and intercepted me with a deft little push to send me spinning back to Paul.

Who pushed me to Rudy in a delightful game of *who's got Bess,* and I'd have happily done it the rest of the trip, ignoring everything else.

But I couldn't. The next time Nia had me, I grabbed her, too. We drifted as one, face-to-face. "I am Paul's secret. I'm why he stayed away."

I ignored his soft protesting, "Es."

"I'm why he died and you lost him," I finished because she had to know, and I hoped with all I had this me was easier for her to forgive.

Blue eyes gazed at me. I couldn't read her expression—didn't know her well enough to guess what she thought. *She didn't push me away.*

A blink and a single glistening drop floated free from her eye. "You brought him back, didn't you? For his sake, not yours."

All at once, I was wrapped in Nia's arms. She'd softer places than Paul's, making it more comfortable to be held. Not that I'd ever tell him.

Suddenly, there were more arms and firmer body parts, and if ever there was a time I mustn't explode from surprise, it was in the midst of this crush of apparently overwhelmed-with-joy Humans.

My friends, who were friends again.

Though if they kept it up, this me was going to have trouble breathing.

Paul would rescue me. *He always did.*

Rudy brought out a fourth seat and we strapped in, there not being much time left, as Paul put it, to rehearse our plan to deal with the Null.

As arranged, we'd dock with the *Mistral.* Everyone but me would go over to the safety of the Survey ship, Paul explaining to them that Esen hadn't come after all. He'd give Captain Clendon the excellent news that *Swift* had brought a trap specifically designed to destroy an extra-dimensional space monster with lightning tentacles like the one coming their way. The Library to the rescue again!

Not that we were to promote that part because Survey might want some credit too, but it would make a nice addition to our brochure.

If we succeeded.

My part? To make our trap irresistible by coating the boom in web-flesh. *Me.* Once done, I'd act as the *Swift's* remote control systems—something this bucket most certainly didn't have, but the *Mistral* didn't need to know that—and on receiving Rudy's "command" I'd lock the hatch on the cargo hold and set it to vent, releasing our trap into space. The *Mistral,* the *Swift* attached, would move out of range, leaving the trap to do its job.

That was the plan they knew. *Mine contained some modifications.* None of which Paul would ever approve so I didn't bother sharing.

Our end goal remained the same. The Null would take the bait, swallow the boom, and, well, *BOOM.*

Rudy sighed. "There go all the presents."

"'Presents?'" I echoed with dismay, those being something this and other mes quite enjoyed.

"I'd filled the hold with treats for the family. They can be replaced." He grinned at me. "Even yours, Gloria. Bess, I mean."

Nia looked a question. "Sometimes I'm Gloria," I explained. "It's Rudy's name for me when I'm his pretend niece." *Who gets presents,* I thought, cheerful again.

Her attention shifted to Rudy. "Wasn't 'Gloria' your pet mousel?"

"A mousel?" I glowered at him.

The former patroller made a quick recovery. "Gloria was cute. Like you. This you. And the *Swift.*" Patting a bulkhead.

I was surprised it didn't rattle.

"And that's it." Nia's long fingers toyed with the end of a strap, her expression impossible to read.

Paul studied her, then asked quietly. "If you see a problem, now's the time."

She looked up. "I see nothing but. All this—it's based on guess-work. That the boom will kill it. That it will take the—" an under-standably confused glance at me, "—bait and not the ship."

"That part's no guess." I retorted. "The Null hunt my kind."

Earning an unhappy look from Paul. "You're sure it can't detect you as Bess."

We'd discussed this. I squeezed my cheek then stuck out my tongue. "This flesh is Human," I reassured him. Then, because he'd given me the opening I needed, I pointed casually at his chest. "That's not."

Paul pulled out his medallion, cradling it in his palm. "It contains a speck of Esen," he told the others, stopping there, it being my special gift and private.

"Enough for the Null to sense." *Not that I knew any such thing.* I held out my hand. "It goes with the boom."

Silently he took the chain from his neck and passed it to me. The medallion was warm from his skin, frozen inside, and the living sym-bol of our bond. I blinked quickly as I pushed it inside my coveralls.

"If you have to evacuate, take the lifepod," Rudy ordered. "Remem-ber how to use it?"

I raised an eyebrow. "You told us."

"Perfect memory doesn't take the place of practice, Old Blob," Paul insisted, sounding a little grumpy. Maybe it was giving up his medal-lion.

I unstrapped, gave a well-aimed push—*having practiced*—and grabbed the bright red handle. There should have been a second lifepod in the crew quarters, each capable of holding the *Swift*'s maximum crew complement of five, but Joel had had it removed for repairs. "Turn the handle halfway in either direction," I recited. "The hatch opens, and I hold my nose. Just kidding," as Paul gave me *that* look.

I wasn't wrong. Rudy had warned us the pod, while checked out and reliable, needed a good cleaning. Something else he hadn't had time to do. My guess was he'd preferred polishing his new ship over tackling body odor remnants.

Or he didn't want anyone to use the lifepod for anything but a life-or-death emergency.

"Once I get inside and close the hatch, I have five seconds to step into a safety restraint cubby before the pod blows itself clear of the ship and begins transmitting an auto distress signal. Cupboards contain e-rations, water, and spacesuits." I gave Rudy my most innocent look. "Did I miss anything?"

He shook his head. "Just remember it's one-use-only. Joel'll have my hide if we have to replace it."

"I've no intention of using the pod," I assured him.

Later, I'd remember saying that.

Nia didn't appear convinced. "We're using an explosion to destroy a creature that feeds on energy. What if we end up feeding it? What if it grows?"

Paul shrugged, his hair floating distractingly. "We won't know until we try."

"And if it can't die?"

"Everything dies." They stared at me, implying it sounded grimmer from this me than when Ersh said it. *As she had on a regular basis, usually accompanied by a lecture on protecting my form-self, whatever it was.* Her point being life was a fight against entropy and, while it must ultimately lose, there was no need to hurry the process through stupidity.

"If a Null could consume vast amounts of energy in one gulp without risk to itself," I said in my calmest, most reasonable tone, "it would feed on stars, not ships." *Or Web-beings.*

"The boom is what we have, Nia," Paul said with a note of finality. "It's more than any of the Kraal ships or the *Mistral* possess."

"Thanks again for putting it on my new ship," complained Rudy.

It lightened the mood, as I was sure he'd intended. At least that of my Human friends.

I pretended. If Nia and Rudy hadn't been there, Paul would have noticed and worried. He knew me in any form. Would have seen I was keeping something from him.

I was.

I felt the press of the medallion over this me's heart, its secrets within my grasp, and reviewed my plan, the one Paul didn't know and wouldn't, unless it worked and I chose to tell him.

I would be leaving the *Swift,* but not in the lifepod.

It was time I remembered how to fly.

Nearby

"THIS is the captain speaking. We're clear of the Confederacy and standing down from battle stations. Passengers are to remain in their quarters until further notice. I repeat, standing down from battle stations."

Evan eyed the door. When it didn't suddenly open, he went back to searching Strevelor and Decker's luggage, a task he'd assigned himself when it became obvious he'd be in here a while.

"We told them where you were," Wort assured him.

"And insisted. Didn't we, Harps?"

A popping sound, then, "Harps is busy saving us. Don't bother him. We did insist, Goosebumpies."

Evan smiled at the holocube on the table. "I know. They'll come for me when they can." His smile faded. He wasn't about to tell his friends that the delay in retrieving him probably meant Kamaara and her people hadn't found the faction agent. They would—a ship being finite— but given his door would need power tools to open, the pragmatic head of security would consider his location to be more secure than most.

Given Strevelor's claim the faction had been involved in the *Mistral*'s design, he preferred not to think about what the agent might do to the ship in the interim. Or had already done—

Nothing he could do about that. He opened the next bag. There were five in total. Two Strevelor had emptied on the floor; Evan kept a wary distance from their contents, not that he knew what most of it was. A third had contained the clothes the pair had worn on Pachen IV, including sandals, along with the oddments anyone needed for protracted travel. None of it personal or labeled.

All of it lies. He'd paused, his outrage at the agents' trespass in their home returned a thousandfold, and decided, then and there, that no matter how hospitable Great Gran was, nor how generous her nature, he'd insist she never let strangers through the door again.

After which Evan had envisioned her reaction, right down to her furious *and whose house is it,* and almost laughed at himself. She'd never change. *She mustn't.*

He was the one who had to adjust, starting with a com in his room he'd leave on at all times, so people who mattered could reach him. So he could reach them.

"Did you find any secrets?"

He'd had to tell the Dwelleys what he was doing and why—mostly to stop their effort to enlist him in a game to pass the time. They'd taken to his hunt with fierce glee. "Nothing yet. Going into the next one."

The fourth bag was Decker's, judging by the size of the garments, and for the first time Evan hesitated. He didn't know Decker was a faction agent.

He'd apologize later. Resolutely, he emptied the contents on the bed and began going through each item. Everything appeared absolutely normal.

He pulled out a pair of undergarments printed in a dramatic eyeball motif.

To each, their own. He went to repack the bag. "What's this?" he murmured aloud.

"What's what?"

"He found something. Harps, he found something!"

Pop pop. A *SMACK* that made Evan wince in sympathy, despite knowing Dwelley skin was tough. "Don't bother Harps! What did you find, Goosebumpies?"

"The bag feels heavier than it should." He poked the bottom and sides, shook it. "I must be wrong."

"Stealth field." Harps' voice, dry and distracted. "Should be a trigger. Bring it here. I'll find it."

"Goosebumpies is trapped!" shouted the Dwelleys in unison.

"Right. Not fun."

Evan half smiled. *It was certainly more bearable with these three around.* "I'm open to ideas."

"If it was me, I'd hide a trigger in something no one would steal. Something easy to grab."

"Like underwear with eyeballs?"

A pause, then, "I'd steal those." "Me first!" "Can you bring them?" *He'd been joking.*

On the other hand, Evan had nothing but respect for the minds of the hilarious trio. He picked up the flamboyant article of clothing, inspecting it closely. Almost finished, and slightly embarrassed, his fingers discovered a thicker spot. One of the eyeballs wasn't like the others. "I may have found it," he announced wonderingly. "What do I do with it?"

"Release won't be on the inside."

"Blue Spider, shouldn't Harps go back to work and save us?"

"Think I'd stop for this if I hadn't? Fifth Rule of Harps. Don't fail."

Evan stared at the cube. "We're safe? You've stopped Strevelor?"

"Can't say. Did scramble a signal that wasn't mine, wasn't the ship's. That do?"

"Genius," Wort said with feeling.

Genius. Hardly daring to believe, Evan sank onto the clothes-strewn bed, bag still in one hand, eyeball underwear in another. The two touched on his lap.

The bottom of the bag vanished, replaced by a foam-filled space. There were shapes carved in the foam. One held a translight com, identical as far as Evan could tell, to the device Strevelor had given him. Another, empty, resembled the foghorn on Great Gran's boat, only smaller.

A weapon, and Decker had it.

"It worked," Evan said numbly. "Decker's one of them and he's armed."

"He isn't here."

"Haven't seen him since the alert."

"Should we tell the captain?"

"Wait, please." He pulled out the com with the vague idea of seeing if he could use it. Wedged underneath was a folded piece of plas.

Evan put aside the com and pulled out the piece, unfolding it, somehow unsurprised to recognize the neat handwriting. He mouthed the words as he read aloud:

Esen, Esolesy Ki, Bess.

Decker had stolen his notebooks. Had torn out and kept this half of a page, the one where Evan had begun his questions about Paul's friends, and he had to assume Decker had read the rest.

Why?

"Goosebumpies? You good?"

Not in any sense. Evan roused himself, taking the paper and, after a second's thought, the translight com, then pulled back the undergarment to close the stealth compartment.

"I want to keep this—Decker—between us, for now. Will you do that?"

"Will do," from Harps. Evan had a sense of the professor giving the Dwelleys a daunting look. "You good?"

Busy repacking the bag as quickly, and well, as he could, Evan shook his head. "I need answers," he said forcefully.

"Copy that."

His hands froze. "Harps. Wort. Blue Spider. These are dangerous, scary people." *And you're the furthest thing from it.* "You stay out of this."

"We're just play'n our game, Goosebumpies." Harps' voice developed a grin. "You should try it."

He almost smiled, then couldn't. The faction. A space monster. Now, Decker spying on his most private thoughts. Evan shook his head and resumed packing the bag.

He stopped and picked up the translight com. Decker had used it. Who had he called?

Evan hit the auto connect. *"Redirecting,"* murmured a machine voice. *"Redirecting."* When that was all it did, over and over, he put it on the bed and sighed.

"Largas Swift."

Paul's ship?!

Why—how—*It didn't matter,* he decided, snatching up the com with relief. "Paul? Esen? Are you there? Can you hear me?"

There'd be time later, he hoped, to worry why Lieutenant Decker had a secret com keyed to his friends.

The crewmember put away her torch. "Careful. Edge's still hot, sir."

Buoyed by the knowledge Paul and Esen were close—and having recognized the voice of the formidable Rudy Lefebvre, who must be the captain of the *Swift*—Evan hopped into the corridor, his fervent "Thank you!" winning a chuckle.

"Can't say I've seen anything like this since Dresnet locked down the Stinker Bar in the lower fifteen. Fun times." She sounded wistful.

Evan looked over his shoulder at the bags, repacked and piled as they'd been, except for what Strevelor had dumped and the precious translight com bulging inside his jacket. Until the agent was caught—a problem he'd warned Paul about—the *Mistral* wouldn't let the *Swift* dock. "This room has to be locked and secured. Against anyone."

She grinned, bringing out the torch again. "Was hoping you'd ask, sir."

The security guard behind her spoke up, "Polit Gooseberry. The commander's waiting for you in the guest galley."

Evan nodded. "I know the way."

"My orders are to escort you, sir."

Remembering Strevelor's disguise, Evan's relief vanished. "Show me your face."

At his tone, the crewmember paused, the searing point of her torch halted in midair.

The security guard swept up the front of his helmet, revealing a pleasant round face with brown upswept eyes. "Briggle, sir. I understand your caution. Commander Kamaara warned us Strevelor disguised himself. We'll have him in the brig soon, sir. Count on it."

"He knows the ship's design," Evan said urgently. "He has access." Passing information along secondhand, even if the hands were the capable ones of the Dwelleys, abruptly felt inadequate. "I must talk to the captain and commander at once."

"Waiting for you in the galley, sir." With a patient gesture down the deserted corridor.

Of course. "Sorry. Yes." Evan's walk was an almost-run, Briggle thudding behind. When he turned the corner, he collided with a large solid mass.

Decker.

Evan shoved himself away with two hands. "Arrest him! He's one of them!"

Decker broke into a grin and the security guard chuckled. "Arrest the lieutenant, sir? He's no spy. He's a Survey operative."

"Is that what he claims?" Evan glared at Decker until the other's face lost its good humor. "I know what I found in your bag." His hands closed into fists.

"Which would be classified way over your head, Briggle," Decker commented, completely at ease. "Leave us. I'll bring the polit to the galley with me when we're done."

"Very good, sir."

Don't go, Evan pleaded with his eyes. The guard hesitated.

Decker raised his eyebrows. "Please tell the polit the commander's orders concerning me, Briggle. Perhaps he'll be reassured."

"Yes, sir. You're acting as her second-in-command, sir, when it comes to the faction and any infiltration of the *Missy.*" A glance that slid off Evan like an apology. "We're to obey your orders unless they contravene hers."

"Thank you. That'll be all."

The guard walked away.

Decker stepped close, pressing what Evan had to believe was the weapon missing from the slot in the bag hard into his side. "Into the lift."

Once in the lift and headed down, Evan looked surreptitiously for one of the surveillance boxes.

"Don't worry. I've a fuzzer." Decker hit stop. "We're not on any vids."

For some reason—perhaps Paul—Evan found himself more angry than afraid. "What do you want from me?"

"Why are you after Paul Ragem and Esen?"

Evan started. "What? No. They're my friends—"

"'Friends'? Hardly." The weapon shoved into his ribs, nothing warm left in Decker's brown eyes. "I've read your notebooks, Gooseberry. You've been spying on them since Urgia Prime. What did you tell Strevelor and the faction?" Another, harder shove. "How much do they know?"

"I've nothing to do with the faction. I don't understand—"

"You went with him."

"Kamaara knew what he was. She wanted me to spy on him. And how do I know you're what you say?" Evan held out his arm, heedless of Decker's warning hiss. "You put this in me for him!"

"I put it there so I could keep track of you."

Evan frowned. "You're not Survey."

"Oh, but I am. A full-fledged operative tasked with keeping tabs on the faction. I've been following the one calling himself Strevelor for some time."

Making Decker what Strevelor had claimed to be.

Evan lowered his voice, sure of this much. "What else are you?"

Putting away his weapon, Decker sent the lift moving again. "Someone who's going to keep you close, Polit, until we get Strevelor and they let the *Swift* dock."

18: Starship Afternoon;
Mistral Reckoning

"*L*ARGAS *Swift,* this is the Commonwealth Survey vessel *Mistral.* Hold your position and do not approach."

The four of us glared in unison at the com panel. Not that it did any good, but I felt the solidarity of a species' appropriate reaction. *Which didn't happen to me all that often.*

Paul was doing the talking, my no longer having a voice to impress, and he having more patience. "If it's the *Centos Pa* you're worried about, they're here as observers. Please tell Captain Clendon Paul Ragem needs to talk to him. We're here to help—"

"Hold your position and do not approach."

I knew that voice. Comm Officer Snead. Probably a good officer under normal circumstances but one sorely lacking in the ability to think outside of his orders. Especially when it came to non-Survey personnel. Most especially with anything to do with the All Species' Library of Linguistics and Culture.

We'd history.

"*Largas Swift* to *Mistral. Swift* to—"

Rudy made a throat-cutting gesture meaning we'd been cut off. Or that he wished to do violence upon the *Mistral*'s comm officer which seemed an overreaction. Then again, we'd a space monster lurking and potentially ready to grab us, so maybe—

"New signal incoming." Rudy raised his eyebrows, looking to Paul.

"If it's the *Centos Pa* again," snapped my friend, proving even his patience had limits, "have them hold—"

Rudy shook his head. He gave Nia a dubious glance, then turned to Paul. "It's coming over the reserved channel."

The one used by Paul's Group. *Our Group*, I reminded myself, meaning the person using it had followed a possible threat to us on to the *Mistral*. Had contacted Paul once before.

Was the reason we were here.

Secrecy hardly mattered now. Besides, since Nia knew about me, she joined the Group. *Sort of.* "Let it through, Rudy," I said before Paul had to wrestle his conscience.

"*Largas Swift.*"

"Paul? Esen? Are you there? Can you hear me?"

Evan Gooseberry?

My turn to look at Paul for an answer. His frown wasn't reassuring. "Evan, this is Paul Ragem. What's wrong on the *Mistral*?"

No wonder they didn't want us to dock. A faction agent, out to harm Paul, was loose on the ship. The ship where I'd planned to shelter my friends while I dealt with the Null and—not that they knew it—did my utmost to learn the truth about Veya Ragem and Starfield the Very Strange Pony.

A Web-being could feel persecuted by the universe at times.

"—until they locate Strevelor," Evan finished, "I'm stuck in here."

Rudy scowled. "Explains why they can't let us dock."

"Evan, thanks for this. Sit tight and be careful."

A brave chuckle. "Not much choice there. You be careful too."

"Always. *Swift* out." Paul looked at us. "Ideas?"

"Why don't we send out the—" Nia brought her fists together, then pantomimed an explosion "—on our own?"

Because that was NOT my plan and put them all in danger and— I gathered my wits and tried not to hyperventilate. "We—"

"Too risky," Paul told her. "We couldn't get out of range in time."

She looked to Rudy. "The lifepod?"

His eyes turned cold. "You're suggesting we abandon my ship and feed it to this monster?"

"Yes."

Not that great a ship. A thought I kept to myself.

"Even if I was willing," Rudy growled, "which I'm not, by the way, it wouldn't work. The pod's got no propulsion system. After the initial kick from the ship, it drifts. We'd still be in range."

My friend's expectant gaze rested on me. *Did I have a plan?*

The answer being *yes, I'd had one you'd have hated but it's ruined now so not telling,* wasn't at all helpful.

"We run," I said finally. "Tell the other ships to do the same. Try again."

Paul narrowed his eyes. "It's heading for Botharis. We can't let it—"

I'd never been happier to hear the com make its little sound. Rudy, looking as if he felt the same way, toggled it on. A new voice filled the bridge.

"*Swift,* this is *Mistral.* You're cleared to dock. Make it quick."

I beamed. "There you go. All fixed."

"*Swift,* be advised an unauthorized lifepod has ejected from *Mistral.* Scope shows an unidentified ship dropped from translight, heading to intercept. Once you're on board, we will pursue."

Or not.

There'd been times—*a growing number*—when I'd wished a moment of my life would slow down.

Possibly I was the only semi-immortal being of perfect memory to have such desires. Certainly Ersh encouraged me to *hurry up and mature, Youngest.* Looking back now, I supposed it was also rare for any of us to be in a rush.

I'd put Ersh and my Elders through a plethora of moments they hadn't seen coming.

This one, I did.

"They have to cut the *Swift* loose to pursue. Bess will fine. She always is." Rudy, although he'd strong and often inconvenient parental instincts concerning this me, also had a ridiculous confidence in my abilities.

Nia, who didn't know me, shook her head. "I don't like it. Maybe we should take the boom to the *Mistral*."

I shook my head back. "They wouldn't like that. We'll stick with our plan. The only difference is I'll use the lifepod and the *Centos Pa* will retrieve it." *Skalet owed me.* "I'll be fine. Tell them," this to Paul.

Who knew me best of all, better even than Ersh, and this was the moment. If I couldn't convince *him* I was going to behave, I'd have to do something rash. In anticipation, I'd positioned myself by the tube door, ready to open it. Ready to lock it behind me and wait until they had to leave the ship.

When what I wished for, more than anything, was for this moment to last. To look at my dearest first friend as long as time would let me.

Paul tilted his head, gray eyes puzzling at me. Before puzzling became concern, I scrunched my face in worry I'd no need to feign. "How will I know you're safe? You can't call a ship that's supposed to be empty. There could be," darkly, "more faction agents on the *Mistral*."

His expression softened. "Evan has the translight com. I'll keep in touch with that."

A deep *CLANG* shuddered through walls. "We're linked." Rudy manipulated controls and the lights inside abruptly dimmed; the ever-present back-of-the-teeth whine of the *Swift*'s engines disappeared.

"What are you doing?" Paul demanded.

"It'd look wrong if I left her up and running."

Meaning life support would be at minimal. Being Bess, I wouldn't need to worry about air for days. As for freezing? "I won't be in here long anyway," I assured them. "You should get going."

A crackle on the com. "Move it, *Swift*!"

"I'll set up the airlock. See you later, Bess." Rudy opened the hatch in the floor and launched himself headfirst to the antechamber below, calling back. "Nia."

Who hesitated, looking at me.

"Thanks for the boom," I told her, finding a smile after all. She gave me a grave nod in return, then sailed down as Rudy had, her boots disappearing in the tube.

And then there were two.

"Old Blob." Paul paused at the hatch, regarding me with familiar and slightly impatient fondness. "Set the trap and get clear. Promise."

"I know the plan," I countered, which wasn't the same. Before he noticed, I hurried on. "Nia mustn't get into trouble."

"She won't." He began to frown. "Esen—"

"Was never here," I interrupted, waving at him. "Go. Go."

Unlike the other Humans, Paul Ragem descended feet first. Presumably to keep an eye on me as long as possible, so I stuck out my tongue until his head disappeared and the hatch closed.

My moment, over.

An assortment of noises marked whatever was happening below to remove my friends from the *Largas Swift.* To be on the safe side, I sailed up to the crew quarters and tucked myself in the accommodation. The others had taken advantage of it during the trip, leaving behind a homely smell my Lanivarian-self would have appreciated in more depth.

This me wanted to plug my nostrils. Still, I'd my own bodily requirements, not that I'd be Bess much longer. Once the *Swift* was free and clear of the *Mistral,* I'd climb out, use my helpful Human hands to open what was closed, set the cargo hold to vent, and be myself again.

In more ways than the obvious. My fingers closed over Paul's medallion. I waited. Waited.

A final shudder and a louder-than-before *CLANG!*

The ship was loose.

I began counting to myself, just to be sure. I'd reached five when I heard something else.

A *person* something else.

My initial thought was a glad, if truly foolish, notion that Paul hadn't been able to leave me—

My second was that the faction agent hadn't been on the lifepod at all but had waited for a ship of his own. If he was here to find another way to harm Paul?

I needed living mass.

Nearby

"**I** am Kalesaty Ki," the unexpected Lishcyn introduced herself, flashing a pleasant tusk. It was carved in intricate patterns, a tasteful solitary gem glinting in the light.

"Go eat somewhere else. There's only supper for me," Lesyole's body tilted in a proprietary slant over her meal on Lionel's desk.

"Food can wait." Kalesaty Ki rested a three-fingered hand on the plain black bag at her chest. She was clothed in black-and-red silk, a combination striking against the honey brown of her scales.

An altogether impressive individual, of whom Lionel was in no doubt. "Skalet," he half-whispered.

A second tusk joined the first, a Lishcyn smile of approval. "Indeed. It was *expedient* to appear thus." The thick upper lip came down, turning her expression serious. "I've come to take you with me, Lionel. We've a window—it won't last. Soon nothing will be allowed to leave the surface."

Lesy let out an indignant belch. "What about me?"

"Endure, Elder," Skalet informed her web-kin dryly. "It's what you're best at."

"And what are you *best* at? Running. Hiding. Leaving. You can't *take* him." A plate, already emptied, flew across the room. Lionel ducked and it smashed against the door. "We never *keep* them."

Skalet's huge head lowered in threat, scales swelling. The Human eased out of the way, Lishcyns prone to charging one another to resolve a dispute if projectile vomiting proved insufficient.

To his surprise, Lesy's head tilted up at an awkward angle. *Appeasement.* "Take me as well, then."

"Esen-alit-Quar."

Pulled by the name, the massive *ancient* beings turned to stare at Lionel and he made himself continue because she would. "Esen expects us to trust her. Especially you."

Skalet's ears twitched. "What does the Youngest's trust look like, Lionel? Waiting here, exposed and vulnerable, while what hunts us comes to this system and the greatest gathering of Kraal in their history gathers to feast on what remains?"

"Yes."

"'Hunts us?!'" Lesy's jaw unhinged, dropping to her chest. She pushed it back in place. "No. You're wrong. It doesn't hunt *us*. Not anymore." Her scaled face took on a smug cast. "Esen knows, I showed her. The Null is the mother now. The mother hunts a memory. Her son that was. Oh no. Oh no." She retched without warning, bile and fudge dribbling over beautiful silks, then whimpered, "That's why it's coming here!" Scales swelled. "Stay for Esen if you want," with sudden strength. "I'm leaving this place!"

"Veya?" Lionel struggled to grasp what he was hearing. "What do you—"

"I finished what I had left." Ally Orman appeared suspended between coming in his office and running. "You wanted to talk to me—bad time?"

Lionel couldn't imagine a worse. "Can you—"

"Leaving," Lesy reiterated, striding forward.

"We stay," with an edge to her voice that froze Lesy in place. "Everyone stays." Skalet's Lishcyn-self hadn't looked away from Lionel, not even at the new arrival, but she knew Ally was listening. "For the good of Botharis, the Kraal's Fleet Commander just ordered all ships remain where they are until the present *situation* resolves."

They'd declared a leader. They'd a plan. And all at once a space monster didn't seem as great a threat, Lionel decided, feeling his own stomach roil. *What were the Kraal up to?*

The person who would know stood looking back at him, a tufted ear flipping back and forth, the hint of a tusk showing. *Trust me* that now-calm visage demanded.

Lionel coughed once and turned to the anxious Human in the doorway. "It's not a precursor to invasion, Ally," he said, projecting confidence. *Trusting Skalet to ensure it wasn't.* "As soon as I can, I'll provide details on the situation to staff and our guests. Until then, I ask you to keep this to yourself. I regret your plans will be disrupted."

She looked incredulous. "Forget my plans. You need us, Lionel. The Library needs all of us." An assessing look at the strange Lishcyns. "Shall I escort your guests back to the Lobby?"

"We're fine here," Lionel said as he came forward, taking Ally's elbow to steer her around and out the door, away from two still-unsettled Web-beings. "I need you to find Duggs and Lambo for me. Bring them here, quietly, at once," he ordered, beginning to see what to do, and who best to have do it. "Don't explain. Just tell them it's important."

Trust Esen, he told himself.

Out There

'M going to space, Momma, just like you. You'll see.
Why?
Because I want to meet every kind of person there is.
It would take more than a lifetime.
That's all right. I'll meet as many as I can.

The shard spins away, taking with it the dream in his eyes, the smile on his lips, the possible.

Leaving Veya alone in a crowd of every kind. Hell's core continues to condense, filaments drawing tighter, forming knots of strangers' flesh.

At the same time, her eye—*its eye*—sees further and further. More and more. It isn't her will. It's as if what surrounds Hell, holds it, has begun to thin and crack, letting more *real* through.

But Veya has forgotten the shape of hope.

All she knows, all she feels, is Hell's desperate appetite. Hers for home. They blur. Have become one. She won't make it—they won't.

Unless *they* feed.

Her eye tracks. Finds. Another ship. Two. No, four. Dropping out of translight . . . *HERE.*

HELL IS HUNGRY!

Momma. When are you coming home?
Soon. I'm almost there.

19: Starship Afternoon; *Mistral* Reckoning

SOMEONE was on the *Largas Swift* who shouldn't be, and I wasn't pleased. In fact, had I risked becoming Lanivarian—and succumbing to spacesickness—my lips would have curled back from fangs eager to bite.

That I'd another form, one I must assume as soon as possible, that didn't need to bite at all to cause fatal damage?

Not as relaxing as it might have been.

So it was as Bess I emerged to confront my intruder, a form adept at sneaking through a Humanocentric starship. Had I better known—or trusted the condition—of the *Swift,* I might have used the luggage tube to slip down to the lowermost level, but I refused to risk trapping this me and elected to drift, headfirst, down to the bridge.

Empty. *Well, that was disappointing.*

I eyed the closed hatch.

Tap. Taptaptap. Tap.

Whomever was tapping did so with distinct urgency.

TAPTAPTAP!

That was frantic. Perhaps they'd noticed they could now see their breath. I exhaled a puff of fog to confirm then pushed myself to the hatch. "It's not locked."

The tapping stopped as if my intruder was embarrassed. Hearing some tentative *is this how* movements, I clicked my magboots to lock my feet and gripped the hatch, pulling up.

Hands came with it. Hands and arms followed by a cap of tight curls and a high-cheekboned face dominated by green eyes that went wide with shock. "Bess?"

"Evan." I closed my eyes briefly. *Of course it was Evan.*

I opened them again to find the rest of our feckless young diplomat soaring past me, having used too much force. I grabbed for him, hooking my fingers in his waistband. Evan twisted violently to keep me in sight, "Bess!?" managing to break my hold. He careened into a thankfully control-less portion of wall and bounced back, letting out a little shriek.

All very entertaining under other circumstances.

A spare pair of magboots were clipped near the hatch. I freed them and my feet, pushing off to intercept Evan before he impacted anything important. I caught his outflung hand, then worked my way down to where I could pull off his shoe—dress footwear completely inappropriate—and pushed on the boot, activating it.

Evan's right foot locked against the ceiling, the rest of him coming more or less to a stop. Instead of enjoying being still, he kept looking frantically around. "Where's Paul?"

"On the *Mistral*." I floated where he could see me. "Why aren't you?"

He gave me a woeful look. "Decker."

We'd a Null incoming and who knew what else on the move, but I couldn't imagine Evan's story would take long to tell, since I'd heard the beginning of it—not that he knew—and I needed to know the rest. He'd been waiting to be freed from Commander Kamaara's quarters— *I didn't ask why*—had contacted friends to foil the faction agent's plot to summon the Null—*I didn't ask how*—and, with triumph, Evan said, "I found this hidden in Decker's bag."

Shivering, he reached inside his jacket to pull out what I recognized as the sort of very expensive translight communications device Lenata Mady kept leaving at home. "I used it to call Paul and warn him," Evan concluded proudly.

Making this "Decker" the member of Paul's Group on the *Mistral,* one of ours, and—more significantly to me—this the device Paul had planned to use to be in touch. *Not happening now, was it?* I scowled at Evan.

Who looked as abashed as only Evan Gooseberry could. *Must be practice.* "Decker said he was a Survey operative. He accused me of— of helping Strevelor and the faction." Abashed became devastated. "Bess, he accused me of spying on Paul and Esen. You and Esolesy Ki too."

"Did you?" I asked in a very small voice.

"No! No—I—" He sagged. "I wrote things, in my private note-books. Questions. I—everything in my life was shifting. I'd found out I was—what I wasn't." A heart-wrenching pause, then, "I stopped trusting them. You. I know I was wrong. Lionel told me I was. Do you know Lionel?"

Unable to speak, I nodded.

"Decker stole my notebooks. Read them. I thought I'd started to convince him I meant no harm. And then—"

The only people Evan and Decker encountered in the corridor were security, moving at speed in the opposite direction. As each approached, they'd lift their visor for a second, then lower it, and Evan began to flinch, expecting the next to be Strevelor.

"Calm down," Decker whispered.

"Where are we going?"

"We've a problem. Strevelor's compromised the com system. I think I know why. We have to hurry."

"Why aren't you taking some of them?" Evan angled his head at the passing trio of black-garbed—and well-armed—ship's security. "Unless you're faction," he accused.

"Shut it." Decker pulled him around a corner and leaned close. "I'm not. I don't know if any of them are."

Defiant, Evan stared back. "Prove it. Where are we going? Or you'll have to drag me there—that'll get noticed."

For an instant, Decker looked sorely tempted, then he blew out a frustrated breath. "They think Strevelor's trying to escape. You and I know he's got more to do."

"He's after Paul. Esen." Evan swallowed. "You think he's waiting for them at the docking port."

"After sending a false come-ahead." Decker pulled back. "Can we go now, Polit?" He didn't wait, looking both ways before breaking into a run.

There were no more security personnel in sight. *Not good. Not good.* Evan ran behind Decker, his head seething with the questions he should be asking, the objections he should be making. *Why them?*

Why just *them?*

He'd have to start a new notebook— *No. Notebooks weren't safe.* He'd keep his notions and worries in his head from now on.

The corridor opened into a bulb, and Decker kept to a wall. He slowed to a stealthy walk, a hand raised. *Quiet,* that signaled. Or as Lisam at the embassy would say during his lessons, *your feet can get you killed, Evan,* so he copied the other's movements as best he could.

The bulb ended in a huge door; as he stepped over its tall sill, Evan recognized his surroundings. The hanger deck. He'd been brought on board through here, down an airless tube from the shuttle instead of through the main airlock as he'd entered on Botharis—*had it been a year ago?*

The ceiling was festooned with cargo moving tracks heading into the distance. Nearer, hoses crisscrossed the floor. A chill emanated from the metal around them, unless it was his nerve failing. To check, Evan brushed his fingers along the wall. *Ice cold.* He could do this. Help protect his friend. All of his friends, he thought. Everyone on this ship and on the *Largas Swift.*

This door would have been closed and locked during the alert—

Not to Strevelor, Evan realized as an armored form stepped in their way, weapon in hand.

He'd time to tense and wish he'd never left Great Gran's before the weapon lowered and the guard's free hand lifted the visor. "Lieutenant Decker. Polit," Briggle acknowledged, quickly coming to attention. "Nothing to report, sir. A-nought-sweep didn't find a trace."

"Very good," Decker replied, as if he hadn't whipped away his own weapon. "The polit and I are here to greet our inbound guests. You're relieved, Briggle." He started walking forward, Evan forced to follow.

Briggle didn't budge, making them both stop again. "No, sir."

Resolute and firm. "Standing orders. Not even the captain enters after an A-sweep unless accompanied by security personnel."

Without showing frustration—or suspicion—Decker gave a short nod, his face bland. "My mistake. Please accompany us."

The guard visibly relaxed. "My pleasure, sir." He turned to lead the way.

Evan hesitated. If Strevelor, as Decker suspected, was in the hanger— was Decker using Briggle as bait to draw him out?

Or with the guard's back to them, would Decker stun him or worse?

Not while he was here. Evan seized Decker's arm, the one over the weapon, with both hands and held tight. "Briggle, wait," he said quickly. "That's not why we're here."

The guard swung around, frowning as he took in the situation. "Polit? What's this about?" No "sir" this time, and his hand dropped to his weapon, staying there. "I'll call the commander."

"Belay that," Decker ordered, twitching his arm free. "The faction agent's tapped into coms." Ignoring the guard, he glared at Evan. "I hope you know what you're doing."

So did he. "Briggle," Evan said calmly, "Strevelor's goal is to kill Paul Ragem and Esen as well as everyone on this ship. We think he'll try something as the *Swift* docks. We have to check it out, now."

The guard looked from one of them to the other. "But—"

Decker drew his weapon, aiming it down. "Deadly force, Briggle. We can't risk the ship."

"Belay *that.* Both of you." The young diplomat drew himself up, unaware his eyes had a new fire nor that his demeanor had shifted to that of someone who didn't take orders but gave them. "Strevelor has to answer questions." This to Decker. "I assure you he isn't the source of this threat. To Paul or to the Commonwealth."

An eyebrow lifted, very slightly. *Respect.* "Set to stun, Briggle." They waited, watching the guard make the adjustment.

But as they started walking again, Evan noticed Decker hadn't done the same.

The hanger deck wasn't only where supplies entered and other ships could dock with this one in space; it held the heart of what the *Mistral* could do on the ground. Aircars and ground transports stood in their rows, secured and shrouded in protective sheets. Towering over them were the servo machines that, using the most minimal local material, could fabricate any type of structure a mission required—including the essential Survey emergency shelter, should the ship be stranded on an alien world, or first contact specialists be left for a longer period.

Any other time, Evan would have been fascinated by the place and equipment. Today, walking among the looming shrouds, he felt the skin prickle at the back of his neck and his stomach clenching. There must be a hundred hiding places in this huge room—a thousand. *Strevelor could be anywhere.*

He'd whispered that aloud, for Briggle winked at him, pointing to what Evan had taken for an ordinary strap around an aircar's shroud. "A-nought tape, Polit," he explained, keeping his voice low. "Marks what's been thoroughly searched, then seals it. If it's disturbed in any way, turns red. Low tech and reliable."

Evan nodded, smiling with relief. The white straps were everywhere, now that he knew where to look.

Decker glanced around. "Strevelor knows the procedures. Trust nothing."

"Yessir," the security guard replied hastily. He bent to look under the nearest shroud.

"We can't search for him," Evan heard himself say. They weren't even close to the docking port the *Swift* would use and time wasn't a friend. "We have to anticipate. That's your job," he declared, turning to Decker.

Who nodded. "We check the ports. And stay together," when Briggle started for the near wall.

It turned out the *Mistral* had two ship docking ports, one for tubes and one for a direct connection between ship airlocks. *He'd have preferred that.* There was also a wall-sized door that opened when the ship was finsdown.

Their concern was for access outside and *Mistral* had two maintenance airlocks in its hanger. They found what Decker had anticipated outside the second: a discarded spacesuit.

"Ship's suits were accounted for, sir," Briggle said, careful not to touch it.

Decker squatted next to the suit, also not risking contact, and examined the *Mistral* patch on the chest. He stood with a muttered curse.

"Fake. You were right, Polit. Someone left this for Strevelor during the sweep. All he had to do was mute the sensors and hide outside on the hull."

Meaning the faction agent was inside, with them, and it was as if Evan could feel his piercing blue-eyed stare, see that mocking smile. He tried to swallow but couldn't. Briggle put down his visor, anonymous again, ready for action. Decker studied their surroundings. "This way."

As they began to run, a klaxon sounded, then lights flashed red, then white.

The *Swift*!

The next minutes raced by in a blur. Evan ran with the others, not that he'd a weapon or could help in a conflict, but because he couldn't stay behind and they'd no time to make him. They reached a row of tied-down crates, ducking behind them. Strobes of light shot everywhere, turning their surroundings into a puzzle of bright and dark, and Evan found himself composing a complaint to send later about being half blinded at such a crucial moment.

As Strevelor would be.

It wasn't a comfort. He was squeezed between Decker and Briggle, the latter's armor harder than it had looked, and as much as Evan Gooseberry was worried and afraid—

—most of what he felt in this moment was anger. The faction made the Kraal seem reasonable and civilized. *How dare these people try to harm the innocent!*

The flashing stopped and Evan blinked, startled.

Decker gestured. Briggle, crouching behind the crates, moved off. Evan twisted, tried to see.

A hand pressed him down. He felt breath against his ear. "Listen to me, Evan. They're in the airlock, cycling through. I think I spotted Strevelor on the other side of the port. Shooting starts, get to Kamaara." Decker pressed something into his hand and began to rise.

It was, as he feared, another weapon. Putting it down, Evan grabbed Decker's sleeve. "You can't kill him."

Decker shook his head. "He knows about Paul."

What did that mean? "Paul lost his mother because the faction made a mistake. Lost fifty years because someone in Survey made a mistake— and we can't make another one now. Decker. *Decker*," as the other started to pull away. "If you want to keep Paul safe, it's the faction we have to deal with—"

A burning look. "No promises."

Then he was gone and Evan was alone, his back to flimsy crates wondering how he'd explain any of this to Great Gran.

And that's when it started—

"And that's when it started," Evan said, eyes wild. "Shouts. Weapons going off. A crate caught fire and I had to move. I ran for the port, to make sure Paul and the others were all right."

Of course he did. I tensed. "Were they?"

"I think so. Yes. When I last saw them, they were," he corrected. "Rudy took cover with Paul and one of the crew." *That'd be Nia.* "Briggle was with them, firing. Decker—" He sagged. "Decker was on the deck. Bess, he'd been hit," with very Evan outrage. "His arm burned—his body—I tried to drag him out of the way. Strevelor, and maybe someone else was firing at us. Decker—I don't know how—he got to his feet and shoved me in the airlock. Told me to get in the ship and stay there until it was safe. Started it cycling so I'd no choice."

Paul and I were going to have a talk about his Group. If Decker had known the *Swift* would be set loose and left behind, he'd deliberately put Evan in greater danger. If not—

He still had.

"The *Mistral* crew will take care of them all. As for you, Evan," I said brightly, "sorry to tell you this, but you can't stay."

"Pardon?"

I finished putting on his other boot. "This ship is about to be attacked by the Null. You and I, my brave friend, are leaving before that happens." I released his boots and pushed us to the lifepod handle. "I open the door, you get to the nearest safety cubby. You've had the standard drill?"

"Yes, but—"

"Good." I opened the door. "In you go. Don't worry about the auto distress. You've got the com." *Much as I wanted it.* "Call for help. Paul will answer." I started to close the door.

"Aren't you coming with me?"

"I'm taking the other pod," I said glibly. "See you on the other side!"

He didn't move. "Bess—I'm not going to ask why you're here or why Paul would leave you alone." Resolve filled Evan's voice. "I'm not asking because it's time I trusted you even when I don't understand what's happening. You and Esen and Esolesy Ki. Paul. Just—please be careful."

I hooked my arm through the handle, studying his earnest, honest, dear face. I'd no idea if I'd run out of time or had an hour to spare. *Most likely the former.* But here was the chance I hadn't expected, looking back at me, to give Paul what he deserved. *In case I couldn't.*

"Listen carefully, Evan. A portion of Veya Ragem, Paul's mother, isn't dead. Her implant continues to function."

He blinked. "That's what Harps—what we've followed. The Null has it."

"It's more than the tech, Evan. Something of *her* has continued, struggling to come home, to find Paul." I paused at his gasp. Let him absorb some of that horror before I went on. "I believe Veya's fought to protect him. That all this time, she's tried to warn us. Warn him. The frames aren't abstract meaningless symbols. Combined, they're a representation of Paul's favorite childhood toy. Evan, tell Paul it's Starfield. He'll understand."

"Why can't you tell him?" Evan started to come back. "Bess?"

I closed the hatch and pressed my hands to it. Seconds later, I felt the *thump* as the lifepod self-ejected, spinning into the void with Evan and what might be my final gift to Paul.

Then I got to work.

I set the timer for the cargo hold to open to space, then soared through the air and up the tube. In the crew quarters, I unzipped the bags we'd brought.

Duras leaves erupted from their tight pack, floating like the veils from Lesy's dress. Leaving them, for now, I went up to the cargo hold, opening that hatch.

Amid presents for family, the boom squatted like a red-and-black spider within its transparent case. Skalet-memory knew what it was, how it worked, what it could do. The knowledge came with a frisson of unfamiliar fear.

Good.

I pushed aside any thought of Evan. Of the injured Decker and our Group and how we must no longer let them act without us. Of Lionel and those on Botharis. Of Nia and Rudy and those on the *Mistral*. Of the *Centos Pa,* her crew atingle at the prospect of a noble death under S'kal-ru's orders.

Humans.

Fragile and annoying. Precious and stubborn. If it was being on the cusp of leaving this me that gave me this rush of affection for them all?

High time I was myself.

I opened Paul's medallion and deactivated the cryounit. Before that tiny piece of me thawed completely, I cycled . . .

Web-flesh.

The metal tang of the ship, the sharp cold of the thinning air, vanished to be replaced by other, deeper sensations. Energy throbbed within engines, waiting. Closer, a feral *pulse* I knew was the boom, until a vibration signaled the venting of the cargo hold.

Ferried by ship's atmosphere, the boom tumbled away, surrounded by presents I could no longer detect.

Around me, the rich dance of light and magnetism, the slow roll of gravitational waves and sharper tasty notes of high-energy particles. Within, I sensed starships. Specks of artificial gravity and harnessed power and one held my first best friend. I couldn't tell which.

I would protect them all.

After I answered an imperative as old as my kind. Web-flesh called to me, the irresistible taste, and I snapped up what waited.

Ersh-taste. Esen-taste.

Once more, I remembered what a Web-being was. What I truly was.

A creature of space.

Nearby

EVAN Gooseberry tumbled, holding his hands over his face to fend off chunks of his own vomit, as miserable as he'd ever been.

If he never went to space again, that would be absolutely fine with him.

Though of course he would because he'd work to do. Work he loved that didn't take place in the next fishing village over from Great Gran's house or happen in the next city or the next. Space it had to be.

And there were many tried and true medications for spacesickness, he told himself, thinking of Aunt Melan Gooseberry's very helpful book.

Which was better than thinking about poor Decker. Better than thinking of little Bess, tumbling in her own lifepod. No, Bess was experienced and very clever. She wouldn't have forgotten to get in the safety cubby and be snug in the autoharness. She wouldn't be—

Tumbling tumbling—

Evan took it as a personal triumph when he didn't throw up again, although his stomach had to be empty by this point. He remembered, all at once, what Bess had told him about the boots she'd put on his feet. *Which didn't actually fit—*he clicked the heels.

And found himself standing. On a wall but standing was wonderful. Standing helped his brain finally work and Evan hurriedly brought out the translight com. He pushed the talk button.

"Polit Evan Gooseberry calling, assigned to the Survey Ship *Mistral*. I'm presently—I don't know where I am," he admitted. "I'm in a lifepod from—" *what was the name,* "—the *Largas Swift*. Can anyone hear me? This is Polit—"

"Evan?"

Paul's voice! It erased the horrible, vomit-filled space around Evan, like a clean warm breeze off the ocean. "It's me. Are you all right?"

"Yes. Hang on. We can't come for you right away. Let me talk to Bess."

"I can't. She's in the other lifepod."

Silence. Evan gripped the device, dread sinking into every bone of his body. "Paul. The ship had another lifepod, didn't it?"

"I have to go, Evan," the voice of a stranger, thin and strained. "You'll be fine."

No, he wouldn't, not if Bess was still on that freezing dark ship. Not with the monster coming—

"Paul—Paul!"

The connection was dead.

"Your mother's a hero," Evan whispered.

If Bess had sacrificed herself to save him, as he now feared, she was a hero too. Numb, he went to the safety cubby and let the harness take hold, surrounded by people braver and better than he.

What did that make him? A poor friend. A failed one. A burden—

"*Centos Pa* to lifepod."

A Kraal? Evan stared at the device as if it might bite.

"*Centos Pa* to lifepod."

Not just any *Kraal.* He knew that deep rich voice. "S'kal-ru?"

"The irrepressible Evan Gooseberry." *Was that a smile he heard?* "Are you intact?"

Not on the inside. Evan took a breath, steadied. "I'm unhurt. There's a Human child on the *Swift*—she put me in here and stayed behind to use the other lifepod." Which would sound utterly reprehensible to anyone who hadn't met the child in question. "Her name's Bess."

"I know who she is." No amusement now. If anything, the formidable Kraal sounded annoyed. *Who would be annoyed at a child in danger?* "Bess can take care of herself. The *Mistral*'s engines have failed. She's sending out a distress call as the other of her kind flees. Tell me,

Polit. Do I render assistance to one or chase the other?" With cold curiosity.

Strevelor. He must have sabotaged the *Mistral* before he'd fled, leaving it for the Null. If a ship was running, it had to be his.

They needed answers . . . Decker, burnt and in pain . . .

Strevelor'd warned him. *The faction was ruthless* . . .

His face set and grim, Evan gazed down at the com. "Those on the fleeing ship sent Johnsson to Botharis. They harmed Paul's mother and are directly responsible for arousing the Null and the deaths it's caused." He paused, then nodded to himself, knowing this Kraal. "They threaten Paul and Esen."

"No longer." *Satisfaction.* "*Centos Pa* out."

He'd signed Strevelor's death sentence.

Evan closed his eyes, listening to the hum of the pod's life support, and wondered who he'd become.

20: Space Time; Null Time

IT was when I oozed out of the *Largas Swift,* bloated to three times my normal mass courtesy of the Duras, that I comprehended why Ersh named our predator the Null.

To my senses, the vast sweep of space below and ahead of me was empty. Space couldn't be empty, meaning *something* had to be there to erase all else. We weren't waiting for the Null to arrive.

It was already here.

Instinct took over and my exterior *solidified,* an experience as novel as it was painful as my web-flesh sent out a desperate message of *nothing to see here. Just another space rock.*

Not helpful, I realized an instant later. Well, yes, it must have been once. We'd lived the long slow life until Ersh assimilated the first ephemeral mass and I'd no doubt hiding as a rock for an eon or so until drifting far enough from a Null for safety would have been fine by my ancestors, being all they knew and could be.

Things were different now. I was. And I'd a boom heading toward that ominously *empty* portion of space, along with ships and lifepods, requiring me to *not* be a rock because even if the Null couldn't sense my presence, I couldn't sense anything either.

I reanimated microscopic portions of my exterior—*here a spot, there a spot*—until information about my surroundings began to trickle in to me.

Rock-me was moving along the same course as the *Swift*'s cargo, gaining on the assorted presents and boom because I'd given myself a good push. At this rate, we'd enter *Null* space in about a month.

STOP!

Not that I stopped but my mental processes screeched to a gibbering halt because now I sensed the other thing about the Null.

Filaments of otherworldly energy were everywhere, insubstantial and faint as if not yet fully awake. They stretched beyond the limit of my reduced senses, busy wrapping around everything, including me. Including the ships and lifepods.

The Null's trap. We were caught already. Its core—its *mouth*—would be open, waiting for an exit or entrance into translight to swallow its prey. I felt remarkably insignificant.

Stay a rock, whimpered the sensible part of me.

Another, possibly foolish but braver part? Focused on Veya Ragem.

I believed what Lesy'd uncovered. Something of Paul's mother was in there. Had survived.

If ending the inconceivably vast and terrifying Null was as impossible for one Web-being to accomplish as it now seemed—

Maybe I should try to find a lost piece of Human.

Keeping my leading edge *rockish* as best I could, I freed the rest of me and sacrificed mass for energy. Sublight at first, to ram carelessly through presents and boom, drawing them along, then—

I soared from real space into the—

Nearby

L AMBO Reomattatii loomed like an ominous statue in one corner, granting space to those gathered in front of Lionel Kearn. The former Survey operative had done his part, using the com equipment hidden in the basement to send a warning to those who needed to hear it.

Not, Lionel thought, *that the Commonwealth would risk confronting a united Confederacy over one remote planet.*

The Null, however, was everyone's concern.

Duggs Pouncey leaned against the Carasian, arms folded. It was more a statement of *gotcha* than camaraderie, Lionel judged. A wary eyestalk remained bent to regard the much smaller Human.

The Library's seniormost staff stood waiting, bells muffled. Had it only been this morning they'd rung Paul and Esen on their way? Only this morning they'd thought they'd time left?

"You remember the drill, people," Lionel told them. "The story is a difficulty with orbital traffic control." *Not a lie.* "While it continues, our priority is to care for those who can't leave the premises. This time, many of our scholars have ships still finsdown at the landing field. Rhondi, you and Carwyn will coordinate getting them back on board as soon as possible."

Carwyn spoke up. "Some, like the aquatics, won't want to go. They're more comfortable in their habitat zone."

"Those who prefer to shelter here may." Lionel looked around, making sure to catch everyone's eye. Skalet/Kalesaty Ki was a reassuring presence at his shoulder, not that anyone here could know. *Not even Duggs.* "Unlike our last, ah, situation, this one should resolve quickly. What is it?"

A stir at the back. The staff parted to let Constable Mal Fletcher step forward and, seeing the urgency in his approach, Lionel's pulse began to race. "Something's missing from my office vault," the Hamlet's sole officer announced grimly. "A restricted and very dangerous piece of equipment." His steely gaze swept the room. "I've traced it to the landing field and the only departing ship was Rudy's. Did anyone see something this size being taken on board?" He held his hands out the width of a hayberry basket.

"Just Paul and Esen's bags," Henri replied.

"And Lesley's," Ally chimed in helpfully.

"Samgo made a delivery," said someone.

"No, he didn't," said someone else.

"Sure he did. His truck was pulled up to the ship," from several, "and left before takeoff."

"Wasn't Samgo. He was ringing a bell with me."

Mal held up his hand for silence. "Onlee Naston?"

"Here." Nia's assistant was at the back of the room, sitting apart. She lowered the hand she'd raised and curled it in her lap.

"Good. I've been trying to raise your boss on coms about this."

Faintly, "She's otherwise occupied." Her distress was palpable.

Seeing it, the constable gentled his voice. "Onlee, where's Nia?"

If ever Lionel had seen guilt on a face, it showed on hers. It was almost anticlimactic listening to Onlee stammer out the truth: that when they'd learned the truck was to be driven out to the ship and back, they'd paid the driver to take it themselves. That Nia climbed a ladder into the ship.

That she hadn't come out.

"Paul arranged it," Onlee finished. "Not—not what we did, or Nia, but the truck. The driver said he was to wait there in case Esen changed her mind at the last minute, to let her avoid any crowds. He thought— he thought it was funny, an alien afraid of space travel. Nia told him Esen was very brave and he should try it himself and see if—if he laughed then."

"Esen didn't get off."

Onlee shook her head.

"And Nia took the equipment from my office and brought it with her." Her lips closed in a flat line.

Mal nodded slowly. "Well, then." He turned to the rest, glancing at Lionel, then suddenly smiled. "That's it then. I'm satisfied. If anyone's the right to do all that," he proclaimed, "it's the hero of the Mavis Peace Accord."

"What hero?" shouted someone, their voice full of fear. "The Kraal are back!"

Kalesaty Ki took a step forward, startling everyone, including Lionel. "There are events occurring in your heavens, good people of Botharis. Not all," with a warning rumble of her stomachs that encouraged those in direct line to shift quickly, "concern those on the ground."

"Exactly," Lionel confirmed. "We've our scholars to look after. I'll update you on the private staff channel when there are developments." When they didn't budge, he made a tiny shooing motion.

"Let's get to work," Henri said loudly. "Who knows what's happening out there without us?" Eliciting some groans and a welcome laugh from the staff.

Mal lingered. When the door closed, he dropped in a chair. "I don't like this." He gave Duggs and the two non-Humans a meaningful look. *Do we need privacy?*

Lionel shook his head. What he needed—what they all needed—were allies. With Lesy/Esolesy Ki unpacking at the farmhouse, this was the moment to pull them together. "There's little to like," he agreed, sitting himself and waving Duggs to a chair. "Paul and Esen—and Nia—" However *that* would work out and he was very conscious of Skalet's presence. "—have gone to meet with their Survey counterparts. What they're facing—what we are, Mal, is a powerful force of nature. A monster," he said, feeling the biting irony of saying that, again, on this world. *Believe me,* he begged with his eyes. "It's heading for our part of space and the Kraal fleet is here to stop it."

"So the embargo is for our benefit." With less scorn than it warranted. "I don't suppose you've any proof."

"Lambo?"

The giant creature clanked forward, stopping with great claws tip down. "I was sent here to investigate Veya Ragem and the illicit actions of a group within Survey called the faction." Eyestalks lifted. "I now work for Lionel Kearn because what he tells you is the truth. This monster has taken starships and their crews for years. It has destroyed a world." The claws rose ceilingward. "WE MUST DEFEAT IT!"

"Hush, you." Duggs rose and got the bottle and a handful of glasses from Lionel's cupboard, serving one to Mal who took it with a dazed look on his face. After a swallow, his eyes sharpened. "That's why Nia took the warhead. To use against this thing."

"A Null." Skalet paced slowly across the office floor, drawing their attention.

She hadn't Lesy's elegance in the form, Lionel observed. Instead, she'd an economy of motion, a confidence. This wasn't a Lishcyn to knock over a priceless antique in a shop.

Unless she wanted to do just that.

"And you are?" Mal asked.

"Esolesy Ki's—the most useful Human correlation would be aunt. And you are the redoubtable Constable Mal Lefebvre of whom my *niece* has spoken." A courteous, if brief, flash of a tusk. "Carasian. The Pouncey." Without tusk.

Lambo had subsided, his every eyestalk riveted on the new Lishcyn in admiration.

As Duggs' curious gaze followed Kalesaty Ki, Lionel held his breath. Then she looked at him. "What can we do?"

Both tusks and forked tongue showed in a wicked smile. "Perhaps sacrifice a small animal—to curry the favor of your deities."

Lionel held up his hands. "That's quite—" The flash of the com on his desk caught his eye. He pressed to let it through. "Lionel Kearn."

"This is S'kal-ru of the *Centos Pa*. Are we secure?"

Her voice, utterly convincing to someone who hadn't experienced the simulation in her quarters.

Exemplary.

Thrilled to his core, Lionel composed himself. "Yes, S'kal-ru. I'm with Constable Lefebvre, Lambo, Duggs, and Kalesaty Ki."

"Acceptable. The *Centos Pa* has accompanied the *Largas Swift* to its encounter with the Null at the request of Paul Ragem. I agreed to convey our observations to you as well as to the Kraal Fleet Commander and wish to make my initial report."

"Go ahead, *Centos Pa.*" Eerie, hearing her voice through the com as the real Skalet stood nearby; he kept his face averted as if to better listen, uncertain of his ability to control his expression.

"At the behest of Polit Evan Gooseberry, we have destroyed the ship he identified as carrying enemy agents working against the Commonwealth. Glory to House Ciet and affiliations. We are now engaged in ferrying the polit's lifepod to the Survey ship *Mistral,* itself disabled. An act we trust will be compensated."

A minor house, of little account until the powerful S'kal-ru clarified her own affiliation and sent its fortunes skyward. Overhead, as they sat here, power began to flow along different lines as priorities changed and spread like a contagion throughout the conveniently gathered fleet, for affiliation, Lionel had heard her say, had read in her book, was earned, not claimed. Deserved, not taken, and for its *failed* presumption of leadership, Great House Virul would crumble to dust.

A victory he'd applaud, Lionel thought with a shiver, if not for the blood being shed in ship corridors. Still he could—*did*—admire the accomplishment.

Mal leaned forward. "Constable Lefebvre. What of the *Largas Swift?*"

"Those aboard transferred to the *Mistral.* The ship itself has vanished from scans and the working assumption is that it has been consumed by the Null."

It took the bait. Were they able to spring the trap? Lionel's surge of triumph turned to dread. If so, there'd be an explosion—"*Centos Pa,* you must leave that area of space at once. Advise the *Mistral*—"

"We cannot. The *Mistral* warns our ships and this entire region have in some way been penetrated by the creature. We cannot risk translight and urge all ships in range to refrain until further notice."

Then, in such a Skalet-way as to freeze Lionel's heart, even knowing she was here and safe, "We aspire to highest of honors, to die with such a formidable enemy beneath our knife. *Centos Pa* out."

The room fell still. Lionel looked up to meet the steady gaze of Skalet's Lishcyn-self and couldn't help the question. "Will they survive? Can—can they all survive?"

She knew he meant Esen, who had to be in the midst of it—was doubtless in the worst of it.

A thick-fingered hand stroked the air. *Indecision.* "As I advised the Pouncey. Sacrifice a small animal."

But he heard the distressed workings of her stomachs and knew.

Skalet feared for Esen too.

21: Null Time

*L*IFE.
 Surprised, I came to a stop. Rudy's packages, accompanied by the deadly boom, drifted gradually onward, slowed by the goo.

Life, gooey and otherwise, pressed close on all sides, and I realized I'd matched it, unconsciously shifting my outermost limit from rockish to something animate. It was web-flesh but wasn't, as if instinct assured me I had to hide my true self, the energy coursing through my every molecule, by encasing myself in quiet.

Having fed myself to my enemy.

I had to stop doing that.

The thought, and the realization if I could think it I must be alive shook me out of an almost stupor.

Not having expected life inside a Null.

Not that I'd known what to expect, but it certainly wasn't this.

It felt *old.* Older than Ersh—which I'd trouble imagining at the best of times—and rotten. I drifted inside an enormous core of organic debris confined to a loose ball by listless filaments. Some reached for the packages, touching then curling away. Some stroked me then flinched, as if I'd a bad taste.

Promising sign.

Most filaments were strewn with parts, as if displaying wares in a crazed market. Legs. Arms. Organs and fluttering skin. A cacophony of agonizing death that wasn't, completely, dead. Had the Null's own nature kept the fragments nourished and living?

Tentatively, each time I bumped a bit, I tasted. Human. Sacrissee. Human. An unexpected Ganthor. Human. Human. I began to suspect—to hope—the Null couldn't taste me back, being stuffed with so much else.

I'd never find Veya.

Unless—I flowed deeper inside the core, then began to assimilate whatever touched me into more me, working as quickly as I dared because at any moment, the Null could notice it had swallowed its favorite treat.

Of course, at any moment, the boom might go off and we'd both die.

It should need me for that. The going off part. Rudy had supplied a simple timer, attached to the outside, with enough explosive to cause a sympathetic reaction, but neither he nor Paul had anticipated I'd be delivering it in person. *And I hadn't been about to tell them.*

Before sending it into space, I'd jammed the simple timer on the exterior with, well, me. Once I'd found Veya, I'd planned to reclaim my web-flesh and make a speedy escape—assuming I could.

Might have been optimistic.

I kept assimilating. Kept growing. There was a natural limit to how much of this mass I could take from the Null, namely when I'd reached the point where gravity preferred I became a rock in truth though, before that, the urge to bud off new mes would likely take over.

Inside a Null.

Or I could expend mass as energy to move around. Something I couldn't do without attracting the attention of what surrounded me.

Did the Null have a similar problem?

It was supposed to hunt us. A trapped wild Web-being would try to escape by releasing energy, an attempt as ultimately futile as a glow in a bottle. The Null would absorb what was released until there was nothing at all left.

But this one had been contaminated by what it couldn't assimilate and use, as we could. Its core was bloated with flesh, a hoard it couldn't remove on its own.

Could I save it?

Admittedly, compassion was the trait Skalet most abhorred in me.

Ersh hadn't. She'd tried to use it—use me—against Death in their final battle.

Compassion aside, there was the not-inconsiderable factor that I was no longer at all sure I could kill something this massive even with the boom. The Null's outside, like a shell, held firm against the strange forces of unreal space.

Perhaps not for much longer. Stars showed, here and there, as if it began to crack. Or was moving into real space to attack more hapless ships—and Paul.

Assimilating more and more mass, I bumped and drifted, pondering what to do. What if I could cleanse it? Could I lure it to a hunting ground without ephemeral life? As if I'd used up my ability to be shocked and horrified, it seemed an unexpectedly peaceful pondering.

Until it wasn't. I felt a sting. A filament had stuck to me. Had begun to *radiate* as if I fed it.

I stripped memory from the tiny portion and cut it free. Other filaments reached for it, then more.

NOT GOOD.

Trying to put as much flesh as possible between me and my sacrifice, I found myself near the edge of the core. I went back to taste and assimilate. Only to stop.

Metal?

I'd found something not alive, that had never been alive. A sliver of a helmet or some such. I went to keep moving.

Then stopped again.

Veya-taste.

I knew it, for I knew her scent. It had been on the suit fabric wrapped around Paul's toy. More, this genetic sequence said *PAUL* to me.

I hadn't really wanted to be right. Hadn't wanted to find anyone I could name in this horror of forgotten rent-apart flesh.

But I had.

I knew what I must do. What Paul would want—and Veya, if she could speak.

Making an outer portion of me more corrosive than usual—a trick Mixs taught me Ersh had forbidden in her house—I touched everything in reach that wasn't living mass. The bit of metal. Shards of plas and wires. Made-things.

Then I drew in all I could find that sang *Veya* to me, assimilating what remained of my friend's mother.

And ended it.

Out There

ALMOST home—
Things move past. Filaments reach only to curl back only to reach—

Hell's indecision catches Veya's eye. *Things* move past. Tiny things. Not shards, yet like those splinters of memory, with intention and purpose. *Things* brought and arrived. Lost and—

Are they found? Filaments reach and curl, reach and curl—

Another *thing* moves past, this one blue like the richest summer sky, shocking in a place where she's seen everything but a color, but a sky, and for the first time Veya feels the filaments holding her *flinch*.

Sees others *flinch*.

Then sees the impossible.

Everything around her, the bits, the wrack and ruin—she sees it vanish—how can it vanish—

Hell seizes her eye, bends it, turns it, tries to control it, tries to aim its flight—

Momma. Momma? Are you listening?
Always—

All at once, what Veya's eye sees, the one that wasn't hers but is again, the one that's been Hell's favorite and her torment, but isn't now—

What that eye sees last—

Is blue—

22: Null Time

I'D taken Veya Ragem from the Null.

And stuffed Rudy's presents for family inside an extradimensional space monster with tentacles, but I chose to focus on the positive, that being less terrifying than what I had to do next.

I'd grown convinced what I detected was damage. There were holes in the Null. Maybe from its encounter with Noam, natural aging, or rot. Whatever the cause, this wasn't the indestructible monster of Lesy's nightmares.

I hoped.

Time to find the boom. Keeping my exterior disguise—though by this point I was far larger than I should be and only a rotting Null wouldn't have noticed a giant Web-being flowing clumsily through its insides—I retraced my path through the core.

In the end, I relied on the presents. The filaments so disliked them that each hung within bubble-like gaps of *no flesh/don't touch* and I grew more and more curious what Largas Freight was using to wrap its cargo. *Clearly the stuff had anti-Null potential.*

Right now, they were my guides, because the boom should be drifting near one of the small gaps. I'd check each until I found it, remove the bit of me and escape.

Me! There!

Unfortunately, my ability to detect web-mass was equaled by the filaments'. A number were wrapped tightly around the boom's case, glowing and crackling as they took what they—and the Null— needed.

Freeing the timer.

Time to head in the opposite direction.

I shifted a good hunk of mass into energy, aimed for what looked like a hole in the fabric of space and was *hopefully* one in the Null, and I—

—wound up outside. WAAAY outside, because by the time my terror was replaced by a more thoughtful, *how far do I run?*

I'd gone a long long LONG way.

Paul was not going to be happy.

Still, I sensed no *empty* anywhere and WAAAY behind me there was a sharp drumming as if gravity and light poured down a new well. *I'd done it!*

And, on the plus side?

I'd more mass than I'd ever need. I began to hum to myself as I reached out my senses, interpreting the spectra of stars.

Ah. There.

I began my journey home.

Nearby

"**W**OW!" Evan raised his head from his arms to stare blearily at Harps. "What?"

"You gotta see it." Goggles went flying. "Full replay. Of—the—explod—ing—space—mon—ster. WHOOO! Definitely a black hole forming. Bet there'll be talk others might have been the result of, say it with me, Space—Mon—sters!"

"Oh." Evan lowered his head. "That."

Harps sat beside him. "Not fun?"

He sighed, cheek on his arm. "Sorry. No."

It hadn't been fun when grapples from the Kraal ship grabbed his lifepod, scaring him half to death. It hadn't been when he'd stumbled out the hatch into the *Mistral,* only to collapse and wake up in the medbay after it was all over next to the cocoon holding the still-critical Decker.

And where the worst had happened. Rudy and Nia had told him Bess hadn't been on the ship at all. That he'd hallucinated under the strain. That they were all glad he'd saved himself.

Which wasn't true. Bess had saved him. *Hadn't she?*

"Bess wasn't on the ship," Evan said, as if repeating it to himself might help.

Then why had Paul asked for her?

An arm draped over his shoulder. "You did good, Goosebumpies."

Had he? There'd been no survivors from the faction ship, according to the *Centos Pa,* though Kamaara had requested their vid feed of the *incident,* not trusting Kraal to be entirely truthful and prisoners with technical secrets of great value. The *Centos Pa,* flushed with glory, had refused, politely for Kraal.

"Paul's avoiding me."

A feather's touch of lips to his ear.

Followed by a wet "*Pttthp.*"

Evan sat up, wiping his ear in disgust. "What was that for?"

That pursed grin. "For being so dumb. Your Paul was by earlier when you were busy snoring. Said he'd be by again soon."

"He's not *my* Paul," Evan said stiffly.

"Good."

And before he could figure out what *that* meant, Harps was up and away.

"Regarding the actions of Lieutenant Kelce Decker, herein reported. We recommended he not be suspended, pending a review. There remains his assault on the person of Polit Evan Gooseberry. You've the right to press charges, Polit." Kamaara raised her eyebrows. "He did toss you off the ship."

"To save my life." Decker couldn't speak for himself, not yet. He'd lost the arm and not even the head med-tech would say how long it would take to regenerate the tissue lost on his torso, so he remained in an induced coma. He'd broken regulations—a stack of them—stolen his notebooks, scared him half to death—

Then saved the ship and Paul, with Briggle's help.

This meeting being official, Evan spoke clearly and firmly. "I, Polit Evan Gooseberry, attest that Lieutenant Kelce Decker performed his duty to Survey and the *Mistral* to the highest standards of service to the Commonwealth. For the record, I am confident he put me on the *Swift* to save my life. No. I will not press any charges."

"Accepted by Commander Ne-sa Kamaara, Security Chief acting, *Mistral.*" Kamaara keyed off the recorder. "Damn straight about

Decker. As for you, Polit?" With a stare that flared into a grin. "Congrats on taking out the enemy."

Evan sighed inwardly. They persisted in appreciating an action he wished he could forget. *But mustn't.* "I wish I'd found another way."

Captain Clendon tapped the table smartly. "I appreciate your sensibilities, Polit, but Strevelor and those with him were willing to kill everyone on board this ship—and would have, if not for you and the others. I'll not waste a tear. I'd like to give you a medal. You know I can't, of course. This isn't a mission Survey wants public."

Evan nodded, more relieved than otherwise. "I'd like to stay on the *Mistral* while the experts finish up. To write my report, among other things. If that's possible?"

"Technically, you're still assigned to us," the captain said. "Happy to keep you if that's what you want. After Botharis, we're heading to Dresnet Shipyards to be sure we've found all of Strevelor's tricks. We can drop you at Pachen IV if that suits you."

He'd a game of *Turn of Light's Edge* to play. "Yes, sir. It does. For now."

Paul Ragem was waiting when Evan returned to his cabin, sitting on the one cleared chair. He looked haggard and worn, but the smile was as warm as he remembered.

The diplomat went to his cot and sat. "I know Bess was there."

The smile disappeared. "Evan—"

"No. Listen, please. If you have to keep her presence on the *Swift*— her, her loss—" his voice threatened to break, "—a secret, I will. You don't have to explain. Ever." The room seemed empty of air. "But that doesn't matter, Paul. There's something Bess wanted me to tell you."

Gray eyes studied him, cool and intent. He couldn't read anything from Paul's face. "Go on."

"She said the frames around the images have meaning. To you, specifically. That together they're a representation of—of Starfield."

Paul's hand grasped the arm of the chair. In anyone else, it would have been a shout. "Go on."

He understood, Evan thought suddenly, his heart aching for his friend. Bess had been right. "Bess said to tell you that something of your mother survived in the Null, fighting to protect you and everyone from it."

"That's what this was about," Paul whispered, almost too low to hear. "Brave, precious Old—" He came to himself, looked at Evan. "Have you told anyone else?"

"I had to tell you first." Evan hesitated. "Paul. Your mother's a hero. People should know."

Paul rose to his feet. "'People.'" Grief thickened his voice. Grief and a terrible rage. "They put her in that ship. They fed her to the monster. *People* deserve nothing of her."

Standing, Evan had to say it. "What does she deserve?"

Paul bowed his head. "A better son."

The words clouded the room, ached in his heart, and Evan fought the impulse to reach out and fold his friend in his arms. There was no comfort for this—no answer.

But possibly comfort. He made himself smile. "Some friends and I are about to start a new game in the galley. *Turn of Light's Edge*? We could use another player."

Evan couldn't imagine what it cost Paul Ragem, in will and courage, to take a breath and shake off that momentary darkness. To look up at him with the beginnings of a twinkle in his eye.

"Room for Nia and Rudy?"

"Seven's the ideal number." If it wasn't, Evan didn't care.

"Count us in." The twinkle deepened. "Be warned. She's good."

"Wait till you meet the Dwelleys and Harps." Thinking about his friends, together and safe, brought to mind the ones missing. "How's Esen taking all this? Rudy told me she'd had to stay behind with Esolesy."

"She'll be more upset to miss you, Evan." Paul put a hand on his shoulder. "You're always welcome. Stop over with us."

"Another time. Great Gran's waiting. And my job—I think I feel up to it again. Isn't that strange?"

"After what you've been through, I'd say it should feel like a vacation." Lightly said, inviting laughter.

Evan found he couldn't. Found the touch of Paul's hand as true an anchor as Great Gran's gentle hand and stood mute, not knowing where to start or how, desperate to tell *someone* about his nightmares, about the haunting *click, clicks,* about not being Human.

"The game can wait," Paul decided, his hand gently pushing Evan back down to sit on the cot. He sat beside Evan, shoulder to shoulder so they didn't face one another—made no demands on each other—but simply shared warmth and space. Then, soft and kind, "Talk if you want. Or not. I'm not going anywhere."

It was as if he walked in the door to his home, his hat waiting, and Evan hadn't felt this safe since that moment.

Making that where he started. "I found out what I am. About my twin, Evie. That's when the nightmares began. I couldn't sleep. I kept hearing that sound."

"Describe it."

Click, click. Click, click.

"I—I can't." He trembled and was ashamed, knowing Paul could feel it. "I don't know why."

A companionable shoulder bump, like Esen would do. "Then don't. Tell me about your home."

And so he did, bringing out the holocube to show Paul images of his family and Great Gran and *Sparkles* and Scintillation Bay.

The nightmare fading away.

23: Garden Afternoon;
Library Morning and Night

I returned to the Library Garden with the snow. Not intentionally, the snow that was, but there's always a first snowfall each year and, as it happened, it arrived with me.

I licked a flake off my nose, checking out the place.

Our new addition appeared finished. More or less. There were workers at the lovely big window I'd only seen in blueprints and someone shouting from the roof.

The plants had grown wild and the paths were a mess, but I'd expected that. My web-kin weren't gardeners. I headed for our place, having told them I was coming.

Having given Lesy permission to be creative with the stone patio where the Web of Esen met—*not that it had, officially, making this a first too*—I was curious what she'd done. And a little anxious, creativity being a moving target for our Elder, but I was in a mood to forgive anything, almost.

Being home.

Sure enough, the stones were gone. In their place was an intricate tile mosaic wrapped around an ambiguous blue question mark. *I might have guessed.*

Lesy, as a magnificent Lishcyn in beautiful silks, stood at the dot of the question mark. Skalet, also Lishcyn, to my surprise, stood where it curved. I ran to the middle, tongue out in a smile. "I'm back!"

And then, before they could ask a single question or voice a complaint, I cycled into web-form, sending my invitation into the air.

Share . . .

When we were done, Skalet was Kraal again and Lesy her Human-self, as if they sought those forms for comfort the way I sought mine. *Not that I'd point it out.*

We'd learned things from one another, that being the point. Skalet, despite remaining at the Library, had solidified her position as courier to a new association of formerly obscure Houses, several of the Great Houses certain to fall apart within the coming year, meaning she'd been successful. As for the fleet that had massed at the edge of the Botharan System?

S'kal-ru's personal triumph at the battle of the Null—a Kraal missile proven to have destroyed the monster—had so outshone the would-be Fleet Commander from House Virul he'd courteously committed suicide.

Or not. She'd tasted disturbingly smug on that point.

Lesy, meanwhile, had declared herself unsuited for work in the Library. *Probably for the best.* She had, however, developed a fondness for the making of elk cheese and now worked for Rhondi four days a week. *Possibly for the best.* I remembered a Lishcyn's delight in fresh dairy.

Though how Lesy managed it without growing wide remained a mystery.

From me, they shared the experience of being inside the Null, if not how. And a fair bit of time being spacesick, since Esen-alit-Quar couldn't fly.

Not where anyone else could see me, that was.

I made that choice for them, not to share what we could do. Skalet knew and accepted. Lesy? Caused sufficient trouble confined to ephemeral transports. She did take credit for Ally Orman leaving the Library and going off planet. To my relief, and I'm sure Lionel's, Kalesaty Ki had agreed to work in the Response Room.

I glimpsed Lionel, Ally, Duggs, and other Human friends in their memories. Some of the interactions were entertaining, to say the least. To a Web-being.

I shunted theirs of Paul aside.

It was time to make more of my own.

As suited a being of my many years, I'd developed some skills and one of them, I was proud to say, was that I could send a letter through the Botharan postal system and have it arrive most of the time.

I'd sent one timed to arrive with me and, I looked cross-eyed at another flake, the snow. Which was why, having left my web-kin to assimilate monsters and a spacesick Lanivarian—*and how brave Nia was and how true Evan was and how much I'd enjoyed the bells*—I was sitting on the stone wall at the base of the Ragem's oak tree.

That was a fern, but I'd stopped telling him.

Not that I sat for more than an instant, being just a little nervous and my tail alternatively trying to wag and tuck between my legs. *We'd never been apart this long.* Long in Human terms, but Paul was Human, and we'd left under a set of circumstances that potentially meant he wasn't happy with me.

Then I sniffed.

Still sniffing, I turned around, following what I sniffed, and looked up.

The face of my first best friend grinned down at me. "Took you long enough, Fangface."

"There's snow," I informed him haughtily. Which would have worked better if my tail weren't beating my legs. *Not that I cared.* I watched Paul climb down, slipping once because the trunk was damp and he was wearing his office shoes.

He landed and stood looking at me. "Esen-alit-Quar," he said in a very firm voice, with a very stern frown.

I angled my ears, detecting insincerity. "You're not mad? Because if you are mad," I asserted, "I can explain—oooff."

He'd fallen to his knees and grabbed me, burying his face in my fur.

It had been a while, I told myself, putting up with it. There'd been the whole terrifying "almost died" part, which I'd tell him in cautious small installments.

A mumble in my fur. "Evan told me about my mother. About Starfield."

And there was that. I pushed my snout in the vicinity of his neck and snorted, moistly.

"Esen!" he protested, pulling back.

I laughed. "You missed me!"

"Everyone did," he stated.

Which I found very satisfying indeed.

There was one more thing to be done, not that Paul knew it. The next morning I pulled him from our most excellent new apartment atop the addition, through the Library, and out the doors onto the platform, refusing to explain.

If I had, he wouldn't have come.

Having mastered letter sending—and with help of the best kind—everything was in place, even better than I'd hoped.

For what waited for Paul was his family. As many as we'd been able to find and Lionel had been relentless in his search—and provided funds for travel. Ragems and Camerons. Terworths and Powells. Names and faces that echoed the past and forecast the future, all of them standing in yesterday's snow, with Uncle Sam and Paul's father Stefan at the front.

There was a small stage backed by a curtain, thanks to Duggs, and Lambo stood holding up umbrellas in his great claws to be sure no snow fell on it, and on the stage, in front of Paul and his family?

A bench held Lionel Kearn and Reeve Joncee Pershing and Constable Mal, as well as Lenan Ragem from the Preservation Committee, smiling for once. Special Envoy Niala Mavis stood by a podium I recognized from the Iftsen Habitat Zone and hoped they'd cleaned.

"Esen—" Paul whispered desperately, in his *what have you done* voice.

"Don't blame me." I pointed.

Polit Evan Gooseberry, resplendent in his finest diplomat suit—if likely chilly because he'd forgotten to check the season—stepped down from the train. With him were two Dwelleys and a thin strange Human with goggles and a thick colorful scarf around his neck, and together they marched to the stage. Leaving the others, our Evan stepped up to the stage and turned. "Would Director Paul Antoni Ragem come to the stage, please?"

I pushed Paul ahead as my web-kin came to stand on either side of me, blocking the view until I pushed forward. *Family.*

Once Paul was standing with them, and some cousins in the back row stopped clapping, Evan produced a black velvet case from his pocket. With a bow, he passed it to Nia.

Who looked gorgeous and smiled through very non-official tears as she turned, case in hand, to face Paul.

"It is my great joy and privilege, as a representative of the Botharan Planetary Government, a citizen of this world, and friend, to present this medal, the Commonwealth Star of Valor blended with the Botharan First Settler's Circle of Merit, to Navigator First Class Veya Ragem, in recognition of her skill, courage, and love for us all. Paul, will you accept for your mother?"

She held it out and I saw it before anyone, that he wasn't going to take the medal. That Paul's hate for those who'd taken his mother from him—*he'd left first, but Humans weren't always rational*—that his hate was going to spoil this, and it would harm him forever.

I covered the distance to the stage as only a Lanivarian could, *on all fours in public*, in front of the family who still weren't that sure about me, *not going to improve their opinion,* and bit my friend on the ankle.

He hopped, letting out an uncharacteristic *bad word*, then stared down at me.

I wrinkled my snout at him, then looked at Nia, still holding out Veya's medal.

Paul straightened with a shudder, gave me a wild-eyed but sane look, then took it.

Those gathered erupted in cheers.

We weren't done. The cheers were a signal. Lambo tossed aside his umbrellas, narrowly missing Sam and Stefan. With both great claws he ripped down the curtain—likely with more force than planned, so we'd need new tablecloths for the staff room, but it added a nice touch of drama.

Revealing a Human female, in uniform, perhaps thirty years old, perhaps younger. She stood smiling, holding hands with a small boy with tousled hair. The pair were looking up, the boy on the tips of his toes as if ready to fly, for her free hand was raised to the sky.

And on her palm rested a six-legged pony.

It was the work of the rightly famous—and reclusive—ceramic sculptor, Lesyole, inspired by current events and informed, I'd learned, by pilfering family albums. The glazes were subtle, breathing life into the faces of mother and son.

Except for a familiar brilliant blue on the pony, and if I found a question mark on its rump—

Paul took a step toward it, his hand rising to echo his mother's, and I found myself oddly glad I couldn't see his face. This was a private reunion.

Until his gathered family began a chant of "Ve-ya Ve-ya" interspersed with "To the pub!" as they swarmed the stage, everyone intent on seeing the medal, that being important, the statue, that being beautiful, and hugging Paul, that being something most hadn't yet done.

And about time.

I slipped away before anyone stepped on my tail.

The snow was the playful sort, ideal for an evening of joy and celebration. And of tears—I knew Humans, and there'd be some. Long overdue tears and probably an excess consumption of the Ragem family tradition meaning headaches and grumbles tomorrow.

I curled in the sofa that was even better for curling in than Samgo's—and all mine—to admire the fluffy flakes passing the window. Lesy had, as I hadn't expected, taken one of the smaller apartments on a lower floor. Then again, I'd the feeling her bags were packed and it was only a matter of time before the itch to find inspiration consumed her again.

Though Paul planned to write to Evan's Great Gran if that inspiration included a visit to check out the Gooseberry Lore, Lesy convinced she'd find a name she knew. *Quite possibly.* I'd leave explaining how to my Elder, who'd proven to be much better at schemes than I'd expected.

This floor and the roof were ours. Paul hadn't shown me its secrets, being busy showing me which parts were his and which parts *weren't to be shed upon.* There was time.

A scent announced him and I angled an ear to enjoy his footsteps. Paul trying to sneak up on this me was always amusing.

"Boo!"

I flicked my ear. "They're waiting for you at the pub."

He sank into the other half of my new sofa, legs outstretched. "Sure you won't come, Fangface? There's chips."

This was his night, with his Human family. *Not that he'd accept that truth.* "My stomach's still upset," I claimed, also true, wrinkling my snout at him. "All that space travel."

"About that." Paul reached behind his neck, then pulled a chain over his head. Dangling from it was the medallion I'd taken from him.

I stretched my neck to look more closely. This one was new, of course. It appeared to be a perfect reproduction. No, something was different.

Instead of the logo for *Cameron & Ki,* it was inscribed with the image of a starship and book, and if the starship bore a striking resemblance to Rudy's lost *Swift*—which I'd promised to replace with something *not-a-bucket*—and if the only paper books in the All Species' Library of Linguistics and Culture were in Paul's half of our apartment, as well as the majority of homes on Botharis—

"I like it." *Though I missed our names.*

He smiled as if hearing the thought. "I added this." He turned it over.

Just as on the Ragem family oak, there were letters scratched by hand into the metal.

ES/PR

I put a leg over my tail to hold it down and flattened my ears, doing my best to hide my delight. "Those are your initials. They aren't my initials. Why didn't you use EAQ?" I squinted. "There was room."

"I'm the one wearing it. To me, you're Es." As he delivered this declaration with a fond scritch under my ear, I accepted the inevitable, raising my ears with a grin.

"I love it," I told him.

"Thought so." Paul kept dangling the medallion in front of my nose as if waiting.

I pulled out of the scritch, lowering my ears. "What?"

Though I could guess, there being a cryounit inside.

"Why don't I leave it here?" my first and very wise friend proposed, getting to his feet and pulling on a sweater. His head popped out. "When you're ready, you can put your secret back inside. If you want."

"You knew? When did you—how did you?" I stopped before I asked the revealing *then why didn't you try to stop me?* with its powerful wave of confusion. Paul always objected to my risking myself. *Hence my being sneaky.* "You let me go when you knew," I finished, my ears flicking in a distress I didn't understand at all.

"Silly Old Blob." Paul came back around the sofa to kneel in front of me, taking hold of the fur to either side of my head. His gray eyes were moist. "Leaving you on the *Swift* was the hardest thing I've ever done."

As if he'd been wrong. Paul was never wrong. "You had to," I protested. "Or I couldn't fight the Null and find—" I hesitated.

"My mother." Said with unexpected peace. "You did what you had to. And I knew you would save us if I let you go."

"I didn't know that." With a hint of whine. *I'd been scared.*

"You were very VERY brave, Esen-alit-Quar. I knew you would be."

Paul had known a great deal I hadn't.

No, he hadn't, I realized. My friend had relied on something else entirely. On the cusp of grasping what felt scarier than the Null, I made myself ask. "Why?"

His nose touched mine. "You're growing up."

Back to confused. "This me will exhibit no observable relative change for—"

"Hush." He pressed his lips to my forehead. *Likely picking up a few hairs; space travel made me shed.* "The thinking you. The part that makes decisions. The part," his voice grew thick, "the part I've learned to trust and believe in."

I'd been right. *This was scary!* Fortunately, I knew just how to fix it. "You built me a slide?" Bounding off the sofa, right over his head—bounding what this me did particularly well—I began racing around the apartment on all fours, nose down as if hunting. "Where? Where? Where?"

Which, having started thinking about a slide, and racing being fun, might have been more serious than he realized.

"There isn't a slide," Paul half shouted over the din of my paws. "And there won't be. It's a bad idea!"

I slid to a stop, tongue out, feeling rather smug.

He gave me that exasperated *Esen!* look, then threw up his hands. "Fine. I take it back. You haven't grown up at all. I'll question your every decision."

"Unless there's an emergency," I suggested, head tilted. "Like a space monster."

Giving up, Paul's laugh filled our home.

And all was right again.

Nearby

DUGGS slapped her hand on the table. "Told you."

Harps laughed. "That you did. Best seats in the place."

Evan eased back to let a tray of beer-filled mugs reach the table. "Put it on my tab," he told the server. "Evan Gooseberry."

"That's the spirit!" Duggs roared. "More beer! Evan's paying!"

Lionel leaned forward. "I'd set an upper limit if I were you."

"How bad could it be?" Evan replied, feeling remarkably cheerful.

Blue Spider giggled. "Depends how many tables take you up on it." His fingers hovered over a plate of purple jelly cubes.

Lionel slipped it out of reach. "I've ordered you both some local cider. You'll love it."

"And won't kill you," Harps added. "Seventh Rule—"

"—of Harps," they all joined in, including Evan.

For the first time the Hamlet of Hillsview had hosted aliens, things appeared to be going very well. Lenan Ragem had gone out of his way to make the Lishcyns feel welcome, the species now familiar to anyone who bought cheese, and Evan thought he'd seen Esen.

He'd been wrong. It had been a local canid. He stared into his beer.

"What's up?" Duggs asked quietly.

"I'm leaving tomorrow. I'd hoped I'd see Esen."

"She's still not so popular in the village. And it's Paul's night. Never seen someone with as many cousins. It was a good thing, what you and Nia did."

He looked up at her. "It was the right thing."

"Not always the same. Paul—he needed a way back to his family. Veya's coming home like that? It's what did it. Because of you." A nudge that rocked Evan sideways.

Right into Harps who laughed. "Fun?"

Evan found himself laughing too. "Absolutely."

The next day, Evan Gooseberry said his farewells—just not to Esen— and boarded the train to the landing field. He could have flown to Grandine with Harps and the Dwelleys, but he'd arranged passage on a freighter. A slower way back. Time to reflect.

To think. Paul had suggested it. Had urged Evan to analyze what his nightmare—wonderfully absent these past nights—might be telling him, rather than fear it.

The car was empty, being the first out of the morning. He found a window seat that more-or-less fit his Human posterior and gazed outside.

"May I join you?"

Esen stood there, her lovely ears somewhere between happy and uncertain.

"Please. Yes! I'm so glad you're here." He let her arrange herself, and tail, on the opposite seat. "Why are you? Here, that is. Not that I'm not delighted." He stopped there, flustered.

Delicate nostrils flared as if testing his scent. "Decker. He told Paul about your notebooks. And that he destroyed them because he felt what was in them wasn't safe. It wasn't Decker's decision to make and we're sorry."

"Please, don't be." Evan's face grew warm. "I'm the one who's sorry, Esen. I've told Paul, whatever secrets you have to keep are yours. I promise to trust you. I didn't always, I admit. But after Bess—" He had to stop and wipe his eyes. "I'm so sorry about Bess."

An ear flipped. "Why?"

He frowned. "Surely Paul told you—surely you know—she died."

"No, she didn't. Bess got into a spacesuit and ejected. S'kal-ru picked her up before the *Swift* went into the Null. You can ask her if you don't believe me."

It was the best of news and he believed—

Didn't he?

Surely Paul hadn't known on the *Mistral*—

Had he?

He did believe Esen, of course he did, because it was such a relief and explained so much. And what it didn't explain, Evan thought solemnly, wasn't his to know.

"Paul was worried," Evan said, instead of all that.

Her jaw dropped in a grin. "He does that."

They sat in companionable silence. The train rolled along, passing forests and open fields, slipping into the hills. Shadows began crisscrossing the interior of the train car.

Esen put her paw on Evan's knee. "You're our friend, Evan Gooseberry."

It seemed oddly like a plea. He smiled. "And you're mine. I'd like you to visit my Great Gran. She'd love to meet you. And Esolesy Ki and maybe Bess, one day."

"Anything's possible." A tongue-lolling grin. "It always is."

He'd wonderful, special friends. Had made Paul happy and honored his mother, a brave officer, and if Evan's step had an extra bounce, it might have had something to do with a message from the Dwelleys.

Or something to do with a shy two-thumbed hand slipping into his as they walked back through the snow last night to Sam Ragem's, who'd offered rooms to those not from the family. There being some dispute about a sofa and his grandmother.

So when the crewmember of his ship handed him a com and said, "Private call, Polit," Evan smiled happily and took the device to his cabin, anticipating any voice but the one he heard—

"It's time we met, Brother."

And any sound but the one from his nightmares—

"Click, click."

Main Characters

Author's Note: Esen would like to point out this is a tiny sampling of the many beloved, semi-reasonable, or outright unpleasant beings in her memory and she sincerely hopes no feelings are hurt by omission.

Web-beings (in order of arrival in known space)
Ersh
Lesy
Ansky
Mixs
Skalet
Esen-alit-Quar, Esen in a hurry, Es between friends
Death *Author's Note: Esen wishes you to know the stranger was named by those attacked. A Web-being not of Ersh's Web.*

The Trusted Few (who know of Esen, her abilities, and the Web)
Author's Note: Don't blame me. Esen wants their loyalties made clear for you. Those of the Group remain a puzzle.
Paul Antoni Ragem—Human; former First Contact Specialist, Survey, Esen's first and best friend; went by the alias Paul Cameron while pretending to be dead for fifty years to protect Esen's secret

Duggs Pouncey—Human; Library's head contractor. *Author's Note: Esen says this wasn't her fault. Paul disagrees. They do agree Skalet and Lesy shouldn't find out that Duggs knows.*

Joel Largas—Human; owner of Largas Freight on Minas XII; father of Char Largas; grandfather to Paul's twins with her, Tomas and Luara Largas.

Lionel Kearn—Human; Paul's boss while in Survey, former First Contact Specialist; led the hunt for the so-called Esen Monster (Death) while Paul was pretending to be dead to—you know the rest. Now in Paul's Group and dedicated to protecting Esen's secret

Rudy Lefebvre—Botharan Human; Paul's cousin; former patrol; searched for the truth while Paul was pretending to be dead, etc., now captain of the *Largas Loyal* and in the Group, etc.

Staff of the *All Species' Library of Linguistics and Culture*
(those named in this book, in order of responsibility)

Director: Paul Ragem

Administrator: Lionel Kearn

Curator/Head Gardener—Esen-alit-Quar (Esen as Lanivarian)

Assistant Curator/Gardener—Esolesy Ki (Esen as Lishcyn) *Author's Note: Esen hopes you've noticed this means she does twice the work. Oh. Now Paul points out she's only one of these at a time and leaves the conclusion to you. Also, the staff wish to add that while they adore Esolesy, she's more a big softie than boss.*

Assessment Desk—Henri Steves (Botharan)

Response Room—Ally Orman (Botharan) and Lesley Delacora (Lesy as Human)

The Anytime Chow Inc. Food Dispenser Operator and acting Head of Security—Lambo Reomattatii (Carasian)

Head Contractor/Maintenance Chief—Duggs Pouncey, Botharan who built the Library and remains on staff and in charge of maintenance/repair. *Author's Note: Esen's convinced Duggs stayed to make sure no one—especially Skalet—messes with her work. Paul agrees.*

Head of Security—Skalet (who remains in her Kraal form but doesn't use S'kal-ru on Botharis among non-Kraal). *Author's Note:*

Skalet is in no doubt that Duggs remained in order to make her life more difficult.

Flight Controller, Landing Field: Lenata Mady (Botharan)

Greeter/Coordinator of Intersystem Passage—Carwyn Sellkirk (Botharan)

Greeter—Brooks Louza (Botharan)

Greeter—Envall Ragem (Botharan)

Greeter—Quin Spivey (Botharan)

Maintenance Personnel (exterior)—Correa Faster (Botharan)

Maintenance Personnel (night shift)—Zel Doctson (Botharan)

Maintenance Personnel (night shift)—Travis Doctson (Botharan)

Train Operator—Rhonda Bozak (Botharan); also maintains herd of Botharan Elk used to produce cheese for village

Train Operator—Goff Cameron (Botharan)

Train Operator—Kelly Kiser (Botharan)

Botharan Authorities

Author's Note: Esen would like to point out that considering the small population of the planet and their stubborn nature, Botharis has a well-functioning democratic system despite the way each level of government ignores the others unless absolutely necessary.

Assistant to Special Envoy Mavis—Onlee Naston

Constable Malcolm (Mal) Lefebvre—was a Commonwealth patroller; now retired to care for the Hamlet of Hillsview; Rudy's uncle

Preservation Committee Member, Hamlet of Hillsview—Art Firkser; author of historical romances; publisher of the *Hamlet Times*

Preservation Committee Member, Hamlet of Hillsview—Lenan Ragem; architect

Preservation Committee Member, Hamlet of Hillsview—Ruth Vaccaro; retired school teacher

Reeve Joncee Pershing—elected head of the Hamlet of Hillsview Council; also runs the post office and claims office; volunteer firefighter

Special Envoy Niala (Nia) Mavis—currently assigned to negotiate with non-Botharans on behalf of the planetary government in Grandine; was once involved with Paul Ragem

Deputy Constable—Merri Higbee; normally mobile livestock med-tech

Deputy Constable—Teri Terworth *Author's Note: Esen says to keep an eye on any relative of Jan Terworth, close or not. Now Paul adds she's overreacting and Teri's a very nice person. To which Esen adds: Jan is not, and she'll stay cautious, thank you.*

Deputy Constable—Tuggles Cameron; Paul's cousin; raises scruffs (Botharan pet canid)

Paul's Family

(those mentioned in Web Shifter's Library series, in alphabetical order)

Char Largas—Paul's temp contract partner, mother of their twins, Tomas and Luara

Delly Ragem—Paul's grandmother on his mother's side, now a sofa in Sam's attic

Envall Ragem—distant cousin, works at Library

Jan Terworth—cousin

Kevin Ragem—cousin

Lenan Ragem—Paul's Uncle Sam's distant cousin, architect and member of Preservation Committee

Luara Largas—daughter of Paul Cameron and Char Largas, sister of Tomas

Rudy Lefebvre—cousin; captain of the *Largas Swift*

Sam Ragem—Paul's uncle on his mother's side

Samgo Cameron—nephew of Tuggles; owner of the Hillsview Pub

Stefan Gahanni—Paul's contracted father; drive machinist; lives on Senigal III

Teri Terworth—distant cousin

Tomas Largas—son of Paul Cameron and Char Largas, brother of Luara

Tuggles Cameron; Paul's cousin; raises scruffs (Botharan pet canid); nephew Samgo

Veya Ragem—Paul's mother, starship navigator: died on the *Smokebat* 18 years before Paul stopped pretending to be dead. *Author's Note: Esen reminds us Human relationships are complicated.*

People of Importance to Evan Gooseberry

(those mentioned in Web Shifter's Library series, in alphabetical order) *Author's Note: Evan adds those from his first adventure* with Paul and Bess as set out in the e-novella "The Only Thing To Fear."*

Aka M'Lean—Human; Senior Political Officer, Commonwealth Embassy on Dokeci-Na and Evan's boss

Alis Poink—Human; Survey captain; Project Passerby expert on Survey ship *Mistral*

Asukun Sun Gooseberry—a tenured professor who remains in a coma

Bess*—Human; the "Esen" Evan meets and befriends on Urgia Prime *Author's Note: Esen wants to remind everyone this seemed an excellent choice of form when she picked it.*

Betts Colquitt—Human; steward on the Survey ship *Mistral*

Blue Spider—Dwelley; Project Passerby expert on the Survey ship *Mistral* (see also Wort)

Celonee Jefer Buryatsea Gooseberry—Human; aka Great Gran, keeper of The Gooseberry Lore and responsible for assessing the legal status of claimants to being real Gooseberrys; raised Evan

Dane Strevelor, Commander—Human; Survey operative; in charge of Project Passerby on *Mistral* (aka Petham Erilton, aka Eller Theelen)

Decker Theelen—Human; Tourist who arrives at Great Gran's (aka Lt. Kelce Decker)

Ekwueme-ki—Dokeci; Leader of the Mariota Valley Project on Dokeci-Na

Eller Theelen—Human; Tourist who arrives at Great Gran's (aka Petham Erilton, aka Dane Strevelor) *Author's Note: Evan wants to add that Eller's real name remains a mystery.*

Evan Gooseberry—Human; Political Officer, Commonwealth Embassy on Dokeci-Na; one of the few accredited Gooseberrys of his generation. *Author's Note: His Great Gran wishes everyone to know Evan is the most eligible and sweetest Gooseberry. Interested parties should get in touch with her directly.*)

Gooseberry—the only Human surname with an unbroken legal line of descent from fabled Earth, as set out in The Gooseberry Lore.

Great Gran—see Celonee Jefer Buryatsea Gooseberry.

Hymna Burtles—Human; manager for Burtles-Mautil Intersystems Holdings on the Mariota Valley Project on Dokeci-Na

Ionneanus—Human Contriplet; Project Passerby expert on Survey ship *Mistral*

Joen Haula—Human; Survey captain; Project Passerby expert on Survey ship *Mistral*

Justin Gooseberry—Human; Evan's cousin, eldest son of his Aunt Melan

Lisam Horner—Human; security at the Commonwealth Embassy on Dokeci-Na; friend of Evan's

Lucius Whelan—Human; acquaintance of Great Gran; friend of Justin Gooseberry

Lynelle Owell—Human; security at the Commonwealth Embassy on Dokeci-Na; friend of Evan's

Melan Gooseberry—Human; Evan's aunt

Ne-sa Kamaara—Human; Commander of the security detail of the Survey Ship *Mistral*

Ny Wimmerly*—Human; Ambassador at the Commonwealth Embassy on Urgia Prime

Petara Clendon—Human; Captain of the Survey Ship *Mistral*

Petham Erilton—Human; Admin Staff at the Commonwealth Embassy on Dokeci-Na (aka Eller Theelen, aka Dane Strevelor)

Pink Popeakan*—Popeakan; nickname Humans give Prela on Urgia Prime

Pre-!~!-la Acci-!~!-ari*—Popeakan; also known as Prela or the Pink Popeakan; Evan encounters this individual on Urgia Prime

Prela—Popeakan; Esen's nickname for Pre-!~!-la Acci-!~!-ari; she and Evan encounter this individual on Urgia Prime

Professor Harpesseon (Harps)—Human/Modified; expert on the Survey ship *Mistral*

Sammy Litten—Human/Modified; xenopathologist at the Commonwealth Embassy on Dokeci-Na

Sedemny Gooseberry—recorded as having "died by carpet" in The Lore

Sendojii-ki—Dokeci; artist particularly famous in capital of Dokeci-Na

Simone Arygle Feen*—Human; Senior Political Officer at the Commonwealth Embassy on Urgia Prime; Evan's first boss

Snead—Human; Comm Officer on the Survey Ship *Mistral*

Stan Gooseberry—Evan's uncle; known for his cider

Tam-ja Gooseberry—Evan's uncle; known for his Extra Sizzle Sauce and the dreaded fruitcake

Teganersha-ki—"Dokeci"; historical figure: the infamous leader who united Dokeci-Na and established their moral system as well as plumbing; in reality: Ersh's name in this form. *Author's Note: Esen has her doubts Ersh would appreciate Evan carrying her image— a small bust—with him for inspiration, but she has yet to figure out how to tell him.*

Terry Koyak*—Human; Evan's co-worker and friend at the Commonwealth Embassy on Urgia Prime

Tonphiger—Human Contriplet; Evan's friend at the academy

Trili Bersin—Human; Political Officer at the Commonwealth Embassy on Dokeci-Na; Evan's closest friend there.

Warford—Human; Senior Med-tech on the Survey Ship *Mistral*

Wenn Gable Gooseberry—Evan's cousin; called a "Putrid Gripe" by Great Gran for tormenting Evan, when a child, about his phobias

Wort—Dwelley; Project Passerby expert on the Survey ship *Mistral* (see also Blue Spider)

Others Who Appear

Author's Note: Esen wishes several didn't, but admits every past has its trouble spots. Paul has moved the Kraal to their own category for clarity and because it worries Lionel to blend them.

Acklan Seh—Sacrissee chimera; Emboldened

Aran—a name used in her story by Bess (Esen)

AULE-TB356994 (Aule)—Sacrissee; male who escapes Molancor Sacriss

Ben Draven—Human, Botharan; former Hamlet of Hillsview Reeve; would-be Drattle farmer

Bob*—Human; alias Diale gives his Sweat Provider and colleague

Briggle—Human; security guard on the *Mistral*

Bunkabo Del—Anata; scholar visiting the Library

Celiavliet Del—Anata; who refused to leave the Library *Author's Note: Esen firmly intends not to let another being hide in her Garden. Firmly.*

Cureceo-ki—Dokeci; curator of the museum on Dokeci-Na about to host a show of Lesy's artwork

Daisi Largas—Human; from Minas XII; crew on *Largas Swift*

Diale—Hurn; security tech specialist from Minas XII; worked with Paul to set up the Library; has history with Cameron & Ki, Paul and Esolesy's company

Elfien—Vlovax

Ginny Filer—Human; Botharan member of Paul's Group Esen refuses to meet

Gloria—Rudy Lefebvre's name for Esen's Human-self; also the name of his pet mousel as a child.

Janet Chase—Human; was captain of the *Vegas Lass* while Paul was pretending to be dead, but turned out to be a criminal; alias used by Victory Johnsson; murdered by Skalet

Jumpy Lyn—Ervickian; henchbeing of Chase; murdered by Skalet

Kalesaty Ki—Skalet's name as a Lishcyn

Lance Largas—Human; crew on the *Largas Regal*

Lesley Delacora—Lesy's Human-self

Lesyole—Lesy's Lishcyn-self

Maston Sah—Sacrissee chimera; Emboldened

Myrtle Rice—Human; Soft Companion to Oieta Fem Splashlovely

Nesel Gabbert—Human; Senior Researcher Molancor Sacriss, a division of Molancor Genomics

OOLA-TB333401 (Oola)—Sacrissee; female who escapes Molancor Sacriss

Osmaku Del—Anata; "head of off-world inquiry" who led delegation to the Library

Palrander Todd—Human; henchbeing of Chase; murdered by Skalet

Pearl—Vlovax

Pearlesen—Esen's name as a Mareepavlovax

Pretty Bill—Ervickian; sent by Kraal with question for the Library

Rampo Tasceillato the Wise—Carasian; philosopher quoted by Lionel Kearn

Reeto—Carasian; Paul's roommate at the academy

Riosolesy-ki—"Dokeci"; Lesy's name in this form

Saxel Sah—Sacrissee chimera; Emboldened

SeneShimlee—"ShimShree"; Esen's name in this form

Ses-ki—"Dokeci"; Esen's name in this form

Sindy—a name used in her story by Bess (Esen)

Siokaletay-ki—"Dokeci"; Skalet's name in this form

Sly Nides—Human; henchbeing of Chase

Splashlovely—Oieta visiting the Library; Soft Companion Myrtle Rice

Tallo—Iedemad; Library client and entrepreneur

Thielex—Lexen; Library client and musical prodigy

Tisken Uppet—Human; Lionel Kearn's "first love"; a classmate

Tory—Human; alias of Victory Johnsson

Vanekaelfien—Mareepavlovax

Victory Johnsson—Human; birthname of Janet Chase/Tory

The Kraal Confederacy

Cieter-ro—Kraal; House Ciet; Captain of the scout class ship *Septos Ank,* attached to the *Trium Pa*; affiliated with S'kal-ru

Dal-ru—Kraal; Commander of spy outpost; House Bryll; from Skalet-memory of Battle for Arendi Prime

Haden-ru—Kraal; Captain of the *Trium Pa*; House Arzul

House Adana—ancient house in myth of "S'kal-ru and the Great Serpent of House Adana"

House Arzul—affiliated with Bract

House Bract—Noble house and S'kal-ru's first real affiliation, via the Bryll Courier involved in Battle for Arendi Prime

House Bryll—Noble house; in Skalet-memory betrayed during Battle for Arendi Prime to House Bract by S'kal-ru and House Bryll's Courier

House Ciet—lesser house

House Conell—lesser but ancient house, but one to which Cieter-ro and S'kal-ru are both affiliated

House Noitci—affiliated with House Bryll and House Bract; once invaded Botharis

House Oalak—an ancient affiliate of House Virul

House Ordin—affiliate with House Bryll and thus House Bract and House Noitci

House Virul—as one of the Great Houses, responsible for guiding the future of the confederacy

Maven-ro—Kraal; Lieutenant at spy outpost; House Bryll; from Skalet-memory of Battle for Arendi Prime

N'Kar-ro—ancient Kraal philosopher

Nadaneo—Kraal; Admiral; House Virul

S'kal-ru—Skalet's name as a Kraal; highest rank: Courier *Author's note: Esen says there's no point listing affiliations as her web-kin's stuck her nose in the business of every House, including those now extinguished—and some of those were Skalet's fault.*

Shirt—Kraal in cave; House Arzul; Esen's name for her

Socks—Kraal in cave; House Arzul; Esen's name for her

Sous—Kraal noncombatants; by custom safe from attack

Suecop-ro—Kraal; comp officer on *Trium Pa*

Vest—Kraal in cave; House Arzul; Esen's name for him

Virul-ru—Kraal; Courier for House Virul and the Inner Circle of Great Houses; sent to negotiate with Botharis

Ephemeral Species

Author's Note: Esen would like you to know this is far, far, far from a complete list. Her universe is a large and lively place. Also, that as a Web-being, she and her kind are not ephemeral, being semi-immortal and originally from space.

Acepan—species extinct before Humans arrived in this part of space, multi-legged and not fond of the cold.

Anata, Anatae—herbivorous species who have yet to live down mistaking performers dressed as edibles for edibles during a Festival of Funchess

Articans—inhabitants of Artos *Author's Note: appear Human but have significantly different biology.*; xenophobic religious fanatics who view the boneless as sin; responsible for the death of Ansky

Blimmet—species that lives in middle atmosphere of gas giant and propel themselves by passing gas out of the requisite orifice.

Botharan—a Human from Botharis. For example, Paul Ragem. *Author's Note: In Esen's opinion the finest of his species. She admits to prejudice.*

Carasian—species with hard carapace/shell, claws, multiple eyes, and significant sexual dimorphism

Cin—one of two communal species (see also Rands); in their case, varied cognitions are present in a roughly humanoid body.

Author's Note: Esen points out Ersh forbade taking this form, citing "one personality is enough".

Crougk—largest land-based sentient species, horse-like *Author's Note: While Paul disputes this, Esen remains convinced.*

D'Dsellan—insectoid; a Panacian from the homeworld, D'Dsel, or living there. Mixs' preferred form under the name Sec-ag Mixs C'Cklet.

Dokeci—species with five arms/three eyes; pendulous abdomen drags with age; Ansky's preferred form for cooking; Lesy's preferred form for art, as Riosolesy-ki. Esen as a Dokeci is called Ses-ki, being too young to be taken seriously.

Dwelley—species more amphibian than mammal; cheeks puff in polite conversation

Efue—species about which the Anatae come to the Library, there being confusion about certain substances and good taste

Elves—what the Dokeci call the aliens they find and transplant from the moon around S'Remmer Prime (see also Mareepavlovax)

Engullan—species with a cinnamon tang; bright yellow makes them wince

Ervickian—species with two brains, two mouths, and pliable morals; most are con artists or petty thieves

Feneden—species new to Esen until Ersh memory informed her this is a species Ersh preyed upon; locate themselves using polarized light

Ganthor—species vaguely like warthogs; tough, with a herd instinct; often mercenaries; need implants to use comspeak, otherwise use olfaction/physical gestures/clickspeech

Grigari—species known for their music; black and white stripes, 2 pairs of feet, 3 tails (one prehensile), long fingered hands; mane collects sensory input; Ersh considered them "show-offs"

Heezle—species resembling pillars of ooze; no interspecies hangups; bats eye covers to assess interest in mating and inattention means "come hither"

Human—humanoid species, bipedal; wide variety of shapes and sizes; prone to curiosity. They are loosely organized within a Commonwealth, although at the far reaches a new Trade Pact is forming. For example Paul Ragem. Esen as a Human is called Bess.

Hurn—species enamored of Human sweat, ring of lip-smacking mouths around the neck; For example Diale, security expert on Minas XII.

Iberili—species that hibernate for 300 years at a time *Author's Note: Esen has no intention of wasting so much time asleep, even if Ersh found it restful.*

Iedemad—slug-like species that must wear osmo-suits to tolerate anything but a water-saturated environment

Iftsen—theta-class species, but live in such a chemically "rich" environment they use non-oxy facilities; known for "party" habit; several subspecies (See also Mobera)

Jarsh—extinct species with memorable voice; Esen sings to Paul to show him what the Web remembers

Jylnics—aquatic species; tentacles; move with reckless speed; one made advances on Paul

Karras—species that hunts by detecting electromagnetism and infrared (body heat); also known as Karras Slug *Author's Note: Esen would like some appreciation for her patience while in this form, as it stops to emote between every major action even when she's in a hurry.*

Ket—species, humanoid but extremely sensitive hands; work as masseuses and always have a hoobit. Esen as a Ket went by Nimal-Ket, the name on her acquired hoobit.

Kraal—Humans belonging to the Kraal Confederacy; strict hierarchy organized by affiliation to Houses; do not interbreed with non-Kraal Humans and may go extinct or become a subspecies. Skalet's preferred form, in which she is known as the Courier S'kal-ru.

Lanivarian—canid-like species known for its loathing of space travel; Esen's birth-form. As a Lanivarian, her name is Esen-alit-Quar.

Lexen—species who employ respiratory tubes in their music

Lishcyn—species with scales, five stomachs liable to react violently, and poor night vision; their homeworld is a Dokeci protectorate; as Paul's business partner and friend, Esen remained Lishcyn while he was pretending to be dead, under the name Esolesy Ki.

Lycorein—aquatic species resembling a very large otter

Machinii—species infamous for killing their own children in a failed attempt to modify them into what could survive a climate disaster; led to the Machin Protocol, an agreement not to impose genetic modification on a population without informed consent. *Author's Note: Esen says that despite Ersh's admonishment that "biology is all they have," she wishes ephemerals would take better care of the rest.*

Mareepavlovax—species the Dokeci discovered and called Elves; also known in Web memory as Ancient Farers, Final Scourge, and Last Reapers (See also Vlovax.)

Mobera, Moberan—subspecies of Iftsen (there are several); frilled face

Modoran—species, feline, dirty (except under UV) white fur, aggressive and large, needs implant to speak

Nabreda, Nabredan—subspecies of Iftsen (there are several); protruding forehead

Nideron—species that inflates a nostril hood in disdain; aggressive toward weakness; 7-digit hands

Nimmeries—aquatic species; thrum when impatient; engaged in border dispute with Oietae

Nerpuls—species that burrows; got into Library planters

Octarian—species with multiple chins, pouch, auditory tentacles

Odarian—species with trunk (sputters in conversation by exhaling moist air) and elbow pouch

Oieta, Oietae—aquatic species; filter feeders (shrimp-esque); color changes with emotion; size of a Human. Esen's name as an Oieta is Esippet Darnelly Swashbuckly.

Ompu—species Ansky watched go extinct

Panacian—general name for insectoid species living in the Panacian system and elsewhere. (See also D'Dsellan.)

Petani—species; associated with ShimShree offworld as translators and transport

Popeakan—arachnoid species known to be reclusive and to work within groups: to interact with other species requires the Offer; twelve jointed limbs, 3 eyes. For example, Prela.

Poptians—species who deals in gems on Picco's Moon; gloved tentacles; green faceted eyes

Prumbins—species that grows larger with age; vertically pupiled eyes; not aquatic

Quebits—species that resemble little Electrolux vacuums with extruded flower-like appendages; work as janitors/repair crew on starships; known for their intense focus on minutiae *Author's Note: Esen will not travel as a Quebit again. Unless she has to, and if so, she expects something to fix.*

Queeb—species with tentacles and six eyes, forked tongue

Rands—one of two communal species (see also Cin) who travel/live in clusters of less than 20

Refinne—massive aquatic species; lives in deep water and is blinded by light

Rrabi'sk—extinct freshwater species, its scales and teeth resembling a Botharan creature from a cautionary tale. *Author's Note: Esen admits to being one in Ragem Creek, but no one saw her. She thinks.*

Rrhysers—species that are standard tripeds, thump chest plates, broad nostrils, infamous for their temper, and will let offspring play anywhere

Sacrissee—species deer-esque; evolved from solitary, shy herbivores; architecture is designed to provide peepholes and prevent interaction

Screed—species with knees at height of Human waist

Seitseits—species who generate internal hydrogen while asleep so need weights or will float away

ShimShree—species adapted to below freezing temperatures; build structures using spew; associated with Petani; Esen's name in the form is SeneShimlee

Skenkrans—space-faring species with leathery wings (not skyfolk)

skyfolk—non-space-faring species with wings; gliders; doleful and solitary

Smoot—species who illegally homesteaded the waters under the south polar cap of Urgia Prime

Snoprian—humanoid species, similar to Humans except for their voices and vestigial feathers

Tly—Humans who live in system of the same name

Tumbler—crystalline species native to Picco's Moon; excretions considered rare gemstones; Ersh's preferred form and Tumblers called her Ershia the Immutable.

Twillex—species who regards intestinal upset a sign of imminent metamorphosis.

Urgian—species with no calcified skeleton, four arms; hosts of the Festival of Funchess *Author's Note: Esen experienced her first festival with Evan in "The Only Thing to Fear"*; known for poetry/dance

Vlovax—small creature that rises from the ground to complete a Mareepavlovax (see Elves); named Devil Dart by the Dokeci

Wz'ip—species like stone; graphite filaments and exterior vents; what Esen sometimes becomes to sulk *Author's Note: Esen points out she doesn't sulk. She mopes. Cutely.*

Ycl—amorphous coalition of cells; obligate predator of "living flesh" so their world has been declared off limits to anyone tasty

For more information, visit the *All Species' Library of Linguistics and Culture* on Botharis. A fact for the collection, delivered in person, will be required in exchange. Please refer to the Library's guidelines before planning your trip. Pamphlets are available on Hixtar Station. Watch for updates on the opening of Botharis Station.